Up
Above
the
Woodpile

A novel by Mark Rait

Up Above the Woodpile:

LITERARY FICTION
LITERARY REALISM

2017 Polygraph Publishing edition.
ISBN-13: 978-1999738709
ISBN-10: 1999738705

To Maggie, Beau and Gracie, for their love and support.

The wind has died and the fire is lit.

And with special thanks and appreciation for their generous insights, support and encouragement to: Aran Jess, Hellena Briasco, Toni Lowrie, Samantha Chesler-Leiman and Toby Dharan-Gibson. Thanks also to the many unnamed others who provided support and encouragement along the way.

Contents

A letter

Saturday, 2 January 2016

Dear Willem,

Y ou didn't know, but I was in the audience on the evening that you presented from the stage at the University of the Western Cape. My daughter, Themula - a student of nursing at the University at the time - had returned home one evening with a marketing pamphlet for the event. 'Have you just seen a ghost?' she said, as I read the information, blissfully unaware of my connection to Glen Cleaver. I felt compelled to attend.

I left just before the end of your testimony - some memories are simply too painful to bear - then driving back with Themula, I opened-up for the first time in my life. At home, she sat me down in front of Thembi, my wife and asked me to tell them everything. (If you knew these women, I had little choice in the matter).

Five hours later, in the quietest hours of the night, I had drained myself of every chilling memory and emotion. I was too tired to sleep, but Thembi lay with me a while, then got up and fixed me a cup of Ubulawu, which helps people to reach their ancestors in their dreams. For the last part of the night, and long into the morning, I slept and I dreamt and I floated up above the woodpile with old friends. When I awoke, a deep peace and tranquillity had washed over me. I hope your ghosts are now silent, Willem. I hope your dreams unfold in the bright light of day.

On Saturday 30th January, I will return to Glen Cleaver for one last time, to check on the fynbos I planted above the estate in the year before your return. Perhaps I will summon the confidence to drop in and say hello after all these years. They say if you want to run fast, go alone. But if you want to run far, go together. You and Victor are never far from my thoughts.

Ubuntu, my old friend.

Lifa (George)

1
Errand

'Can Lifa come out?' I heard the boy ask my mother.

'Come out for what?' replied my mother without looking up.

'Fishing. We are building a net from old pieces of rope and string to dredge at the beach. We will return with fishes . . . lots of fishes. Just like Jesus did.'

'You know the story of Jesus at the Sea of Galilee?' she enquired in disbelief.

'Oh yes Madam. It's my favourite story of Jesus.'

'And what fish are you going to catch, boy?' she enquired further.

'Big ones, Madam. Only big ones. Good for eating, Madam,' he said with a nervous glint in his eyes.

'Lifa, you go fishing if you want to, but make sure not to drown each other with any net.' I was out the door before she had finished her sentence.

We ran for three blocks until my shack was out of sight. The boy slowed to a walk and turned the corner. There in front of us was my father. He was sitting on the dry dirt, leaning against the patchwork partition of a shack, smoking a cigarette, acting like he was surprised and excited to see me. I could tell from his speech and the fumes that he had been drinking.

'Lifa! Hello my boy. Come and sit with your father, boy. No more work for me today.' He was laughing to himself and grinning widely with dilated pupils. The boy was becoming impatient.

'I want my cigarettes,' he told my father with an outstretched hand.

'Have them, stink.' My father handed over two cigarettes to the boy. Before he ran off, he looked down at me as if to ask how I could have been so gullible. Fishing? Really?

'You know, Lifa, they don't smoke cigarettes where he lives, they light them to cover the stink of piss and shit; they the rats of Tolongo.' He slapped my thigh then hunched his arms over his knees in his blue overalls, spluttering out a hoarse, coughing laugh. When he stopped laughing it became clear why he had bribed the boy to fetch me.

'So, Lifa, you'll have to make yourself useful today. I have an errand for you to run.' He pulled a small, dirty envelope from the top pocket of his overalls and passed it to me. I took it into my hand and looked at it indifferently, noticing sheets of money poking out from the edges.

'Money from working, Lifa. Not for you, boy . . . not for you.' He reached up and tightly squeezed my arm as he made his point. I looked back silently and curiously. He looked a little crazy and emaciated, like a stranger that I had randomly bumped into, not my father. The lack of mass around his bones and the gauntness of his face meant his eyes and his eye-sockets appeared much larger than average - out or proportion with the rest of his face.

'It's good cigarettes I want, Lifa . . . the best cigarettes . . . silky smooth and *nice* to taste. Yeah, *very nice* to taste.' When he accentuated the word *nice* he shut his eyes and let it linger on his tongue with a guttural, lustful hiss as if the taste had arrived that second.

'I don't smoke. How can I know what are the best cigarettes?'

'Shut up and listen, boy. I'm telling you now.' My father raised his head as if a fog was clearing in his mind.

'Put the envelope into your underpants and hide it. Don't let anyone see it until you find Mama Blues. You go find Mama Blues.'

'Mama Blues?' I enquired.

'That's what I said, boy. Mama Blues.'

'Who is Mama Blues?'

He pulled his knees into his chest and rocked back and forwards on his backside, spluttering and wheezing, his hands on his head.

'Inner Tikki, Inner Tikki,' he repeated over and over, between coughs and his rabid, drunken laughter.

The Inner Tikki is an area of market stalls and shop traders in the middle of Tolongo that pumps blood to and from the main arteries of the township. In time, I found out that it pumped blood literally, but it also generated an oxygen for life; a microcosm for the very best and worst of human behaviour. Local business was conducted in the Inner Tikki, community meetings took place in the Inner Tikki, crooks coordinated their operations from the Inner Tikki and the Afrikaner police patrols only ventured as far as the Inner Tikki in the direst of circumstances. At twelve years old, I knew the Inner Tikki as a place where my mother occasionally bought provisions – although I had also heard stories about the place, worthy of the shamans.

Father stood up, dusted off his overalls and crouched down to meet my eyes. 'Go to the Inner Tikki. Find Mama Blues. Give her the envelope and tell her your father wants the *best cigarettes*. They must be cigarettes

9

with the sweetest smell and the freshest taste. The *nicest* taste - like honey and watermelon all in one. Do you understand, Lifa?'

'I don't think honey and watermelon will taste nice. I will tell her for a taste like honey and mango,' I replied, staring into his twitching eyes.

'Good Lifa. Honey and mango. Yes. . . Better. . . Honey and mango is very good. . . *Very nice.* . . Yes. Honey and mango.' He turned around and walked off with his cigarette hanging from his lips, mumbling about honey and mango, leaving me to ponder what I should do next.

When I arrived at the Inner Tikki I thought it would take me the whole day to find her. There were hundreds of stalls, and small shop fronts selling their wares; all sparsely populated with products and a limited choice of foods which did not deter the bustling custom. I approached a lady behind the first stall. She was selling chicken; alive, dead, raw, feathered, boned, skinned, dried, diced, minced, fly encrusted - all sorts of chicken.

'Do you know where I can find Mama Blues?'

'Mama Blues!' she said. 'What is a young boy like you wanting with Mama Blues? Go home to your mother, boy.'

She clearly knew Mama Blues but was in no mood to help. I got close to the same reaction from the next six women I asked, sensing I must be close from the consistent strength of opinion. I decided to approach a man. He was an old man in a bowler hat a size too large for his head, with not enough fat or muscle to fill his skin. Short grey hairs were poking out from his hat near the ears and clumps of grey beard had grown in irregular, wiry patches across his chin and neck. He was sitting slumped against the wall on an orange crate with his eyes closed. I knew that he was not asleep.

'I'm looking for Mama Blues.' I said, standing directly in front of him. He slowly opened his eyes and propped his head forward, studying me briefly, seeming neither interested nor disinterested in my statement, before pointing to the doorway at a concrete building on the far side of the stalls. He quickly returned to his drowsy slouch.

I passed the line of stalls and arrived at an alley of raw concrete blocks supporting a corrugated iron roof that led to a thick, metal door. The door was imposing, with large iron hinges, locks and brackets for fixing padlocks. I knocked, and a small metal shutter on the top half quickly opened to reveal two large eyes. The person on the other side did not speak; simply looked.

'Mama Blues?' I asked.

The shutter closed. Silence.

After half a minute I knocked on the door again and the shutter opened once more. The eyes behind it belonged to a different person.

'Mama Blues?' I asked.

'What do you want with Mama Blues?' asked the women.

'My father has sent me to buy cigarettes.'

'Cigarettes you say?'

'Only the best that you have – ones that taste like honey and mango.'

'Honey and mango you say?' The lady looked at me like I was the strangest thing she had ever seen.

'That's what he asked me to buy. I must give this to Mama Blues.' I reached into my underpants and pulled out the envelope.

The clink of locks and chains pulling apart preceded screeching as the door opened and scraped along the concrete. A tall, thin lady was standing on the other side wearing black silk shorts and a white t-shirt.

'Come in,' she said, locking and bolting the door behind me. 'Wait here.'

The space was dark, with a lonely paraffin lamp on a wooden table next to a chair. There were no windows and I had no idea whether I had arrived at a home or a place of work. When the lady returned, I had decided that my father did not need all that money for cigarettes; two of his notes were rolled-up and tucked neatly against the interior stitching of my underpants.

'Follow me,' she said.

We ascended two flights of cold concrete steps, passing an open corridor on the first floor. I had never been in a building that had steps up to another floor - up to two other floors. There were no windows in the stair-well and the first shard of natural light appeared at the landing on the second floor. The lady pointed to a blue door at the end of the corridor, half-stripped of its paint.

'In there.' she said.

Mama Blues, I assumed, was sitting on an old upholstered paisley pattern armchair, with a blanket draped over her feet. She wore a glamorous azure-blue dress with a matching headdress and around her neck was a circle of gilded metal from which hung a circular, translucent-blue mineral. Her eye-shadow and her lipstick were the same colour. A portable gas fire in the corner was flaming on high, heating two canisters of water containing drops of eucalyptus oil - the source of the sharp smell in the room.

The lady stood up and bangles clinked on her arms like pieces of percussion, while large, pearly blue circles swung from her ears as if their purpose was to entice parrots to swoop and perch. This was Mama Blues alright - either that or some elaborate practical joke.

There are many well-endowed women in Tolongo, but it is fair to say that the contents of Mama Blues' bra far surpassed maternal necessity. She moved forward to me in a processional slow march, reaching with an unnatural length on each step; a variant form of cantilever to counter the overwhelming effects of gravity.

'Are you a prince, or a wise man or a fool, little boy?' This was not the introduction I had expected.

'I'm not sure, Madam.' I replied with an instant courtesy. Five other women - much younger than Mama Blues - were sitting on chairs spread out against the wall on my right.

'Mama Blues. Not Madam,' corrected one young lady.

'I'm not sure, Mama Blues,' I said.

The young women looked at me curiously, waiting to see what the exchange would reveal.

'You can't be a fool, because a fool would think they already knew the answer. That is good news for you, little boy. No?'

'I think so Mama Blues.' Two of the young ladies on the back wall were holding their hands to their mouths to cover growing smiles.

'You are either a prince or a wise man. But if you are a wise man, why would you come to Inner Tikki looking for Mama Blues?'

'I was asked to come by my father, Mama Blues. I am running an errand to buy the very best cigarettes; ones which taste like honey and mango.'

The women at the side burst into repressed laughter which Mama Blues silenced abruptly with a short glance in their direction.

'Who is your father, boy?' she asked, immediately holding up her hand to delay my answer. 'No, wait. Siseko Tshabalala, Ntando Bonani, Degana Asanda? Yes. Your father is one of those. Which one, boy?' I could not believe that she had narrowed it down so easily.

'Ntando Bonani,' I replied. Mama Blues started to shake her head and looked around the room with disgruntled eyes at the younger women. They all began to mirror her expression.

'I have not seen your father for some time. It's a serious business when debts are outstanding in the Inner Tikki. Too frightened to show his face, is he? So he should be. I see he's happy to send his son though. What sort of a father is that?' She looked at the young women, who all nodded in agreement like pre-wound mechanical dolls.

'He's the only father I have. I didn't choose him.' I immediately regretted having spoken.

'Wise young boys run errands for their mothers - not their fathers,' she said. 'So, if you are not a fool or a wise man, then you must be a prince. A prince is rich with money, no? Is that envelope for me, boy?'

I was holding the envelope of notes tightly in my hand, reluctant to let it go.

'It's the money for the cigarettes.'

'You see, what did I tell you girls? . . . A prince. . . I knew he was a prince all along.' She took the envelope from me, placed it in a metal box on top of the portable fire, then pointed to the girl nearest the door.

'Coca will bring your father his cigarettes shortly. That concludes our business.' She turned around and slow marched back to her seat. I was standing in the same spot feeling uncomfortable, not because of the heat and humidity.

'How will I know that my father gets his cigarettes?' I asked, more worried about the repercussions that might result from me returning home empty-handed.

'Ask your father when you next see him if he received his cigarettes.' she retorted, closing the matter.

As Coca escorted me out, Mama Blues maneuvered herself back into her chair, which I heard creak under her weight as footsteps scurried across the room; presumably to replace the blanket at her feet.

Outside, the old man was sitting up wide awake and staring at me. He kept staring until I reached him.

'Get what you want boy?' he said, like he already knew the answer.

'Thanks,' I replied.

'Thanks for what?' he asked.

'For showing me where to find Mama Blues.'

He cricked his neck, took off his hat and scratched at his thin grey head of wiry hair. 'Ain't not worth thanking me for showing you to the devil, boy. You believe in the devil?'

'I don't know,' I said.

'I believe in the devil.' He nodded with certainty. 'I seen the devil myself and I tell you . . . hell don't burn no red . . . it burn blue . . . bright blue, boy.'

I walked on, but not in the direction of my mother, which would have been the most prudent decision, and one which I relived in my mind many times. But curiosity is a powerful force, especially for a twelve-year-old boy on a solitary adventure. Coca emerged from the door to Mama Blues shortly after me. She was wearing a tight red dress and high heels, clutching a purse, and must have been one of the prettiest women in Tolongo at that moment. Not even the wisest counsel from my ancestors could have prevented me from following her. She headed for a shebeen, which my mother had warned me about, certain it would bring me the same fate as my father.

I watched Coca enter the shack, then boxed around to the back, where I squinted through a crack in the plywood. She was sitting next to my father as a metal bucket of maize beer - umqombothi - was passing from person to person, followed by a stick of mountain dacha - Zambezi gold, as it was known. Everyone inhaled, and the noise of laughter increased in proportion with the flushing of their throats.

When my father pulled Coca up by the hand and lead her into the adjoining room, I found a new crack in the partition wall, and my curiosity turned to fear. They stood kissing, before my father picked her up and forced her, face down, into the mattress. She tried to resist. He lifted her dress, pulled, then ripped her underwear. She strained to breathe as he covered her mouth with one hand and gripped her neck tightly with the other. As he began to rape her, her will relinquished. She lay idle and compliant as he banged his hips into her behind with an animalistic reverence. When his gratification arrived, his grip relaxed, and the corners of his lips lifted in a wry smile. Coca sat up, fixed her dress, then spat in his face, shouting *bastard pig* repeatedly. He laughed at her and playfully slapped her cheek, as if to say she had nothing to bother about.

I hoped never to see him again, but hope is a beggar.

2
Glen Cleaver

In his stupor, my father blindly stumbled into my collection of glass bottles - thankfully for me, without cutting himself. It was less than a day and a half after I witnessed him assault Coca in the shebeen.

'Get up, Lifa! You coming work with me, boy!' he said, shaking my shoulder roughly then flicking a warning-slap that landed above my ear. It was so early and dark that I could not see him. He threw down a set of overalls and a wooly, moth-eaten hat onto the thin blanket covering my legs.

Behind, my sisters pretended to sleep, lying silent and prostrate, like field mice in the presence of a boomslang. In shock and disquiet, I fed the overalls up my legs, half asleep. They were far too big, so I turned up the sleeves and legs, transforming into a comedy-like character from one of the silent movies Mr Mpendulo projected in church. I stepped tentatively over mother's body on the earthen floor. She was lying quietly on her side, on lengths of well-used cardboard, also pretending to sleep. I crouched-down, sitting on my heels, seeking a better view of her face. Her eyes flickered open, trying to focus as I whispered into her ear.

'I must leave for work, mother.' Her full lips thinned and tightened, and her face radiated a vague sense of sadness. She propped herself up, onto her side, using her forearm and elbow, then wheezed.

'Them bottles better for catching rain from the roof, boy.'

She had a point. Life was hard when it rained. Life was always hard, but it was especially hard when it rained. Thin cardboard insulation and shared body-heat is no remedy for a penetrating wet. The rickety door to the shack flung open, stopping hard when it hit my boney backside. I wanted to kick it back into my father's face.

'Out, I said! *Kafferkont*!' he shouted, in Afrikaans.

I walked barefoot into the lane, clutching my hat. My emaciated, pole-of-a-father was already on his way, so I burst into a jog to catch him up. He had the distinct advantage of old, leather boots. My bare, calloused soles bore the discomfort of the dusty, potholed lanes well enough, but they could not resist the cold. We moved silently through quiet, welded lanes and fifteen minutes later arrived at a main road intersecting the sprawling township. He joined a huddle of six men in similar overalls just as a white

15

bakkie stopped beside them. Every man jumped on. I was the last to climb over the tailgate, squeezing into a small space against a jutting wheel-arch.

Beginning my life as a man, at the age of twelve or thirteen, was not unique. Those without a father or mother to exploit them were forced to beg, or steal, or run petty errands for unscrupulous, empty souls. An unlucky, anonymous number were ensnared and subjugated into a life of crime and depravity. The less unlucky lived homeless and alone, in the undergrowth by the roads adjoining the township. I knew all of this. I didn't like it or understand it, but I knew it.

The distant glow of Cape Town's lights diluted as we climbed through pine trees over the mountain pass, down into the deserted main street of a small, pristine town in the valley below, then turned and crossed a rickety bridge. It was not long before Glen Cleaver's imposing, whitewashed pillars came into view. My father had worked at the prestigious vineyard for the last five years.

Whitewashed rocks stretched out in equal intervals on the grass verges of the dusty driveway, with rhododendron bushes and mature oaks lining the route; a dramatic guard of honour. As the vehicle twisted and turned, the headlamps unearthed a kaross of vines in the foreground of a grand, whitewashed, estate-house, framed by the Hottentots Mountains.

I never could have imagined a house so big; in our tribal homelands and in the township, every shack or hut consisted of one room. We continued past, uphill, over crunching gravel onto a rough track under the cover of bushy karee trees. For the last half-mile, the bakkie bounced and bruised on the potholes and gnarly tree-roots. At a small, brick hut in a clearing beside the track, we stopped.

'Get off!' shouted my father. I climbed over the tailgate and followed to the hut. My father knocked on the door. When it opened, an old man stood hunched in the doorway, his short, grey curls accentuated by the light behind. His eyes were cloudy and blueish, and his skin was dark, cracked and loose, like it belonged to an old black mamba struggling to shed it.

'This my boy, Mister Ringidd,' said my father.

'Come in.' he replied, seemingly debating whether he could be bothered with the interruption. My father returned to the bakkie, which crunched into gear and continued up the track without me. The old man shuffled over to a small table by a wood-burning stove and ushered me in.

'Wait there while I finished eating. You calls me Mister Ringidd . . . or sir . . . or Mister Ringidd, sir. Unnerstan'?' His pulled a seat from the table with one hand, stroking the prickly, grey stubble on his chin with the other.

'Yes, sir, Mister Ringidd, sir.'

16

'What your name, boy?' he asked from the seat, pushing a spoonful of steaming porridge into his mouth.

'Lifa, Mister Ringidd, sir.'

'It's not Lifa anymore. You is called *George* now.'

Thirty minutes later I was in Glen Cleaver's vast press shed. My mother had told me about Kalahari bushmen crossing vast salt pans in feats of superhuman endurance, to reach seasonal watering holes overflowing with prey. With so much concrete expanding out in front of me in the press shed, I felt at the edge of my own remote salt pan . . . but suspected there would not be any glory for my efforts in crossing it with a mop.

After more than seven hours of mind-numbing, back-breaking drudgery, following Ringidd's orders, I slumped down behind a high tank intending to sit and rest, but sleep's seductive melody overpowered me.

'George!' shouted a man. I bolted upright, startled and fearful that he had been calling my name for a while. My father was standing, unimpressed, in the doorway, when I appeared with the mop, pretending to have been working.

Hurry up . . . hurry up . . . were the only two words he uttered all the way up the track. I followed as best I could, surrounded by an enthusiastic choir of crickets and grasshoppers . . . a sound I rarely heard in Tolongo, but which offered a fond reminder of my earliest years in the bush.

We passed Ringidd's hut and continued to a clearing hosting a wooden shed, capped with a dark, bitumen-soaked roof. My father creaked up the wooden steps onto a thin stoep and pushed open the door.

It feels strange to call a place home when it's not home. That's how I felt about the bunkhouse for every moment I lived there. The dilapidated construction was the estate workers' accommodation from Monday to Saturday and comprised one, long, open space, barely catering for the rudiments of fourteen men - twelve men and two children to be exact. The eating area encompassed two stained, scratched, oak tables with bench seating on the sides and wooden chairs at either end. A rusty, wood-burning stove sat to the side of two crooked antique dressers containing an assortment of old, cracked, chipped crockery, pots and worn, sticky utensils. The other half of the room was set up like an abandoned military barracks from the Great War, with six bunk-beds lined up symmetrically down each side.

'Eat, then go to the bottom bunk, second-last on the left,' said my father, pointing to a pot on the stove.

Men lay on their bunks or sat at the tables drinking umqombothi, smoking and playing cards. Some wore dirty white vests with their overalls half-off and hanging from their waists. Behind the smell of cigarette smoke was the smell of the bunkhouse - a smell I never adjusted to, like a busy, low-grade car-mechanics' garage; never quite losing that greasy, sticky, sweaty stench of a hard day's work, even though it might be tidy.

A lonely paraffin lamp flickered on one table. I sat quietly, anxiously, at the unlit table eating thin, tasteless vegetable stew with pap as my father joined the gamblers. A young worker was holding his hand out in front of an older man, smirking, until his palm was begrudgingly greased with three unsmoked cigarettes. He took them to his nose and sniffed.

'Ummhhh . . . smells best when them free, Duke,' he said, grinning.

'You is paying for them later, Bostock, don't worry 'bout that,' replied his irate senior.

'Gonna take some money off you old bulls as well,' said Bostock, looking at the group on the neighbouring table.

'Got my eyes on them pickings Franklin hiding up him bunk,' said one of the older men. It was Franklin, I assumed, that stood up and scurried off to his bunk, returning just as quickly with a small package in his hand. Four, thick, half-smoked cigar-butts rolled onto the table as he unwrapped the rag.

'Big baboon's fingers,' said old Duke. Laughter was followed by the licking of lips at the sight of this newly discovered tobacco royalty. Franklin was the only one brave, dumb or desperate enough to pick up the remnants of Mister Vorster's treasure during the working day.

I rinsed my bowl and walked barefoot to the end of the room, arriving at my bunk in darkness.

'What's your name?' said a quiet voice. I noticed the silhouette of a boy on the top bunk next to mine, up against the back wall.

'Lifa,' I answered.

'No . . . your *English* name? Always use your English name. What's your English name?'

'George.'

'I'm Victor.'

'Is that your English name?'

'What do you think?'

'What is your real name?'

Victor paused, wondering if he should bother telling me.

'Best you don't know . . . keep you out of trouble.'

'Do you work on the wine estate, Victor?' I asked, hoping to receive some information about my new life. He sighed quietly before answering.

'Everyone in here works on the estate. Anyone else is on the household staff.'

'How long have you been here?' I whispered.

'Six months . . . and I'm glad you've arrived. I've been stuck here doing two people's work with no help.'

'Does that mean I will be working with you, Victor?'

'I hope so.'

'What work do you do?'

'You sure ask lots of questions, George. Cleaning, mostly always cleaning,' he replied with a raised voice.

'What sort of cleaning?'

'It doesn't matter what sort of cleaning. Cleaning is cleaning . . . but now you're here, we'll finish work in the bunkhouse by lunch and Masta Baas will get us onto the estate in the afternoons . . . that's what Ringidd said.'

'Who is Masta Baas?'

'You'll find out soon enough.'

A hoarse voice interrupted us from two bunks along, although in the dark I could not see a face. 'Shut up, go sleep.' Victor turned away from me and rested his head on a spare set of overalls, which he had rolled up as a substitute for a pillow.

3
The Bunkhouse

There was not one morning in the last twelve years that I had not awoken in the same room as my mother. A blanket of dark covered the bunkhouse and I wished I was back in Tolongo, feeling increasingly aggrieved to be near my father. He had barely acknowledged me since surprising me the morning before. In the last two days, he had turned my life upside down.

I searched blindly for my oversized overalls and dressed, then my small, bare feet tentatively shuffled past the passive, brooding bodies lying asleep on their bunks. The gambling table was full of empty umqombothi bottles and stained, chipped cups full of cigarette butts, not cigars, from the previous evening. Victor filled a pot with water and showed me the log pile. He scrunched up paper and lit kindling in the wood burner with a match. We prepared a breakfast of pap, tea and coffee. Without any meat or vegetables to accompany the bland, cheap, white-maize staple of all poor people across Southern Africa, pap is little more than flavourless starch. But to eat a bowl of it every day is a luxury I can hardly describe.

Instructional is the most objective way to have described my first impression of Victor. He avoided play and small talk, relaying directions and information about each task like a parent mentoring a struggling child.

'Johnson's always up first,' he whispered. 'He gets angry if anyone reaches the pits before him. He's been here longest, apart from old Duke. Then there's your father, Kenneth . . .'

'Kenneth?'

'Kenneth, your father,' he said again. I could not believe my ears. My father had worked at Glen Cleaver for all those years and never once mentioned they had called him Kenneth.

'And there's Charlie - a big, friendly Zulu - Herbert, Robert and Gilbert . . . they keep by themselves; quiet and out of trouble.' Victor continued. 'Bostock, Peter, Franklin, Barclay, and Eugene are the younger guys . . . they're ok.'

'What if I can't remember their names, Victor?' I replied, concerned everyone would instantly dislike me. He shrugged his shoulders.

Just as Victor had predicted, Johnson was up and out in his underwear before anyone else had stirred. Duke shuffled distinctively over to the table with small steps, in dwindled bones that held his skin. His dark eye sockets were overgrown, either that or his skull had shrunk around them.

Men trickled slowly, in ones and twos, over to the pot with their bowls. I ladled in generous helpings. Some half-nodded, but nobody spoke. A big head, a foot taller than most, with shoulders wider still, reached the front, and a single eye gazed into mine, followed by a deep, wide grin showing an assortment of yellow teeth in differing shapes, sizes and states of repair. The man stretched out his great earthen clod hand, inviting me to shake. My hand disappeared into his, like a newborn child's.

'Welcome to them bunkhouse, boy. You Kenneth's boy, no?'

'That's right, sir,' I said, fearful and polite, as if meeting the chief of an old Zulu tribe for the first time. This overgrown, one-eyed man with the two deep, white scars running across one side of his face was no Zulu chief. He broke into an unforgettable, deep laughter, that even now I could not impersonate with any accuracy, lest my vocal chords are lowered by two whole octaves. He shook my hand vigorously until his laughter subsided.

'Good Goad, boy. You'll meet them mastez an' them baases an' them surz in all good times. Me is Charlie. No baas and no surz . . . Charlie, boy.'

'Sorry, Charlie. I'm George. I met you once before,' I said nervously, expecting him to remember and finish the scolding he had started.

'No. I'm not think so, George. Where we meet?' Charlie looked down at me with a vacant expression on his face.

'In Tolongo . . . when your plastic sheets were flying in the wind.'

Charlie paused for a moment. 'I'm not remember,' he said, looking like he was trying to requisition information from a small pocket of air inside his head.

'My mother told me who you are. Jama . . . you're called Jama.' I said.

'Not calling me Jama. Never calling me that, see? I'm is always Charlie, boy . . . at Glen Cleaver, see?'

'Sorry, Charlie,' I replied, my eyes fearful of looking up into those of the giant before me.

'Victor told you how it works here in them bunkhouse, George?' Charlie continued. I remained silent, concerned that whatever I said would get me into trouble.

'Come on, Charlie man, you tell the boy how it work in the

21

bunkhouse,' interrupted Franklin. Charlie stepped back and opened his stance towards the tables.

'Them two times in them bunkhouse. Them morning times . . . them early, dark morning times is sad times . . . them very serious times. All mens is unhappy in them mornings. Them never smile and them never happy. Them never joke . . . even them good joke . . . joke is very bad. Don't speak to nobody in them morning times. Eat and drink and do them work like them mouse or them grass snake – hidden and quiet.'

Charlie paused for breath, and the men tuned in, pausing the filling of their stomachs momentarily and replacing expressions of fatigue with growing amusement.

'Now . . . them dinner times, that is them time of different times. That is them time of good times. Them good times for umqombothi and smoking and eating and joking and dancing and gambling. Understand them different type of times, George?' Charlie gave me a smile after his conspectus.

'I think so,' I replied, still unsure if he was playing with me or not.

'Good. Very good, George.' His friendly pat on the side of my shoulder almost knocked me over. 'Remember, them morning times is like them burial ceremony - them beginning of them funeral. But night times - dinner times - is them party after them funeral. Them all good party times, George.'

Eugene spoke next. He was in his early thirties, with a mischievous grin and a lisping whistle - born of a lost front tooth.

'No, Sarlie, man. Mornings not all bad. Sarlie doing gumboot dance in mornings. True – no, Sarlie?' he said, looking around the room and raising his arms, willing on agreement. 'Show the new boy your gumboot, Sarlie. No more funerals in the morning, eh?' Charlie looked back at Eugene like he had just been set up for a fall.

'How can I show them boy, man? I'm got no gumboots, man,' replied Charlie.

'Go on, Sarlie, man. You don't need 'em gumboots. Be a good Zulu?' he said.

'Okay, one small time them gumboot, special for them new boy, George.'

Drummed cutlery sprang from metal bowls and metal cups were banged on the tables, accompanied by loud whoops and jeers. This was followed by much bending over at the stomach from laughter in anticipation of what was coming.

To see a grown man - a bulky, ungainly man - jump and bounce with difficulty from foot to foot, extending and twisting his legs uncomfortably in different directions, was about the funniest thing I ever saw in the bunkhouse. Charlie's broad grin was dominated as much by gums as teeth and his half-closed, white eyeball belied an unplaced confidence in his failed attempt at delicate, rhythmic gumboot dancing. He gambolled on regardless, like a gargantuan *izimu* - that fabled, cannibal Zulu giant.

Charlie was in full flow, dancing his mocking, cumbersome routine with his hands flailing and slapping and his knees and ankles searching helplessly for a rhythm his audience could follow. The circle of enraptured, bating manikins continued to jeer, shout, whistle and clap. It was partly his unruly size, partly his rusty routine and partly the fact that he was proud of it that made it funny and ridiculous. Not even the most stoic or repressed or burdened person could have contained their laughter.

Charlie raised his body a whole two-feet off the ground as he jumped, preparing to land with legs and arms outstretched for his finale. Without adequate flexibility and coordination, his bulky, muscular chassis was not equipped to deal with such exuberance. He landed on the back edge of his heels, slipped and fell hard onto his backside. This sent the men into a more virulent epidemic of laughter and bewilderment at the giant Zulu in their midst. Charlie sat on the stained floorboards, staring up at his audience, strangely pleased with himself, unaware that every man was delighting in his ridicule.

4
Masta Baas

'I was slow like you when I started,' said Victor.

'I'm not used to this,' I admitted.

'Don't worry, you'll speed up. Doesn't matter much anyway, soon we'll be working on the estate with the men.'

'What sort of work?'

'Producing the famous wines of Glen Cleaver . . . anything to avoid the cockroaches and maggots in the pits. I hate those damned crawlers.'

'Maggots? You serious?' I thought he was playing with me.

'We'll be out there shortly, see for yourself. I saw old Duke pick up a handful of maggots once and inspect them. He said they healed cuts and you can eat them . . .'

'I ate a live grub one time in the bush. My father made me. It was wriggling around in my mouth and I thought it would choke me. I'll never forget the slimy stench in my mouth for as long as I live,' I lied.

'You should have washed it down with some wine, that would have taken the taste away,' said Victor.

'I never tasted wine before. My father said it's a white man's drink.'

'Really? I've seen your father drink plenty of dop in the bunkhouse . . . and take it away with him at the weekends,' disputed Victor.

'What's dop?' I asked.

'Sometimes they give the workers wine they don't want, instead of money . . . Anyway, white men drink beer and so do black men. So why can't we drink wine if we want to?' he said.

'I never seen a black man drinking anything but umqombothi,' I answered. 'But I've never been near a wine estate, until this week.'

'One day you will drink wine, George,' Victor confidently replied.

Two boxed pits stood behind a thicket, fifty yards from the back of the bunkhouse. Victor led the way, and with each footstep the thickening smell usurped his role as guide. He climbed two wooden steps, stopped, pulled a rag and a small bottle of eucalyptus-oil from his pocket. He doused the rag with the oil then tied it around his head, covering his nose and mouth. After opening the door to the first pit, he flicked a latch on top of the box, lifting it up on its hinges. As it swivelled, a hole in the board used for pissing and shitting came into view. I was still out in the open, a few feet behind, but the stench of fermented gases and a plague of well-fed flies flew out at me like a puff adder striking a lame impala calf. I flinched unconsciously, ducked and ran to the side as quickly as I could.

'Pass me the bucket,' called Victor urgently, with a rusted tin in one of his hands. I stepped up and passed in the metal bucket with my free arm, covering my nostrils. Victor's head and half of his body disappeared into the box and he began scraping hard and fast with the tin.

'I tell the men to piss in the bush. Insects love the moisture. It's not so bad when the shit is dry.' He climbed back out to empty his tin into the bucket then plunged back into hell. When the bucket was full he stepped away and untied his rag. His hands were splattered with drops of excrement.

'I wretched my first three times . . . even with eucalyptus soaked into the rag . . . but now my nose has switched off to it a bit,' he said, grimacing. I didn't believe a word and reluctantly picked up the handle of the bucket. We emptied everything into a wire casket in a septic tank a hundred yards further downhill. The dried remains were burnt at the end of each month.

'So, you meet Masta Baas yet?' asked Victor.

'No . . . nobody has mentioned him apart from Ringidd and you,' I answered.

'He's the estate manager . . . works for Mister Vorster, the owner.'

'I thought Ringidd was the baas?'

Victor laughed. 'Ringidd is a worker . . . senior worker . . . but he doesn't do any work, not real work anyway. He's like one of the baases, but he's too lazy to be any trouble. It's Master Baas you gotta be careful around,' he said.

'Why?' I replied, with a nervous break in my voice.

'He's scary. You can't tell what he's gonna do,' said Victor.

'How scary?'

'Never look him in the eye. Remember what I told you . . . never look him in the eye . . . and never speak back to him unless he tells you. Do anything he says.'

I didn't want our conversation to continue, a deep, dark mesh of anxiety and fear was taking a permanent hold in my chest.

'Did you hear me George? I'm not playing tricks,' said Victor, changing his tone from informative to serious.

'I heard you.' I looked down at my feet wanting to be back in Tolongo with my mother. I had never missed her so desperately until this moment.

'Promise me you will do what I say, George,' he urged.

'Yes. Of course.'

'Then repeat it to me.'

'Never look Masta Baas in the eye and never speak to him unless asked.'

'And do anything he says, immediately,' Victor reminded.

'Yes, anything he says . . . immediately.'

'Do that and you'll be okay.'

'My mother used to be the only person who told me what to do - and my father for a while, but I don't do what he says anymore,' I said.

'Well, make sure you do what Masta Baas and Ringidd says,' he replied. 'Those two are no mother and father,' he mumbled under his breath.

Ringidd fetched Victor and I after lunch, then drove us to the offices on the outside of the courtyard. He told us to knock and wait for a reply before entering, but disappeared before Victor's knuckle had tapped the wood.

'Enter!' boomed a gruff voice. I walked in behind Victor, both our heads to the floor. Two menacing, brown beasts jumped to attention, growling loudly and straining on their leads.

'Christ min, Victor, what have you brought me? Another kaffir for the family?' said the mousey-haired man sitting behind a plain desk with his camel-coloured shirt sleeves rolled up showing strong, tanned forearms laden with bleached-white hairs.

'Yes, sir, Masta Baas,' replied Victor, eyes still to the floor.

'What's your name, little kaffir?'

'George, sir, Masta Baas.'

'George, eh? . . . like the fokin' King of England, eh?'

'I'm not sure, sir, Masta Baas.' I heeded Victor's warning and kept my eyes on the stone floor.

'Are you going to behave yourself, little kaffir king?'

'Yes, sir, Masta Baas.'

'You had better - or Mallie and Toppie will teach you a lesson you'll never forget.' He pointed at the two Rhodesian ridgebacks. There were dogs in the township, mostly scavenging, shameless mongrels, quite different to these well-groomed, well-fed, supremely athletic animals. They stood to the side of Master Boss with glossy, caramel coats and an upright, regal posture. On closer inspection, I noticed they were covered in scars, lightly peppering their faces and bodies, like the faint remnants of a past life.

'Don't think I'm joking about these dogs, little kaffir. They'll rip you apart one limb at a time if I ask them to.' He turned to the dogs, unable to hide his pleasure, pointed at Victor and me, then shouted at the top of his voice.

'Kaffir! Fetch!'

In a swipe of lightening the dogs near snapped their leashes, lunging towards us, barking ferociously, showing sharp, ivory-white teeth and spraying saliva at our feet. I was so scared that I urinated. Thankfully, I had emptied my bladder not long before and the incident passed unnoticed.

Master Boss could not contain his laughter as he ordered the dogs to retreat and sit. But it did not take long for his sombre, aggressive tone to return.

'Self-discipline. Success at Glen Cleaver requires self-discipline, my little kaffirs. If you can't discipline yourselves, I guarantee I will do it for you.'

'Yes, sir, Masta Baas,' replied Victor and I in unison, eyes still at our feet.

'Take these buckets and brushes and dilute the lime powder in water - one part powder to ten parts water. You will clean the inside wall of the press shed in preparation for whitewash. You know the routine, Victor. If it's not clean enough for me to lick my dinner off it, then I'll crack you, boy. I'll fokin' crack you. *Duidelik*?'

'Yes, sir, Masta Baas,' we replied firmly.

Victor jumped into action and I followed immediately on his shoulder. The remainder of our afternoon was spent in the press shed at the long, tall back wall, ascending and descending wooden steps, scrubbing black and green mildew from the thick render. The muscles in my arms were cramping in the first hour, although Victor did not hold it against me; he just kept on scrubbing – like his life depended upon it.

Master Boss arrived later with a shrill, metal tapping that got louder with every step of the slow march he undertook in our direction. Segs fitted to the soles of his boots echoed up into the rafters of the press shed, imprinting a signature on my memory that I will never shake off. Among the dusty, earthen tracks of the vineyard, the segs were impotent, but in the press shed, in the courtyard and around the workshop offices where the ground was hard concrete, the sound had the effect of thunder before lightning. A dark, unsettled foreboding followed the noise of those boots and now an unsettling silence ensued as Master Boss stopped by a section of the wall, half-way towards us. He turned and faced it, stepped in close and squatted low on his haunches, inspecting a small area at the bottom.

Energy and vigour returned to Victor's arm as soon as he was aware we had company and he scrubbed with a speed and intensity that would not previously have been possible. His eyes glanced momentarily at mine as his brush sank into the solution of water and lime powder, suggesting I scrub like I wanted to make a hole in the wall.

'Stop and run here, little kaffirs,' Master Boss said without looking away from the wall. Victor and I dropped our brushes and ran towards him, coming to attention by his side with heads bowed towards our feet.

'Mildew destroys a harvest. I have already made that clear. Have I not?'

'Yes, sir, Masta Baas,' we spat out in unison.

'So what is that?' He pointed at a very light patch of tiny yellow spores, indicating mildew was present.

'Mildew, sir, Masta Baas,' replied Victor.

'I said like I could lick my dinner off it . . . lick my fokin' dinner off it . . . or I'll fokin' crack you, boy.' His voice got louder and quivered as if he was about to lose control of his temper.

'Yes, sir, Masta Baas. It's my fault. I did the bottom section,' said Victor, immediately lying on my behalf. He had used the wooden steps to tackle the more physically demanding, higher section for most of the afternoon.

'Get on your knees, Victor,' shouted Master Boss.

Victor obeyed instantly.

'Now lick it . . . lick it like a dog lickin' a fokin' bowl . . . domb fokin' kaffir.'

My eyes were still at my feet, but Master Boss wanted my full attention.

'This is what happens, little kaffir . . . when you lazy, fokin' dogs cut corners.'

Victor stooped for a few, long, uncomfortable minutes licking the sour, sharp, poisonous lime residue and yellow spores from the wall with Master Boss, Mallie, Toppie and myself observing at his side. It took until his tongue had turned fully white and his eyes were pickled and dripping from the potent fumes for Master Boss to drag him back up by the scruff of his neck.

'Be thankful Mister Vorster is not here. What do you say, Mallie and Toppie? Am I going soft on these domb little kaffirs?' He looked down at the dogs who looked back at him with quizzical eyes, indicating they knew the answer; confounded about why he was being so lenient.

'Get this wall finished quick-sharp and get back to the bunkhouse before I change my mind.'

Our arms moved like pistons, scrubbing furiously at the last, small, length of mildew-stained whitewash on the wall. We evaporated so many layers of old paint that the age of the press shed unravelled like the age of an oak tree is deduced by its rings. My arm went limp for a moment as I pondered it all. What poor souls came before me - from a bygone era - gripping brushes in their hands, growing calluses on their palms? Could they foresee that two young boys would exhume a record of their lives, their toil? Victor nudged my elbow, interrupting my thoughts, and the muscles in my arm reconvened.

5
Church

We filled then placed steaming bowls on the table in front of the men and laden spoons rushed into their mouths with a collective zeal. The desire for second helpings was habitual even though the chance was doubtful. Within a few moments, a cloud of contentment spread out across two fully occupied tables. *Them evening times is them good times,* Charlie said on my first morning. Perhaps he was correct, relatively speaking.

The second bottle of umqombothi passed around from cup to cup but emptied just before arriving in front of my father. He chugged down his last dregs and stood.

'Fok man, Franklin. Fokin' snake,' he said. Franklin had finished the remains before handing over the bottle.

'Take some dop, Kenneth man, and shut whining,' replied Franklin, shaking his head.

'Not want no dop - want umqombothi,' he protested. 'George! Come here.' He pointed right at me as he shouted. I walked over to the table with the men either side of my father staring at me. Victor stayed where he was, putting crockery into the crumpling dresser. My father passed me both empty bottles.

'Fill them from the stash. Hurry up!' he said, turning back to the tables.

'I don't know where the stash is,' I said.

'Go fokin' find it . . . idiot piece of shit,' he replied, still with his back turned.

'I'm not your errand-boy,' I said in defiance, frightened as a shrew.

'You is what I tell you you is, boy. Get out 'fore I drag you out.' My father pushed his chair back and stood up with clenched teeth and fists, flaring his nostrils.

'Sit down, Kenneth man . . . Victor and I show him. Night times them good times, not them bad times,' said Charlie, walking over from his bunk and interrupting before I had a chance to say anything else or my father had a chance to do anything else. Charlie looked at me then nodded towards Victor.

'Run quick, Zulu boy, 'cos I'm thirsty,' my father called out as we reached the door. Charlie ignored him. I was glad to breathe in air that was not mixed with alcohol, smoke and sweat, relieved not to be in the presence of my father. When we returned, Ringidd was standing in the middle of the room.

'Uh huh,' he tutted, shaking his head slowly from side to side, looking at the bottles we were carrying. 'Be careful this don't turn into some damn shebeen other than the bunkhouse. You be workin' dog hard early morning now.'

'Yes, sir, Mister Ringidd' replied old Duke with the force of habit, as he lay carving a small block of wood with a rusted pen-knife on his bunk.

'Duke the only worker in here or something?' shouted Ringidd.

'Yes, sir, Mister Ringidd,' came the reluctant, tired reply from the rest.

'Remember . . . without me you ain't got no sway with Danie or Mister Vorster.' Ringidd always referred to Master Boss by his first name.

'What sway you got with Master Boss or Mister Vorster, Ringidd?' quizzed Johnson. 'You got about as much sway as this new boy here . . . and that's no more than the rest of us,' said Johnson, pointing right at me.

'What you said, Johnson man? Say it again. Go on.' Ringidd was angry now.

'Ah nothin', man. You got all big sway you need, Ringidd. Yes, sir, Mister Ringidd,' he said.

'I got enough sway to get you all pork the other week. That enough sway for you, Johnson? I don't like no pork, so I passed it on . . . suggested the bunkhouse might be grateful. I got that wrong eh, Johnson? Well, I don't make no two mistakes twice, man. Ungrateful swine! You want the hard way, Johnson? I can make the hard way.'

Ringidd scrunched up his nose, eyes and forehead. His illusory sense of grandeur about the power of his position at Glen Cleaver was perhaps an over-compensation for the plain fact he was a turncoat. For twenty-nine years, he had worked the wine estate and lived in the bunkhouse - just like the rest of the men - until the day he was promoted to senior worker and bunkhouse charge. Then he moved into the dingy, two-room hut on the track; charmed by the plumbed toilet, a small kitchen with a gas hob and enough electricity for two lightbulbs and a radio.

'Let this be learning for you two. Don't end up a bunkhouse worker all your lives,' Ringidd remonstrated, pointing at Victor and me then leaving, shutting the door firmly behind him.

'He's not fucked for thirty years,' said Robert chuckling to himself.

'Thirty years? He's *never* been with a women, man! That's why he's a grumpy, old fool,' whistled Eugene.

'He was okay when he was in the bunkhouse with us,' said Duke, mumbling to himself. 'Used to keep himself to himself and didn't have a bad word to say about nobody.'

'You talking about a different man, Duke? I like him more now he's all way down in that brick hut. Never once saw him take a slurp of umqombothi or a drag on the dacha or tell no story about good times. Always just sat there reading him's bible like some sort of witch doctor. Dull as toothache . . . I tell you, Duke,' said Johnson.

'Well, I'd more have him bunkhouse charge than that crooked bastard Samuel before him. Ringidd's harmless . . . too lazy to care and always forgetting things. Remember when Gilbert went missing for a day? Didn't even notice,' said Duke.

'I just don't like how Ringidd gets away with being the only black man I ever met allowed to call a white man by his first name,' said Johnson. 'You gonna tell young George and Victor how that came to be, Duke?' urged Johnson. 'What about you . . . Peter, Bostock? Bet you never heard it,' he said, glancing over at them. Peter, Bostock, Victor and I turned to face Duke as he sat up on his bunk, readying himself for the story.

'Quite simple . . . 'bout eight years ago, Ringidd did some driving 'round the estate for Masta Baas. Ain't nobody else could drive in the bunkhouse at the time and he had nowhere to go anyways . . . Transkei too far for no weekends . . . so it wont 'cos he was no favourite or nothing. After a while he was asked drive Mister Vorster and his family to church, Franschhoek, every Sunday morning - chauffeuring - what them rich peoples calls it. Sounds good at first, 'til you see he's working on his day off. After a few months of him driving Mister Vorster, his wife and kids, the next thing we heard is he invited in from car by minister to sit on them wooden chair up back. All the peoples at church called it Ringidd's chair. He did some good job on them all with the bible jargon he speak, and always smiling at children and patting them heads like he them old grandfather or uncle or something. But all that fuss don't get him invited into the shade of the white marquee in the garden for lunch with the congregation.'

'What *con-grey-shun,* Duke?' asked Bostock.

'Congregation?' said Duke. 'Congregation is like what they call the people who goes church each week for religious and Christian,' explained Duke with Bostock sitting up straight, blinking in confusion like a meercat drunk on fermented jackal berries.

'So while them local baases sipped on cold white wine from Franschhoek and Paarl and was quenching mouths with freshly squeezed orange juice and filling bellies with them freshest sandwiches - with the crust cut right off - Ringidd was all time sitting waiting in the car. He not included in no white-man garden party, for sure. He sat in the car, reading him's bible, getting stewed by the sun, more pious than a disciple his Jesus Christ. Some the wives gives him odd sandwich or piece of fruit going to waste - and for all his God-fearing, Ringidd knew how to smile good and wide. He showed real meekness and thankfulness whenever them wives gives him their scraps. I fancy he more like Mallie or Toppie in that regard, and it did him no harm.'

'So why he get to call Masta Baas by his real name *Danie*, Duke?' said Peter.

'I'm comin' to it man . . . After 'bout three years him going church and sitting up back, the church committee is voted put a small plaque on him chair. They is engrave it with his name. Danie Rousseau - Masta Baas - also went church with him wife and kids each week. He done the carpentry and engraving see . . . Now, come church time when chair all finished . . . at the end one sermon, minister asks Masta Baas to make presentation to Ringidd on behalf the congregation. Masta Baas get up and says words 'bout how Ringidd come such a fixed part worship each Sunday, then gives him the chair . . . In this moment, Ringidd saw an opportunity he not pass up. Like an experiment to test his faith in God or something - though I reckon it more like he so desperate to be friends with those white peoples . . . So what happens is, he walks right up front of the congregation and takes the chair. He reach out his hand toward Masta Baas - Danie Rousseau - and shakes it warmly . . . like they is old friends and says; *Thank you, Danie. Thank you so much, Danie. And thank you to God for bringing us all together.*

'Buffalo kak, Duke! No ways! Least tell me he got a beating from it,' interrupted Peter.

'I don't know 'bout no beating, but you could see them shock in every face the congregation,' Duke replied. 'Even the Minister's. But 'cos they in them God's house, nobody do nothing 'bout it . . . case they look stupid or ungodly in front everyone. And neither did Danie Rousseau. Ringidd had him by the short and curlies, man. Won't nothing Masta Baas gonna do about it standing right in front of them Jesus Christ dying up wooden cross. From that day on, Ringidd made it stick. Not a thing Masta Baas could do, unless he wanted to come off bad Christian and whole town hear 'bout it. Ringidd boring all right - but not one man I never met in the last thirty years called a white man by his first name and got away with it.'

'Shit, Duke, how d'you hear about all this? Ringidd's the only man ever going tell that story and could've lied it,' said Bostock, not at all convinced.

'Rubbish man, Bostock. I heard it first-hand from my friend James - he caretaker at church and slept every night, right up the eves. He saw, heard *whole* thing. Eyes near popped out his head, man.'

'I ain't never heard of no James, Duke,' said Bostock.

'Well there a whole lot you not heard, Bostock. You not heard no James 'cos he dead near six years now.'

'Shit . . . Ringidd, man. I can hardly believe it, man' said Bostock, now accepting the story must be true. Johnson was shuffling uneasily in his chair, desperate to speak.

'Well it worked with Masta Baas, but it would never work with Mister Vorster. Can you see Ringidd going up to him in the courtyard and saying; *Good morning, Koibus?* Shit, I would pay all good money to see that one, and then to watch him unleash Mallie and Toppie. They would rip him into a thousand pieces,' he said. 'Remember . . . no black man ever going to be taken in proper by no white man . . . it don't matter if you is calling him by his own name or nothing. Don't forget it, boys.' Johnson's warning landed with a thud. I nodded in agreement, but Victor stared back at Johnson as if decoding a riddle. That was the unsettling thing about Victor, he looked like he was always thinking, although he was never in a rush to speak.

I reckon Ringidd wasn't the only servile sycophant with an insincere smile. Johnson would have traded places with him in a flash; leniency and tolerance from his white masters, privacy in his own accommodation, the material comfort of a sprung mattress, electricity and radio, cooked meals prepared by the estate-house kitchen every evening. Ringidd's life was a tendon-tearing leap away from the spartan nature of the bunkhouse. Over twenty-nine years, he had climbed to the summit of a high, black mountain; where the air hangs thin and stagnant . . . and the blood runs cold.

6
Forbidden Friends

My father didn't reduce himself to a *goodbye*. He shot an unimpressed glance in my direction, then disappeared down the bunkhouse steps into a cloud of dust as two bakkies turned and stopped. He was returning to the township, like the men did every week, from Saturday lunch, until early Monday morning. My confinement to Glen Cleaver would last for the next twelve weeks, as part of my induction.

I resented the lighthearted, jovial atmosphere as men passed Victor and I at the table. They bounded out, pockets lined with wages, arms laden with bottles of dop. Victor poured me a mug of rooibos, then smiled.

'It won't be as bad as you think,' he said.

'What do you mean?' I replied.

'Staying here at the weekends. You could enjoy it,' he said. I sighed and lowered my eyes, unaware he was lifting up a small sack from the seat beside him. 'Mary sent up sandwiches and fruit for lunch,' he said. I peered inside. Not even the softest, thickest pieces of bread with the most sumptuous fillings could kick-start my appetite.

After his sandwiches, Victor got up and left without a word. I hadn't managed a single bite, and found myself lying completely alone on my bunk. For the first time in a week, I was aware of silence. Even in the dead of night, with every man lying deeply asleep, it was never silent. The sound of sleep was deafening, especially the collective trammel of twelve exhausted vineyard workers recovering from eleven hours' labour under an African sun. Sleep is meant to be a time for the body to repair itself, but for me in the bunkhouse, it was always an elusive basic human right. I was forced to listen to an ugly, extemporaneous orchestra snoring repetitive tunes each night. The sound reminded me of where I was and how my life was unfolding. I was a child in a man's world, without the privileges of a man; if you can call them that. At least it is something to have your own view of the world and to be listened to or to make your own decisions, about what you would like do with your life.

Our ancestors were warriors and hunters. One day you will be a warrior and a hunter, Lifa. My mother said these were my father's only words when he saw my wailing, infant speck for the first time. He constantly relayed that sentiment to me when I was a young boy, young and innocent enough to believe the words that came from his mouth.

All I wanted to do was skip forward five or six years to seventeen or eighteen - an age when I would become my own master. 'Shut up, boy!' my father would always say to me. 'When you are a man, you can decide what you want to do. Until then, you do what I say.'

'Yes, Father,' I would say. I didn't want to say it, but what choice does a young boy have? That is why I longed to be older. Maybe there are some children with a better start in life; born into those rich people, or born in the rural homelands far from the townships, with enough space to grow food and keep animals. Apart from Victor, my first week at Glen Cleaver felt like a life not worth living. I would have rather gone straight from birth to adulthood in one day. Childhood is a thankless, pointless apprenticeship for life . . . that's what I thought.

I turned around on my bunk, noticing Victor had left the door wide open. The rustling and chirping of nature was being gently blown in on the breeze. For a brief moment, I felt like I was lying comfortably, hidden in long grasses near our family homestead. We used to live in a mud-walled hut, clustered together with seven others in a clearing in the bush, surrounded by hills, twenty miles from the town of Wellington.

Animals roamed plentifully and freely among us. Goats were the main source of livelihood. They provided milk, cheese, meat and money when sold to neighbouring communities, or at the market on the outskirts of town. Life was simple and straightforward; we lived safely and shared the burdens and the blessings with everyone in the settlement. There was always enough food and plenty of fresh water.

When two white men in pressed shirt-sleeves and slacks, holding national government papers, drove into our clearing in a tall, military jeep, everything changed. They called an impromptu meeting with the men. There was great anger from the men and wailing from the women after that meeting. Three weeks later we packed up and left, walking as far as Wellington with all the belongings we could carry or drag. Forty-four departed; men, women and children, an hour before sunrise. We arrived, exhausted and sore, on the outskirts of Wellington an hour before dusk, then climbed onto three lorries that drove us towards the coast. Nobody told me where or why we were going. We arrived in the burgeoning, township metropolis of Tolongo, a settlement designed as an outcast state, part of the government's master-plan to segregate our black population from their white privilege.

Victor sat at the end of my bunk prodding my shoulder. I had been asleep for most of the afternoon.

'I've been shaking you for a while. It'll be dark in a couple of hours,' he said, when I finally stirred.

'Can you keep a secret, George?'

'What sort of secret?' I replied wearily, rubbing my eyes like it was nearing dawn rather than late-afternoon.

'Doesn't matter what sort of secret. Will you keep it . . . if I show you?'

'Yes, I promise, Victor,' I said, intrigued and curious about what he was inviting me to see. I didn't know what I had just agreed to, but my mother and Mr Mpendulo always told me that if I made a promise, I must keep it, it made a person a man. This was the first time I had the chance to keep a secret since returning from the Inner Tikki.

'Follow me,' said Victor, walking to the door.

'Wait. Victor?' Victor stopped underneath the doorframe and gave me a look that said if I wasn't quick I would miss it. I yawned, needing the full expansion of my ribcage, then joined him outside and began my inquiry.

'Where are we going, Victor? Masta Baas says I must not leave the estate.'

'I know what Masta Baas says. You worry too much, George.' The sun was still in the sky and slowly descending towards the horizon with a wide, reddish hue as I followed. 'We'll avoid the courtyard and the estate buildings. Keep hidden behind the trees - we don't want to bump into Ringidd.'

'Why would we bump into Ringidd?' I asked.

'He strolls around the estate sometimes . . . must be boring in that hut of his.'

Victor led the way, weaving from sugarbush to tree-trunk, always in cover. Without shoes in Tolongo, my feet were hardened to the dusty, prickly floor of leaves, twigs and needles under the trees. We passed assorted vine plantations, stretching out in perfect symmetry like ten-thousand, thin, stunted, pea-green infantrymen standing obediently for inspection.

'They call the vineyards after mountains,' whispered Victor. 'Cederberg, Overberg, Pilanesberg, Drakensberg' The first few all looked similar to me, sloping and arching gently over the ground, separated by wooded areas that never gave-way to grapes. Below the Drakensberg vineyard, I felt like we were on the other side of the world.

'We'll have to run across in the open,' said Victor, pointing at the track beside the thin, spindly, empty rows of the Drakensberg vines. He set off without waiting for my confirmation. At one point we crawled, bruising and scraping knees and elbows, for the thirty-yards gap to reach the oak trees high on the estate boundary. Halfway across, Victor turned to check I was behind.

'Keep low until we are in the trees . . . then we're free.' Victor used the word *free* rather than *safe* or *out of-sight*. It struck me as a strange choice at the time.

We sat shoulder-to-shoulder with our backs against the trunk of an oak, catching our breath and wiping dust and dirt from our overalls. Our laughter was driven by the adrenalin, the relief and the sheer audacity. We had survived unscathed, although I was still confused about why I had just run this gauntlet, blindly following Victor.

'Willem? Willem?' Victor whispered loudly, expecting company.

From behind another tree, walked a chubby boy, of around my own age, with bright, blonde hair. He was dressed in a uniform - pressed black shorts, knee-length green socks that were at his ankles, highly polished black brogues and a starched, white, short-sleeved shirt. He had unbuttoned the collar of his shirt and a green tie hung low, with a loosened knot. His shirt seemed not to have soaked up an ounce of sweat or gathered one speck of dirt. Willem was Mister Vorster's son, his only child and the fifth generation of Vorsters, who was expected to go on to inherit and manage Glen Cleaver when his father gave way, or passed away - whichever came first. Willem lived in the grand, whitewashed estate house at the end of the long, oak-lined driveway in the distance below.

I had not seen or heard of Willem before now, but had glimpsed his father a couple of times on the estate with Master Boss in the week before. Mister Vorster was imposing in stature and always immaculately dressed in pressed brown trousers or tailored khaki shorts and a clean, smart shirt. Mallie and Toppie roamed freely by his side, displaying a loyal obedience to his every word. Master Boss may have been the dogs' keeper, but Mister Vorster was their master; *Master Boss the Mister - Mister Vorster the Master.* I used to say that silly phrase over and over with Victor until it got us tongue-tied.

'George, this is my friend Willem. Willem, this is my friend George,' said Victor looking at both of us, brokering the introduction.

We briefly said hello then Willem's face lit up with excitement.

'Come Victor, let's show George,' he said.

The further we walked from Glen Cleaver's boundary, it became more rugged and unkempt underfoot. Thick clumps of wild grass, sugarbush and fynbos forced us to meander aimlessly, without a path.

'Make sure not to step near the sugarbush, George . . . puff adders,' said Willem. I did not like snakes. Willem could see my concern and wryly smiled at Victor. I responded nonchalantly, pretending not to be afraid.

'I never saw a puff adder. What do they look like?'

'You don't *see* puff adders, George . . . brilliantly camouflaged,' he said confidently. 'And they strike fast . . . way too fast.' I believed him, from the way he was speaking, all serious all of a sudden, like he knew everything there was to know about snakes.

'Father said a worker once got bitten on his calf-muscle and they cut off his leg at the knee. It swelled up like a rugby ball and turned black and yellow from the venom. They called a doctor but he came too late . . . and didn't have the correct serum anyway. You've got to give the serum within four hours for a puff adder or you're in big trouble,' he continued.

I didn't know what serum was, but deduced it must be some type of medicine for snake bites. Two threatening clumps of sugarbush, directly in front of me, now looked life threatening. I made an abrupt, wide detour, half-expecting a puff adder to be hidden in wait among the foliage, ready to strike and puncture one of my own, spindly calf-muscles.

'He got you good, George,' said Victor. He and Willem slapped high-fives and smirked. 'You nearly turned white like Willem,' he said. This sent them further into hysterics. I kept quiet, not wanting to risk further ridicule.

At the end of our walk from the oak trees, Victor's secret revealed itself; a beautiful, crystal-clear pool. There was enough water to swim across and it was deep enough to jump safely from high above. The most exciting feature was that it was completely hidden from view of the surrounding countryside. Unless you were a high-flying bird, you had to be ten paces from its edge to know it was there.

'Look, George! . . . A fish eagle . . . above the trees,' said Victor, pointing back at the tops of the oaks at the boundary. I strained my eyes, struggling to see anything other than a perfectly still, landscape painting. Screams made me quickly turn around again. Willem and Victor had disappeared. The sound of two splashes preceded a short silence, then ecstatic laughter echoed up into the sky. Two small piles of clothes lay on the ledge overhanging the pool. I walked to the pile and shuffled tentatively nearer the edge on hands and knees. The stream had bid a temporary farewell to the earth and relinquished its will to gravity. Against my better judgement, I inched further forward and peered over the sharp, rocky lip. Willem and Victor were treading water below.

'Come on, George. Jump. It's easy.' Victor was first to speak.

'Take off your overalls, but keep on your underpants,' shouted Willem with a wide grin and the essence of glee on his face. The look on my own face said there was a bigger probability of lightening striking from the clear blue sky than me jumping from the ledge.

'George?' shouted up Victor. 'Walk down the side. There is an opening in the bank of the stream and you can walk back up to the pool.' He pointed down in the direction that I was meant to go.

'Okay,' I said, thankful I did not have to endure any undue persuasion.

'Heh, George?' shouted Willem as I stood. 'You're going to jump off that ledge one day. Not today, but one day . . . and you're going to love it.'

I smiled back, my way of saying thanks for understanding. When I reached the pool, it looked more beautiful than it had from above, and bigger. I turned up my overalls and pulled the legs up above my knees then sat on a nearby rock, immersing my feet in the cool, inviting waters. There was nothing to see but a wall of stone rising towards the cloudless, blue sky. The only visitors to this part of the mountainside were rock thrush, warblers, sunbirds and siskin . . . and the occasional fish eagle, observing us from a floating fortress high up in the thermals.

I played along as best I could from the side, splashing and watching as my proficient, new friends climbed out and scampered downstream then back up the bank to the ledge to jump again. They jumped and jumped, then swam, and held their breaths after diving below the surface to see who could stay under longest. As they played, I watched dragonflies hover above the water, searching for snacks, and threw pebbles into small, stagnant pools below.

Willem taught Victor how to swim in this pool and when he had mastered it, Victor gave Willem lessons in fearlessness; jumping and pirouetting from the high ledge without a blink of his eye. I may have been lagging behind in friendship, swimming and jumping, but it would not be long before I caught up in all three.

7
Cigar Smoke

Ringidd told Victor and I to eat in the estate-house kitchen after dark on my third weekend. During the afternoon, I had taken my third trip with Victor to the pool, the second with Willem, who had been visiting relatives the weekend prior. As dusk approached, we hopped from rock to rock in the stream below the pool, towards the clothes on the bank. I had not yet jumped or swum, and stood dry as dust, watching Victor and Willem's clothes streak and stutter over their damp bodies.

'When did you learn to swim, Willem?' I asked.

'When I was five,' he replied nonchalantly as if it was nothing special.

'But how did you learn?' I asked.

'I had lessons at school. All we do is train for swimming galas. It's *so* boring. My dad says I must keep on practising but I'm only in the second team for my age.'

'You go to school? A school with a swimming pool?'

'I have to go to school. Everyone has to go to school and all schools have swimming pools,' he replied, confounded and chuckling that I would even ask the question.

I was embarrassed to mention that the last time I attended school, I had only managed three days, before escaping unnoticed and unreported for over a month. The trouble came when my mother found out, but she never got through to me and always asked Mr Mpendulo to take up my case instead. It was his school after all. If Mr Mpendulo's school had a clear, blue swimming pool, maybe there would have been some incentive for me to attend more regularly. I had never seen a swimming pool in my life . . . I thought the only place to swim was in a river or the ocean.

'Why don't you go to school, George?' said Willem. I shrugged my shoulders.

'School in the townships is for kids,' said Victor. 'I stopped going because it's more important to be a man and do man's work. That's why I came to Glen Cleaver.'

'I hate school, all everyone talks about is rugby . . . *rugby, rugby, rugby*. I hate rugby. I'd rather come live with you in the bunkhouse than play blinking rugby. Father says I'm going to run the estate one day anyway,' said Willem, with an air of entitlement.

'You can be our *baas*, Willem. Yes, sir, Mister Vorster,' said Victor, standing to attention. 'You'd be a better baas than Masta Baas or Ringidd, that's for sure.'

'Hey! Boy! Fetch my clothes.' Willem pointed at me, mimicking his father.

Victor laughed. 'Nah, I don't think you're gonna be my baas, Willem.'

For those two hours I completely forgot about my mother and father and the bunkhouse. But at the shade under the cover of the oak trees on the boundary I received a stark reminder that I had left one world and was re-entering another. I wished that my life might exist only with my two new friends at our deep, blue pool . . . but that life was only available in dreams.

'See you, George. See you, Victor. Still on for next Saturday?' said Willem hopefully.

'You bet, Willem. As long as Masta Baas doesn't have any surprises, we'll be here.' Victor spoke on my behalf.

We left the trees at the opposite end from Willem. He took quite a detour; walking back uphill, entering the woods on the far side of the vines, then moving towards the neighbouring vineyard, far from the view of the estate buildings and the estate-house.

'Why doesn't Willem walk right down the track?' I asked Victor, confused about the need for such an elaborate detour.

'That's the safest route,' he replied.

'But he can come and go as he likes. He's Mister Vorster's son,' I commented, still unhappy with Victor's answer.

'Yeah, he can come and go as he pleases, but not with us. He can't be seen with us.'

'But we're not working now, Victor.'

'We don't need to be working, George.'

'I don't understand.'

'You will. Willem is raised so not to be friends with us; with a black person. Remember what Johnson said. Ain't no white man ever going to take in no black man. Not ever . . . no Shauna, no Xhosa or no Zulu . . . not proper anyhow.'

'But Willem is your friend. I saw for myself.'

'Yeah. For now. But one day he'll stop being my friend. He'll have to listen to the other white people. It won't be his fault. They'll tell him. They'll show him. He'll be forced. You watch, George. You'll see.'

In the bunkhouse after dark, Victor put on clean overalls and we ambled down the track in still air with a quarter-moon struggling to penetrate a thick blanket of cloud. A light and the thin hiss of a radio leaked from inside Ringidd's hut, interrupting a chorus of crickets and grasshoppers, which resumed after we passed.

The facade of the estate house was illuminated by powerful spotlights, hidden behind balustrades on the paved terrace in front. Under the heat of the spotlights, the house was less white than during the day - like the buttery teeth of a middle aged man next to the milky white of a young child.

'You see the two small lights beyond the trees?' Victor said, pointing. 'That's Masta Baas's place . . . keep well away.' He needn't have worried, because I wasn't planning going anywhere near him, unless I had to.

'Don't ever walk in front of the house . . . or over the grass. Always follow the track in the trees behind the hedge and come down from behind. There is a gap at the far end and a small path straight to the back door . . . just in case I'm not with you.'

'How d'you know all these rules?' I asked.

'Mary came and got me on my first weekend. She showed me the way and told me things to watch out for.'

'What's Mary like?'

'Like a big sister . . . when she's not asking questions about Barclay that is. Barclay's all she talks about when nobody else is around. Charlie says to keep friends with her though . . . and we'll always eat well. She gave me pastry tarts with fresh strawberries and whipped cream the weekend before you arrived. They had this fine sugary dust sprinkled on top. When I'm older I'm going to have my own shop and that's the first thing I'm going to sell. Best thing I ever tasted, George,' he said, looking like his hunger had just been satisfied by the thought.

'I would eat them all myself before selling them,' I replied. 'One time I had honey and mango and banana all mixed together for my sister's birthday. That was the best I ever tasted,' I continued, feeling rather inadequate alongside strawberry and whipped-cream, pastry tarts. Victor was less than a year older than me, although sometimes I felt like he might as well be five years older with all he had experienced.

Voices and laughter echoed from an open window on the ground floor of the estate house. 'Come here,' said Victor quietly, stopping and crouching down behind the tall conifer hedge that rose like a fortress-wall between the lawn and the woods. He lay down flat on the ground and pulled at some branches to see through.

Double doors opened onto the terrace, radiating a flickering warmth, the mixture of bulb and candlelight. Three men walked forward, holding delicate, bulbous glasses, full of wine. The wine was dark as the silhouettes, so must have been red, according to Victor. Two glowing cigarette tips moved like fire flies as the arms gesticulated and danced with the conversation, occasionally resting to burn more brightly with each new inhalation. A third, brighter cigar-tip rarely moved. It was comfortably resting between the thick fingers of a man who was unmistakable.

The smell of the cigar and cigarette smoke crept across the lawn like fog invading a calm sea. Behind the men, the Vorster's dining room was full of people sitting at a long, antique table. It was hard to make out any detail, apart from the outline of the adults and of one child running in and out of the room, before being firmly escorted away by a short, chubby lady - presumably his mother.

'It's the Vorster's dinner party,' whispered Victor. 'They host up to twenty people on a Saturday every few months. The parents eat and get drunk and the kids play in the drawing room. Everyone dresses up in fancy clothes and shoes . . . you gotta have big money to be friends with Mister Vorster.'

'Is Willem there?' I said.

'He'll be inside somewhere, probably with the other kids. Sometimes the adults come out onto the terrace to smoke. They start with the white cigarettes, then after dinner they smoke these big thick brown cigar cigarettes, like Franklin finds; long, fat boerewors. It takes five or six goes just to get one lit,' he whispered.

Victor said he often sat hidden behind the hedge, watching the dinner parties unfold on his way back from the kitchen. On still, dry nights he could hear every word spoken on the terrace. He was nearly rumbled once, when a tickle in his throat made him cough. He ran like a springbok back to the bunkhouse, jumped into bed and pretended to be sound asleep. Nobody came, although he was sure they heard him.

As we finished our observation, Victor put his finger slowly to his mouth and fell back to the ground, lying on his front. 'Quick. Stay low.'

I lay next to him on a bed of dry leaves at the bottom of the hedge, peering through a small gap. Victor's ears were perfectly attuned to the Afrikaner dialect. Sometimes they spoke in English, other times in Afrikaans, and sometimes in a mixture of the two languages in the same sentence. Apart from a few common words, I could not speak Afrikaans - but Victor could. The three men walked into the middle of the lawn, stopping in a huddle, thirty yards from our position.

'Breeberg is completely different, Hendrik. Glen Cleaver never has a bad harvest. We have not had one year in the last twenty without a medal-winning wine . . . Twenty years! Not many can say that. Brockendaal, Grootgelegen, Tokenkop are the only others I can think of,' said Mister Vorster to the man on his left.

'So why is Breeberg struggling, Koibus?' asked the man to his right, with a distinctive English accent.

'They are not a wine estate like Glen Cleaver. We obsess about the technicalities of our growing process and run the farm like a machine. Don't get me wrong, I like Paul Van Horst, but he's not a winemaker. He's more interested in a lifestyle, with visions of becoming a restaurateur or hotelier. South Africa is not ready for diversification. It's all about good wine . . .' explained Mister Vorster. He took a sip from his glass and then inhaled forcefully from the wide, brown stick in his puckered mouth before swelling his cheeks like a puffer fish and exhaling.

'And an uncompromising regime of course. We squeeze every ounce from our kaffirs,' he said, with a cloud of smoke hanging above the huddle. 'We don't tolerate any of the shit Paul Van Horst puts up with . . . *Never* compromise on kaffir labour - Danie Rousseau will testify to that.'

'I've heard different about Danie,' said Hendrik, chuckling then looking knowingly at the Englishman opposite.

'What do you mean by that?' snapped Mister Vorster.

The laughing ceased abruptly as the man tried to erase his comment.

'Nothing at all, Koibus. I'm trying to be funny with all this medal-winning wine inside me,' he said.

'That wasn't nothing, Hendrik. Tell me. What have you heard about Danie?' insisted Mister Vorster.

'Seriously, Koibus. Just rumours. Nothing I can vouch for,' said the guest nervously with his twitching hand flicking cigarette-ash onto the lawn.

'What rumours? You had better tell me, man,' repeated Mister Vorster, sounding increasingly irate.

'I just heard that, eh . . .'

'Come on, man, spit it out for fok sake!'

The Englishman took a step backwards, clearly disassociating himself from the conversation or any prior knowledge he may have had in the formation of the rumour. But with the absence of information from Hendrik, he was next in the firing line.

'Come Adrian. What's so funny? I am hosting you two for dinner and you are pissing all over me.'

'Apologies, Koibus. No harm intended. Hendrik and I heard some rumours, that's all. We don't want to make trouble for Danie when it's probably only gossip.'

'So tell me then . . . if it's all kak,' said Mister Vorster, fixing his stare on the guest.

'It's my fault, Adrian' interrupted Hendrik, acknowledging to the Englishman that he was responsible to own up to a loose tongue in the wrong company.

'I just heard on the grapevine . . . that Danie might be compromising his marriage so to speak. It was funny . . . you know . . . the play on words . . . what you said about him not compromising on the kaffirs.'

'You mean he's fokin' one of my kaffirs?' Mister Vorster came straight to the point and there was a tentative, embarrassed reply from Hendrik.

'That's what I . . . eh . . . heard . . . Koibus. Sorry you had to hear it like this,' said Hendrik; a guilty child in front of a strict schoolmaster.

'Shit. Is that all? You had me worried for a second. As long as my estate runs like clockwork and my wine keeps winning medals, he can fok who he likes . . . he can fok anything he likes for all I care.'

Hendrik and the Englishman chuckled along with Mister Vorster but the tension was palpable and the relief on their faces more pronounced than that.

'Now come, we have the main course coming and another red I want you to try. Goes great with Kudu . . . Just be sure to hold your fokin' tongues in future,' said Mister Vorster, stepping back towards the terrace before the others. Both guests nodded profusely in obsequious obedience.

'I wished we hadn't heard that,' I said to Victor.

'Yeah, that's trouble,' he replied.

8
Miss Johanna

Miss Johanna tutted when she opened the back door, unimpressed that we had been crawling around on the ground before arriving at her kitchen.

'Victor? What in God's name you been up to? And you must be George. Come in, come in, quick, quick. We is about to serve main course.' Her arms hurried us and Victor walked ahead of me into a vestibule with high shelves packed with everything from old shoes and boots to rugby balls, fishing nets and rods. The highest shelf was reserved for dusty, empty wine bottles crammed together so tightly they looked in danger of falling over and shattering on the terracotta tiles.

'Wash your hands and faces. Don't forget the soap,' said Miss Johanna, opening the door to a washroom containing two deep, white, porcelain sinks.

Hoses hung down from taps on the walls above - one for each of us. The water flowed lukewarm and clean. I picked up a bar of soap which smelled like the rose I had inhaled in the walled garden. It reminded me of when Victor and I were ordered by Ringidd to rake up the cuttings and fallen leaves from the paved pathways that spread across the garden. In the central quadrant, at a large, stone weather-dial, lived one hundred rose bushes exuding an unavoidable, delicate, lingering aroma.

Victor bent down and stuck his face into the largest red rose with the widest petals, breathing in deeply then lifting his head and acting like he was drunk on umqombothi. When it was my turn to step into the rose-bed and smell, I chose a smaller, half-open, swan-white bulb. The smell pulled me in towards it and increased in intensity as the end of my nose was tickled by petals. As I breathed, I drank in the enchanting, hypnotic fragrance. Such a simple thing, such a beautiful thing; the sight and smell of a flower, the majestic rose, in bloom. I refer to that moment as the one which started my love affair with flowers, with horticulture. My adult life has, for the most part, been devoted to growing and caring for flowers. I am never more at home than when I am surrounded by flowers.

The dreary lye soap my mother used, if you can call it soap, was made from the fat of old cuts of meat, mixed with wood-ash. It was all she could afford and she treated it like gold bullion. She forced my sisters and I to wash with it every day. On the worst days, the bucket was placed in front of us containing water that had been used for cleaning clothes earlier in the day. A film of fat from the lye and grey bubbles formed on the water, but this never deterred my mother who was always first to wash. My eldest sister was next. She plunged her hands in and out of the bucket so fast I swear they were still dry when she wiped herself under her arms and around her body. We hated doing our faces. I hated it most of all, not least because I was the last person to use the bucket. I felt like I was wiping myself dirty and constantly protested at the imposition. My mother never budged. She may have had uncontrollable, under-educated, hungry children . . . but they always went to sleep clean.

Miss Johanna did not have the time nor inclination to wait for us in the washroom. When we entered the kitchen, she called loudly to Mary, asking her to find a brush and tidy us up. Mary was all dressed up in a black skirt and white blouse with a tight fitting hair-net pressing down on a full head of hair tied up in a large knot. The kitchen was huge, the size of the bunkhouse and a thousand times cleaner; spotless I would say, and definitely not smelling of moldy old grease, sour umqombothi and old cigarette smoke, all of which had oozed into every grain of our wooden floor.

Five polished, bronze pots sat on top of a huge stove with four big oven doors. The stove was partially hidden behind a dominating oak table for at least twelve people. Every member of the staff, all women, had their heads down, engrossed in different culinary tasks: cutting, washing, dressing, stirring, kneading. Miss Johanna was conducting an ensemble, regularly shouting orders and asking for updates on progress. Including Mary, I counted seven in total, then suddenly two others appeared, dashing in from the dining room with cutlery, dirty plates, dishes and glasses, constantly attending to the needs of the guests.

Mary was the prettiest of all the women and at the younger end of the spectrum, probably in her early twenties, which was a lifetime away from a twelve-year-old boy like me. She brushed us gently, with a mother's touch, displaying an air of apology at having to put us through such a fussy ordeal. Soon the hairs of the brush had adequately stroked and wiped away the few remaining needles. Mary had a soft spot for Victor - I could tell. She smiled at him warmly and stroked the top of his head with her hand when she was done. He was a little embarrassed, but her attentiveness instantly waned when Miss Johanna walked towards us.

'Dauphinoise better not be burnt,' she said with a raised voice. I found out later that dauphinoise was some fancy way to cook potatoes with cream and cheese. Mary scuttled back towards the oven and Miss Johanna grabbed us both firmly by the arms, sitting us down on two wooden stools at the back of the room nearest the door.

'When Mary finished with the potatoes, you can have soup. Sit here and don't move 'til she's ready.' Miss Johanna could never be described as motherly, which is just as well, because she was responsible for serving twenty guests four courses of dinner and I imagine the presence of Victor and I five minutes before her crescendo was an unwelcome distraction.

'Always listen to Miss Johanna,' Victor whispered to me when she turned her back to taste the gravy and inspect the half-dressed plates waiting to be finished and served. 'She's real nice, just don't get in her way when food's to be served.'

Mary had two dish cloths wrapped around each hand and was carrying a hot tray that looked too heavy for her. Her arms strained and shook as she bent down to put it back into the oven. She sighed, wiped her brow, closed the door, then picked up a bunch of fresh parsley, chopped and sprinkled it onto the generous swirl of cream that had been poured into our butternut squash soup. I could not believe my eyes.

'Right you two,' she said with a warm smile. 'Take them bowls of soup and two pieces of bread. Sit quiet on the stools until I am done.'

'Thanks, Mary,' replied Victor who was already off his stool and halfway towards the pot with the wooden bowls in his hands. He looked around the room quickly, peered into the jug of cream on the table, then ladled an extra spoonful into each bowl, simultaneously winking and smiling at me after successfully evading detection.

Mary quickly forgot about us, lost in the frenetic business of helping get twenty immaculate plates out of the kitchen and placed down carefully in front of guests while the food was still piping hot. The women were sweating profusely as each waitress was toweled down by Miss Johanna's stained cloth before entering the dining room. Someone once said to me that it's not lady-like for woman to sweat; so until Mrs Vorster entered, there must have been no ladies in Glen Cleaver's kitchen.

My gurgling stomach rapidly filled with soup which tasted better than anything that had ever slipped down my neck before; all rich and salty and mopped up with that soft, malty bread - bread with butter. Bread with butter! I tell you. That made me smile all through my body. They kept the butter and the milk and cream in huge fridges. How was I to know they were called fridges? The kitchen had three of them. Victor was patient, answering all of my questions as we perched together on the stools watching dinner-service unravel. I had too many questions if I am honest. I wanted to know the names of the foods, what they tasted like, the names of the equipment and utensils they were using and what the wine tasted like. I still had not tasted wine. There was plenty that Victor could not answer, but he did try and describe what wine tasted like. He said it was better than umqombothi. I had not tasted umqombothi either, so that was not very helpful. 'It's smooth like silk and not bitter or sour like lemon' he said. I had tasted lemon. He was getting a little frustrated, because no matter how he described it, I could still not imagine what wine tasted like. 'You'll just have to try drinking it yourself. It's the only way,' he said defeated. I could tell he hadn't tasted it either.

A waitress walked urgently through the connecting door to the dining room with a tray of glasses and I glimpsed a large mahogany dresser holding two silver candlesticks, an empty silver cake stand and a sizeable bronze gong with a wooden hammer containing a soft bulbous head about the size of a small potato. In the polished bronze face of the gong I could see reflections of a large, roaring fire-place, piled high with logs. I now realised the flickering warmth was not simply from candles and lighting. The night was not cold, so the fire must have been for show or to create what white folks call *ambience*.

Every time the connecting door from the dining room to the kitchen was opened, a noisy gaggle of conversation and laughter erupted, overpowering the faint sound of clinking cutlery on plates. The twenty china plates waiting on the kitchen table were all bright white with an ornate, delicate blue crest adorning the rim. I could not begin to describe or name all the different vegetables and salads that were being neatly placed onto the plates. Mary's potatoes didn't much look like potatoes to me. With her knife, she cut small square slabs from her tray and lifted them one at a time onto the plates. At the other end of the table, three joints of meat - beef, I thought from the colour - were strung out like freshly skinned boa constrictors. The meat was added to the plates in thick wedges, with enough on one plate to have made a generous stew for a family of eight in Tolongo. It was only when steaming, glistening gravy was added to the plate that it became unrecognisable, exuding such a deep glaze that the food might have been painted on from an easel with a fine-haired brush.

My mouth filled with saliva as I excitedly anticipated the meal that Victor and I were to enjoy this evening. What a treat? What a picture? This was going to be some story to brag about to my sisters. My father would never have been into the estate house. I bet he had never seen so much meat in all his life. I had . . . and I could not wait to tell my mother. I got that same feeling of anticipation, a hurtful excitement, many, many years later when I took my family to a restaurant for the very first time. I was in my forties and I paid for the whole meal with my own money. That was some meal, I can tell you. The setting was not nearly as grand as the table in the main house at Glen Cleaver - and it was not accompanied by a selection of red and white wines - or dessert wines as I came to learn. Imagine that, a wine made especially to be sipped with a dessert. Imagine dessert? I had never heard of dessert until that evening in the estate house. In the bunkhouse we had two meals a day and only because without the extra energy we would not have worked as hard. Only the dogs of Glen Cleaver got one meal a day, and we were not dogs. Even today, people in townships all across the Cape Flats are lucky to find one meal in a day. I grew up as one of those lucky ones if I am to be honest, but only because after arriving in Tolongo - much to my father's disgust - my mother turned devoutly Christian and became good friends with Mr Mpendulo. We had something to eat nearly every day, even if it was only boring old pap with watery gravy. Mother regularly reminded my sisters and me of this fact.

9
Ostrich, Beef and Kudu

Gwendoline Vorster walked into the kitchen carrying a plate of the main course which had not been touched and I knew immediately that she was Willem's mother. It was the nose and the mouth and her pale, freckled complexion that gave it away. The similarities between mother and son were as marked as the differences. Her slender frame and pristine, strawberry-blonde head of hair, trimmed short and conservative around the nub of her neck, was passed down from a gene pool Willem had avoided. And I could not imagine Willem pouting with tight, corrugated lips in such an unamused fashion. Willem preferred smiling to frowning.

The kitchen staff were in the middle of a well- rehearsed performance and I felt like a member of the audience, even if I was uninitiated and a little intimidated by such new and unknown surroundings. Mrs Vorster's unsettling arrival was a pressing reminder that the dinner party was not a show organised for my amusement. I was in the Vorster's private kitchen and all of the people around me - myself included - were at their behest.

'Johanna!' she said in a repressed, clipped voice.

'Yes, Madam.' Miss Johanna put down the sharp knife she was holding and shuffled urgently towards her.

'*What . . . is . . . this*?' said Mrs Vorster, holding out the plate in one hand and pointing to it with the other.

'Yes, Madam?'

'No! . . . Johanna . . . no! I specifically stated a trio. I typed it onto the menu cards. Two pieces of beef and one of kudu is not a trio. *What an embarrassment!* In front of all of my guests. And whose plate is this?' Miss Johanna knew Mrs Vorster's question was rhetorical.

'Not Willem's or Pieter Krauss's boy . . . no . . . it only belongs to the senior magistrate in Paarl - Jeppe du Toit. *Jeppe . . . du . . . Toit.*' It was as if repeating his name more slowly elevated her opinion of his position in the community further. 'Of all the people? Plate it up again, this time with ostrich fillet.' She threw the plate down onto the table. It should have smashed, but it bounced and spun, swirling a couple of times on its underside before coming to rest.

'Yes, Madam. Straight away, Madam.' Miss Johanna turned around and her eyes changed from obedient to fierce. She looked at the two women who had been in charge of plating the meat but could not tell which one was to blame.

Mrs Vorster waited impatiently over the girl charged with fixing the plate of food and gave a detailed commentary of what she should be doing before she did it. She could have returned to her guests, but seemed more comfortable hiding here in the kitchen, the only place she was revered like Judge du Toit. The young woman was trying her best, but became increasingly nervous and flustered. When she placed the last spoonful of gravy on the meat, she turned and accidentally wiped the edge of the spoon across Mrs Vorster's waistline. She didn't notice her mistake and looked confused when Mrs Vorster screamed.

'Don't stand there you idiot. Look what you've done.' The girl froze and noticed the streak of gravy, boldly traversing the floral greens and whites of the expensively tailored dress. A drop of the gravy fell onto Mrs Vorster's patent leather, high-heeled shoe, but she remained, thankfully, unaware of it.

'Come here!' Mrs Vorster shouted loudly, this time close to the girl's face. She reached for her wrists and pulled them in towards the stain to be certain she knew what she was talking about.

'Cloth! Now!' The cloth was already at her side, placed down by another member of staff who had anticipated its requirement. Mrs Vorster released her grip of the young girl's wrists and flung them back towards her in disgust. She snatched at the cloth and dabbed the dress herself. She then attempted to compose herself, slowing her breathing, lowering her voice and assuming an expressionless pout as if realising her guests might have heard the outburst.

'What is her name, Johanna?' she said in a more reasonable, but still angry voice. Miss Johanna was standing next to her boss and about to answer. 'Actually, don't say a word, I don't want to hear her name spoken in my presence. You can tell her she no longer works in my kitchen.' Mrs Vorster smiled at Miss Johanna with pathological ease. She gave the cloth back to the girl that had placed it onto the table. 'Now, clean my dress!' she said.

I noticed a tear running down the dismissed girl's cheek as her hands untied the knot of her apron and she walked towards the back door. Miss Johanna hadn't needed to say anything. I looked at Victor and his head was bowed, eyes focused on the terracotta at our feet. I followed suit. Victor hadn't prompted me to do it, but I felt like I was back in Master Boss's office on my first day. Miss Johanna did not appear surprised or remorseful at the outcome; all in the course of a day's work for the kitchen staff, as I came to learn.

I hope that trio of beef, kudu and ostrich tasted good for that poor soul Jeppe du Toit when it finally arrived. How inhumane to have a man restrained at a table, close to starvation, watching every other guest gorge themselves on a feast. And to have been at first teased with the unthinkable prospect of two pieces of beef and one of kudu - lying alone, all desolate and dejected without the good company of ostrich. How you can reasonably expect a person to tolerate such an abomination, I do not know? Ostrich fillet? Can you imagine? Seriously? Ostrich fillet? At that time, I could not tell you if an ostrich was a bird or an animal. Victor and I pondered on the question later that evening. He had heard Ringidd talking about collecting the meat from a local butcher in Paarl. They used Klepper's farm on the outskirts of the town which specialised in breeding ostrich for eating. 'They can run as fast as a horse,' Ringidd said. 'But they can't fly like no bird. Can't get themselves off the ground, not even for an inch.' On account of that, Victor and I reckoned they must be an animal.

Mrs Vorster continued making a nuisance of herself. She fiddled with utensils otherwise needed by the staff and re-arranged bowls, glasses and towels.

'Everything must be just right, Johanna. You *must* know that by now. Everything in my kitchen is to be just so. Twenty guests for dinner is no excuse for letting anything slip. Let that be a warning to you. Do you understand?'

'Yes, Madam. It won't happen again, Madam. Two new girls in training next week, Madam.' She informed her boss with such an earnest extenuation that Ringidd would have benefited from the lesson, although I would say Miss Johanna was a more accomplished actor. Ringidd in comparison had accepted the hierarchy of life at Glen Cleaver like an absolute truth.

'I should hope so,' replied Mrs Vorster, clearly pleased with Miss Johanna's deference in front of her staff. It was not only Miss Johanna's words that were intended to please; a more accurate judge of character and behaviour I have still to meet. She instructed one of the girls to fetch Mrs Vorster's empty wine glass from the table and refill it. She returned and passed it to Miss Johanna who immediately and personally handed it to the lady of the house.

'Madam, please, you are without wine. Even the most attentive hostess must not be neglected in her own home.'

54

'Quite right, Johanna.' Mrs Vorster took the glass of wine like a small child does their silken comfort-blanket. The gesture softened her immediately, for Miss Johanna knew well which levers to pull. Gwendoline Vorster's patterns of behaviour were routinely exhibited and could be forecast by the hands on the large antique clock which ticked, tocked and chimed from the wall of the kitchen with reassuring familiarity. Gwendonline Vorster's unpredictability was a predictable unpredictability and Miss Johanna knew every marker.

Lunch at Glen Cleaver was taken at noon during the working week. For Mrs Vorster it was usually an informal affair in the kitchen, around the oak table with her husband; sandwiches, baguettes, cheese, salad, fruit and cold meats, that sort of thing. There had to be food on the table before she could justify opening her first bottle of wine - always the same bottle - a 1954 Chenin blanc, cultivated six years earlier. She had selected it as the family's house white during the first tasting in that year and had grown accustomed and attached to it - I daresay she was reliant upon the loyal friendship it languished. She only ever poured two glasses at lunch - two large glasses - nothing exceptional by most standards, not for a housewife with little work to do aside from directing Miss Johanna and loosely monitoring her troupe of household staff. Willem posed little inconvenience, being picked up and driven each morning to Paarl Gimnasium, one of two large Afrikaans and Christian schools in the centre of town, by a friend of the Vorsters who worked nearby. Willem returned during late-afternoon by school bus. Gwendoline Vorster's next glass of Chenin blanc had to wait patiently, chilling in the fridge, until her son walked through the front door. From then until bed, a glass was always by her side; two full-to-empty bottles a day.

Miss Johanna knew that before dinner and at the end of her first bottle, Mrs Vorster was highly strung, intent on organising and checking the next evening's menu, adamant that all preparations must be complete. Dinner was a formal affair in the dining room, attended by all three; Mister, Mrs and Willem. They sat like small pebbles in a large cave at one end of the long dining table, enduring a review of the day, luxuriating in three courses from silver cutlery and pausing intermittently to prod at crumbs on the side of their mouths with beautifully laundered, linen napkins.

It was always between the start of dinner and the end of the main course that Mrs Vorster became irrational and unreasonable. Whether it was intentional or unintentional it is difficult to say. Alcohol took hold and goaded the officious, needy and controlling streak in her personality to take charge. Nobody was spared, not even her husband or Willem. In this state she was incapable of relaxing, forever getting up and out of her seat to make some observation or complaint in the kitchen, then returning to the dining room to sit and continue with the incredulously mundane conversation that batted back and forward between them like a hot stone. No wonder Willem greedily quenched his thirst for frivolity with Victor and I up at our secret pool.

Miss Johanna was always cautious, overly attentive and obedient when Mrs Vorster was in this stage of her libation. She understood that a manageable inebriation - the most subtle and underrated form of inebriation - could draw unsuspecting people into the milieu without their knowledge, more often leaving them regretting their involvement. If there was one time to avoid Mrs Vorster, this was it.

Mrs Vorster's final furlong was *'her saving glaze'* according to Mrs Johanna. This always happened near the end, or after, dinner. Her eye-balls went from dry to wet, filling from the bottom up with a clear, viscous liquid; rising in a straight line like a high-tide climbs the watermark of an imposing cargo vessel in port. For the uninitiated, you might think her eyes were welling with tears, but the tears never fell and the liquid didn't stop until it had covered the entire sphere. At this point the kitchen staff had the confidence to breathe more slowly and deeply.

With the filling of her eyes - for some scientifically unknowable reason - Gwendoline Vorster transformed for the better. She surrendered her entirety to the will of the alcohol in the wine. The sound of her fingernails scraping behind a doorway of inhibition quietened and her vain, desperate, exhausted acquaintance with self-consciousness, temporarily slipped. She sank into the intoxicating warmth of her unequivocal, yet strangely manageable, inebriation. All was well. Fear abandoned. Alcohol is a mysterious remedy but a likely companion for a person who has not experienced the liberation of unconditional, unbridled love in their lifetime. From what Willem said, his mother was one of those unfortunate souls.

Mrs Vorster's short-lived escape from self-loathing lasted until a hazy dreariness overcame her. In those two blithe hours, she behaved like your favourite, doting auntie Gwen on a white family's Christmas-day afternoon. She indulged in self-deprecating jokes, laughed, overlooked imperfections, embraced nonchalance and initiated displays of overemotional affection - rebutted by her husband but inhaled deeply by her son.

'Hey, Willem!' I shouted, smiled and waved from my stool at the back of the kitchen when he walked in from the dining room. He heard me - I knew he heard me, but he didn't flinch or give as much as a glance in my direction, not even for a fraction of the smallest second. If it was me, I could not have helped to look automatically in the direction of someone calling my name. That is a common, natural reaction; but not for Willem. He blanked me. I did not think it was normal to hear your name being called and be capable of ignoring it.

Everyone else in the kitchen heard me loud and clear. A chain of heads moved like a munitions belt being fed through a hard-working, large-bore machine-gun shooting out expressions of shock and disbelief. None of the staff dared hold their stares on me for any longer than a passing moment, returning immediately to their work with bowed heads, hoping not to attract any unwanted attention.

I laugh about the absurdity of it now, but at the time I felt smaller than a mosquito; and the look on Mrs Vorster's face quickly hardened the cement of my *insectification*. If I had been more confident or impervious to the good opinion of others, I would have stood and firmly slapped her on the back, to help pull out the sharp chicken-bone stuck in her throat, choking her half to death. The look of shock and disgust she threw in my direction, was not nearly as strange as the glance she gave Willem. Blink and you would have missed it. I saw it, like a huge question mark and a judgement all rolled into one. Good old auntie Gwen recovered quickly though, having in no uncertain terms registered my irreverent interruption and logged it as ammunition for future use.

The pain in my left thigh was Victor's pinching thumb and forefinger. It was a protracted pinch that said *shut up . . . shut up now, don't say another word.* I had already received the message without his pinch. Seeing Willem's cold denial was a source of unexpected disappointment, not least because we had been playing together at the pool only hours before. He had seemed so friendly and full of fun, but now a new boy was standing in front of me. He even looked different, pristine, expressionless and unruffled. Not one of his hairs was out of place, all neatly combed and slicked down close to his head. I didn't see any guilt or pain in his face, but on reflection I saw something well concealed behind his masquerade. Fear. I saw fear.

'Why are you in the kitchen, Willem? Go back to the table!' His mother placed her hand at the top of his back and guided him towards the door. 'It's very rude to abandon our guests. Why don't you tell Mrs Fourie about your piano lessons,' she advised.

'Yes, Mother,' replied Willem.

He was two paces from the dining room door when it swung open, nearly hitting him with a force that would have sent him flying backwards.

'Christ, Willem! Watch where you are going, boy,' said his father, stepping into the kitchen and commandeering the space with his overbearing height and puffed-up torso.

'Sorry, Sir,' Willem replied, although from where Victor and I were sitting it looked like Mister Vorster should have apologised. He was lucky not to bound into a member of staff carrying a stack of dinner plates or a tray of glasses.

'Where is the wine, Willem? The whole table is waiting with empty glasses.'

'Sorry, Father,' he quickly replied, rushing over to the sideboard where at least a dozen bottles of red and white wine were all neatly arranged in a row.

'Gwen, what in hell is going on? I sent the boy to choose two bottles of wine five minutes ago.' It was more like one minute ago, but the patriarch in the Vorster household had generous leeway for poetic licence. His wife looked at him and placed her hand on the edge of the kitchen table to steady herself.

'And what about me, Koibus? You going to fill me up? You never fill me up anymore.' Her lewd euphemism was picked up by more than just her impotent husband. He stared at her with contempt as she laughed fatuously, revelling in her comment and holding out her glass towards the bottle of Chenin Blanc on the table beside her. A few drops of her wine fell and splashed onto the table. 'Ooops!' she gasped and giggled. Her husband had already turned and pushed open the door to the dining room, followed closely by Willem who was carrying a bottle of wine in each of his hands.

10
Interrogation

Monday morning, before dawn, there was a gentle roll of rubber tyres on dusty ground and mild screeching of brakes as two rusted bakkies came to a standstill in front of the bunkhouse. From inside, hearing no audible voices, there was little indication that Glen Cleaver's workforce had returned from the weekend. That was before the clunk of doors being opened and shut, and the scraping of bolts unlatching tail-gates hinted at the herd being brought in from pasture.

The sound was distinctively eerie; like prisoners being set free in a desolate forest before the fate of the firing squad. Still there were no voices. Feet shuffled and dragged their way up to the door and then one-by-one, men filed into the bunkhouse and kicked off their boots. Some went straight to fill a bowl with pap and sit at the table, others to their beds, lying in relative warmth for an extra twenty minutes, before roll-call.

What was it Charlie said? Morning times is like the funeral . . . all bad times. He wasn't joking either. Monday was worst of all. Everyone looked tired and weary, like it was the end of a hard week, not the beginning. Young or old, it didn't matter. The only difference was the younger guys lethargy was more mental than physical. The older men, like Duke and Johnson - Charlie even - their weariness was more physical.

This particular morning, after another carefree weekend spent with Victor and Willem, felt like my own, personal funeral. As far as my father was concerned I might as well have been dead for the last three weeks. He walked in near the end of the line and didn't so much as look in my direction or seek me out to say hello. Not that I should have expected anything else, he had behaved the same way for my whole life. I was foolish to think that because I was now working with him - in the same place at least - he might become slightly interested in me. Part of me was glad he wasn't though. It made it easier to hate him.

As I grew older I realised I definitely wasn't the problem. He was the problem. He never said two words to anyone in the bunkhouse during the day, kept himself to himself, all reserved and unassuming. The only time he left the shadows was after dinner, when his voice rose in unison with the rest; assertive in making sure his cup was filled with umqombothi or dop, or that his cigarettes were promptly lit, or that the playing cards were adequately shuffled and dealt as he kept a keen eye on the sums of money he had spent and lost, or occasionally won.

Contagion was the only reason a worker could return to the bunkhouse during the day - with the express permission of Master Boss, and only in the direst and rarest of circumstances. Most men carried on working at all costs. Mr Vorster didn't tolerate physical weakness from a workforce. In the days before a vineyard operation was more heavily mechanised, the job demanded endlessly challenging, manual labour over long hours. Mr Vorster instructed Master Boss to be uncompromising on the principle of hard work. There were no second chances - do a full day's work, even if you are bent over double in pain, or most likely lose your job on the spot.

So when the bunkhouse door swung open hard on its hinges just before lunch and slammed into the inside wall with a loud clatter, Victor and I jumped with an anxious startle. Charlie was panting heavily, sucking up all of the remaining free air into his lungs. He was bent right over with his head to the floor and his hands on his knees helping to hold his weight.

'Good Goad, man,' he puffed. 'I only got quick time. Just been done running from Overberg. If Ringidd or Masta Baas catch me, them all big troubles, see?' Charlie cricked his neck as he looked at Victor and I anticipating a grateful response for his altruistic gesture. But he had yet to explain what all this commotion had to do with us.

'What's wrong, Charlie?' asked Victor as I watched on silently. Charlie stood up, expanding his lungs with outstretched arms. He pointed towards me with a grimace on his face; although you could be forgiven for thinking that Charlie had a permanent grimace on his face - what with that one blind, closed eye and the pink tapestry of scars that dominated the left side of his face.

'I heard them Masta Baas and Ringidd talking. All them bad things. Them says Mister Missus Vorster all bad unhappy with George. Them says maybe you too, Victor. Them boy, Willem . . . them is worried him all friends with you two kaffirs.'

Victor let out a sigh as if this was the reprisal he had been expecting. I knew straight away that it was because of the way I had spoken to Willem in the kitchen the night of the Voster's dinner party. It had taken five days for news of my naive misdemeanour, of greeting Willem in the presence of his mother, to reach Ringidd. Now I understood why Victor and I had been ordered to report to the estate office at lunch.

I didn't know what the Vorster's would think was worse - having a kaffir-lover for a son or having two young kaffirs on their workforce with such misguided audacity in thinking they could befriend a white boy in the first instance - even had he been someone other than the owner's son.

I felt sick to my stomach. In the course of one month I had become the source of constant problems for Victor. He hadn't needed to include me in his friendship with Willem. I didn't understand how I could have been so stupid.

'If you tells me, Victor, I is help, see.' Charlie said sincerely. Victor didn't need my approval to decide whether he should tell Charlie and stood in front of our large friend as calm as ever.

'I've been friends with Willem since I started work here, Charlie. We meet lots and play on the estate - when nobody is around. I've invited George to come along too.'

A grin appeared on Charlie's face. He couldn't help to grunt and chuckle as Victor's revelation sunk in. 'My Goad, Victor boy . . . you is more mischief than them Tokoloshe.'

'It's okay, Charlie, I drink lots of water!' said Victor. Charlie's laughter expanded, despite our precarious circumstances. It was rumoured that those evil mischievous spirits the Tokoloshe - the scourge of the Zulus - could make themselves invisible by drinking water.

'You better drink them more big water before Masta Baas and Ringidd is finding you.' Then a serious expression returned to his face. 'Them don't know nothing, boys. Say you is never been friends with Mister Vorster's boy. Say you is good kaffirs; got no place to be friends with no white boy.'

'What about when they ask how I know his name, Charlie?' I said, knowing I was not a very convincing liar.

'You is heard it from other people. You is called him that name by mistake. You is never speak to Willem before. You is very sorry for the mistake. Understand, George?'

'Okay, Charlie. Thanks.' I can't say I felt any relief on receiving his advice.

'Don't worry about it, George. We'll stick to our story. Everything will be fine. You watch,' encouraged Victor, with greater magnanimity than I had thought possible.

In my experience, there can be a joyful absence of fear when something is experienced for the first time. Fear requires expectation. Weeks earlier I had walked down to Master Boss's office for the first time with much less tension in my body. Despite my briefing and the warnings from Victor, I had not bubbled up into the panicked state I now found myself in.

Charlie, Victor and I headed downhill through the karee trees in the direction of the estate office. Charlie left us halfway, preferring the cover of the trees to get back to spraying the Overberg vineyard, from where he had temporarily taken leave. He left his equipment on the edge of the forest in case anybody noticed his absence, with an excuse that he was relieving himself in the woods.

Victor was in the process of forging our story. 'There are only three things you need to say, George. Repeat them after me.'

'Okay,' I said. 'Okay.' My breathing raced and my legs wobbled. Victor knew it. He stopped in the middle of the track and grabbed my shoulders, giving a serious glare.

'Breathe slowly, George. Think about breathing slowly. Deeply. That's it. Yes . . . That's it.' I did what he was telling me and slowly the feeling of dizziness and nausea disappeared and I focused on the task at hand.

'I am not friends with Mister Vorster's son, Masta Baas, sir,' he coached. I repeated.

'Again,' said Victor. I repeated.

'I am a kaffir worker, Masta Baas, sir. No kaffir be friends with no white boy.' I copied Victor again.

'Again!' said Victor. I repeated.

'I have never spoken to Master Willem before, Masta Baas, sir.' Victor's final summation hammered a large, sharp nail of a lie into the coffin and sealed it, I hoped forever.

'Again!' said Victor. I repeated.

Victor got me to repeat all three lines, one after the other. By the time we reached the cluster of estate buildings, I had repeated them twenty times. Thank goodness Victor was with me. What if they had called me in by myself? That would have been the end of it. With Victor present, there was at least a fighting chance, no matter how slim.

Ringidd was waiting for us outside the office door and shook his head when we appeared along the outside wall of the courtyard. He was standing straight up in his white overalls, his head stooped slightly with his chin near his chest revealing the top of his short, grey head of hair. His eyes rolled towards the top of his head.

'What sort of trouble you caused me, Victor? Eh boy? Ain't never heard nothing like it,' he said.

'Excuse me, sir? Mister Ringidd, sir?' Victor said innocently.

'You'll be sorry, boy, if what I heard is true. I'll make you pay if you gone behind my back. Do not be deceived: *God is not mocked, for whatever one sows, that will he also reap. Galatians 6, Verse 7,'* proselytised Ringidd, something he would do again in front of Master Boss at the inquisition which followed.

Ringidd knocked on Master Boss's door, walking in first, closely followed by Victor and me looking at the floor. Mallie and Toppie were conveniently leashed to a metal down-pipe on a radiator fixed to the wall. They had been lying leisurely on their sides, but rolled over and assumed a formal posture on their fronts when we appeared; their attention sharpening and focusing on the three imposters that had entered their territory.

Master Boss invited Ringidd to take a seat in the corner and he duly obliged.

'Do you know why you are here, Victor and George?'

'No sir, Masta Baas, sir,' replied Victor. I repeated the line with a fraction of a delay.

'No sir, Masta Baas, sir,' he sarcastically mimicked with a high pitched tone, achieving a reasonably accurate impression of our young, black dialects. He looked over at Ringidd - ever the sycophant - who was grinning and chuckling in deep approval, rolling up his sleeves into neat cuffs below the elbow.

'Look at me!' said Master Boss. We raised our heads.

'No more *Master Boss*. No more *sir . . . please*, call me Danie. You two are practically part of the family now.' His advice was delivered sincerely enough, but I suspected it preceded a cruel game. Without the wealth to underwrite the bet in calling him by his Christian name, neither of us answered.

'Why so shy, boys? . . . Am I not correct, Ringidd?' He handed over to the person who was meant to represent our interests.

'Yes, sir, Danie. They be moving into the big house anytime soon. Nice soft beds, hot running water and all them toys of Master Willem to play with.'

'Ringidd's spot on, eh, Victor?' He looked back menacingly, always focusing on Victor before me. Ringidd settled comfortably into his seat - as comfortably as it was possible for a black man to be in the same room as Mallie and Toppie - evidently excited about the ensuing pantomime. He chuckled louder with each new derisive sentence that came from his boss's mouth.

'I'm sorry, boys. How rude of me, I have not offered you a thing to drink.' Master Boss turned and lifted up a glass jug full of water from the shelf on the wall behind his seat. Drops of condensation fell from its sides as he placed it on the table in front of us. He reached below the desk for two glasses.

'Victor? George? A glass of water to quench your thirst?' He smiled kindly.

I don't know why I always deferred to Victor. It was always my choice rather than his imposition. Being the new boy, I knew instinctively that he was better prepared to navigate Master Boss and his twisted amusements.

'Thank you, sir, Masta Baas, sir,' Victor said. True to form, I repeated.

Master Boss poured fresh water into each glass until they were three-quarters full, then stood over the desk and beckoned us forward. Victor's hand reached at a glass first, but before he had a chance to pick it up, Master Boss interjected.

'Hold on, Victor. Let me fill that up properly for you.' Victor's grip released and his hand came back to his side. Master Boss slowly picked up the glass without moving his eyes from Victor's. The glass stopped a few inches below his chin and Master Boss vigorously coughed up phlegm and saliva from the back of his throat, letting his mouth fill with a hazardous, toxic fluid before letting it discharge slowly into the glass, where it settled in a thick, aerated globule on top of the water.

'That's better.' He placed the glass down onto the table, not having taken his eyes off Victor for a second. 'Now *drink . . .* you fokin' kaffir.'

Victor drank. The expression on his face was no different to that of a boy savouring a chocolate-powdered milkshake. I was next and I am not ashamed to say that my discomfort was, unlike Victor's, not easily hidden.

From that moment on, the inquisition began; all sorts of questions and insinuations. They said that Mister and Mrs Vorster spent a long time questioning Willem and he had owned up to all sorts of activities in our company - none of which made any sense. The longer it went on, the clearer it became - even for the uninitiated interviewee like me - that they were calling our bluff in the hope of forcing a confession. I don't know how I managed it, but those three lines Victor schooled me in were all I could think of in the course of those twenty minutes. It was just as well, because on a few occasions their questions flummoxed me and I could not think of a thing to say. Victor always came to my rescue and answered instead, somehow advocating on my behalf, rather than giving an answer of his own.

Ringidd said that despite our insistence of innocence, he was still grounding us to the bunkhouse each evening after dinner and during our free time for the next four weeks - weekends included. There was a spring in my step as we walked back up towards the bunkhouse. Victor whispered to me as we turned away from the courtyard at the end of the office wall.

'Don't smile or speak until we are out of sight.' We walked tempering our pace, with excitement and adrenalin swelling in our veins.

It felt like we had just escaped the clutches of two lions during a hunt - which is rather an exaggerated feeling of life and death, for two boys whose only crime was friendship. But a victory is a victory. When we reached the path at the karee trees and were sure that Ringidd was not following us, we relaxed and held a small, memorable, victory celebration. We high-five'd, then we high-ten'd, then we danced in circles and laughed. I was laughing relief; intoxicating relief. Victor's unshakeable confidence and assiduous preparation had paid off. There was one question which still remained unanswered though, the answer to which seemed out of our control. Halfway up to the bunkhouse I plucked up the courage to ask.

'But how did you know Willem wouldn't tell them anything?' I said.

'I knew,' Victor replied, as if that was the most obvious thing in the world.

'But how can you just know?'

Victor stopped and extended his arm, splaying his fingers to reveal the palm of his hand. 'We made a pact, Willem and I. See there?' I looked down at his finger pointing to a faint scar on the meaty underside of his left thumb.

'Willem and I are blood-brothers. He has a mark in the same place on his hand.'

Victor and Willem used an old pen-knife to draw a scratch of blood from each of their palms before shaking and sealing an irreversible bond of friendship. The act was more symbolic than physical I suppose, but what it said was that their friendship was more important than anything else. I wished that I could have smiled and told Victor how great it was, but I was jealous. I wished more than anything I could have been Victor's blood-brother, even though I had only known him for a shade over four weeks.

'That's dumb,' I said, turning up my nose in the process. Victor put his hand down slowly without trying to defend himself.

'Yeah, well . . . maybe it is.' It was the first time I had seen his feelings hurt - and I was the cause - after all that he had done for me. I wished I'd never turned up at Glen Cleaver. That would have been better for everyone.

The silence between us didn't last too long - and as usual it was Charlie that knocked our heads together to help us forget ourselves. After dinner he walked with us, out beyond the turning circle and sat down with his back to the trunk of a tree and lit up a cigarette. He hadn't told any of the other men about our problem, and could hardly wait to hear the news - although he knew fine well it hadn't ended badly because we were still in one piece and our spirits were high.

I told Charlie about the personally flavoured water courtesy of Master Boss and how Victor had drunk it without blinking whilst I sucked and gagged like it was snake venom. Charlie couldn't help laughing hard at that part . . . and he didn't feel bad for us one little bit.

'My Goad,' he said. 'Better him spit than piss.' The comment sent us both into hysterics and all of a sudden Victor and I were friends again - not quite blood-brothers, but that didn't matter . . . blood may be thicker than water, but it is not as pure.

11
Adultery

Willem's interrogation came the day before ours and he evaded every enquiry, but worried that we would not be so lucky. Before breakfast on the day of our interrogation, he gargled with egg-whites and salt-water to make himself sick. The trick worked perfectly and he was forced to stay off school and told to retire to his bedroom. His parents would have called the doctor had he not made a miraculous recovery before lunch. He had not been ill, of course, but he was very concerned for Victor and I, and the serious repercussions that would arise if we cracked in front of Master Boss and Ringidd. He overheard his father giving Master Boss stern instructions to get answers from *those two insolent kaffirs*, as he called us.

Later in the day, Willem saw Master Boss in the vestibule at the kitchen entrance, waiting for his father to appear. Mister Vorster grabbed a brown, wide brimmed hat and sunglasses from the shelf to shield him from the low hanging sun. He was holding two recently opened bottles of chilled Windhoek beer between the fingers of one of his hands and passed one to his manager. They walked around the rear of the house beside the shaved, green lawn, towards two ornate oak benches below the walls of the terrace. Willem raced to an upstairs window and carefully opened it just as his father sat on the bench. He watched him place his hat on his thighs, lean back and prop his elbows up onto the back of the bench, then take a long, slow sip of his beer.

'Shit . . . that's good. Sometimes I wish I'd inherited a brewery instead of a vineyard. It's easier to produce good beer than good wine.'

'That's the truth. Thanks for the beer, sir.' Master Boss held up the bottle, placed it onto his puckered lips and sucked out a mouthful. In different circumstances, the bench and those cold beers would have been a relaxing unwind after a hard day's work, but in Mister Vorster's eyes there was a serious matter to confront - one which had rocked his foundations.

'So, Danie . . . what's the verdict? Gwendoline and I can hardly bear it. She refused to come out here with me in case you are about to confirm her worst fears.' He paused . . . 'Is our son a fokin' kaffir-lover?'

'I believe Willem is telling you the truth, sir . . . no doubt . . . We rung those little kaffirs out like a wet flannel. That new one, George, is a bonehead. He's not clever enough to cover up any lies.'

'What about that Victor?' asked Mister Vorster, still not entirely convinced.

'Victor? . . . He's the best little kaffir we've ever had - better than most of the men. He doesn't have much of a kaffir's constitution; he's a hard worker, reliable, intelligent . . . honest as a bottle of Pinotage . . . I've come up against all the rebels and he's not like them. Ringidd said as much.'

'Well if Ringidd echoes what you say, then I feel better. He knows which side his bread is buttered.'

'Sir, you have nothing to worry about. We've grounded the kaffirs for the next four weeks, and you can keep an eye on Willem. He's probably wandering the estate looking for his butterflies and the like - you know he's not one of the cricket and rugby types.'

'Christ, those fokin' butterflies. I hope you're right, Danie. Fok me! You had me worried.' Mister Vorster took another sip from his beer and his body slouched in growing relief.

Willem witnessed a hint of doubt and vulnerability in his father - something resembling powerlessness. He seemed truly relieved and thankful that Danie had put his mind at ease, although the next four weeks would provide the harder evidence he sought. Since Gwendoline had spoken to him about the possibility of Willem's forbidden friendship with those two insignificant kaffirs, he had not been sleeping and his usual straight-to-the-point, self-assured character had recoiled. He seemed torn about how to deal with Willem in the event of some collusion with the kaffirs, and it was news that he did not want leaving the confines of Glen Cleaver. Danie was clearly enjoying his new role of mentor, confidante and advisor. He seemed glad of the opportunity to bond with Willem's father over a family matter as opposed to viticulture and annual award applications. But the feelings of parity did not last long.

'Danie, since we are having this chat about the line between the estate and the kaffirs, there is something else, of which you need to be aware.'

'Yes, sir?' replied Danie, looking unsure of where the comment was leading.

'There are rumours, Danie . . . rumours from careless mouths that had the misfortune of falling on my ears . . . although, perhaps it's good fortune from your point of view.'

Danie stopped breathing through his nose, opened his mouth wide and took in a long deep breath as if to prepare himself for the worst. The inhalation was a childlike admission of guilt before the charges had been brought against him; he knew that only one misdemeanour was serious enough to be confronted in such a solemn manner.

'How should I say this, Danie?' Mister Vorster didn't have the correct words at hand, if there were any correct words for this predicament.

'You have a good job, a wife and two young kids, Danie . . .' Mister Vorster then abandoned his gentle introduction, deciding the only way to approach the topic was head-on. Directness was his genetic birthright.

'If you have to fok that kaffir, don't ever bring emotion into the equation. You understand where I'm coming from, man?'

Danie's face turned a dark shade of red as more blood gushed into his capillaries. Willem's father had not noticed the bottle of beer shaking in his manager's hand, which he quickly placed down at his side and pulled tight into his hip in an attempt to steady it. Willem thought Master Boss would feign ignorance, or plead innocence, or aggressively defend himself - but his mind seemed temporarily disconnected from his nervous system, frozen with that natural anaesthetic called fear. He seemed incapable of preventing physical paralysis. Mister Vorster was aware of Danie's body language and in an unusually empathetic gesture, decided that he need not suffer unnecessarily.

'You don't have to speak, Danie. Simply listen.'

'I'm not saying these rumours are true or false. It doesn't matter to me. I need a productive and efficiently managed wine estate, and I've never had any cause for concern with you on that front . . . But beware . . . for over a century kaffirs have been fokin' their masters. They are a wily breed of animal. All the gratification and the carnal tuitions you may receive can come at great cost . . . play with fire and you can get badly burnt.'

Mister Vorster rose from the bench and stood in front of Danie Rousseau with his arm outstretched offering his hand. Danie stood and shook it in silence. His red face had turned to ashen white.

'We won't speak about either of these matters again,' said Mister Vorster.

Danie Rousseau nodded back sheepishly at Willem's father, still not able to summon the power of speech. He left the unexpected encounter with his tail between his legs, dragging it heavily across the lawn and back towards his office soaking up pangs of anxiety and regret, exhibiting a tinge of annoyance that he had been so easily caught and humiliated.

12
The Lotana Blue

Being confined to the bunkhouse for four weeks was a greater imposition than it sounds. There was freedom to be found in countless acres of beautiful, undisturbed grounds; that mix of neatly planted vines, forest and hillside left to its own devices, with enough space to get lost in if you are not careful. This inadvertent gift was stolen from Victor and I for the period of our incarceration. Nobody in the bunkhouse cared whether we would break the rules, but the self-evident risks of wandering beyond the turning circle to find Ringidd waiting behind a tree to catch us felt real enough. Johnson said we should not let such a pointless curtailment bother us for a second - that Ringidd was too lazy and forgetful to meander up to the bunkhouse after work, unless there was an unforeseen errand to run for Master Boss.

The days were long and the nights longer. Nostalgia for my mother and my sisters returned, with all the time I had to lie and think about them after work. Victor was not much better, I think he had coped well with the daily regimen because he looked forward to seeing Willem each weekend or on the odd evening. His spirits visibly waned. Not even Charlie could cheer him up with scary stories about the Tokoloshe. The bunkhouse became suffocating; a cauldron of sour, testicular soup with no female ingredients to soften the taste. Apart from Willem, our intermittent exposure to the household staff - Mary in particular - was the biggest loss. She enhanced our muliebrity with gentleness and lightness, and an attention and care that countered our incarceration in the singularly masculine bunkhouse.

All work and more work makes for a dull existence, although it is not as dull as a life without work. Our parole came five Saturdays later, when the bakkies arrived to take the men to the townships. Victor and I sat in peace, greedily chomping through an oversized water-melon brought up from the kitchen. Victor discarded the last piece of skin and wiped his mouth, then winked at me, smiling. I knew exactly what he was suggesting.

Thirty minutes later we crept quietly and lightly on dusty ground through the karee trees and uphill towards the boundary of the estate. Beyond the oak trees, the open hillside looked different with the sun directly above, casting no shadows. The plants were in full bloom and vibrant blues and purples sprung in every direction as we contoured the terrain towards the stream. The pool was bathed in sunlight, glistening and rippling in the light breeze. In its chasm, the breeze died and the shrill of birds chirping from the undergrowth muted. Victor decided that it was time I learnt to swim and, without any sign of Willem, appointed himself to the role of instructor.

My lesson began in the shallows. I could not believe how much energy was required to keep afloat in three feet of water and I could not grasp it at all. Whatever Victor said, I sank and sucked in water. Each time I panicked, jumping up quickly for air, spluttering and coughing with my nose streaming and my eyes wincing. He was patient, showing me first what to do, then coaching me as I attempted to copy. After half-an-hour we were both defeated. Victor suggested we stop to relax and play.

'I think Willem would be a better teacher,' he said.

A loud shout and the sight of a body in a tuck position, arms around his knees, silhouetted by the sun, rapidly approached from above. There was a hell of a splash when Willem's tubby, compact cannonball hit the surface of the water. Small tsunami's bounded across me and I clambered quickly out onto the rocks, losing sight of a shadow under the water. Willem held his breath for an age, longer than I thought humanly possible, then leapt like a predatory great white, his body rising above the waterline, then diving back down below. The flurry of splashes and loud shouts of *"Yaaah whooh"* eventually waned and he treaded water in the middle.

'Hi guys,' he said, rather pleased with his ambush.

I felt very awkward. This was the first time I had seen Willem since the kitchen incident and I had no idea what was going to follow. I had secretly been dreading seeing him again, and the mild consolation I felt in being grounded was knowing I could not bump into him. Victor made his way into the middle of the pool to meet his friend and was instantly comfortable in his company. I was isolated at the edge, unable to join them because I couldn't swim or tread water. They were whispering to each other and I couldn't make out a word. Shortly afterwards, Willem swam towards me, crawled out of the pool and plonked himself on a shiny rock beside me.

'No hard feelings, George? Sorry I ignored you in the kitchen,' he said holding up a hand, hoping I would grab his palm.

'Thanks.' I nodded back, slapping his hand.

'I'm afraid my parents don't want me to have anything to do with *kaffirs* - I've got to make it look like that when they are around. They told me white and black people are very different and you cannot trust black people. They always go on about it . . . it's so boring.'

'Why do they think that?'

'I don't know - they're not interested in the same things as me. All my dad cares about is wine and sport. It's the way he was brought up.'

'So why are you different if they are teaching you the same things?'

'Who knows? I'm weird, eh?'

'What about your white friends? Do they know you play with us?'

'You kidding? I would get kicked around the rugby fields like a ball for being a kaffir-lover. They're the same as my father . . . rugby, rugby, rugby. *Boerewors, farming and rugby* actually - they're the three things people care about in Paarl.

I looked back at Willem and shrugged my shoulders. He was weird, but I guess I liked weird. All I knew was that Willem wanted to be my friend. If he was good enough for Victor, then he was good enough for me.

'We've got four more weeks to get him swimming, Willem . . . before he goes back to the township at the weekends.' Victor shouted over to his friend.

Willem looked at him, then at me, then at the rock I was sitting on. 'George, that rock you are sitting on is a better swimmer than you. But if I could get Victor swimming, I can get *anyone* swimming.'

Willem braced unexpectedly, straightening his back, startled and flustered, blinking with excitement. Beneath his ruddy complexion was the advent of a crisis.

'It can't be?' he murmured, studying something across the pool. 'It is! . . . It totally is!' he shouted and a huge grin appeared across his face before panic overcame pleasure. Victor and I glanced across at each other curiously, wondering whether Willem had gone completely mad. Then he pointed at it; a magnificent, blue butterfly dancing above the surface of the water, flapping its wings with such syncopated grace it could have been leading an ancient, tribal war-dance.

'The Lotana Blue! That's the goddam Lotana Blue.' Willem was up to his waist in water and thinking fast. 'We've got to get it. Quick!' he shouted, starting to swim across the pool as the butterfly gently rose to a height just out of reach. He swam towards Victor nearest the path leading away from the pool.

'Victor! My net! It's on the high ledge. Quick! Go!'

Victor looked bemused but loyally jumped, high and fast as a pursued springbok. We raced to the top. Victor was in front with Willem not far behind. He nearly pulled my arm off when he grabbed it on his way past, splashing out of the water with such ferocity that I was drenched. 'Come on George. Come on! It's the Lotana Blue for God sake.' Not in all my life have I seen a person become so animated about a topic other than death or injustice.

It turns out that Willem had two obsessions: Butterflies and biltong - dried African game meat. When he got to Victor he grabbed the net from him and spent the next five minutes, with the help of our shepherding, catching the supposedly rare and famous, Lotana Blue butterfly.

'We did it. I can't believe we did it,' said Willem, star struck at the sight of his delicately winged friend.

Willem's passion was to collect butterflies, study their characteristics and document his findings in a small notebook with a pencil sharpened by his pen-knife. The notebook, the pencil and the pen-knife accompanied him everywhere. This Lotana Blue was going to stay with him for longer than normal, in a mesh container in his bedroom prepared fastidiously for the rare and unexpected eventuality. His small butterfly cage was furnished with foliage and food, as his first concern was always his butterfly's welfare. He unscrewed a perforated lid and tipped the shimmering blue trophy in his net into the glass jar, then screwed the lid back in place.

We sat together on the high ledge above the pool, sharing Willem's satisfaction. He passed me a stick of biltong. I rarely saw Willem without biltong. Sometimes it was a small bag of soft and moist shavings, other times it was dry and tough as leather. Most of the time it was long, thin strips or thick chunks of dried beef, kudu or springbok, stuffed into and sticking out from the chest pocket of his short-sleeved shirt. All of it vanished in his mouth like cubes of ice in a cup of hot water.

'Can you believe it? They say the Lotana Blue is extinct. What you doing here little fella? You're a long way from the Limpopo,' said Willem to the glass jar he was holding up in front of his face.

'I better get him home before he cooks,' he said, carefully standing and gathering his notebook and net. 'No way father or mother will suspect I've been up here playing with you guys when I show them this beauty.'

We said goodbye to Willem and he walked off briskly, desperate to run, but knowing a stumble might risk dropping his jar and losing his rare prize. It was only when my love affair with flowers developed that I understood how Willem must have felt on that afternoon with his rare butterfly - with his deep interest in and appreciation of nature. There is nothing ephemeral about nature. It is the window to timelessness. A flower is a flower, as always a flower. A butterfly is a butterfly, as always a butterfly. But a man? . . . I cannot say that a man is a man, as always a man.

13
The Berg Reservoir

True to his word, Willem got me swimming. I did not believe it possible that one week before returning to Tolongo, I would swim across the pool and back unaided. I'm not saying it was pretty and I'm not saying I enjoyed the ordeal, but I managed it. And swimming across the pool was not the only challenge my two friends had in store for me.

'All you got left now, George, is to jump off the ledge,' said Willem from next to me in the water. 'You've seen us do it a hundred times before, you can do it,' he urged.

On this occasion there was no reason for me not to. Victor and Willem stayed in the pool and I walked down the stream and climbed up onto the bank towards the ledge above the pool. I knew if I hesitated I would never pluck up the courage to jump, so I ran at it, closing my eyes and letting my leg push me off into the air. My breath froze and I exhaled without enough air to scream. My legs wanted to run away as I fell, but it was no use, I could not escape. I broke the surface of the water like a nail being hammered into soft pulp and hurtled to the bottom. I noticed tingling in my arms and pulsating in my head and did not know if I had enough oxygen to return to the surface. Then, suddenly, I was there, expanding my lungs, inhaling a grateful enthusiasm for life. Victor and Willem whooped and cheered and punched the air in encouragement.

'I said you would do it, George,' said Willem. 'Scary as hell first time, eh?'

I could only laugh, elated. It was as if the sluice gates of a large dam had opened wide and a heavy weight of water had been released from captivity.

'I can do it again,' I said enthusiastically, using my arms to row to the edge as I reached waist-height in the water. I jumped three more times with Victor and Willem watching below. Each attempt got easier. On my last jump I had my eyes wide-open and wanted the experience to linger for as long as possible.

'You're a natural, George,' said Victor. 'You'll be jumping the pier at the dam if you carry on like this.'

'I'd dare five whole sticks of biltong if anyone ever jumps the pier.

74

Alistair van Horst from Breeberg says he did it a couple of times . . . although nobody was there to see him. It's gotta be three times higher than the ledge,' said Willem.

'Let's do it,' I said, buoyed by the hormones that had drowned my fear of heights.

'You must be crazy, George,' said Victor.

'Alistair van Horst was seventeen . . . at least seventeen . . . and he was the best swimmer at Paarl Gim,' said Willem. 'You could break your legs, George,' he warned. I could not believe the tables had turned so dramatically.

'Come on, dassies. I'm doing it. Why not? If we can jump fifteen feet, then we can jump thirty . . . or forty . . . who's coming?' I said, deadly serious for once in my life. A deathly, suspicious silence came over Victor and Willem.

'He's gone baboon mad, Willem,' said Victor, looking at me walking out of the pool to fetch my clothes.

'He's mad for sure . . . I'm definitely not jumping, but I've gotta see this with my own eyes. Come on, Victor,' said Willem. He was now excitedly hurrying after me with Victor close behind.

For the first half of the journey, we ran down the stream towards the Berg River. Victor and Willem persisted in asking me the same two questions: 'Are you being serious? You really gonna do this, George?' They must have asked twenty times. When I gave up answering, Willem squeezed out some more drama and tension.

'Years ago, some poor old guy drowned himself off the pier. He tied rocks to his ankles and threw himself over. Nasty business...' said Willem. 'And there's carp down there . . . big ones . . . I mean, really big ones. They're not fished in case of contaminations . . . some as big as penguins in the deepest water . . . you sure are brave, George,' consoled Willem. I don't think he was intentionally trying to frighten me, but none of it was in the least bit helpful.

Thirty minutes later, we approached the fence surrounding the pier. It must have been six or seven-feet high. Black and white warning signs saying *Swimming is Prohibited* were attached every fifty yards or so. Heavy, padlocked gates obstructed our view of the high, stone pier protruding into the water, offering the best place to climb over. Willem gave Victor a leg-up. He climbed over and waited on the other side. I was next, swinging over a leg and waiting at the top to give Willem a helping hand.

'I can manage,' he said, waving me off the top. I dropped down. Sure enough, Willem jumped, pulled, then swung his legs over and landed with a thud, falling onto his side, narrowly avoiding cracked bones.

'That's one way to do it,' said Victor, laughing.

We all walked away from the dam wall along the extended, concrete pier, protected by wide, black railings on either side. The level of the water was near the high-water mark, saving me a few feet in distance to the water. The surface was black and still as ice. It looked a hell of a long way down.

'You don't need to do it, George . . . even though we came all this way. Just take a look and we'll go back if you want. I don't mind,' said Victor, giving me an easy way out. Willem raised his eye-brows and grimaced in agreement.

At the end of the concrete, the railings disappeared and the entire width opened to the water. Victor and Willem seemed less inclined to shuffle to the edge for an examination. A couple of feet from the drop, I lay down on my front and crawled forward, allowing only my pink fingertips, my hair, my forehead and my eye-balls to cross the threshold. A steel ladder, bolted against one of the thick pillar holding the pier, ran deep into the water.

'Shit, that's a long way down, George. You don't want to go breaking your legs now. Seriously, this isn't a good idea,' warned Willem, now genuinely concerned. He was with Victor a few yards behind, cradling the railings.

With the sun's heat baking everything in its path, you might think that plunging into a dam is an inviting prospect for a hot, tired, thirsty, sweaty body.

'Van Horst said the water is freezing cold . . . maybe not at the top, but when you get down a little,' he said, still clutching the railings.

I shuffled backwards, stood and joined them. When I smiled, Willem must have thought I was conceding to common sense; finally owning-up to an elaborate bluff.

'Phew, I actually thought you were going to do it, George . . . man alive.'

He hadn't reckoned on my overalls slipping from my shoulders. My shiny, black, bony body stood out in stark contrast against the grey of the pier, and more so against the marbled stains of my underpants.

I lifted my ankles from the heap of overalls at my feet, turned and ran towards the end of the pier as fast as I could. For a few, long seconds, I felt like I was flying with the fish eagles across a sea of black gold. I screamed - a confused mixture of fear, panic and uninhibited joy. I reckon my scream travelled as far as the Cape Flats.

My feet and legs landed perpendicular to the water, with a hard, sore slap. The bracing cold hit me like an avalanche. I didn't see any penguin-sized carp, but Willem wasn't lying about the freezing cold: like nothing I had ever experienced, not even in the ocean at Muizenberg. Adrenalin pumped around my body and I was hyperventilating when I came up for air, slapping the water and yelping. I looked up at the towering pier and saw two faces peering down at me. Victor and Willem could not believe I was alive. My frothy swim to the ladder was six yards in length, but it sapped every ounce of my energy. My arms and legs were stiff and numb by the time I reached the last rung of the ladder and my warm-bodied, fully clothed friends helped pull me back up onto the flat concrete surface. A small puddle ran the length of my body as I lay recovering from the shock of it all.

When Willem took the pen-knife from the pocket of his shorts, I thought he was going to cut some biltong into strips and start honouring his promise. Neither he nor Victor had said a word since I had jumped and climbed back up to the top of the pier.

'Hold out your hand, George,' said Willem. Victor looked at me and nodded.

Willem held my hand in his and nicked a short, thin line with his sharpened blade on the fat below my thumb. A small bubble of blood appeared, no more than you might expect from a pin-prick. He turned to Victor then cut into the old wounds on their own palms. Willem offered his hand first. I raised my arm six inches above the concrete, still recovering on my back, dazzled by the azure-blue sky.

'Blood-brothers,' he said, shaking my hand, making sure the smears of drying, red blood in our palms mixed.

'Blood-brothers,' I replied.

Victor was next. 'Blood-brothers,' he said. I repeated.

'That jump was the gutsiest thing I ever saw, George,' said Willem. Victor smiled in agreement, but this time he was shaking his head, looking at me with wide-open eyes, like I truly was mad. Nobody had ever referred to me as gutsy before. It is probably the last word I would have used to describe myself. I felt like I was floating, enjoying the refreshing breeze and observing myself from above the clouds, in a dream.

Two loud, high pitched barks unexpectedly interrupted our impromptu ceremony, and a loud holler came from the opposite side of the reservoir. An old man with a balding head of white hair had rumbled us. He was shouting and waving his walking stick in dissatisfaction.

'Shit,' said Willem. 'Mr Goosen. He knows my father. Let's make like a banana,' he said. Victor and I looked at him, confused.

'And . . . *peel*?' said Victor.

'Let's make like a banana . . . *and split*,' said Willem, already sprinting down the length of the pier towards the padlocked, iron gates at the fence.

'Grab your clothes, George . . . no time to put them on,' said Victor.

We all reached the fence at the same time. Willem could not stop laughing - he was practically crying with laughter and barely had the strength to lift himself up over the gates. Victor and I pushed his backside hard and he clambered over, falling over on the other side - still laughing. Victor pulled me up last. I would have been trapped behind the railings, like an animal in a zoo, without his helping hand. I was exhausted; the last thing I wanted to do was run uphill.

The old man was two hundred yards away but quickly lost distance as we romped upstream. I must have been some sight - bounding along in nothing but wet, revealing underpants. We climbed halfway back up the slope and sat behind a thick sugarbush to catch our breaths. Willem poked his head out and saw the old man's white head bobbing beyond the reservoir. He had given up his chase long ago and was on his way back to town.

14
Father

My father was the first person to walk through the door of the bunkhouse on the first Saturday I was scheduled to return to Tolongo after twelve weeks' initiation. He stood in the doorway, balanced with an arm pivoting on the doorframe, painfully prising off one boot from its heel. He pulled the second free with a rueful expression before mild relief appeared and he stepped free. Neither boot belonged to each other, or my father; they were outcasts - illegitimate children that had found their way to a run-down orphanage on the underside of his feet.

My father's swollen blocks were covered in red blisters and fungal sores. No worker wore socks with their boots, issuing a fetid odour that continually reprimanded me with its reprobation. He picked up the boots and threw them neglectfully towards his bunk. They landed some distance away, clattering into a tin cup on the floor, half full of water. He was completely indifferent to the shallow puddle that formed in the small gap as he pulled a crumpled envelope, alongside a fresh carrot, from his pocket. He crunched on the carrot and chewed loudly with an open mouth, then turned his attention to me for the first time in twelve weeks.

'Get you to the road before 4.30 Monday morning. You no kid no more. If you late, you lose your job and don't getting no other,' he said in a cold, matter-of-fact voice.

His warning paired with a look of inconvenience as he threw the envelope in my direction. It wobbled and dipped in the air, then landed at my feet with a thud. I opened it to find three crisp, clean bank notes and half-a-dozen coins. I could not read words, but knew my numbers well enough.

'I get half the money of the men. This is much less than twelve weeks pay,' I said, challenging him for the first time in my life. If I was to be a man, then I must act like one.

'I take half your pay . . . my cut. Without me you don't have no job. Better you work harder boy . . . I heard you near kicked bad hard by Masta Baas.' A vague smirk appeared through the orange pulp on his teeth, enough to highlight his amusement that his wage increase was at my expense.

I used to accept this sort of manipulative swindle. It was what my sisters and I did to temper his threatening behaviour, and what my mother did - on those rare days - when he returned unannounced to shrink her self-respect, pulling her from the insipid to the disconsolate. Perhaps on some level I thought I could win his favour; get him to accept me, to like me . . . to love me. But here, now, I didn't care about any of that.

'More money for honey and mango cigarettes from Mama Blues?' I said, knowing my sarcasm would entice a backlash.

'What you said, boy?' His nose and lips curled up tightly and his brow furrowed, then he took two, slow steps towards me in a threatening manner.

'I saw you . . . with that woman in the shebeen. You're not my father, you're a pig.' How I managed to stifle my words and stop from shouting I do not know. I was incensed, and for the first time in my life, unafraid of the consequences. A few of the men filed into the bunkhouse behind us, unaware of the developing confrontation.

My father covered his face with dusty hands. His fingers tightly knitted and he rubbed his eyes, leaving opaque marks around his sockets like the remnants of tribal war paint. Franklin, Eugene and Barclay walked in just as he lunged for an empty glass bottle on the table. He lifted and smashed the end on the table, stopping the three men in their tracks. A fistful of sharp, glass shards splattered across the floorboards and he lifted the jagged weapon in his hand, poking it, threatening my fate.

He moved directly towards me, but his first step landed on a thin slice of the broken bottle, puncturing the sole of his foot. He screamed and threw the bottle at me in fury and frustration, from three yards. He got lucky. The bottle bounced off my forehead just above the eye, and carried onwards, smashing off the wall behind. A sharp edge lacerated my skin and my legs gave way. My head dropped like a watermelon onto the floorboards - which was thankfully softened over time with the ritualised soaking in umqombothi, spilled slops and mopping. The cut above my eye was bleeding profusely, but I had yet to feel any pain. I lay flat on my side, still conscious, as the searing, electrical surge arrived. I looked at my father hovering over me, one leg either side of my body. His cold, spiteful eyes locked onto me like Mallie and Toppie in Master Boss's office . . . but he wasn't tethered.

He lowered himself to my chest and with a clenched fist pulled back his arm, cocking the weapon like a hunter does the bolt on a powerful rifle. Time slowed to a standstill, giving me what felt like an unlimited opportunity for reflection - the strangest sensation. His fist travelled towards the end of my nose, but before it arrived I had time to wish he was dead . . . I saw my mother and my sisters eating from a rusty, blackened pot around the stove in our home in Tolongo, then I found myself floating alone in the air above the secret pool. Willem and Victor, my blood-brothers, were standing at the ledge, curious observers, watching me float and hover - the conqueror of gravity. I felt warm and comfortable up in the thermals, but I had not completely forgotten about my father.

My mind drifted from the pool, and the grease of the bunkhouse reappeared at my nostrils. My saliva was mixing with blood from my head. The fist that I saw was not my father's. It belonged to a different arm; a club fist, competition for a sledgehammer.

Barclay and Franklin waded in quickly behind my father, but it was Charlie who grabbed his arm an inch before it collided with my face, prohibiting my impending pummelling. He swiped my father up from the floor like a lion playing with an emaciated rat and pulled him by the scruff of his overalls towards the door. A line of blood smeared across the room from my father's dragging foot as he shouted and protested.

Victor missed the beginning of the ruckus, strolling back from the pits. He halted when he saw Charlie drag his prey across the turning circle, into the cover of the karee trees. He followed and watched as Charlie pulled up my father and pushed him into the middle of a tamarisk bush, trapping him among prickling branches and hard leaves. Charlie descended upon him and inflicted a lasting reparation.

Victor ran back to the bunkhouse, deeply concerned about what he had seen. He pushed open the door and saw me sitting on a chair, near to where I had fallen, covered in blood. The blood had trickled from above my eye, down my face, neck, chest and stomach to my waist, staining the inside of my overalls and the top of my underpants. He walked to the sink and returned with a damp cloth and some old rags which he soaked in water and applied in short, stinging dabs, before fixing them in place around my head.

He asked no questions other than about my injury. The rest of the men quickly lost interest and dispersed to smoke out front or lie on their bunks and wait for the bakkies to arrive. When Charlie returned, he was without my father. He looked at my forehead and lifted the underside of Victor's rudimentary bandage.

'You be okay, George. Me think not bad deep,' he said.

'Thanks, Charlie,' I replied, frightened to ask about my father. The worst outcome turned me pale and cold, draining clammy sweat from my forehead.

'Them cuts and bruises means you is fit in well Inner Tikki, George,' said Charlie before bending underneath the doorframe to go outside. 'Your father not bother you no more.'

'You two lucky having a friend in Charlie,' said Johnson, lifting his belongings from his bunk. 'Ain't no man stick-up for me when my father gave a damn beating.' I didn't know whether he was complementing Charlie or chastising me for not deferring to my father - even when the father in question was abusive and full of hatred. I didn't give Johnson the benefit of the doubt and I never trusted him again after that.

Victor's dressing absorbed more blood than it could hold. He cut up an old kitchen rag into small squares, handed me the pile then gathered my shorts and a singlet from underneath my bunk.

'We better change the bandage before the bakkies arrive,' he said. This was a job for my mother or my sisters, but it could not wait for another two hours. Victor carefully untied the knot at the back of my head and doused the clotted bandage with more water before removing it slowly. He splashed and wiped the wound gently with the water, placed on three new pieces of rag, then re-tied.

Bodies jumped quickly off their bunks at the sound of the vehicles. The first had barely turned when its passengers stepped up and over the wheel arches without thinking to unhinge the tailgate. The engine revved and without having fully stopped, it carried on down the track. The second vehicle was for Charlie and I, but the others were sheepish and in no hurry to get on. I saw them looking at Charlie through new eyes, astounded that this jovial giant had administered such a judicious punishment. Nobody wanted to irritate him.

Victor walked me to the door. 'You really are a blood-brother now,' he whispered into my ear, smirking. Despite the lacerating pain in my forehead, I saw the funny side.

'Wait 'til Willem hears about it,' I whispered back, forcing a smile through my pain.

'You better get going,' he said, and his smile vanished. The men had one foot in the shebeen, so I walked out and down the steps then thanked Victor for helping to nurse me. There was so much else I needed to thank him for during the last twelve weeks, but I didn't have more words than goodbye.

'Don't enjoy yourself too much - you're back here the day after next,' he said before I jumped over the tailgate. There was a numbing detachment in his eyes, giving the sudden and unexpected impression of distance between us - not unfriendly, but as I had found him on my first few days at Glen Cleaver.

His advice was strange, especially from someone who was meant to be my friend - my blood-brother. When could I enjoy myself if not after twelve weeks of forced labour and captivity masquerading as paid employment? He turned and walked into the bunkhouse without bothering to watch us drive off.

Through the cabin window at the front of the vehicle I could scarcely make out the man in the passenger seat. He was slumped against the door like a dark shadow, low down in the chair, cowering with his right hand curled around his head. I could not see any detail, but I knew who it was. It was the man I used to call my father.

There was very little conversation in the back. The heat accentuated the pulsations in my head. I was thirsty - so thirsty. Nobody had any water. The only available liquid was umqombothi or dop. I asked Franklin for a sip from his cup. He looked back at me puzzled, but Eugene nudged his ribs, pressing his approval. Franklin strained forward, passing me his cup. I took it and nonchalantly swigged like I had done it a hundred times before. The taste quickly killed my bravado. Thirsty? Not this thirsty. I held the sour, cloudy, grainy liquid in my mouth for a few seconds with slightly puffed cheeks, then turned to my side and blew it over my shoulder and onto the middle of the road. It hung in the air, like vapour blown from the top of a wave by a strong wind that is about to crash, then landed on the hot asphalt and evaporated in a flash. A few faces were amused, but none were Franklin's. He shook his head and reached over to snatch back his precious concoction so I could not waste any more.

Charlie had not seen my self-imposed initiation in umqombothi. He sat by the tailgate with one arm loosely overhanging, staring out at the mountains. I don't know what he was thinking. He didn't look peaceful or contented to me. He looked angry. This was the second time I had seen him angry, and much angrier than the first, on that fateful day when I trampled his plastic sheeting. If he was going to get angry again, I hoped that it would not be on account of me.

The closer we got to the outskirts of Cape Town, the busier the traffic became. We stopped at a set of red robots and a fancy, shiny, black car drew up next to us. I turned and stared. On the back seat was a middle-aged, white woman and a blond-haired boy, presumably her son. The driver was a white man wearing a military uniform and a stiff, flat hat with a dark blue, polished rim. The boy was kneeling up at the window looking back at us. He waved and I waved back. His mother's head was fixed dead ahead until she spoke. She turned and glanced out of the window at us, then tugged at the bottom of her son's shirt to get him to sit down, reprimanding him with tight, clasped lips that barely moved when she spoke. He sat down neatly and faced forward just like his mother. The robots turned to green and their vehicle accelerated quickly into the distance as we chugged slowly forward under the weight of half a workforce.

'I wonder where they lives?' said one of the guys.

'Constantia or Bishopscourt; big fancy houses with gates and walls as high as trees,' said Johnson.

'Where that at?' asked Franklin.

'Near Table Mountain. I used to do gardening up one them big houses before Glen Cleaver,' he replied.

'Victor and I will have one of them houses when we are older,' I interrupted. Charlie was the only one not to break out in laughter.

'No way you is, George,' sneered Franklin. 'In a few years you getting a dompas, says you is got to stay in Tolongo. If you found in any other place, they is locking you up in jail.'

I was still allocated to my father's passbook which sanctioned travel to Glen Cleaver for work. Apart from that, I was not supposed to leave Tolongo.

'And where them big money come from, George?' said Bostock.

'Victor is real clever. He will do some big business - like Mama Blues does in the Inner Tikki. I will work for him and earn big money.' Charlie shot me a serious look when he heard me mention Mama Blues' name. I thought I had it all worked out, even though I had not given the topic a second's thought until that moment.

The bakkie slowed by a large area of scrub on the fringes of Tolongo. Bostock, Franklin and Peter jumped off before we came to a standstill and walked away in different directions. Charlie unlocked the tailgate and jumped off before Eugene and Johnson. I was last. Charlie closed and bolted the tailgate and then I heard the passenger door open. My father slithered from his seat and stood on the dusty verge a few yards in front of the vehicle with his back turned, struggling to light a cigarette with a shaky hand.

'Don't ever talk of Mama Blues again, George. Never, you see?' said Charlie.

'Sorry, Charlie,' I replied feeling guilty, although I was unsure exactly why.

'I meet you Monday morning. We go pickup together . . . You go your mother now, see,' he said, making sure my father could also hear.

'Okay, Charlie. See you Monday,' I walked off in the general direction of my mother's shack, not knowing exactly where I was going, more in hope than faith.

Fifty yards on, surrounded by scrub, I looked back at my father. He was sitting on the ground with his legs crossed, cigarette hanging from his lips, watching me disappear into the distance. His face was swollen and much less recognisable after the beating Charlie had given him. I stood long enough to see his head nod slowly up and down. I don't know what his nodding meant and I didn't ponder on it for long. It was the last time I ever saw him.

15
Mother

I walked more in hope than certainty. My immediate vicinity was full of rubbish; discarded indiscriminately and without an ounce of shame into the alleys. People didn't care for bed-pans or walking to the communal latrines; they preferred to stand or crouch and piss and shit next to their shacks.

In my twelve weeks' absence, Tolongo had cultivated everything but charm as I walked in the direction of the latrine blocks, arrested by the smell. Their septic tanks must have been full to overflowing and ready for emptying. When I passed, the lanes were surprisingly busier than usual with every sort of inhabitant out on show. None were covering their faces with rags as I would have expected. The wind was blowing in the opposite direction to normal and for a day, or a few short hours, everyone was making the most of it. A group of younger boys were kicking and chasing a cloth sack, stuffed and tied with something soft. Mothers were fixing washed clothes to lines of string across the lanes and others were waiting for the clothes to dry, sitting on the ground preparing food in rusted tins and pots, conversing with their friends. Most women wore old, flowing, dresses with thin scarves wrapped around their heads, in assorted colours. One woman had a large, flat woven hat decorated with beads, alerting people she was a Zulu - and married. Most men were lazing around, socialising in the sun, drinking umqombothi, smoking, or throwing stones into tins and trying to knock them over for money - a game they called *chukka*.

I crossed an empty piece of dusty scrub, walked down two more lanes and turned the corner. When I saw my crumbling shack, I was surfing in clear blue waters upon the crest of a large wave that led to a beautiful white beach. I was excited and happy and relieved to be seeing my mother again. I imagined her swaddling me in an embrace like a newborn child, kissing me repeatedly until I had to pull myself away and wipe the saliva from my cheek. My sisters would also be happy to see me. They would likely spoil me like a visiting dignitary for the weekend; fetch water on my behalf, ladle fatty meat from the pot into my bowl. They would have cleaned and polished my coloured bottles, or probably collected new ones as a gift. I wondered if they had unearthed any new colours? Orange? I always struggled to find orange bottles.

In my last few steps, I realised for the first time how poor I was - materially at least. At Glen Cleaver, Willem had a radio in his bedroom. His family had a television-set in the drawing room, although it had never been turned on because there was no television to watch. Still, they had it there, waiting for the day when they could switch it on and see some moving pictures. On his radio, Willem listened to music and educational programmes about all sorts of different things. He turned up the volume loud so he couldn't hear his mother and father shouting and arguing. He ate food from countries I had never heard of and drank freshly squeezed fruit juice, chilled in electric fridges. He bathed in a bath, big enough to drown in, with hot water that ran from taps and foamed into bubbles. He lived better than a tribal chief with the richest lands.

I bounded through the thin, rickety piece of wood that we called a door, shouting 'I'm back, I'm back.' Everything was dark and silent, giving the feeling of emptiness. The shack was empty.

My eyes adjusted to the dark and some changes were noticeable: my bottles had vanished from the shelf, my sleeping space was now filled with two wooden crates, each with an embroidered cushion on top. There was a clean, white sheet tied neatly against the back wall, allowing a full view of my mother's space, which had been arranged quite differently. It was like I had never existed.

I sat on a crate, feeling deflated. Maybe they thought I was returning the following weekend? I waited for an hour, pacing between the partitions, sitting or pacing out in the lane, watching life pass. It started to rain; torrential rain, as if my ancestral spirits reckoned I wasn't disconsolate enough and had decided to relieve their bladders right on top of me.

Stuff this, I thought to myself. I'm going to see Charlie. Even if he's still in a bad mood, it's gotta be better than this. I walked away in the direction of my Zulu friend just as my mother and my sisters ran around the corner, huddled tightly together, poorly sheltered from the downpour by a flimsy umbrella held up by Mr Mpendulo. My eldest sister, Duhele, saw me first.

'Lifa! Look. Lifa!' she shouted and pointed.

Their reception was moderately affectionate, but fell well short of my expectations. The rain cannot have helped, so we ran inside and my mother lit a paraffin lamp.

'How are you, Lifa?' asked my mother.

'Good. I've been working hard,' I said, wishing Mr Mpendulo was not present.

With a bloody bandage over the cut above my eye and rags

wrapped around my head, I cannot have looked very good, but nobody showed the slightest bit of concern. I noticed my mother was wearing a necklace I had not seen before. Since I can remember, she had always worn a cluster of brown, carved wooden bobbles on a leather band around her neck. It had been replaced with a delicate silver chain with an ivory cross hanging from it.

'Where is your old necklace?' I asked.

'Oh, you is noticed my new necklace. Mr Mpendulo gave it me, as a present. He is very kind to me, Lifa.' She smiled at Mr Mpendulo, not with a look of gratefulness, but of something less innocent. He shook his head modestly, trying to downgrade the generous and intimate gift.

'They call me George now, not Lifa,' I said, uninterested in the fancy gift.

'Don't speak to your mother like that, Lifa,' said Mr Mpendulo. He loved the sound of his own voice, almost as much as he loved the sound of my mother's voice and everything else about her.

'Did you not hear me? I *said* . . . my name is George. I am a worker now.' There was a look of abhorrence and shock on my mother's face, less so Mr Mpendulo, even though he demanded more respect.

'I expect it's this insolent attitude that got your head cut,' he replied, the first to acknowledge the stained bandages hiding the gash above my eye.

'You know nothing about it. I'm going out,' I said, walking to the entrance.

'You are not! Come here and sit down. Stop making this scene in front of Mr Mpendulo, Lifa,' said my mother. The preacher man stood up as she spoke, suggesting he would restrain me if I did not comply. Good luck. In a flash I was on my way to Charlie's, trying to get that perseverant preacher from my mind.

My mother knew Mr Mpendulo before he was a preacher and I am sure he was the reason she decided to commit herself to her Jesus Christ. I know by the way she looked at him and how she talked to him and laughed with him that she would rather have been married to Mr Mpendulo than my father. But my mother was bound by the marital contract she had made in front of her ancestors, even if my father wasn't.

Sunday was always the worst day when I was a child living in Tolongo. My father appeared rarely, and we all dreaded his return from Glen Cleaver. Mother's solace was found in her new, devout, unquestioning Christianity. The white missionaries were an adamant and clever bunch, recruiting black converts to do their work for them, and my mother was soft wood to split. Most people followed tribal traditions and were sceptical of this new invention called religion. Church was a small part of life in Tolongo, but when people saw the benefits of belonging, it took off. Church-goers regularly traversed the lanes in their smartest outfits each Sunday morning, like worker ants marching to receive their queen. It seemed like there was always something to give, rather than receive. The women wrapped up in their colourful dresses and equally vibrant headdresses and the men wore cheap, second-hand, three-piece suits and ties. My sisters and I were reluctant participants from the outset, even though my mother and my Aunt Nobule coerced us at every turn.

I remember one of Mr Mpendulo's church sermons vividly; by sight and sound and smell and touch and taste - but not because it was so inspiring. Sermons are boring for any young boy, but in this one, Mr Mpendulo nominated volunteers from the congregation. My mother held up my arm against my will. It was the first one he saw. I must have been eight or nine at the time.

'Young Lifa. Come up to the front,' he remonstrated. I wonder if my mother had colluded with him beforehand in an attempt to indoctrinate me further into their world. I walked slowly, sideways, becoming increasingly visible as I got nearer the stage, hearing a hush come over people anticipating the lesson.

'Stand here, young man.' He placed his hands on my shoulders, turned me around on a spot on the platform to face the congregation, then stood behind me in his long white robes with gold tapestry embroidered across his chest. Any other minister I saw wore a suit like the men, but not so Mr Mpendulo. He had a taste for the theatrical and the ostentatious, as well as the delusional.

'Who loves you most in the world, young Lifa?' He directed his question at the congregation rather than me, and I didn't know if he expected me to reply until he strengthened his grip on my shoulders.

'My mother,' I replied quietly, shy as a mouse. Only the front of the room heard me, so he repeated it loudly. The congregation gently laughed and smiled.

'Well, yes. She loves you, Lifa. But there is someone else, who loves you more than your mother. Someone who loved you so much he died for you?'

'My grandfather? I don't think he loved me because I never met him,' I confessed, slowly understanding that I was part of his act.

'Not your grandfather, Lifa, nor your earthly father. I am talking of your heavenly father, Lifa, and his son Jesus Christ. Their love for you is so strong it is impossible to measure.'

'But I've never met a heavenly father or Jesus Christ. I have a father but I don't see him much.' I listened to my own voice with surprise, not having intended to speak. The words fell out without even my own permission.

'But in the Bible it is written, Lifa, that Jesus was sent by God. That God so loved all people, Lifa, that he sent his only son. To save us. To save us from ourselves.' Mr Mpendulo raised his arms, like the victor in a tribal battle without a shield or spear. The congregation echoed the sentiment, cheering and yelping in agreement. They repeated the words *'Sent to save us',* shouting it out loudly as they looked either at me or the ceiling. The look in their eyes was the same as I had seen in the eyes of men returning from the shebeen. It was the same look I had seen in my father's eyes, before he sent me on that fateful errand for honey and mango cigarettes at Mama Blues.

I walked away from the stage confused, nervous and embarrassed; with nowhere to hide from Mr Mpendulo's adoring audience. I was never comfortable with religion since then. What's the point of faith when you already have all the answers written down for you in some book anyway? Some people may have cause for religion, and I do not blame them for that, as long as they do not want me to be swept up in the same tide.

I arrived outside Charlie's door, knocked and pushed. It was shut tight. I knocked again and waited.

'Who there?' boomed a voice from inside the shack.

'It's me, Charlie,' I called through the gap between the door and the flimsy partition wall, waiting for the door to scrape open.

'Good Goad, George! What you doing here man, boy?'

I walked in with bare feet, my only worldly possessions being the pair of black shorts and the white singlet I was wearing, plus the envelope of half wages I had rightfully earned for my efforts. The look on my face told its own story.

'Sit down man. Sit down,' said Charlie. I plonked myself onto a wooden chair and sighed. Charlie's place was done up nice, like he had a wife.

'Why you not with your mother, George?' he asked.

'She doesn't understand I'm a worker now.'

'So why you come Charlie?'

'It's boring at home, Charlie. I want to work with you for Mama Blues?'

'You is gone mad crazy man, George,' he said. 'Here.' He passed me a scratched, rinsed, metal cup of rooibos tea-leaves which he filled with water from a black pot lying on a portable stove.

'I hate them, Charlie. All of them. I wish I never had no mother or father. My mother treats me like a little boy. But I am a man now. She will never be a worker like me.'

'Good goad, George man. What them all sad times happening?' he said.

'Can I stay here with you, Charlie?' I whispered quietly, worried about daring such a request. I had stormed away from my mother only twenty minutes earlier, now I wanted to make a permanent arrangement with Charlie. I wanted to punish my mother for not caring. She cared more about Mr Mpendulo and his Jesus Christ than me.

'What that you said?' Charlie had not heard a word. I was nervous about repeating it and paused. 'Come on man, spit it out,' he sighed.

'Can I stay here with you from now on, Charlie? When we are not at Glen Cleaver?' I made sure that he could hear me this time, but he did not respond immediately, choosing to sit down and reach for his cup of rooibos. The sound of cogs turning inside his head were audible as I waited for his brain to slowly decipher the options.

'I need to speak to Mama Blues first, George. She is give me this shack.'

'Mama Blues knows me. I met her before I came to Glen Cleaver,' I enthused.

'You don't know them Mama Blues like I do, George. You have to pay your way.'

'I can work for you, Charlie. You've seen me work good in the bunkhouse. Victor says I am getting better and Masta Baas and Ringidd did not give me into trouble for weeks.' Charlie paused and sipped more tea from the mug hidden in his cupped hands.

'You stay for tonight. But tomorrow you go back your mother, yes? One night.'

'Okay, Charlie.'

'Me got to be working soon. You stay. Go sleep. See?'

'Have you got anything to eat, Charlie?'

'Me got no nothing to eat, George. Got eating at work. I bring it some back.'

'Thanks, Charlie,' I replied sheepishly, conscious of my gurgling stomach.

Charlie left the shack an hour later for the Inner Tikki. I had not eaten since Glen Cleaver and my stomach felt like a balloon being slowly deflated by a small puncture. I had gone much longer without food but there are different responses to hunger, especially when a body is conditioned to a certain way of living. Since Glen Cleaver, I had eaten better and more regularly. My stomach was used to being full twice a day. And then there were the little extras Mary dropped off for Victor and I - the finest scraps I ever saw.

So here I was, home, whatever that means, and lonely again. I wondered whether my mother would be upset and worried. She could have come knocking on doors or calling for me if she really cared. I would have recognised Lala or Duhele's voices shouting from a hundred yards and I admit that I did listen out for them for a while. I had never spent a night completely by myself in Tolongo. My mind snapped back to the rumbling in my stomach. I hoped it would not be long before Charlie returned, although the chance was unlikely.

Before sleep, I resolved to wake the following morning as an independent man, for the first time in my life. But when I finally succumbed to the warm blanket on top of the cardboard, it was sentimental thoughts of my mother that sent me to sleep.

16
Aunt Nobhule

Late the next morning, after fifteen hours of sleep, I awoke to the smell of body odour, rubbed my eyes, yawned and stretched. Mild guilt bubbled as I relived running from my mother; a petulant over-reaction because she had not treated me like a servant does a prince. I had not thought to inform her of my whereabouts.

Charlie slept on a thin mattress on the open ground. He was lying, spread-eagled, with his hand resting on a half-eaten portion of chicken, potatoes and pap, which was slowly being pilfered by flies. One of his fingers had made a perfect imprint in the pap; a clean, white mould ready for filling.

His shack was brighter than I was used to, with a second door, normally concealed by a rickety old bookcase, covered in plastic sheeting. The sheeting hung loose and the bookcase lay at the side. The opening led into a tiny yard surrounded by the back of three other shacks. The neighbours had no view, with partition-walls that had been reinforced with plywood panels and plastic sheeting. The secluded space offered enough room for a small wooden bench, a table and a few potted plants that had attracted birds and their song.

Reflections from the mid-morning sun in the yard filtered into the shack. I bent down and peered into Charlie's bad eye. I'd never had a chance to inspect it before and desperately wanted to ask why the Tokoloshe had savaged him so frightfully.

When I stood, folding the blanket, Charlie continued to sleep and snore, spluttering air from his mouth like the old tractor at Glen Cleaver did smoke from its exhaust after starting. Boy, was I hungry! The leftover food on the plate didn't look very appetising with Charlie's open palm greasing it. I crouched down and slowly put both my hands gently around his wrist to free his hand and rescue the food. When my fingers touched his skin he flinched and sprung up, ready to defend himself. The food went flying, some of it scattering into the nearby yard.

'Goad man, George. I near hitting you bad hard, man,' he exclaimed annoyed and weary, sitting in his defensive posture.

'Sorry, Charlie. I was trying not to wake you.'

He turned onto his hands and knees and crawled to the bookcase where he picked up a wooden box. It opened and I heard the ticks of a small brass clock. Charlie looked at the clock face in disbelief then wound a small key in the back.

'Thems not ten o'clock morning, George. Bad times. All bad times,' he sighed, in a deep, slow rumble, before lying back down on the dirt. He had returned four hours earlier, just as dawn had broken. There were no early finishes in the shebeen; early starts, but never early finishes. They shut when the money dried up and customers were soaked full of umqombothi, dacha and debauchery. It was not uncommon for their doors to open on a Thursday morning and close seventy-two hours later.

'Them chicken all bad dirty now, man. Give it here, George.'

I inspected a few pieces that were not completely caked in dust and grit, then handed them over. Charlie dunked the meat in a pot of cold water on the stove, then waved it in the air and dropped it back onto the plate on the ground.

'Still good eating,' he said. I sat down near him, crossed my legs and cautiously chewed on the clean, damp chicken and half a potato, which had escaped the assault. The pap was inedible; like grit and dirt mixed in with a baker's dough.

'Did you speak with Mama Blues, Charlie?' I asked tentatively.

'No, I'm decided not speak with her. You go back your mother, see.' His tone was non-negotiable.

Part of me was relieved. It seemed easier to act the big working man than to live the reality, especially when I still had a choice of returning to my mother, if she would have me. How bad could it be sitting things out with her and my sisters for two nights each weekend? I had managed it for over twelve years, so a couple more couldn't hurt . . . as long as they stopped treating me like a child, that would be my only condition. I don't think my mother wanted me to grow up. She would rather I was a little boy forever, to order me about and give her feelings of importance. She had few worthwhile things to do with her day, apart from rushing around chasing Mr Mpendulo's shadow.

Charlie fell asleep again, or so I thought. As I was about to close the door behind me, I heard him mumble something about being on time the following morning. I am sure he would not have remembered it when he woke. The lane was quiet, but the air carried a sordid solemnity; that strange concoction of people going to church or returning from the shebeen. Thousands had recently fallen asleep and would awaken at dusk, having lost another day of their lives.

94

I had walked the route to our shack hundreds of times before, but never feeling as nervous. The aching hunger in my stomach was a mild distraction, but the other parts of my body felt nourished from so much sleep. I waited outside my mother's shack, thinking about what an idiot I had been and about exactly what I was going to say. I planned to apologise, but to make it clear that my mother was also to blame and that she couldn't push me around like a child anymore.

She didn't bother to turn her head when I edged inside. It was as if I had only popped out five minutes earlier. She sat on the wooden stool consumed with preening, washing herself at the bucket, the first step in her routine of dressing for church. Lala, my younger sister, stood behind, braiding strands of mother's hair. Nobody was surprised to see me.

'I don't care what they call you at work . . . when you is living here, you go by name of Lifa,' said my mother, still without looking up.

I shrugged my shoulders in silence, my way of saying *whatever you want,* but not meaning it in the slightest.

'Where you sleep?' asked Duhele.

'Charlie's,' I said.

'Charlie? . . . Who is Charlie?' said my mother, annoyed that I was implying she should have known.

'Jama. You know . . . the big Zulu with one eye.'

'Jama? . . . What in God almighty you doing with him?' I am sure she would not have used that turn of phrase in front of Mr Mpendulo.

'He is my friend. He works at Glen Cleaver,' I explained.

'Friend?' My mother looked at my sisters and laughed. 'He must be your father's age. What man want to be friends with a young boy?'

'Charlie doesn't care about that. He's good friends with me and Victor.'

'Oh, Victor as well? Another friend at your big man's work, yes?' she said, as if the possibility of me having friends was inconceivable.

'Why do you care?'

'I don't care,' she fired back. 'When you is in my house you is no working man. You is my boy and you better behave, or trouble. Pass me that brush and take some pap for those skinny bones. You is thinner than a blade of grass.' She shooed me away towards the stove. 'This your first Sunday back and we is going church. Mr Mpendulo giving the sermon . . . he is very kind to us . . . very good man . . . a man of God.'

Lala grinned, glad not to be the one on the receiving end for once, but it turns out my mother had been playing me all along. The evening before, Charlie left the shack, going to the Inner Tikki via my mother. He told

95

her where I was and that he would have me back the following morning. *He need to get out from under it all,* is what he said, assuring my mother that my decompression in his shack was better than the shebeen or on the side of the highway - a fact she knew only too well.

'Where are my bottles?' I asked. My sisters looked at each other, but neither replied. Just then the door blew open and my spirits dipped.

'Well, bless the Lord. Little worker boy is returned,' said my aunt Nobule, walking into the shack uninvited. She rubbed the top of my head, with a closed fist, as if I was a garment she was trying to clean with a stone. She finished rubbing and inspected her hand, grimacing as if it needed cleaning.

Little worker boy! She always called me *little* this and *little* that. I would soon be taller than her. She annoyed me just by looking at me. In Xhosa language, Nobule means *Beauty Queen*, but my Aunt was not generously blessed in this department. Six years older than my mother, she was forever single and childless and incessant in her obsession to rectify the situation. I have got my theories about why she never married - and it is not because she was ugly. It has never been difficult for an ugly person to get pregnant in Tolongo. Actually, of all the challenges a woman may face in life, in Tolongo, that has always been the most straightforward.

The problem with Aunt Nobule was that she had ideas high above her station. I think she had heard her name called too often and thought she was the personification of the word. She was the worst kind of annoying; like she knew it, worked hard at it, revelled in it. She was quite different from those people who are annoying but have no idea - that is simply unfortunate. The irony is that aunt Nobule introduced Mr Mpendulo to my mother. What a mistake that turned out to be. Never was a woman so adamant she could snare a man - until my mother showed up. I'm not pretending that Mr Mpendulo was in the slightest bit interested in my aunt, and he wilfully tolerated her company because of the volume of unrewarded work she did for the church . . . or for Mr Mpendulo to be exact, because he and the church were indistinguishable.

Mr Mpendulo was the sort of man that liked a challenge. He had this clever knack of turning the unobtainable into the obtainable; a little bit like my mother's Jesus if you like, only his devices were more cunning than turning water into wine, or bringing sight to the blind. He clearly enjoyed the challenge of my mother, something to do with her being married already - off limits. He was ever so attentive to those lonely women whose husbands worked far away from the township for extended periods of time and he was capable of taking their poverty and turning it into his own wealth. He was the nearest thing to a celebrity around our lanes and plenty of forsaken souls queued up, eager for his counsel.

'You will pay money to your mother, Lifa?' I didn't know whether aunt Nobule was asking a question or telling me.

'What money?' I asked suspiciously.

'Money from working, boy . . . twelve weeks working,' she snapped back as if to ask how I could be so rude. It was at this point my mother's ears pricked up. With the melodrama of the day before, she had forgotten all about it.

'Nobule is right, Lifa. Where is my money?' She paused from drawing lines beneath her eyes with a silver make-up pencil and turned to confront me.

'It's my money. I worked for it,' I said defensively.

'No Lifa! You work for all of us. I looked after you for all these years and now you must pay me back.' I had never seen my mother stuck between angry and desperate.

'I didn't ask you to look after me. I didn't even ask to be born. You should not have made me if you didn't want to look after me,' I spurted out, raising my voice in further defiance. She did not expect my direct reply, which rendered her speechless. Speechless was not a condition ever experienced by her sister. Aunt Nobule was thrilled with the opportunity to go into battle.

'Just like his father . . . stupid and selfish. How dare you treat your mother like this,' she said, pressing all the worst buttons.

'I am nothing like my father,' I hissed back, spraying poisonous venom. I could think of no worse or hurtful an insult. If only my mother knew how unlike my father I really was; how I had protected her by keeping the secret of his horrendous assault on Coca in the shebeen.

'If you are staying here, Lifa, then you need to pay, just like your sisters,' said mother, speaking in a quieter voice, presumably hoping a measured approach would calm me.

'I only got half what I should. Speak to my father, he stole the rest,' I said.

'I told you - just like his father. There's never any money and it's always someone else's fault.' My aunt sneered as she spoke, raising her eyes towards the roof.

'Shut up Nobu . . . let me speak for once,' said my mother, now as annoyed with her sister as she was with me. My sisters retreated to the back of the shack. I felt like walking over to my aunt and swinging the metal pot from the stove hard onto the side of her face . . . the remodelling work might

97

have done her a favour.

'Lifa. Don't you understand? We are poor. We need all the money we can get so that we can eat, or so that we can buy nice things once in a while. When we came to Tolongo, we didn't have nice things, because your father neglected us. Now we can make a better life.' My mother came over to me and placed her hands on my shoulders.

I could not decide whether her argument was compelling, or clever emotional blackmail. I took it as blackmail. What couldn't she get work like me? I did not trust the way she had allowed my father to treat her like a helpless, powerless victim and I did not want to follow in those footsteps. Of course I could not articulate it in those terms as a boy, but I knew that feeling in my gut - the uncomfortable, acidic, gurgling.

'No!' I said, standing resolute and emotionless on the spot.

The slap from my mother followed quickly and forcefully. It didn't knock me over, but my cheek stung bitterly and my eyes welled with tears. The tears came not because of the pain, but because of the injustice. I often wonder what might have transpired had she not slapped me in that moment, if she had stepped back and decided to talk some more, to reflect or attempt to see things from my point of view?If she had just taken one minute to get to know me better, to understand me better. That slap marked a turning point in my life. Perhaps I should have thanked my mother for it. With that slap I became a man, not physically, but in my head. It was like a bolt of lightening re-assembling drawers in my mind. I experienced utter clarity, the sort of clarity that cannot be ignored or challenged - the clarity of truth: I did not want the life that my mother and my father and my sisters had accepted. I wanted something entirely different. So I committed, there and then, never to deviate from the intention.

It is one thing to set out a stall in such rigid terms and it is another to back it up. In the heat of the moment, I had not thought about the consequences, but when you hear something in your heart, I have learned to trust that voice and to cultivate faith in whatever the future may bring. I learned that in much greater abundance from Victor.

'Get out! . . .' my mother screamed. She pushed me hard towards the door, past where my aunt was sitting. 'Get out, get out, get out,' she continued to push and scream at the top of her voice - loud enough to have changed the direction of the winds blowing across the Cape Flats.

I think that in that moment she also let out sixteen years of hatred and loathing for my father, and for herself. She would have pushed me though the door had I not opened it so quickly. I ran to the first corner, turned into another lane, then slowed to a walk with tears streaming down my face.

To be young and homeless in Tolongo was not uncommon; to be much younger than me and homeless in Tolongo was not uncommon. At least I had a job and a place to stay during the week. I didn't know where I was walking, but I kept going. I felt like I wanted to be as far away from my mother as it was possible to be. I thought the distance would help me to forget, but I found out soon enough that a person cannot run from himself.

My tears didn't last long. I convinced myself that I had made the right decision. If I brought kids into the world, they would not have to pay me back for anything. What kid chooses to come into the world anyway? Look at Willem. He was rich and he didn't have to pay his parents back for anything - why should I? I had convinced myself that my decision to leave was absolutely correct, then I heard footsteps running behind me and felt a hand fall onto my shoulder.

'I didn't think I would catch you,' said Lala, panting hard to catch her breath. She was carrying something wrapped in papers.

'Here,' she said, passing me the parcel.

I unwrapped it and found one of my glass bottles. It was my favourite; full of ornate rivets that shone in a rainbow of colours as the light refracted in different directions.

'It's the only one I managed to keep. I hid it from mother and Duhele,' she said, smiling warmly.

'Thanks, Lala,' I said, not knowing what else to say in such awkward circumstances. Lala was two years older, and I was closer to her than anyone else in my family.

'What are you going to do now?' she asked.

She didn't mean now - as in right now. She meant what would I do in the future. Where was I going to sleep? How was I going to eat? But for some reason that I could not comprehend, all I wanted to do was to focus on this moment, happy to let the questions about the future fly by me, as if they didn't matter anyway. For now I was with myself and that had to be good enough.

'I'm going to the beach. Want to come?' I asked, hoping she would say yes.

'I've got to go to Church,' she replied.

'That's okay . . . go to Church if you have to.' Underneath, I was disappointed.

'I could say I needed to find you?' She smiled, changing her mind, liberated from the chore of church.

'Mother said we might go to live with Mr Mpendulo,' she said, unsure if this was good or bad. The news did not surprise me, although I doubted if

Lala and Duhele would feature as strongly in Mr Mpendulo's plans as my mother.

17
The Beach

The Cape Flats expanded all the way to the Atlantic Coast, but it was thirty years before Tolongo's fringes made it all the way to the coastline. Today, pure, white sand provides a boundary fence, but when I was growing up it was about an hour's walk.

By the first dunes our legs were tired. A thick fog hung over the sand and the sea to dampen our enthusiasm, even though it provided a refreshingly cool blanket for us to hide under. Poverty and the beach do not combine well to offer an endless list of activities. When my sisters and I first started visiting, we spent ages devising games to play; running games, digging games, splashing games, building games, jumping games – any games that we could think of. On this particular day, Lala suggested we search the sands for something useful that could have drifted in from the sea; some wood, a container, old rope or string or bottles that she could use to improve the shack.

We walked in opposite directions, agreeing to return after covering half-a-mile in distance. I went towards the city and the mist slowly evaporated, burnt off by the late morning sun. A scorching heat was fighting its way through the cover as I walked up by the high tide mark in deep, fine sand that had not been flattened or dampened by the receding tide. In the wind, light, dry, white grains of sand lashed and pinched my ankles.

Lala was out of view when I turned to witness my line of footprints being quickly covered-up by the moving sands. I walked on, without keeping a record of how far I had travelled, determined to find something unusual. Nothing emerged, apart from some frayed, green netting and a few broken pallets. Then the fog thinned, and I could see the top of Table Mountain and a line of jagged hills curving out into the ocean.

In retrospect, there was a certain irony in standing, framed by the backdrop of the Cape of Good Hope at a large wooden sign in the middle of the beach. The sign was nailed onto a thick wooden stake that sank deep and rigid into the softest sand, above the line of broken shells and pebbles marking the highest tide. I looked briefly at the stenciled black letters, unable to read, then continued on, scouring for treasure.

A balding, middle-aged white man appeared, restraining a large, animated, black dog, at a wooden fence running along the top of grassy dunes. He attached the dog's lead to a fence-post then jogged down onto the sand in my direction, arms flailing. He drew nearer and began shouting. I could make out his weathered, leathery face and thick, hairless arms, but I was not sure he was shouting at me. He reached me, sweating profusely and struggling to catch his breath, although the lack of fitness did not abate his shouts. Afrikaans is a language which I did not speak apart from a few common words, but the phrase he repeated did not require translation:

'Yaye fowkin' kaffir. Fokof. Fokof.'

'Fokof, kaffir.' he shouted again.

I stood in front of him, less in fear than in curiosity. To this day I don't know why I didn't run. I had plenty of time to do so. Perhaps at some level, some unconscious level, I was looking for confirmation of the stories I had heard about the white South African government's policy of apartheid. The bunkhouse was full of treacherous stories of maltreatment, upheaval and wicked, irrational discriminations by the whites against our indigenous population. Every man had his own personal favourite, which they laboured over time and again.

Police raids, theft and brutality were commonplace across the townships. Unfair prison sentences, without trials, were handed out because people had not been in receipt of their *dompas*. In a few cases there were beatings that resulted in the murder of innocent people for nothing more than petty indiscretions or the wrong associations. There were violent protests and riots, but the workers at Glen Cleaver avoided them in the working week.

The man closed in and pushed me, shouting and gesticulating, his heavy hands slamming against my chest. The first thud winded me, sending a burning pain through my thin cage of ribs. I dropped my coloured glass bottle and stepped back. The second thud sent me flying backwards. I landed on my back in the sand.

'Why are you doing this, old man?' I shouted in Xhosa, expecting him to reason. This incensed him further. He pulled me up to my feet like a feather and pushed me again.

"Spek Afrikaans, fok!"

When I fell again, tears streamed from my eyes like the last drips being squeezed from a sponge. My sadness was accompanied by a mix of fear and the deep callings of a Xhosa tribesman. I was no match for this man, but part of me refused to be beaten. I rose with a handful of sand and threw it defiantly into his face. The shouting stopped as he frantically cleared it from his face.

I thought I could outrun the fat, bald, pig-eyed lump but just as I moved, the underside of his thick, brown sandal cracked onto my ankle. I didn't know whether it was broken or sprained. I tried to stand, but the smallest amount of weight was unbearable and I fell again, limply onto the sand. Then I crawled, like an injured animal striving to escape the clutches of a predator.

He pushed and kicked and dragged me all the way back to the sign I had passed earlier. My ankle was badly bruised and swollen like an orange. He pointed at me and then the sign.

'Fokof, kaffir,' he shouted aggressively and marched away.

My back rested on the wooden stake and I held my ankle hoping Lala had seen me. She took a while to appear and seemed more worried about the trouble she would be in from my mother, than in the state of my ankle. It was a long, arduous hobble back to the outskirts of the township. Supported by Lala on one side, I limped tenderly on my one healthy leg. Near the Inner Tikki, Lala used her charms on a man with a donkey pulling a wooden cart. He agreed to take us within a few hundred yards of my mother's shack. On this day, I understood the superstitious rule of three; that bad things always come in threes. With my luck, I might have extended that rule to four or five before the weekend was out.

'I'm not coming with you, Lala,' I said.

'But you've got to. Look at your ankle. We can fix it at home. How will you work?' she asked, genuinely concerned.

'Don't worry about me. I will stay with Charlie,' I said - a bare-faced lie. I was too stubborn to accept her offer of help, especially after making my position so clear with my mother. But I was also too embarrassed to ask for Charlie's help again and admit my frailty. I said goodbye to Lala and she watched her little brother hobble, dragging his ankle towards the highway.

'Charlie lives that way doesn't he?' called Lala, pointing in the opposite direction.

'He'll be at work . . . no rush.' This time she didn't believe my excuse, shaking her head in dismay.

I found a piece of wood in a patch of scrub which acted as a moderately useful walking stick. Unfortunately, it enjoyed bending in the middle, causing me to continually lose balance. After a mile or so, I sat down on the ground beside a bush below the embankment leading up to the highway. I was a few yards from the spot that the Glen Cleaver workers were picked up on Monday mornings. My mouth was dry, my leg was throbbing and once again I was hungry. I lay down flat on my back and found a speck of comfort in the dying warmth of the sun. When it disappeared I felt cold and my thirst merged with hunger to give me severe doubts about whether

I would get any sleep before 4.30am the following morning. I had twelve hours of homelessness to endure.

Had I been able to read Afrikaans, English or Zulu on the beach that day, the three repeated messages in the different languages on the sign from the City of Cape Town Authority might have prevented my distressing experience:

"Under section 37 of the Cape Town beach by-laws, this bathing area is reserved for the sole use of members of the white race group."

I have always been glad that I was unable to read that sign. I would not have wanted the feelings of injustice and humiliation that might have accompanied my compliance. Injustice and humiliation were feelings I would have plenty of time to learn about in the coming years. That sign and many like it had been hammered into our country's beaches five years earlier. It was the last time I ventured down to that end of the beach on Sundays. It is one thing to hear the stories and to have lived for a few months under the threat of abuse on account of my colour at Glen Cleaver, but now I had experienced apartheid directly and explicitly. I realised it amounted to more than the ill-thought behaviours of a few white farmers; it was formally sanctioned by the highest law in the land. The highest law in the white man's land. That was not one to which I or any other black tribesman felt we belonged.

18
Roll-Call

'Wake up man, George,' said Charlie.

The moon was still out, right behind Charlie's head as he stood above me, interrupting the sound of passing cars and trucks with his deep voice. My side was damp, cold and numb because my singlet had soaked up the dew during the night. My ankle was throbbing, but not as badly as before dark. The cold had numbed the pain slightly, but also stiffened my muscles rigid as a bronze cast.

A group of men had assembled to meet the bakkie, which was running late. Charlie offered his arm and I reached up with both my hands and clung to him as he pulled me up. He had arrived at my mother's shack to fetch me at 4am and a sleepy Lala had whispered her account of the previous day's events.

'You is sleep here all night, George?' asked Charlie.

'I didn't sleep much,' I said, unsure how he was going to react. He shook and rubbed his head, then sighed.

'Is you walk?' he asked.

No matter how much I wanted to ignore the searing pain, I could not put any weight on my ankle. The bakkie pulled up off the highway onto the scrub and the men climbed on in silence. Charlie lifted me up like a newborn baby, walked towards the vehicle and bundled me onto the back. I slumped down next to Johnson who shuffled up to make room. The air was thin, fresh and still like we were on the high veld, but Eugene and Franklin quickly extinguished any salubrity with their cigarette smoke, which formed in a tail, like it was coming from the chimney of a fast-moving locomotive engine, as the car drove on. Charlie promoted himself to the passenger seat and the rest of us huddled, silent and cold, pensive and insular. There was no sign of my father.

I sat like a cheap, puppet doll with closed eyes, unable to sleep, as my head refused to balance on top of my neck. It slipped continuously onto the shoulders of Johnson and Eugene, sending me sharp jolts of anxiety, induced by the memory of what I was returning to. I wished I was living another life.

The bakkie took a different route, over the Finkel Pass, high above

Stellenbosch. At the steepest points, the bakkie changed gear and came to a complete standstill, sounding like the engine was going to explode and catapult us off the side of the mountain. There was a collective sigh of relief when we reached the top and I glimpsed the promise of dawn, far away in the East. The bakkie free-wheeled down the mountain, breaking heavily at tight bends among the pine trees and almost losing control. The scent of woodland, pine needles and dried leaves intensified and was joined by the less distinguishable bouquet of grape vines among cleanly tilled, well-nourished soil in the valley below - Franschhoek's valley.

For the first time, I realised what Victor meant when he said I should not enjoy myself too much over the weekend. I had not wanted to fall asleep on Sunday evening near the roadside - not because I was frightened and alone, or cold and hungry, but because when I did, I knew my next waking moment would mean travelling back to Glen Cleaver. The prospect filled my heart with dread.

Charlie carried me into the bunkhouse and set me down on a seat at a table. Victor had already prepared pap and coffee. He must have thought I was haphazard by nature with the amount of trouble I attracted for myself, but he remained as sympathetic and helpful as ever. Charlie was more concerned about Master Boss.

'We is must speak with Ringidd. Maybe two weeks before you can walk proper,' he said to Victor and I.

'How it happen, George?' Victor asked, inspecting my ankle which was still swollen and had turned from dark orange to reddish black. I told him the story and he listened patiently while Charlie left for Ringidd's hut.

'At least your cut has closed up,' said Victor, inspecting my head. I had pulled off the bandages before returning to my mother for the second time.

Charlie returned from Ringidd fifteen minutes later.

'Roll-call in courtyard, thirty minutes,' he said, stomping back in hunched, so that his head would not scrape on the doorframe.

'How will I get down there, Charlie?' I said, worried I might have to crawl.

'I is driving you, boy,' he said with a grin.

'But you can't drive, Charlie,' I replied, confused.

'Victor is going to help me. Yes?' Charlie looked at Victor and received an equally bemused look. 'And Franklin - you is helping too,' said Charlie pointing at him. Franklin screwed up his face as if to say: *No. I'm not.*

'*Franklin* . . . you *is* helping, see.' Charlie gave him a serious stare this time. It is odd that a serious stare from only one eye can double the effect of a threat, rather than halve it. Franklin stood up reluctantly, shuffled to the door, sat on the steps and pulled on some boots.

There was no purr of a vehicle because my car was a wooden wheelbarrow. It was parked out in the middle of the turning circle. The men used them regularly on the estate. It was made from a recycled oak wine barrel, cut in half and bound together with metal clasps and studs.

As journeys go, I have never had so much fun. With the best view of the dark, treacherous path in front of me, Charlie appointed me navigator. Two of my three supporters each grabbed a handle and rotated in turns to carry.

We arrived after the rest of the men and joined the end of two full rows in front of the press shed's double-doors. Muffled laughs welcomed us and didn't fully dry up until Ringidd turned the corner into the courtyard. Johnson was in the rear next to Duke, whispering and chewing on something he was not willing to swallow - perhaps tobacco or the grizzle from an old stick of biltong.

'Shut up quiet now, Johnson,' shouted Ringidd, looking like he had aged ten years over the weekend. In the half-light under the visible moon, his hair was a whiter shade of grey and the look on his face, tired, wrinkled and unamused. Some men are older or younger than others, even when they are the same age. Ringidd was one of the older types, especially walking with his faint limp, hunched over slightly like he was unable to fully stretch his back. He would have struggled to touch his shin bones, even if four men were trying to force him down there.

'Hush quiet 'fore Masta Baas coming, man,' he warned, looking at Johnson again. Johnson made a point of turning his head and taking a long slow spit behind to rid himself of whatever he was chewing.

Master Boss arrived with Mallie and Toppie walking placidly behind on the leads - the first time I had seen such a muted threat of aggression. Perhaps they were not morning dogs, just like the bunkhouse. Or perhaps they had learned that kaffirs are too tired and hungover to cause problems early on a Monday morning. He secured their leashes to the metal ringlet, protruding from the workshop wall then turned his attention to us.

'Ten weeks 'til harvest and you fokin' kaffirs are making life difficult.' Masta Baas spoke clearly and slowly with a loud voice. 'First off, Kenneth is not coming back to work . . . and now his domb, lame, fokin' kaffir son cannot work . . . What fokin' disease is flowing in your animal bones?' His question was rhetorical and his words were delivered like they had been written and rehearsed. Victor told me later that he wanted to point out that blood does not flow in bones, but in front of Master Boss he knew well to keep that insight to himself.

'Kenneth will be replaced . . . but with harvest coming soon, let's hope it's by a kaffir that's worked a vineyard.' He turned and looked at me as I lay nervously in the wheelbarrow. 'And as for you . . . you little fok . . . You will work the next eight weekends to repay me for the two weeks you will lose . . . every Saturday and half-day Sunday.'

'Yes, sir, Masta Baas, sir,' I replied instantly, insinuating gratefulness for such generous admonishment.

'And if one of you fokin' kaffirs don't turn up to work anytime in the next eight weeks, I'll set the fokin' dogs on you.' He turned and looked at Mallie and Toppie, who were listening in attentively, from the metal ringlet on the workshop wall. 'They will tear your limbs and puncture your lungs . . . then I will gut you myself.' He reached for a large bush-knife that was in a holster on the leather belt around his khaki shorts. 'I'll fokin' cut up your innards and grill them on my own fokin' braai then feed you to Mallie and Toppie - cooked to a crisp to rid you of that fokin' disease. . . One whisker . . . one whisker out of line and I'll fokin' crack you. Understand?'

'Yes sir, Masta Baas, sir,' we replied in unison.

He turned and walked back towards Mallie and Toppie, untied them and walked past his office in the direction of his house, leaving Ringidd to deliver an encore. Ringidd paced up and down slowly in front of us, rubbing his face with both his hands, thinking about exactly what he was going to say, but also delaying, generating apprehension and increasing the gravity of our situation. He turned sideways and spoke. Dawn was breaking behind as we stood in the shadow of the large press shed, between light and dark.

'You is have it good with me. You men has it all too good . . . too nice with me.' Ringidd turned to face us again and caught Franklin restraining laughter because the man to his left - Bostock - had taken his penis from his overalls, allowing it to briefly droop in front of him while Ringidd was speaking.

Ringidd remained emotionless, fixed to the spot in front of us, with a clear view through to Franklin in the rear. He stared at him hard but it did not have the intended effect. Franklin's laughter found its voice. Who hasn't been in a similar situation, when laughter emerges precisely because it is inappropriate in the circumstances? Sometimes there is nothing a person can do to control it. And once it starts it is like a gigantic cargo ship coming into harbour - there is forward momentum all of its own - even after you have shut off the engines or switched them into reverse. Victor and I often played a game where we stared at each other with straight faces and the loser was the first one to laugh. It is nearly always impossible for someone not to laugh. Even the strongest willed character will break, given enough time. But this was no game and Ringidd was never going to laugh. He stared at Franklin and he stared. Franklin grew self-conscious and sounded increasingly nervous. And although his laughter was slowly drying up, he couldn't completely stop it. He was fighting a losing battle. Ringidd's stare did not recede as Franklin coughed and gasped against his wishes.

Duke said he reckoned Ringidd was soaking up the humiliation, willing it on like a power source he could plug into. He stepped backwards to the workshop door, one careful step at a time, still without taking his eyes from Franklin. His hand reached the latch on the workshop door, turned it, then opened the door a fraction, enough to slide in his arm.

He fumbled for a short time then successfully grabbed hold of an object hanging on the inside wall - still all the while, staring at Franklin. His hand reappeared holding the ridged handle of a stumpy, polished, ebony baton. An outdoor spotlight, high under the overhang of the workshop's tiled roof glistened off the baton when Ringidd walked forward, swinging it loosely and aimlessly from the leather strap around his wrist.

Any lingering smirks on the faces of the men metamorphosed into passive obedience as Ringidd walked up the middle of our two rows. Not one head turned by as much as a hair's width when he passed, but every eyeball strained to the side of their sockets to witness the outcome of such unnerving intimidation.

Johnson and Duke mentioned Ringidd resorting to violence once before, in similar circumstances. Humiliation was his trigger. From the point that Franklin had let out that first repressed chuckle, Ringidd had not taken his eyes off him - not for an instant. He continued to stare at him as his baton smashed the side of his jaw, chipping two of his bottom teeth. That was the only time he hit him on the head. Franklin screamed and fell to the floor onto all fours with one hand covering his mouth. He whimpered and cried; a grown man crying like a small child, pleading for an acquittal. Ringidd kicked away Franklin's arm to open up his rib cage and hit him with more vigour than a prize-winning butcher has for tenderising prime cuts of beef.

Blood from Franklin's mouth splattered onto the bottom of Ringidd's previously white trouser legs as the vanquished worker rolled over onto his side and lay immobile and whimpering. Ringidd huffed and puffed and hissed when he inspected the speckled-red material at his ankles and raised the baton once more, mocking another strike without following through.

'Johnson, Barclay, Victor . . . go wait for Masta Baas in his office. Rest of you get to work,' he said. No men ever moved as quickly or as agreeably on account of an order from Ringidd before then.

Franklin lay motionless on the ground, ten yards from the press shed doors as we moved off to work. Bostock volunteered to carry me back up to the bunkhouse, having sought permission from Ringidd. For a mile, mostly uphill, I hung off his shoulder struggling to find a comfortable position. All I could think about was that baton smashing repeatedly into the side of Franklin's ribs as he crouched on his hands and knees with nowhere to go and nobody to help him.

19
Mama Blues

We cleaned up after dinner and Victor sat at the end of my bunk and placed a plate at my feet, covered in cloth. He teased back the material to reveal a thick brown crust of pastry.

'Apple pie,' he grinned, licking his lips in exaggerated fashion, bending close to my face. 'I smuggled it out of the estate house at the weekend.'

What a nerve? He could fall into the most overflowing cesspit and rise out smelling of lavender. I on the other hand, could fall into a bowl of rose-petals and crawl out smelling like a cesspit. Luck is a funny thing; but maybe Victor's trick was to rely on his own guile and daring, not luck.

'Did my ankle get you in trouble?' I asked, trying to ignore the apple pie.

'Ringidd volunteered Johnson, Barclay and me to stay behind for four weekends running up to the annual braai,' he said. 'Doesn't bother me 'cos I'm here anyway . . . although I'd rather be mucking around with Willem than working.'

'I'm not going to be much help to you this week Victor, not with my swollen ankle.'

'That's okay . . . at least I'll have company.'

'I can try sitting down to work,' I suggested.

'Thanks. But I bet you are fit enough to walk up to the pool by the weekend. I'll clear out the latrines for a week if I'm wrong . . . wanna bet?'

'No, we better stop going to the pool from now on. We will get in big trouble if we are caught with Willem.'

'Don't be stupid, George,' said Victor, taken aback by my apparently preposterous view. 'If you think like that, you'll turn into Ringidd. That's what we are fighting against.'

'Fighting against?'

'Yeah, domkopf. Fighting against.' He prodded the side of my temple with his index finger.

'I don't understand.'

'Who is the boss 'round here, George?' I knew the answer to that.

'Mister Vorster, then Masta Baas, then Ringidd,' I confidently

111

replied.

'Wrong. All wrong.' He shook his head from side to side.

'No it's not,' I protested. 'Who is a bigger boss than Mister Vorster? . . . Nobody.' I corrected Victor for the first time since knowing him.

'No, I'm telling you. I'm my own boss and you need to be your own boss too. Just because we work here and do what they say . . . doesn't mean they own us. I choose to be here - for now anyway. One day, I will walk out and do what I want,' he said, with absolute certainty.

'You are crazy, Victor,' I said. 'If you walk out of here you will have nowhere to go . . . no job . . . nothing to eat. You will die in a week.'

'No, George, *you* will die in a week because you don't believe you are your own boss. I do, that's the difference,' he replied as seriously as I had ever seen him, like his life depended upon it.

I don't know where he got all this stuff from and why he even bothered speaking to me about it. The strange thing is that if we had had the same conversation ten days ago; before I had jumped off the pier, before I had been back in Tolongo, and my father had attacked me, and my mother had disowned me and that fat, bald, pig-eyed lump on the beach had cracked down on my ankle, I would have let his words flow from one ear to the other and fly out the other side, lost forever in the winds. Today however, they made a little more sense. I'm not saying I agreed with him fully, nor did I think life could be so simple just because Victor wanted it to be, but what I did know is I had committed to a better life than the ones my parents endured. That is what I had resolved before I fell asleep under a bush by the highway on the outskirts of Tolongo.

Pieces of cotton-wool soaked in eucalyptus oil were stuffed into the gaps between Franklin's teeth but seemed to have little effect. We heard him turning and groaning and hitting his forehead with a clenched fist in his bunk throughout the night. There is little worse than toothache, not the kind that gives that dull ache, but the type of zinging, metallic, spearing pain that springs from an open nerve-end. Franklin must have had a few of those open nerves because it sounded like every time he took a breath there was torture to bear.

None of the men slept soundly that night; not despite eleven energy sapping hours of manual labour under the sun. Bostock took Franklin's injuries worst of all. Nobody blamed him, because all the younger guys got up to some sort of mischief at some point or another - but Ringidd was normally too lazy or unaware to do anything about it. The incident and the state of Franklin's injuries definitely dulled Bostock's appetite for frivolity.

Everyone was on edge. Nobody stayed up drinking, smoking or

gambling. It was the first night the tables remained unoccupied after dinner. In the weeks running up to harvest, Master Boss had the men working harder than normal. Most retired to their bunks soon after dark and fell asleep shortly afterwards. Some were so tired they didn't even bother to get undressed.

Victor deserved to get to bed early. For a whole week he was responsible for my work as well as his, without the pretence of help from me. I couldn't walk or stand for more than thirty seconds before I needed to rest my ankle.

'Let's sit out-front before bed,' I said to Victor, bored of the bunkhouse.

I put my arms around his shoulder on my bad side and leaned on him. Victor opened the door and there was Charlie, sitting on the bottom step. He was smoking a cigarette, which he only did very occasionally. We sat down on the steps above him, with our heads at the same height as his.

Victor told me Willem was still basking in the glory of his butterfly catch. He had written letters informing the National Butterfly Association in Pretoria and the Natural History Museum in London, England and reckoned he would get a reply within three months. He also hoped to get a newspaper article written about it in the Cape Argus, with a picture he had taken of himself next to the butterfly and his glass jar. Our conversation intrigued Charlie.

'What him like . . . your friend Willem?' asked Charlie, in a hushed voice making sure the bunkhouse could not hear him.

'I'll tell you about him, if you tell us about Mama Blues,' said Victor, with a devious glint in his eyes.

'You is bad clever, Victor. Where you get so bad clever?' Charlie chuckled and his shoulders bobbed up and down gently. He stamped out his cigarette on the thick skin of his heel and the smoke vanished.

'You first, Victor, boy. I is no bad stupid, man,' said Charlie.

Victor told Charlie almost everything he knew about Willem and the majority of it I also heard for the first time. Victor knew all about his school in Paarl, he knew the names of his friends and how they behaved. He knew the names of the people that had bullied him for a year. Willem didn't fit in too well, mostly because he wasn't good at sport. He could catch butterflies, but not a ball. He was admittedly useless at anything that involved hitting, throwing, kicking or catching. His favourite subjects were Geography and Biology. Victor explained what those meant.

The only sport Willem loved was swimming, he loved swimming, but he was not good enough to make the school team in his age-group. He sometimes found it lonely as an only child and often wished for brothers or sisters. His loneliness was compounded because he hardly saw his mother or father. They were either working hard or socialising; entertaining people from the local community, keeping up appearances and the like. There was much more. Victor could have spoken for the whole night, or unlike me, written a book about it. I couldn't believe that Victor could read and write all on his own.

Every so often Charlie interrupted the flow with a flurry of questions. What him eating? Where him buy them clothes? Where he go away with Mister Missus Vorster in winter? Why him not play white friends at weekends? Why him got that bright, white hair so young? Why him chasing butterflies? Victor answered everything that Charlie blurted out as best he could. It was while Victor was passing on that information about Willem that it hit me for the first time . . . I didn't know anything about Victor - nothing personal at any rate. I knew his character of course . . . I knew that as clear as day. I knew his mannerisms and that he was cleverer than any other black boy I had ever met. But I didn't know anything about his time before Glen Cleaver, his past, his family, his dreams. Victor's life was ghost-like - alluded to but never revealed.

I remember saying to myself on the steps that I would find out all about Victor one day - so that I would be able to talk about him like he could talk about Willem. We were blood-brothers after all, and there should be no secrets between blood-brothers. As eager as I was to dig deeper with Victor, he was more intrigued to find out about Mama Blues. I had met her in person. How many people could say that?

When Victor's stories dried up, Charlie stood up onto his tip toes and stretched, then yawned.

'Me dog tired, boys. Go bed sleep.'

The expressions of disbelief and disappointment on our faces must have been amusing as we sat there with widened eyes and gaping mouths.

'But . . . Charlie . . . *you said . . . you promised.*' Our words came out in tandem.

'I'm not promised, man,' Charlie said, restraining his smile.

'Come on, Charlie. What is Mama Blues like? Please Charlie,' pleaded Victor. Charlie had conned us good and proper. 'Tell us Charlie. Go on.' My pleas were just as forceful.

'Okay, okay,' he conceded in a whisper. 'Don't be waking up them whole bunkhouse.'

'Mama Blues?' He leaned his head towards his shoulder as he pondered on the topic. 'She weird strange . . . very weird strange. She love them colour blue.'

'What else?' asked Victor. 'Is she a gangster?'

'No. She not them gangster. She them boss of them gangster. She all clever . . . all good clever with them read and write and numbers all.'

'How she get so clever, Charlie?' I asked.

'I'm not know. But she speaking all English and Afrikaans, Tsonga, Zulu and Xhosa. She living in many different houses.'

'I thought she lived in the Inner Tikki? I met her there once,' I said, astonished.

'No man, George, she living in all them different places. She come Inner Tikki half-day in week . . . sometimes two or three weeks.'

'What else?'

'She rich with money, big rich with money, bigger than them white mans' money.'

'How she get bigger money than white people?' pondered Victor out loud. We had a hundred other questions, but none that Charlie was prepared to listen to.

'That's all I'm know 'bout Mama Blues,' he said matter-of-fact, before rising four steps and entering the bunkhouse for bed. Victor and I looked at each other in amazement, feeling slightly duped that Charlie's knowledge of Mama Blues was not nearly as extensive as Victor's knowledge of Willem. I hadn't noticed the throbbing of my ankle for the last hour.

'We're gonna be as rich as Mama Blues one day, George.' Victor said with a glint of mischief and desire in his eyes.

20
Braai

Ringidd was very contented. He arrived at the bunkhouse, after lunch one Saturday in the weeks running up to the annual braai, to take charge of his specially selected working group that would forfeit four, workless weekends. Johnson, Barclay, Victor and I sat, waiting for instruction. Barclay was less disconsolate than Johnson about being kept back, probably because he would find time to steal with Mary. Johnson, on the other hand, only had hard, unpaid work to look forward to.

Gwendoline Vorster had every fine detail worked out for the braai and Willem told me that each year was more elaborate than the last. Red bricks, bags of sand, cement and powder-coated metal grates were piled up on the terrace then turned into monstrous, open grills. Large, white, umbrellas, emblazoned with the crest of Glen Cleaver, were borrowed from the tasting rooms and mounted in precise rows across the lawn. Twelve old wine barrels were sanded, varnished and rolled onto the terrace in preparation for being filled with ice, beer and Glen Cleaver's best white wines.

Johnson and Barclay were seconded to begin preparations the week before, under the watchful eye of Ringidd. Irrational meddling from Mrs Vorster was commonplace. She found fault in any job in which she had not been involved. Over the next four weekends we heard it all. She went as far as commenting on the angles of the stakes that were hammered into the lawn to secure the ropes that stabilised the marquee.

Hoisting the marquee was a demanding job. Heavy canvasses were hauled from the tractor trailer, unfolded and arranged in adjoining patterns in the middle of the lawn. Heavy wooden beams were laid flat out and fixed to heavier metal repositories and plinths, then attached to ropes and pulled carefully by the tractor, levering them into position. Every worker was called upon once the high beams were in place. Sheets of the heavy canvass were pulled up by hand in a ferocious game of tug-of-war that lasted for hours and resulted in some nasty friction burns if you were not careful. Tables and chairs were manually loaded and offloaded from the tractor trailer and carried, never dragged, across the lawn and arranged to seat two-hundred-and-fifty people. White linen was pressed by the household staff and draped over each table, then clipped in place with clasps made specifically for the job.

There was a children's playground to assemble. Apart from one, wooden climbing-frame and two seat swings, it was more like a museum exhibition; formed of old vineyard memorabilia and machinery that was scattered at random across the lawn behind the marquee. Any object was fair game - the children would be allowed to climb and clamber over anything they liked.

Far away from the children in the cellar of the estate house, trolleys of malt whisky, vodka and gin were stacked high, replete with boxes of imported Dominican and Honduran cigars; the domain of the Vorster's inner-circle.

Willem's father told him that of all the events and gatherings in Franschhoek's social calendar, their annual braai was the most revered. Glen Cleaver's crest was embossed in gold-leaf on professionally printed invitation cards and addressed to guests in Gwendoline Vorster's shaky handwriting, sometimes containing footnotes and minders of the previous years' frivolities. Over three hundred were invited, including children. There was space, alcohol and meat for double that.

For anyone outside the upper echelons of the local community, it must have felt like Christmas morning when those dainty, little white cards dropped out of their mailboxes or were pushed underneath their doors, or were occasionally pressed into the palms of their hands - for those lucky enough to be graced with Gwendoline Vorster's stone-cold presence. Ringidd drove Willem and his mother to residences across the valley to deliver invitations for two hours each evening over two weeks. A detailed scheme of the logistical operation was hand-sketched and guests were clustered and assigned different colours that denoted the day on which their invitation was to be delivered.

A guest's status depended upon whether Mrs Vorster or Willem, or both, left the comfort of the car to deliver the invitation. Generally speaking, Mrs Vorster remained inside, happy to let Willem skip up to the doorways and deliver the biggest, personal endorsement from the richest family in town. The most notable wine producers attended, although Mister Vorster must have made an exception for that man Van Horst from Breeberg. Willem said he fell into the category *have to invite* rather than *would like to invite*.

The dress code was casual; summer frocks for the ladies and short-sleeved shirts, smart shorts or slacks for the men. The staff complement was dressed formally; Mrs Vorster had arranged for professionally tailored uniforms to be worn on the day. Ringidd, Johnson and Barclay were whisked up like sugary icing on a cake, in white suit jackets with neat lapels. Ringidd's jacket had a line of black silk stitched onto the edge of his lapel, differentiating his position among the other workers. Miss Johanna was the same, apart from she had white silk stitched on the collar of a black blouse. The men's white jackets covered black shirts and silken, ivory bowties. A tailor from Paarl spent an entire afternoon in the estate house, fitting everyone up a month beforehand. The women mirrored the men except for their long, white skirts.My shoes were beautifully crafted works of art - all hired specially from some fancy department store in the centre of Cape Town. We had to hand them back, but I could have got used to those shiny, black, leather gloves on my feet - Chelsea boots, the man from the department called them.

Victor and I were given white slacks, black short-sleeved shirts and the boots; no jackets and no bowties. Our only task was to tidy, clean, dry and return used glasses for guests, on gleaming, silver trays.

With such elaborate planning and advance preparation you might think everything would have been ready weeks in advance - not so. We needed every second to get everything in place, right up to the point when the first guest's car rolled up Glen Cleaver's long, oak-lined driveway. There was an eerie silence across the lawn as we waited patiently, in lined formation, for the guests to appear. The tables glistened with empty crystalware and the sun was reflected off ice brimming from the oak barrels on the terrace. The sight reminded me how light used to bounce off my coloured bottles.

The first fifty cars parked up near the estate house, and the others were forced to find space on the verges of the driveway or on the open scrub underneath the oak trees. No empty piece of ground was left unused.

To reach the centre of the lawn, guests walked through a, welcoming tunnel of neatly assembled household staff. Victor and I were at the end the line, watching the procession of nervous energy and excitement. It was as if there was a penalty for missing a single minute. Men stepped from the driver seats, wives from the passenger seats, clutching fine hand-bags and neatly wrapped gifts. Some fiddled with wide brimmed hats; positioning them perfectly on their heads. Others shepherded and cajoled their children, reminding them of the appropriate behaviours for such a prestigious gathering.

Some folks greeted one another with an unashamedly buoyant, tacit delight at being included. Then there were the *big dogs*; men like Judge Du Toit, Commissioner Bosman and Mr Frank Retief, owner of the Chapel Stile estate. They swaggered up and onto the lawn like they owned the place, as did their wives and children. You would have thought they were doing the Vorster's a favour by turning up; like they expected some sort of a fee for the pleasure. They didn't stay long either. Experience must have taught these people to leave in the same state as they had arrived - like firm, freshly picked bananas in a fruit salad - before they had ripened, softened and blacked, beyond edible. Hot sun, alcohol and small-talk are ingredients that will ruin even the freshest fruit.

Kids scampered onto the grass behind the marquee and quickly clambered onto the vintage equipment on display; an old tractor, some trailers, pyramids of barrels and a tall, rusted copper vat that was once used to store wine in years gone by.

Some overly attentive mothers were clearly less comfortable with the social graces, and followed on the heels of their children, pretending to monitor them as they played. Husbands fetched their wives glasses of wine then vanished to acquaint themselves more intimately with bottles of Windhoek beer alongside their male contemporaries. White folks are no different from black folks in that regard; it is the same in the shebeen, men sit on one side and talk amongst themselves and women sit on the other and do the same.

Those not standing in the sun sat in the shade of the marquee, sipping cool drinks and letting extravagant canopés tickle the back of their throats; clement precursors to the onslaught of red protein. Duck-liver pate on lightly peppered pastry swirls and salted quails eggs with sticks of cucumber were not my idea of a treat, even less so when I nibbled on some in the kitchen.

Victor and I were inundated immediately, but remained somewhere between discreet and invisible. The midday sun was near its highest point without a cloud to be seen and the lawn was sheltered from the breeze. Our punishment was to pace from table to table, sweating profusely until our shirts were damp enough to wring out a full jug's worth of salty sap.

Half-an-hour after the first arrivals, Mister Vorster walked from the lawn onto the terrace next to the grills and faced the audience of guests. He clinked a wet, dark bottle of Windhoek with the tip of a silver knife, but the thin taps were audible only to the closest guests. As they quietened, others slowly followed, helped on by Mister Vorster who raised his arms repeatedly up and down in an attempt to hush the crowd. Something resembling silence was discernible apart from the kids playing on the machinery. He pulled a sheet of notes from the pocket of his khaki shorts for support and spoke up in a commanding voice.

'Before I commence our long-established lighting of the braai on this day of indulgence and excess . . . I would like to welcome you all to Glen Cleaver.' His voice carried easily across the lawn and he left room for applause which appeared in that polite and understated way that only people in floral frocks or starched collar shirts can evoke.

'Can you believe it is sixty-three years since my grandfather first lit this braai?' He was shaking his head in disbelief and stroking the bald patch in front of his half-receded hairline with his thumb and forefinger.

'It feels like only yesterday that I was one of the children playing on the equipment at the back,' he said, pointing. Most of the heads turned to look, smiling or chuckling supportively.

'Now . . . although our wines hold international awards, I can't say that they are better than they were sixty-three years ago, and I still have the evidence . . . but I'm not brave enough to open these last two bottles.' He reached across and grabbed two bottles of wine sitting on top of the nearest balustrade. Feigned awe and amazement at the age of the wine was etched on some faces in the crowd as people gathered more closely together, pressing nearer to the terrace wall to be closer to their host.

'As many of you know, my great grandfather was the founding father of Glen Cleaver. He spent seven years as a young man working among some of the greatest vineyards in France - no finer an apprenticeship exists on this earth. And when he returned, he pioneered wine-making in South Africa, in creating Glen Cleaver. Without his vision, his passion and his determination, it is fair to say there might not have been a modern wine industry in the Cape . . . But come, you are not here for a history lesson. There are some people that I must thank.' He paused and looked at his notes to make sure he had the names in the right order.

'My grandfather did not have the luxury of Pieter Kloppers. Where are you Pieter, man?' He searched the crowd and half-a-dozen helpful guests pointed in Pieter's direction. He was not a man that looked like he enjoyed the attention.

'There you are. There is not a finer butcher in South Africa. Every ounce of meat we eat today is from Pieter. Thanks Pieter . . . and what a generous deal you did me . . . you're definitely invited back next year.' Another bout of lighthearted laughs and smiles and nods weaved between the guests, echoing those coming from Mister Vorster who was beginning to feel more relaxed and consummate in his performance. He mentioned another five or six people, the big noises, those important enough to need on your side; local politicians, law-makers and business owners. When he had finished acknowledging influential friends and associates, he turned to his family.

'There are two other people that deserve a special mention. The first is this beautiful picture hiding behind me.' He turned and beckoned his wife.

Gwendoline Vorster stepped out from beside a red velvet curtain, behind the doors leading into the dining room, holding a glass of Chenin blanc. She self-consciously stood next to her husband while he put his arm around her shoulder, bringing her in close like a man would another man in some strange bonding ritual.

'Is she not a picture in this dress?' he said to the guests, while his wife subtly pulled sideways, releasing herself from his grip, looking childlike, and flapping her hand to suggest the delicately strapped, green and white polka-dot dress she was wearing was not worth commenting on.

'No, but seriously, without my Gwendoline this day would not happen. She has pondered on every detail for the last three-hundred and sixty-four days.' This got a bigger laugh than anything else; the first one that felt close to the bone. 'We owe the finer details to Gwenie. She just wouldn't have it any other way.' She couldn't wait to escape and the mild applause fizzled out by the time she had returned to the patio doors.

'Now, one last special mention.' Mister Vorster looked around, annoyed because the object of his attention was nowhere to be seen. He turned his head to his wife and narrowed his eyes, then hissed 'Where in kak is Willem?' She looked back vacantly, shrugging her shoulders. He turned back towards the audience and decided the direct route was the most effective.

'Where the heck is Willem? You're supposed to be standing at the bottom of the steps,' he boomed. Neither his question nor his statement was heard by Willem, despite both being delivered for his benefit. At that moment he was jumping off the back of a rusty old tractor with some of the other kids on the lawn behind the marquee - well out of sight and sound. One of the guests in the marquee took it upon themselves to fetch him. Willem had completely forgotten about his only task of the day because he was having fun with some boys from Paarl Gim. Even Frank Retief's son was being friendly towards him, and they had barely spoken two words in kindness or civility at school.

Willem's white head of hair appeared in the crowd. He moved from a brisk walk to a jog, sidestepping guests apologetically, towards the terrace. They parted like the red sea near the terrace and he ran up the steps immediately apologising to his father, recognising that well-trodden look of displeasure and impatience.

Mister Vorster gave Willem a playful slap on the back of his head which he instinctively tried to avoid. His father was restraining indignation in

121

front of the onlookers and Willem expected some retrospective discipline later in the day.

'Kind of you to grace us with your presence, Willem,' said his father. 'Punctuality, second only to godliness. Is that not right Reverend Heyns?' He looked over at the local minister who nodded forcefully, mimicking solemnity, looking like he didn't believe a word of it.

'So as I was saying. The last person that *did* deserve a mention is Willem.' He paused for effect before continuing.

'One day Willem will inherit and manage Glen Cleaver. I hope he understands the importance of upholding tradition; not only the tradition of hosting our community at our annual braai, but also in upholding the traditions that we hold so dear at Glen Cleaver. It is these traditions and qualities that have nurtured such deep respect for us as a wine producer here in South Africa - and despite sanctions, in countries as far as Europe and America. I was brought up to engender self-discipline and ambition, all fuelled by the pursuit of the highest standards. It is for that reason that I am pleased to announce Willem will be leaving Glen Cleaver and Paarl Gimnasium at the end of this summer to attend Ascension College near Pietermaritzburg, in the lush green countryside of Natal . . . like his father and his grandfather before him. Ascension is an exclusive boarding school that educates children in the very best English tradition. I can think of no better a role model for that ethos than Henni Du Toit - Judge Du Toit's boy - winner of Ascensions Verwoerd Scholarship last year.' Mister Vorster looked at Judge Du Toit who nodded back agreeably, more certain of the fact than Koibus Vorster.

'So I would like everyone to raise their glasses and toast these three: Willem, self-discipline and ambition.' The majority of the guests called out Willem's name, sipped on their drinks and then applauded, more vigorously than before because it was the end of the speech. Only one thing remained for Mister Vorster as he shouted over the subduing applause.

'Now let's get these fires lit . . .' Everyone cheered and he raised his bottle of Windhoek and whispered encouragingly to himself 'and let's get *pissed.*'

Willem cut a lonely figure. He had not moved from his spot on the terrace, but his father was no longer beside him, purloined by fawning guests, many of whom had formed a neat queue and were waiting patiently for a few noteworthy and distinguished minutes with his lordship.

Nearly every glass was empty by the end of Mister Vorster's speech and the trays were piled high for recycling. Victor walked up the steps to the terrace with a full tray and Willem stepped directly into his path, almost knocking him off balance and sending every glass flying. Victor flinched and moved to the side to give Willem space.

'Third room on the left . . . at the top of the stairs,' Willem whispered to Victor, looking dejected, forlorn, alone and helpless. He walked along the terrace, past the double bass player of a four-piece jazz band, then turned the corner and disappeared.

'Remember how I licked that mildew and lime powder in the press shed in your first week?' Victor said to me. How could I forget? 'You have a chance to pay me back . . . blood-brothers?' he said.

Victor went to the kitchen then collected one last load of glasses and returned to the dining room. I followed him all the way into the kitchen with both my hands full, strenuously balancing a tray of my own.

'Cover for me, George. I won't be long,' he said on our way back through the kitchen doors. He didn't come into the dining room with me, but instead bolted through a door leading into a corridor that ran to the hallway and the grandiose stairway at the front of the house. A minute later he opened the third door on the left from the top of the stairs - Willem's bedroom.

For twenty minutes I covered anxiously for Victor, knowing that I was his accomplice. I felt a sense of deep relief when I saw him standing in the middle of the lawn like he had never been away. He was smiling and thanking guests for bothering to hold out their empty glasses even though they had not turned their heads to acknowledge another human being was serving them. He winked at me as we passed on the steps, and my frenetic approach to glass collection finally relaxed.

It took an hour for Gwendoline Vorster to leave her perch in the dining room in search of Willem. She asked members of staff first, then gave up and decided to check his bedroom herself. His crying had stopped, but his eyes were still red and swollen from the rubbing and his pillow was stained with the dampness of it all. Sympathy eluded her, because she was not yet in that salubrious phase of her inebriation. She stood in the doorway and shouted with greater shrillness and austerity than is conceivable from a Shakespearian actress playing the most villainous witch.

'You don't know how lucky you are. I don't care how you feel . . . get downstairs and make sure you smile. Hiding up here like a damned crybaby!? What on earth will people think?'

Victor told me that until Mister Vorster had made that public announcement on the terrace, Willem had not known he would be sent off to boarding school in the summer. All he knew about Ascension College was the legend, handed down by his father and the younger brothers of a select band of alumni who, like Willem, had an equally formative primary education at Paarl Gimnasium. By all accounts it was a school for scholars or sportingly myopic bone-heads. You had to be one or the other; no middle ground, no re-drawing of the lines. The school motto said it clearly enough: *Animo ac Viribus,* courage and strength.

Johnson, Barclay and the household staff were overwhelmingly busy. Meat was turned and cooked to the exacting preference of each guest, salad bowls were refilled, plates and cutlery were recycled, cake and fresh fruit salad were distributed, towels, soap and wicker baskets of potpourri were replaced in four toilets that were always full of impatiently queuing women. By four o'clock, some guests began to leave and the men gave up queuing, choosing instead to walk to the trees and water the roots in full view of the marquee and the children. With each passing hour, the distance the men were prepared to travel to urinate retreated by a noticeable margin. At one point they were only taking four or five steps from the back of the marquee. Trickles landed and splashed onto the ground, forming in pools; the grass could not quench its thirst quickly enough to meet the abundant supply. An unpleasant smell encroached through the marquee, encouraging guests to move to tables nearer the entrance or to give up altogether and stand on the lawn.

I do not know what state Mrs Vorster was in, but it cannot have been in her early or intermediate stage of inebriation. She left her hiding place in the dining room to circulate with the remaining guests, most of whom seemed more familiar to the Vorsters, compared with those who had departed. A few curious and hopeful newcomers wanted to remain until the bitter end, intent on pushing their acquaintance a little closer towards the inner circle.

She walked up to a table of women on the fringe of the marquee, all sitting observing their husband's demise, lined up like jurors before a dock. One lady pulled out the unoccupied chair beside her for Gwendoline to sit on.

'Well, Gwendoline,' said one middle-aged lady from across the table. 'Thank God your Ringidd actually does some work. The way everyone fawns over him at church makes me itch all over.' The lady finished with a grimace, acting out the words that had passed with fingernails scraping her arms. Some women looked uneasy about the accusation. From what Johnson had said, some of the wives benefited from their peculiar exchanges with Ringidd at church. They dined out on the pretence that their tiny acts of perceived compassion, in passing him some sandwiches or fruit through the car window, or in having him sit behind them during church sermons, made up for all the times they had turned a blind eye to the frequent intolerance, humiliation, degradation and brutality that many black workers experienced in their employment.

'That wasn't my idea Francesca, and you know it. He's just another lame kaffir when his feet are on our estate,' she replied, refilling her glass without looking back at her friend.

'Yah . . . poor thing, you should have driven up his little carved chair to let him rest his weary legs. He looks like he's going to keel over from exhaustion. What on earth are you doing with a kaffir so old as that anyway?' The lips on a few of the women curled upwards slightly at the edges in amusement.

'How do I know, Fran? I leave all those details to Koibus. I run the house - and that's the way I like it.' Just as she replied a baby in the arms of a younger lady two seats away started to cry. Mrs Vorster's glance in her direction could not have been more blunt: *shut that thing up*. The lady hurriedly pulled aside her baggy, flapping dress in an attempt to free her breast and give the child some comfort.

'How old is he now, Cynthia?' asked one of the ladies.

'Olivia is four months next week,' she replied, embarrassed at the growing, repetitive, wailing screech drowning out the women's voices.

'She's a hungry one,' said the same lady watching the young mother take hold of her breast and guide the child's frantically nodding, searching head towards her raw, blistered nipple.

'God - *how bovine!*' Mrs Vorster had not intended to give voice to the thought, but showed no shame or remorse when the women at her table - apart from the breastfeeding mother - immediately turned their heads towards her in shock and amazement.

'*Well it is*. And I'm sorry if you don't like it. But babies ought to be reared on milk from someone built for the purpose. Gnawing and biting until you are red raw or bleeding . . . it takes away all a woman's sensuality and her femininity . . . it's just not right.' Nobody had the courage to challenge their hostess and it was likely that a few of them agreed wholeheartedly. This did not deter the breastfeeding mother from moving to an empty table to continue the task.

'My Willem suckled on one of my women for nearly a year - Mistress Polly - didn't do him one little bit of harm. She was overflowing with milk from a month before he was born . . . like a dairy cow I tell you - bovine - just like I said. A mother's got more to do besides being drained like a bath by her children.'

21
Green Eyes

My first sip was damnation, my second was curse and my third commissioned ulcers on the inside of my mouth. There was an anaesthetic quality to the fourth sip and by the time the fifth arrived, a warm, ephemeral glow feathered the back of my throat and a tingling joy fizzed throughout my entire body. I've heard that it's twelve steps on the way back, but on the way out in 1960, Victor and I only needed five.

We didn't know what we were drinking, but reckoned that if it was good enough for the guests to have been devouring for five hours, then it was good enough for us. We only siphoned the clear dregs - Gin or Vodka, I believe - so that it looked like water. Some of the alcohol had been diluted with tonic and soda water, cubes of ice and slices of lemon. We decanted the ice and lemon then filled our glasses, quickly becoming confident enough to drink it openly in the kitchen. Neat and on the rocks is how I've heard it ordered since. There was nothing neat about it, although it certainly hardened my constitution for the remainder of the evening.

I drank some water in between, which did not subdue the uneasy effects, which came knocking very quickly. Neither Victor nor I had considered the consequences, but it turned out we already had the perfect cover: the guests were more intoxicated than us.

On my way back from the terrace with a tray of cold, freshly opened bottles of Windhoek, I tripped and fell. One bottle smashed, crashing into another, but the rest landed, bouncing softly on the lawn. I had them upright before much of the liquid had soaked into the grass, but a group of men, including Master Boss, saw my mistake and I assumed the worst. They were standing in a circle together competing in volume, telling jokes and stories.

'Shit, that little kaffir is as pissed as us,' said one of the men loudly. They all broke out laughing; hard and bent over at the stomach.

'There be three green bottles standing on the wall . . .' sang another man. This sent them into further convulsions.

'Fuck, George man, stick to the beer - keep off the hard stuff,' shouted Master Boss. I was not yet so drunk that I was incapable of doing my job, but Ringidd and Victor were shortly by my side. 'Sorry, sir, Masta Baas, sir' I replied. He had already turned back to the group of men, who seemed to have forgotten all about me as another joker held court.

'What in hell happened here, George?' Ringidd asked. I forgot that I was supposed to look at Ringidd when he was speaking to me, and I answered with my back turned.

'I slipped,' I said. He pulled me around suspiciously and looked at me. The fear in my eyes was covered by a faint smile on my lips.

'If you is playing games with me, you is going by way of Franklin, see?' said Ringidd. My lips quickly joined my eyes and I scurried off to fetch new bottles like he told me. The cost of the spillage would come out of my pay.

I returned and knelt on the grass with a hand-brush, scouring for tiny shards of glass that might unfortunately slice a guest, as many of the women had discarded their heels and were walking around in bare feet. Mister Vorster joined the group of rowdy alphas - perhaps eight or nine in total - all consumed by the sound of their own voices, but friendly and competitive, conjoined by the alcohol and the occasion.

'So come, Koibus. How much is Glen Cleaver making a year?' asked one of the men - a pointed, thin, tall guy with blond hair, wearing dark green braces.

'Mind your own fokin' business, Kerkhof!' said Mister Vorster, seemingly quite glad that his wealth created so much intrigue.

'I'll have to check the archives at the agriculture department in Paarl for your filed accounts then,' said the man.

'Good luck you gangly rake. My accounts are held privately - and legally, I hasten to add. All you need to know is that Glen Cleaver is a licence to print these crisp new Rand notes we are now using. It doesn't matter to me what the money's called; English pounds, shilling and pence or South African Rands and cents . . . Glen Cleaver is like the National Mint.'

'Yah, yah. Well I suppose you've paid for these Windhoek's Koibus . . . so cheers for that.' The gangly rake lent over and held out his bottle of beer which clinked against Mister Vorster's.

Master Boss looked over from the circle of men towards the corner of the estate house noticing Mary on the terrace with a hard-bristled broom. He traced her every step. I could almost decipher his thoughts playing out like a movie in each of his eyes; lustful and gleeful memories of all he had taken from her and of all she had given.

His wife was engrossed in conversation on the opposite side of the lawn, but I got the feeling that he would have continued the lustful observation had she been right by his side. I wonder what Master Boss would have thought had he heard the rumours Gilbert spouted every time

Bostock and Peter left the bunkhouse after dinner for some *fresh air*.

'They is out watching Mary and Barclay in the woods. She knows it too, I thinks,' said Gilbert, grabbing the attention of Franklin, Victor, myself and Eugene.

Apparently Peter was the voyeur, and Bostock liked to get a little more involved. He crawled in close through the undergrowth to get a good view of the conjugal act and of Mary's flesh in particular. Then he would touch himself. He liked to watch her chest swing and bounce, and he would position himself behind her ass and watch it wobble and clench. If it was too dark, he closed his eyes and listened out for sounds of the couple's skin slapping together and yanked himself in time to their rapid, heavy breathing and groaning. Of course, this was all hearsay. Gilbert had absolutely no proof of anything, but he loved to stir it up.

'Bostock told me himself,' said Gilbert. 'She lets Barclay take her any way he wants: held up against the trees holding her by the legs and ass, lying on her back squeezed down into the ground by his weight on top of earth and leaves and twigs, sat on top of him, bouncing up and down like a bull-frog with her arms pressed hard onto his chest, or even from behind on her hands and knees, like a dog.' There wasn't a sexual position Gilbert couldn't dream up. I wondered whether he was actually the one with the obsession.

He said after sex they curled up for a while and held each other affectionately before repeating their lustful indulgences - sometimes three times. I suppose without many opportunities for such dalliances, two young, athletic, sexually charged adults in their prime had too much temptation not to find a way.

Mary was an arm's length from Barclay on the terrace and I watched Master Boss looking intently, seemingly mesmerised by their interplay. Behind his studious posture he was concealing curiosity. Mary pretended to be busy but Barclay's hand gently stroked and cupped her backside. She shot a pouting smile and slapped the hand away playfully, furrowing her brow as if to say; don't be naughty, we might get caught. I could have sworn that Master Boss saw a ghost. He turned ashen white, paler than you could expect such a weathered, tanned face to turn. He could not prise his eyes away.

'Koibus?' he called over to Mister Vorster. 'What about a little game of *runners* before it gets dark?' he said.

'Fok man, Danie, you are a mischievous son of a bitch,' replied his monarch.

'Runners? Yah, run off and get me another beer, Danie!' interrupted one of the men in the circle, trying a little too hard to get a laugh.

'It's time to unchain the two reasons for our exceptionally industrious vineyard gentlemen. My well-kept secret,' said Mister Vorster with a lubricated sense of importance.

'Where *are* those damned beasts, Koibus? They give me the fear of death. Don't unchain them on my account,' said another of the men, clearly with prior knowledge.

'No, no, Trenchard . . . I won't have you speaking badly of my Mallie and Toppie?' Mister Vorster jovially corrected his guest, then nodded to his estate manager to fetch them. Master Boss ran like a child towards his first bike on Christmas morning, gleeful in his knowledge that Mary's amends would shortly be made.

Mallie and Toppie must have heard the entire conversation from their kennels. When Master Boss arrived, they were sitting up at their gate, impatient and alert.

'It's not right to keep you beauties caged up all day,' he said, unlocking the gate with the bunch of keys hanging from his belt.

Mallie and Toppie pulled hard on their leashes when Master Boss turned the corner of the estate house and joined the terrace. He walked in the direction of Mary and Barclay who were now behaving less conspicuously. They stepped back, seeing the dogs coming towards them, but were prevented from going anywhere safe by the balustrade. Master Boss smiled as he got closer, using most of his muscle to restrain the dogs from escaping his grip. I could never tell which came first for those dogs - the smell of us or the sight of us. Either way, they had telepathic abilities. They knew when black skin was in their vicinity, even from a mile away.

'Say hello to Mallie and Toppie,' requested Master Boss, looking at Mary in a polite, jovial tone. He point blank ignored Barclay. Mary returned a very faint smile and nodded politely as the dogs arrived level, a few yards ahead of their handler. It was then that I thought Mary had seen a ghost.

'*Yeow filthy, fokin', kaffir whore,*' Master Boss whispered quietly in her ear as he walked passed towards the lawn. He said it slowly and deliberately with cold, tight eyes, just loud enough for Barclay to hear. In his following footsteps a relaxed smile came onto his face and he continued towards the lawn. Mary walked briskly back to the kitchen and Barclay picked up some fresh logs and added them to the fires.

A hush came over the lawn when Master Boss appeared with the dogs at the top of the steps where Mister Vorster had made his introductory speech. Master Boss's wife was standing with two couples near the marquee and turned to one of the women, saying sarcastically: 'What on earth is he up to now?'

Mister Vorster greeted the dogs before they had arrived at the circle of men. They jumped up with their paws, reaching high onto his stomach. Master Boss called for them to stand down, but it was no use; Mister Vorster was their master, the one who commanded any genuine authority. He was the leader of a hunting pack and the dogs loved him for it.

'How's my little boy and girl tonight?' he asked affectionately, happy for them to playfully jump up with their hind legs and let their front paws pad his stomach and chest. He hushed them with a click of his fingers and both dogs fell immediately into line at his thigh with no need for a leash. Then he turned back towards the inside of the circle of guests to introduce his animals.

'The secret to my success is a disciplined and tireless workforce . . . administered by my two admirable lieutenants. During my time in the military, I served under a Rhodesian Colonel - a man called Salvesen. He swore that one of these dogs was better than ten armed men . . . *Lion Tamers* is what he called them.' Mister Vorster finished the last mouthful of his Windhoek and lobbed the bottle onto the ground in front of Victor from ten yards. 'Another beer, kaffir!'

22
Game of Runners

The circle of men widened to make space for Mallie and Toppie, or perhaps to create some distance from their threatening gnashers. Mister Vorster took a fresh bottle of Windhoek from Victor and handed the leashes to Master Boss.

'Come Danie - explain the rules,' he said.

'It would be my *pleasure,* Koibus.' This was the one day of the year he got to call his boss by his first name.

'Runnerrrsssss!' shouted Master Boss, lingering on the word until his lungs had fully exhaled. 'It's very simple - a straight up game of hare and hounds . . . or lion and kudu, if you prefer. We'll call the hares; kaffirs 1, 2 and 3. They get a head-start in a straight race against Mallie and Toppie. Any kaffir that can outrun the beasts can climb to safety. Those that can't? . . . well, let's find out shall we . . . Oh, I almost forgot . . . we'll open some betting while we're at it.'

'That's the dombest fokin' game I ever heard of Danie. Count me out man. I'm not running for kak, and I don't have any cash on me, man,' said a man from behind the circle who had only heard half of the briefing.

'Jesus, Venter man - will you listen - *you're* not running domkopf - the kaffirs are running,' said Master Boss, frustrated at not having been properly listened to.

'I thought you were saying we had to run. I near kak'd my undies man.' The others laughed as Venter held onto the guest beside him to stop himself from falling over, the wine having stolen his balance.

'Place your wagers, gents,' said Master Boss with his wide, mischievous grin.

'I wanna see the kaffirs, Danie, 'fore I say goodbye to any cash,' said another man looking around to see which staff were available.

'Ringidd man, fetch me your kaffirs!' said Master Boss whipping himself up into a fervent excitement whilst Victor, Barclay, Johnson and I wished we were in the kitchen wearing skirts.

Ringidd didn't have to walk far to round us up. We walked over to the circle where the men were waiting, already making their assessments.

'Them all the men we have working today, Danie - the rest is gone back township for the weekend.' I could see it still grated Master Boss when Ringidd used his first name, which was unlikely to happen in formal company, apart from church.

The circle of onlookers deepened and wives joined, curious to see what was happening. Mrs Vorster's head poked out from the side of Venter's swaying shoulder.

'Koibus - this is not what I think it is?' she interrupted.

'Don't worry your pretty little head, Gwenie,' he replied. His condescension placed a sour, hard-boiled sweet into her mouth for her to suck on, leaving little room for reply.

Master Boss beckoned us into the circle and pranced like a circus master.

'Who we going with folks? Little to choose from in this paddock.' he chuckled. 'Time to introduce the hares.' Some men cheered and laughed, holding up their arms like loyal, expectant rugby fans watching their team walk out onto the pitch at Newlands.

'Our first runner - and don't let your eyes deceive you, this is not the charity stakes . . . come forward . . . Ringggiddddd.' Master Boss announced his name like the referee of a world title fight and pointed right at him. Ringidd's face was total disbelief, scrunched up so hard the skin had rolled miniature trenches on his forehead. He shook his head, wracking his brains for an appropriate line of protest.

Every onlooker had something to say about Ringidd's selection. *That's a lame horse. Put it down. Put it out of its misery. The game's rigged, man.* Layers of laughter built, layer upon layer, goading from one man to the next, escalating towards an unthinking furore.

'Where's your bible, Ringidd?' asked one man. 'In your undies? Protecting your arse from those incisors?' Ringidd glanced at Mallie and Toppie sitting obediently next to Master Boss. 'They're looking at you Ringidd . . . it's dinner time,' said the last man, pleased with his contribution and the ensuing, drunken hilarity.

Ringidd was on long odds. I had never seen him move faster than a slow, stooped, limping walk. His protestations were entirely in vain. In an instant he was relegated to the same status as the rest of us. His leather-bound King James Bible and those short pious recitals and proverbs he peppered the congregation with after a church service could not wash away the colour of his skin. This was a bear pit and the audience was thirsty for entertainment.

'Please sir, Mister Danie. I can't be doing no running, Mister Danie. Look at my leg, see. I am sixty-two years old.' His desperate pleas bordered on ridiculous and insolent.

'Shut up, Ringidd,' hissed Master Boss. Ringidd opened his drooping mouth wide to respond but was quickly cut off.

'I said *shut up* you lazy, fokin' baboon. If you are fit enough to work at Glen Cleaver - then you are fit enough for runners. Stand over there or I'll unleash Mallie and Toppie right now,' he quipped, finalising the matter.

Mister Vorster looked on in mild amusement. There were no soft touches at Glen Cleaver, especially when kaffirs were involved and Mister Vorster seemed happy for his guests to witness the policy without ambiguity. The recommendation for a second participant took me totally by surprise.

'You! Little kaffir? It's about time you showed us what you're made of.' Master Boss pointed straight at me and my heart almost stopped. It was then that Victor spoke. His interruption was undeniably brave, but irrefutably stupid.

'Masta Baas, sir, I don't want you to lose no money, sir. George breaking his ankle six weeks ago now. Please let me take his place, sir, Masta Baas, sir. I will win you good money, sir, Masta Boss, sir, I promise.' Victor spoke directly and humbly - different to normal, like he was a little simple.

'This little kaffir is the best you will find at Glen Cleaver. A right little workhorse and some say he has something that resembles a brain.' Mister Vorster's unanticipated endorsement was cheered by a few guests who raised their glasses in Victor's direction and gave shouts of *'the little kaffir'*.

'Okay, Victor,' said a surprised Master Boss. 'If it's runners you want, it's runners you'll get. Don't fokin' lose me any money, boy.'

'No, sir, thank you, Masta Baas, sir,' replied Victor. I don't know what it was about my friend. He was like my personal shield made from the toughest, rarest metals from the deepest mines. I never once asked him to step in front of me, but there he was, unflinching and supremely confident in everything he did. He didn't even look nervous, he met every situation calmly, as if he were waiting patiently in a queue to buy a ticket for a bus.

Either Johnson or Barclay was next, but Master Boss had only one card heavily marked. Barclay, after all, was the reason the charade had been instigated.

'And now gentlemen, our final competitor . . . a prized kaffir stud. We usually keep him tied up in the bunkhouse and brought out strictly for breeding. And I hear he has plenty of energy in that department when it comes to our household staff.' Master Boss stepped across and grabbed Barclay roughly by the arm, pulling him beside Victor and Ringidd.

'Get a beer, fill your glasses . . . bets are open,' shouted Master

Boss, enjoying the limelight.

A drunken few pranced around the three participants assessing their capabilities for the race as their wives shook their heads in disapproval. They squeezed Barclay's leg muscles and gently punched his torso to find out how solid and athletic he really was. Nobody touched Ringidd or Victor; the absence of athleticism was plain to see.

Master Boss grabbed the hounds' leashes and strode out into the lawn towards the trees beyond the marquee, followed closely by his three hares. The sun was setting and many of the participating guests were now largely unintelligible and incoherent, slurring their speech, shouting and cheering. Johnson and I retreated quietly to the dining room. He caught me siphoning a half-full glass of white wine and realised why my inhibitions had fast disappeared. Drinking gin and vodka was a tribulation, but the wine was smoother, so that's what I settled on.

If one period of the evening necessitated total intoxication, this was it. As it turned out, Johnson had not been so shy himself, having decanted some vodka into a small medicine bottle that he kept in his jacket pocket. He suggested we stay hidden behind the curtains, and observe from the windows until the game had finished.

Master Boss yanked Mallie and Toppie hard on their leashes, slapping their sides, helping to achieve the most frenzied state. Ringidd's finishing line was at the tractor; a foregone conclusion. He would take a few short steps over the paltry distance, then climb up three steps to safety. Never was a race rigged in such obvious favour.

Victor was told to run to the wooden climbing frame. It was twice the distance Ringidd had to cover and I thought the outcome would hang anxiously in the balance. Victor was fast, I knew he was fast, but he had never raced or outrun two Rhodesian Ridgebacks in their prime - even with a fifty yard advantage.

If Ringidd's race was rigged in his favour and Victor's hung in the balance, it was another matter entirely for Barclay. Master Boss had only one victim in mind, giving Barclay an unfathomably long run to reach the ladder on the copper wine vat that formed part of the braai exhibit. It might as well have been a mile away for all the chance he had.

The kitchen staff, including Mary, decanted into the dining room alongside Johnson and I, peering from behind the curtains, waiting anxiously for the game to commence. We stood motionless, frozen still, holding our breath in apprehension, ignoring the polluting jeers and cheers that echoed across the terrace and through the doorway.

I am slightly ashamed to admit it, but my only genuine concern was for Victor, although clearly I did not have the courage to risk the tearing of my flesh for his. He was standing up straight at his staggered start, looking back past Ringidd who was nearest the dogs but still with the shortest distance to travel. Barclay was another thirty yards ahead of Victor, but with three times his distance to cover to reach safety.

The crowd was ranting, cheering and willing Danie Rousseau to release the dogs and begin the entertainment. Some were beyond fervent, with significant sums of money at stake. At the last minute Mister Vorster announced he was donating a magnum of French champagne to the person that had placed the largest bet. Of course, everyone was too drunk to realise they had placed bets before they knew the outcome of the race was rigged.

The noise of the small, yelping crowd reverberated around the cavernous garden echoing from the trees on all sides. That sound mirrored the omen of dark red that appeared on the horizon as the sun fell from sight. The breeze dropped and the birdsong ceased, as it would have done all across the south-western tip of Africa at that moment.

Barclay looked like a smartly dressed Jesse Owens at the start of an Olympic final, crouched down for a sprint start, ready to spring free. Ringidd on the other hand, looked like a cracked headstone about to topple in a cemetery. And Victor? Well, he just stood there looking over the ridge of the mountains on the horizon in the distance, like he had purposely chosen the spot for the best view of a beautiful, dramatic sunset during an early evening stroll.

Mallie and Toppie were choking with enthusiasm. Master Boss meant to unclip the leashes from their collars, but the fatigue in his forearms, from the two locomotives trying to pull away from the station, proved too much. Friction burns slashed his hands as his grip weakened. Mallie and Toppie broke free, unleashing their rabid, hell-bent fury.

Ringidd hobbled forward, his legs trying to catch up with his arms, which were outstretched towards the grab handles on the rusty old tractor ten yards before he arrived in preparation for his climb to safety. Barclay shot forward like a bullet, focused with all his will on the ladder on the copper wine vat in the distance. His legs moved like explosive pistons in a hard-working engine flowing through the gears, but the hope in his face visibly retreated when his acceleration ended and he reached maximum speed. The unconscious calculations in his mind must have informed him that one extra gear and a stride six inches longer was needed to assure his safety. He didn't dare look behind him, but he could hear the clinking of leashes dragging behind Mallie and Toppie as they powerfully and elegantly leapt towards him.

Victor's start point was close to Ringidd's finish-line at the tractor. He was being filmed by a cine-camera in Mister Vorster's hand. That silent film will only have shown half of the picture, because the sounds in my ears were all the more detailed and frightening. Whenever I have retold this story, there is still not a person who believes me when I say Victor was not interested in reaching the climbing frame - the same structure that was overrun with children only four hours before.

When Mallie and Toppie broke free, Victor turned to face them and did not move a single inch from his spot. Time paused and I am certain Victor smiled and let out the smallest of chuckles. Unlike Ringidd and Barclay, he showed no sign of urgency. He walked slowly forward. Looks of incredulity appeared on the faces in the crowd as they watched him amble, strolling on a lazy summer afternoon along the bank of a beautiful river in search of a picnic spot. After a few steps, Victor turned his head to the side and fixed his eyes on the drunken guests. There was no discernible emotion on his face, only the look of a mildly curious observer. Guests stopped jumping and shouting as the magnitude and severity of the situation uncovered, especially because Mallie and Toppie were closing rapidly on their target. Victor continued strolling on his suicide mission, refusing to be rattled. And as he strolled, he stared. He kept staring, right into the crowd of guests, ever the observer. He intended to catch the eye of every last man before the dogs reached him.

Ringidd was the first to safety, clambering up onto the tractor with twenty yards to spare. Mallie and Toppie continued past him undeterred, chasing down Victor like Ringidd had never been there. Barclay was halfway to the copper tank, but the dogs were travelling at more than double his speed, their leads flying and whipping in the air as they pulled with a regal grace towards their prey.

Victor still had thirty yards to travel and not even the most basic arithmetic was required to forecast the outcome. It was impossible for him to make it to the climbing frame in time. If he had run, he would have had a fighting chance at worst, and a good chance at best. But he had accepted the inevitability of a brutal mauling, one that might leave him maimed and scarred for the rest of his life - or worse. There was a chance he would be torn and chewed and gouged towards a bloody, lifeless, heartless death.

In the dining room, Mary covered her eyes at the sight of impending doom and tears streamed down her face. As the growls and slavered barks drew closer to Victor and Barclay, Mary realised what a terrible mistake she had made in entwining herself with two men. She felt responsible. She *was* responsible. Perhaps she believed her sexual relationship with Master Boss

136

would result in more equitable treatment; that she would be favoured for employment if Miss Johanna's position became vacant. Who knows? Until now it had done her no harm. But when Master Boss saw her flirting intimately with Barclay on the terrace he was already drunk from the beer, then drunker still from that sickly, poison called envy.

Mallie reached Victor first, one stride ahead of Toppie. I think most onlookers had already played out the scene in their minds. There were shrieks and muffled sobs from some of the women. I didn't know what to feel. I was numb. It was like looking at a film on a screen, where the participants were actors. Then for no apparent reason, I suddenly trusted Victor. In every decision he made, there had been a fortuitous ending. Victor only acted when he knew what he was doing. It was as if he trusted himself more than anything.

The reaction of the women was premature, and my instinct to trust Victor proved wise. The dogs approached from a whisker's length behind and he stretched his arms out as if he was about to embrace someone he loved in a bear-hug. Mallie and Toppie completely ignored him. Why they did not touch him I do not know. Victor continued walking for another twenty yards and sat on the bottom rung of the climbing frame, feet planted firmly on the ground.

I will spare you the exact details of Barclay's final, dying sprint to the copper tank. There was no practical use in his suffering, other than for Master Boss's tormented, salacious soul. Mallie and Toppie reached him ten yards from the ladder. Nobody expected him to get that far with such unfavourable terms. He held his arms tight over his head, which was one saving grace, but his legs and his arms and his rib cage sacrificed themselves. Mallie and Toppie ripped and gorged him like a straw dummy basted in freshly minced beef.

Master Boss was meant to be adjudicating. He could have called off the dogs immediately, but wanted to give them a meal, not a taste. Mister Vorster ran shouting and screaming, ordering them to come to heel, but they were so consumed that they cannot have heard his shouts. Master Boss stood on the start line hiding a wicked grin until Mister Vorster's voice eventually penetrated the dog's killing fury and they withdrew, scampering back to their master. It would not have taken much longer for them to have inflicted mortal damage. Barclay lay on the grass rocking from side to side with his hands and arms tight up against his head, his white trousers seeping red.

Apart from the few insensitive, drunken gamblers exchanging cash, a deathly silence pervaded the guests. Most had watched the race and nobody missed the chaos in failing to call off the dogs in time. Mary ran out of the dining room, through the kitchen and out of the back door of the estate house, screaming and wailing.

Victor sat quietly and peacefully on the climbing frame, increasingly serious and studious as he observed the fallout following the incident, like he was a tree in the forest behind. When I walked outside to resume my duties at the dying party, I looked over for my friend on the climbing frame. He was nowhere to be seen.

23
Amnesia

Johnson sat at the first bunkhouse table with both feet resting on a chair in front of him. He looked over at me on my bunk with a cup of steaming coffee clasped between his thumb and forefinger then slowly shook his head. He slouched backwards resting the nub of his neck on the back of the chair with his head facing the ceiling, then closed his eyes and let out a lingering yawn.

One of Victor's legs hung over the side of his bunk above and to my side like a length of taxidermy in a museum cabinet. Barclay was no better. He was three beds further down, also on the lower bunk and lying flat on his back, arms stretched out straight and neatly by his side. His arms and legs and the right side of his chest were covered in rolls of pale brown bandaging with purple smears escaping at the edges.

The purple was thick iodine solution a doctor had buttered onto his wounds before applying an accretion of bandages onto the array of deep punctures and lacerations from the dogs sharp teeth and claws. Luckily, Barclay's face escaped similar punishment. Mister Vorster agreed to the local doctor at the end of the evening, protecting his own investment in harvest six weeks hence. The doctor had attended the early part of the braai but left before the game of runners and did not expect to return so soon. There were no broken bones but a couple of ruptured and torn tendons meant the next six weeks would be a challenging rehabilitation. The wounds in Barclay's body would heal better than the wounds in his mind.

I was thirsty - so thirsty. As I rose to vacate my bunk for some water, the smell hit me. I don't know why I didn't notice it the instant I woke, because it was not timid. When I stood up and looked at Victor on the top bunk to side, the slimy culprit introduced itself. He had been sick across his chest and down one side of his shoulder. A pile of viscous mucus and bile had congealed and dried throughout the night, although it still looked alive enough to kill an entire tribe. How Johnson could sit fifteen yards away, seemingly oblivious to the odour, I do not know. I could taste the smell lingering on my tongue like it was goading its relatives from my own body. Nausea came first, then the surge. I ran to the door, catching some of the eruption in my mouth with my hand, afraid that Johnson would demolish me if I let it go anywhere near him. Each step leading down from the stoep was varnished with my acidic discharge.

Sitting hunched over my knees, it was an effort to breathe as I wiped clammy moisture from my brow. My sweat smelled like the bi-product of disease. What or who had invaded my body with such loathing?

'Bucket. Cloth,' said Johnson, pointing to the sink when I returned. It took six full buckets of water to be thrown over the steps before I was brave enough to start wiping. I moved in with the damp cloth each time holding my breath - a cunning trick to delay a second, imminent eruption from my mouth. Inside, I also wiped away the discharge surrounding Victor. It was a poor attempt by any standards, more of a gentle dabbing; a weak, cowardly pretence. He did not wake for another two hours, but heavy breathing proved his heart was still beating.

At the sink, whilst rinsing the bucket and the cloth, Johnson interrupted me again. I had placed the cloth inside the bucket and slid it underneath the sink.

'No! Cloth in the bin,' he pointed again, this time to the front door which led to the two bins at the gable end. I did as he ordered, returning empty-handed.

Johnson said Barclay would wake up when the morphine wore off. The doctor had given him an injection, as much to calm his state of shock as to numb the pain. I drank three full cups of water at the sink, one after the other, then pathetically shuffled back to my bunk. I lay there waiting for Victor to wake, but could not sleep with the constant reminders of nausea and an overactive mind. Victor and I were meant to meet Willem under the line of oak trees in the middle of the afternoon, but that journey felt like an impossible and futile endeavour in this condition.

My eyes closed and my mind wandered into the moment of my assault by that fat, bald, pig-eyed brute on the beach near Tolongo. I re-wrote the scene in my head: The Afrikaner pig missed my ankle when he tried to stamp on it and became disorientated and frightened when I threw sand into his eyes. There was a piece of drift wood next to me that I picked up and used to bludgeon him repeatedly at the side of his knees until he fell. His dog was whelping and barking in the distance, unable to give support from the fencepost he was tied to higher up on the dunes. I spat on the pig's face then told him to start digging. *Dig with your own hands*, I shouted at him. He obeyed immediately with fear in his eyes. *Keep digging,* I shouted, hitting him again with the driftwood to hurry the process. When the hole was big enough for a human body he tried to scramble away on his hands and knees, just like I had done. But he did not get very far as I scolded the back

140

of his raw, bloodied knees once again. *Get in.* I shouted. He climbed into the pit and I covered him with sand.

Creaking from Victor's bunk interrupted me just as the pig's body was about to disappear under the sand - only one thick ear and a sliver of his bald head was poking through. I opened my eyes and looked up and across at Victor's bunk. He was turned on his side with his eyes open looking down at me, now with his arm hanging like a lonely pendulum in a broken grandfather clock. Although his eyes were open, the engine behind was not yet turning. He looked like a sleepwalker ready to take his first steps from bed.

'Morning,' I said. He didn't reply, just kept on staring down at me. 'Are you okay?' I continued. Still no reaction. He had never completely ignored me before and I was struggling to think of what else to say.

'Johnson said Barclay should be okay,' I continued. Still nothing in reply. I don't think Victor had heard a word I said and he couldn't see Barclay lying in bandages from above because his view was obstructed by bunks. I turned away and closed my eyes again, and that is when he finally spoke.

'What happened?' he said with a sticky voice, like glue was in the process of setting on the underside of his tongue.

'What do you mean?' I replied. He was struggling to untangle the string of our conversation - confirmed by his distant, confused gaze. He waited for his brain's processing to complete, then replied.

'I don't know,' he said, still trying to work it out. 'I really don't know what I mean.' Then he asked again. 'What happened? What happened yesterday?'

'Do you not remember anything?' I quizzed.

I remember being at the Braai and I remember being in Willem's bedroom. He was upset - very upset. I don't remember anything after that.'

'*You don't remember the game of runners?*' the pitch of my voice rose an octave.

'*Runners?*' he said. I looked over at Barclay then back at him.

'You better see this, Victor.'

He slowly shuffled to the edge of the bed, swung his legs over the side and stepped onto my lower bunk with one foot then landed on the floor with his other. I did not need to say anything, he saw Barclay right away, more in bandage than in skin.

'He's lost a lot of blood, but the Doctor says he's going be okay . . . as long as he doesn't get infected or nothing,' informed Johnson, now lying on his bunk. Victor could not take his eyes from Barclay's mummified corpse.

'What happened?' asked Victor for the third time.

141

'Mallie and Toppie is what happened - on account of that evil prick Danie Rousseau. It could have been you, Victor,' interrupted Johnson again without giving me a chance to speak.

I fetched a cup of water for Victor which evaporated at his teeth. He paused, then noticed the stains on the chest of his shirt and across his shoulder. He gave out a weary, knowing sigh.

'We have to meet Willem later,' he whispered to me, making sure Johnson could not hear.

'I know,' I replied. 'I can tell you everything on the way up if you like?'

He nodded gratefully then climbed up onto his bunk and lay down again until it was time to leave.

24
The Three Chwamas

Victor and I swallowed two more cups of water then stepped away from the bunkhouse. We couldn't stomach food but were expected in the estate house kitchen later in the evening for sumptuous leftovers from the braai. On any other day we would have been impatient at the prospect.

For a Sunday afternoon, the estate grounds felt even quieter than normal. The sound of birds chirped but there was not a breath of wind to rustle the trees or bushes. We followed our usual route, concealed from the main pathways. I told Victor everything I remembered from the evening before. We stopped and sat on the thin trunk of a fallen tree while he questioned me. He could not believe what had happened and it quickly became clear that his appearance of calm and contentedness during the game of runners was the positive enhancement of the alcohol he had consumed during the braai. Neither of us remembered the end of the evening, or getting back to the bunkhouse. Those slices of history had been stolen by our introduction to distilled grains and juniper berries, then fermented grapes.

Willem was sitting waiting for us under the umbrella of the oak trees with his legs crossed. His pencil was sketching a butterfly in his notebook that he would colour-in later on in his bedroom to achieve the truest likeness. What is a butterfly without colour? I looked at his drawing, envious of his talent, then up at the sky, which was now sketched in the same black and grey's in Willem's notebook. A storm was brewing.

'I don't fancy being at the pool if lightning strikes,' said Willem when we reached him. 'If you follow me, we can miss the storm,' he said, waiting for an accord.

Victor and I had trampled sluggishly uphill to see Willem only because we felt obliged to honour the arrangement. We could not have been more relieved.

'Everyone has been asleep since lunch and I think Danie Rousseau has gone to Paarl with his wife and kids for the afternoon' said Willem.

'What about Ringidd?' I asked.

'Ringidd will be holed up in his hut. I don't think he will care anyway - not after what you told me,' said Victor, referring to Ringidd's involvement in the game of runners.

We stepped out of the cover of the oak trees as the skies dumped their cargo. The drops of rain fell heavy and hard, drenching us before we had travelled across the open ground above Drakensberg. We slid as the earth turned to fine silk underneath our feet. I fell three times, smeared in mud, unable to accelerate and catch Willem or Victor, with no friction on the soles of my bare feet.

Willem jogged towards the estate buildings and found temporary shelter under the overhanging roof at the back of the press shed. He waited for me to arrive then peeked around the corner into the courtyard, checking if it was clear. We followed him into the open, running past the office block and onwards to the walled garden.

The potting shed ran long, thin and parallel to the main, high outside wall of the garden. Three small terracotta plant pots were lying upside down next to the door and Willem toppled the middle one, picked up an old, rusted key then returned the pot to its original position. Once we were inside, he closed and locked the door behind us.

Three puddles formed on the concrete tiles beneath us. We stood in dim lighting, relieved to be sheltered from the downpour and satisfied that our daring had paid off. The shed was a long, thin greenhouse with a work-bench, equipment store and an unintended museum of horticulture antiquities. The double doors at the far end were bolted on the inside and only opened to avoid dragging lawn-mowers and wheelbarrows down the narrow length of the shed.

Willem was on his tip-toes, feeling around on a high shelf for matches and a paraffin lamp that he assured us he had seen before. He passed the box of matches down to Victor who dried his hands on a piece of rag from the floor. He struck the side of the box for the first time and found a flame, then lit the moist wick in the lamp.

'What is this place?' I asked Willem.

'It's the potting shed . . . where they grow things for the garden.'

'Do you smell that?' he said. 'Herbs for the kitchen are planted in here before they move to the garden. Parsley, chives, tarragon, mint . . . all of it. My mother did the growing until Miss Johanna took over,' said Willem, walking down the paving stones in the middle with his lantern illuminating tables of potted green plants on trays in dark, damp compost. He stopped half-way and pulled some leaves from their stalks.

'Try this,' he said.

'I don't want to eat leaves,' said Victor, studying the thin, green, velvety object in his hand, rubbing it curiously between his fingers.

'Look,' said Willem, biting and chewing with his front teeth. Victor and I copied.

'It's a little sour and spicy at the same time,' I said.

'It's not spicy, George. Mint isn't sour or spicy - mint is mint,' replied Willem rolling his eyes in the light of the lantern. So mint tastes like mint. There is something new to learn every day.

There has always been something exciting about an adventure for me . . . any adventure. They slap encouragingly on the back of the human spirit and spark that acute feeling of aliveness. My nausea was fast disappearing and Victor's grin suggested likewise. The best was yet to come.

'Don't tell me you've brought us here to eat leaves, Willem,' said Victor, partly in humour but mostly sincere.

Willem sighed and shook his head slowly. 'I'll give you three guesses, Victor, and a pair of my shoes if you get it right.'

'It's not wine is it? I'm not drinking any wine,' said Victor.

'Not even close.' Willem contorted his face to show the thought abhorred him. Drinking wine for the purpose of drunkenness was an idea that he would be unlikely to have for another four years - if at all, knowing Willem.

'I give up,' said Victor, rubbing his head and sighing as if his nausea was returning with a vengeance. 'Just tell us Willem . . . I feel sick.'

'Okay,' said Willem. 'Follow me and keep very quiet. Only whisper, okay?'

He walked to the furthest corner of the potting shed, holding the lamp out in front of him to guide his way. Apart from the lawnmowers and the wheelbarrows, the tools and equipment hanging on nails on the wall were all old, rusted and abandoned. Most of them were covered in a layer of fine dust and cobwebs that were so decayed their creators must have lived in a different century. It was the same in the rafters, where old iron implements were placed for storage; forgotten and obsolete.

A tall, flimsy cage, erected with planks of wood and chicken-wire, at the back of the shed looked awkward and out-of-place.

'In here,' whispered Willem, crouching down and placing the lamp on the floor then undoing a small latch on the loose doorframe. He picked up the lamp and walked in ahead of us. There was barely room for two people to stand and the compartment was fitted with wooden shelving on three sides. The top shelves were empty, but on the first shelf and below it on the ground were a dozen, old wooden wine cases.

'Someone has moved the boxes around,' Willem whispered,

sounding surprised and frustrated. Then he grabbed one nearest the back and slowly, gently slid it out along the concrete floor from underneath the bottom shelf. He turned to look at us with an excited smile, now whispering more quietly, barely audible. He put his forefinger to his lips to repeat the need for silence.

Victor and I knelt down beside each other and the smell of old, crafted wood intensified as Willem slid open the lid on a case. Half a dozen holes were drilled into the top, for a reason which became clear when we saw what was inside. I could make out the Glen Cleaver crest stamped into the wood along with a date - 28 May 1948. Inside the case, lying on a bed of dry grass, were three newborn puppies, perhaps only a week or two old. Their eyes were shut tightly as they slept, huddled together in a soft pile of warmth.

Victor's face lit up with joy and amazement. Willem turned and smiled, raising his eyebrows to encourage acknowledgement of his sensational find.

'I overheard my father and Danie talking. Mallie gave birth just over a week ago. Father told Danie to separate the pups from her immediately. They are being isolated for socialising, whatever that means?'

"Poor little pups,' said Victor, sticking out his bottom lip with a sad expression.

Willem reached into the wooden case and tenderly pulled up a cosy bundle of milky brown in each hand. Both pups continued sleeping despite the intrusion. He passed the first one to me, which I cupped in my hands, unconfident and unsure if I was holding it properly.

'Hello,' I whispered in the darkness.

It was not long before the little pup was nestled beneath my chin being lovingly petted. I looked at Victor who was also engrossed in the soft, delicate warmth nestled into his chest. We three, mischievous adolescents had succumbed to an unanticipated, doting, paternal instinct.

'Danie will be back in an hour . . . he feeds the pups milk every few hours,' warned Willem.

'What are their names?' asked Victor.

'I don't think they will have names until they are sold . . . I don't even know if they're boys or girls,' answered Willem.

'We can give them names,' said Victor. I agreed. Willem didn't seem bothered either way.

'What about the three chwamas?' said Victor.

'I like it,' I whispered.

'What is a chwama?' asked Willem.

'It's Xhosa for bushmen,' replied Victor. 'The three bushmen,' he repeated in English.

'The three bushmen?' Willem pondered on it for a while. 'Yeah, I like it. But how will we know which one is which?'

'We'll know, Willem. You see how one is smaller than the other two?'

'Just like you next to Willem and me,' I said to Victor jokingly, although there was barely an inch between us.

'Yeah, this little one is going to be stronger than all the rest. You will be a famous warrior one day, little chwama,' said Victor, holding the pup up in front of his face.

'We should go,' said Willem.

'Can we come back?' asked Victor.

'You know where the key is,' said Willem. That was all the encouragement Victor needed. He put the last chwama safely back into its wooden case, replaced the lid and we left quietly, unnoticed. The rain was still falling. Willem headed for the front door of the estate house and Victor and I walked in the opposite direction towards the estate house kitchen.

Water was dripping from my chin and elbows as Victor knocked on the back door of the estate house before walking inside. Just as he did, Mary turned the corner from the opposite end of the building, pacing fast towards us. Her head was down and the length of her stride was limited by the narrowness and tightness of her skirt below the knee. Her skirt and blouse had shrunk in the rain and both clung to her like she was vacuum packed. An empty wooden tray hung down by her side and her hand was shaking. She brushed passed us without a word, sniffing and wiping her nose, then turned the handle and leaned hard with her shoulder to push open the door. Victor and I watched her stride through the vestibule into the kitchen, throw down the empty tray onto the table, and then turn and run back out of the building. You could be forgiven for thinking it was rain covering her face, but tears flow from red eyes. She ran passed us for a second time and continued into the trees towards the women's quarters.

She looked weary and disheveled; not the pretty, desirable woman lusted after by every man in the bunkhouse. Despite the rain, from a distance her outfit looked smart and appropriate, meeting the expectations of a woman on the Vorster's household staff. But on closer inspection, she appeared to have given up all care for her appearance, ignoring the finer details deemed requisite in all pretty, well-groomed women. Beautiful, poor women with none of the accoutrements afforded wealthier ladies can manage to upgrade themselves with clever little touches; in the way they set their hair, or in supplementing with subtle jewellery, or in choosing what parts of their body to reveal and what parts to leave to the imagination. Mary was one of those women who found it hard to keep her beauty hidden.

Tonight told a different story; her unkempt, ruffled hair was matted and damp and her crumpled, stained skirt and her large, painted white fingernails were dirty black and scratched at the tips. Miss Johanna followed quickly behind her but stopped at the door, watching her disappear.

'Porcelain dolls shatter when they are dropped,' muttered Miss Johanna from under her breath, letting out a sigh. Victor and I heard her comment even though she had not intended it.

'What is wrong with Mary, Miss Johanna?' asked Victor. She glanced down to the side of the door, noticing us for the first time.

'Mary is unwell . . . she better in morning.' Her answer deflected a truth which Miss Johanna was unwilling to reveal. Mary had just returned from delivering food to Master Boss's house. Something ugly had transpired.

25
Harvest

On the morning of harvest, I slept right through. Victor pinched my nose with his thumb and forefinger so that I could not breathe. For months he had experimented with the most effective way to waken me; shaking my shoulder - which only rocked me like a baby into a deeper hypnosis - whispering in my ear, pinching me. His preferred method was suffocation. I awoke shortly before death, a few minutes after half-past three in the morning, a full three hours before daybreak.

My first job was to take in and fold the overalls from the drying racks out back and lay them neatly at the bottom of every bunk. I had forgotten to fetch them the previous evening and everything was coated in a thin layer of condensation which had settled during the cloudless night. I opened the wood burner and filled it with kindling while Victor brought in logs from the store under the stoep, then sparked a match. We arranged four chairs in a semi-circle around the oven door and hung the clothes, hoping they would dry in time.

Victor arranged cups, plates and cutlery in neat piles in the middle of the table then boiled water and prepared fresh, thick, strong coffee in pots that stewed. I didn't know whether time was passing twice as fast, or if I was moving at half the pace; either way I was always behind and hated having to rush. Victor was supremely efficient. He had developed a routine, a precise procedure for each task, which he followed to the letter. Every one of his tasks was completed to the same standard and with time to spare, but instead of sitting down to relax he always came to my aide - and never complained.

Ringidd requisitioned Charlie, Peter, Bostock and me to drive down with him to the estate house before breakfast and pick up extra food. Peter walked back into the bunkhouse first, dragging a heavy metal urn full of fresh cold milk. Charlie was behind with two large sacks of maize, one carried under each arm. Anyone else would have needed both arms, strong legs and a strained back to carry one, but they hung from Charlie like soft pillows filled with air. Bostock carried in two wicker baskets of bread for twice our number and Peter went back outside, returning with a heavy tray and a large square object wrapped in brown paper. My responsibility was for four, rusted paraffin lamps that I placed on the table beside the tray.

Underneath the brown paper was a factory slab of lard, intended for mixing in with the pap. I find it hard to describe what it smelt like, but not like it was supposed to be eaten. That lard may have trebled the amount of energy in each spoonful of pap, but it more than halved the quality of the taste - which was hardly agreeable in the first instance.

Victor placed a pot of cooked pap in the middle of one table, signaling breakfast was ready. Charlie was up to the table first with overalls hanging from his waist and a white vest covering his torso. He cut three, thick slices of bread and spread on lard in the same thickness as the slice, finishing each piece in two bites with a minimum of chewing and some forceful swallowing. He sat smiling joy, like he had just devoured a fillet steak and mashed potatoes served up by Mister Vorster at the dining room table in the estate house. Victor was bemused, intently watching Charlie's bread and lard vanish.

'You really like that bread and lard, Charlie?' he said.

Charlie used his last half slice to scrape up pap from his bowl and shoveled it into his mouth. As the final gulp slid down his throat, he wiped his lips with the back of his hand, smearing a lump of the white, lardy residue half-way across his cheek. The smear glistened like white lipstick applied by a drunk.

'All busy working harvest. Not good time for eating,' he replied, sitting back with his hands on his head in a satisfactory salute to the morning's filling of his stomach. 'When you is eating pap for as long as me, you is very happy when different foods is for eating . . . very happy with them bread and butter.'

His use of the word *butter* was entirely misconceived. Victor and I had tasted bread and butter in the estate house during the weekends - real butter - the soft, waxy, creamy yellow kind that irresistibly melts in union with warm bread. What Charlie had smothered on top of his bread was not *butter;* it was dirty white, marbled and grainy in parts - because it was *lard*. We didn't bother convincing him of the difference. If Charlie wanted to believe it was butter, then good luck to him.

The men sat in moderately dry overalls, filling second mugs of coffee when Ringidd pushed open the door unannounced and walked into the middle of the room. He stopped in that hunched-over stoop, steadying himself with one hand on the edge of the nearest table and held up a crumpled piece of paper expecting silence and everyone's undivided attention. He picked up a slice of bread, chewed on it slowly and spoke before his mouth was empty. Not everybody was aware he was in the room.

'Better be no damn meddling this harvest. We is got two weeks of dog hard work. Unnerstan'?' Largely inattentive ears pricked up and a disgruntled wave of silence washed slowly across the room, starting with those nearest him.

'I am *said* . . . do you understand?' his question was louder than the first time, making sure nobody had an excuse to ignore him for a second time.

'Yeah, Masta Ringidd,' came a sluggish, mumbled, incoherent reply from around the room.

'You is better understand me. Is it more of Franklin and Barclay what you want? Is it?' He pointed at both men. Franklin was fully healed from Ringidd's assault three months earlier, but with only six weeks since the annual braai, some of Barclay's wounds were still covered in iodine-stained, old bandages. He was lucky to escape a secondary infection and would not be adequately healed for another few weeks. The legacy of those lacerations would remain with him forever - scars as deep as they were wide, across his legs and arms and around his ribs. The ancestors were definitely protecting his handsome face though, it didn't bear a single scratch.

Any remaining vestiges of respect for Ringidd had entirely vanished. He called out instructions and timings from his piece of paper and pointed at Johnson.

'You is responsible for it, Johnson man. If them one little thing not right, you is in trouble.' Ringidd followed his threat with a facile smile then walked out of the bunkhouse. Johnson refused to look back at him or acknowledge the responsibility that had just been imposed upon him. Nobody resented Ringidd more than Johnson . . . besides Franklin that is.

When it came time to go to the press sheds, Johnson was the first up. He walked to the door, opened it and turned towards the rest of us.

'You heard Ringidd - we got twenty minutes.'

A handful moved immediately on Johnson's warning, pushing back chairs and picking up woollen hats and caps from the tables, then moving to the stack of boots on the rack by the door. Woollen hats keep heads warm in winter and provided protection in summer. Even those as black as the ebony tree can be susceptible to sunburn.

A small group formed below the steps smoking and chatting near Eugene and Franklin who were standing by themselves, fighting the impulse to lie down on the ground and sleep. Johnson waited at the top of the steps until Barclay shuffled out. He then shut the door, turned around and took a deep inhalation of breath. The wind was blowing harder than normal, bringing a slight chill into the air. Although it was the middle of summer, cloudless skies and higher altitude meant cold early mornings, that were usually usurped a few hours later by that bellowing furnace called an African sun.

Without the sun and with one sprinkling of distant, dim stars and no visible moon, the turning circle was very dark. Old Duke handed out paraffin lamps, passing one to Victor and I. We were instructed to join opposite ends of the line - Victor at the front and me at the back. Charlie chaperoned me.

'Cold and wind. Not good for grapes,' said Charlie as we set off. He sucked his index finger and held it up in the air. 'Wind always colder from the sea.'

Four specks of light bobbed from side to side on the track in front of us as our line carefully trod for a mile, down towards the courtyard. We arrived and two lines formed as usual without direction. I was in front of Victor with two lanterns at my feet, feeling cold and tired and thinking about lying in the hot bath of bubbles Willem had spoken about, when snaking headlights on high beam and the noise of engines bounced up the main driveway. The vehicles drew nearer and the chatter quietened. Shortly headlamps lit up Master Boss and Ringidd walking across from the estate offices and the convoy arrived in the courtyard shortly afterwards. Each vehicle reversed into formation by the wall on our right-hand side. There were six in total. Engines turned off but the vehicles dimmed headlights remained, draining batteries and illuminating the courtyard like illegal poachers searching for big game in the bush. The drivers - all white men - vacated and shepherded workers off the back.

Master Boss shook hands with each driver and introduced himself to one he didn't already know. Fifty temporary workers formed in front of the vehicles, blocking the light from the headlamps and relieving my eyes. We looked at their boots first. These men had an assortment, in varying conditions and states of repair - not dissimilar to the collection that lined the racks in the bunkhouse.

Most were dressed in overalls, although a dozen or so wore shirts with flimsy collars underneath grey or black jerseys tucked into their trousers. One hardy, pitiful soul wore a thin, ragged shirt that was tucked into trousers and held up by string.

The drivers relaxed in a huddle at the edge of the workers, lighting up cigarettes and pouring cups of steaming liquid from flasks. Next, Master Boss walked into the centre of the courtyard folding and unfolding a piece of paper, closely followed by Ringidd. He opened the paper, revised the contents then whispered words back to himself and folded it shut again. Ringidd was on his shoulder, hunched forward with hands clasped, hanging motionless in front of his privates like a goddam baboon. If I had been a sheep, I would not have followed these two, not even out of curiosity.

A large, recognisable shadowy figure emerged from the corner of the office building and the sound of slow, heavy footsteps crunched on gravel then clicked onto the smooth concrete of the courtyard. Each step tinged like a conductor's baton demanding the attention of an ensemble, but the gentle patting of the accompanying paws was barely perceptible. Mallie and Toppie's leashes were wrapped tightly around Mister Vorster's wrist and their shadows elongated menacingly against the workshop wall as they passed the end of the line of vehicles, caught in the wake of the headlamps.

Mister Vorster came to a standstill halfway along the workshop wall and coughed. I didn't dare look in his direction for fear of bringing attention to myself. His coughing was strained and wheezy, sounding painful and not easily releasing in accordance with his wishes. His rib-cage was working over-time, fighting hard to banish uninvited visitors from the shelter of his lungs.

Master Boss waited for the coughing and spluttering to stop, pretending he was not aware of it, then spoke in a loud, authoritative voice.

'The Glen Cleaver harvest is two weeks of toil on a biblical proportion. We have borrowed workers from the Roggeland farms who will be coordinated by their foremen. There will be no mixing of the two groups and there are two vital rules: timings and behaviour.

Timings: Between 9am and 4pm on each day during the first week, we will be joined by young Master Willem Vorster and half a dozen boys from Paarl Gimnasium. Do not speak to these young men, unless you are told to. You will not work alongside these young men, unless you are told to. We are seventy in total. When picking starts, there will be two breaks either side of lunch, of twenty minutes each day, and water to drink at each vineyard until the job is done.

Only Mister Vorster decides which rotation of vines is for picking - which is weather dependent. When he gives the order to harvest a specific vineyard, we do so immediately - Drakensberg, Cathkin and Pilanesberg are reserved for Glen Cleaver employees only.

My name is Master Boss. I do your thinking for you, and Ringidd here will keep a close eye. Right Ringidd?' He turned to Ringidd, inferring the man was his second-in-command.

'Yes, sir, Masta Danie, you kaffirs going to work long, hard and obedient.' He made the statement staring at our line of bunkhouse workers, certain of the derision we felt towards him since Franklin's beating.

'My final point is behaviour,' said Master Boss. 'Over the last twenty-five years, Mister Vorster has built a reputation for excellence . . . in South Africa and overseas, despite strict sanctions. We have a very professional operation at Glen Cleaver.' Master Boss pointed at our two lines to reinforce the point.

'These kaffirs live it. We expect the same high standards from Roggeland. Be early for everything. Move immediately when you hear a command. And for God's sake, make hygiene your priority . . . we will inspect you three times a day. Next to your water stations are sanitising chemicals to keep hands free from organisms that can infect the vines. We cannot risk contaminating our crop or spreading fungus and mildew between vineyards. If anyone fails a hygiene inspection you will be immediately dismissed and escorted from the estate. Understand?'

'Yes, baas, yes, sir, Masta Baas,' came loud, disjointed replies from the two groups of men.

'Mister Vorster will finish with a few words,' he said.

Mister Vorster waited until his manager fully retreated then waited some more, until the silence was audible. In that moment there was a celestial intervention; a ray of light from the rising sun shone in a gap between the mountains and cast a long strip of light and shadow across the courtyard. Mister Vorster's weathered cheeks were visible for the first time - although his head was bowed-down solemnly like he was lost in prayer after a powerful sermon. He raised his head and transferred Mallie and Toppie's leash from one hand to the other, then marched slowly, purposely forward. The dogs followed gracefully at his side and stopped when he did; the most faithful of servants.

Mister Vorster's nose must have been broken on several occasions in the past - rugby or boxing in childhood perhaps. The bone and cartilage cannot have reset correctly - not that his nose was crooked, but rather flattened slightly and pushed down nearer and wider towards his top lip. And the whites of his eyes? You could hardly see them, so narrow and puckered were his eye-lids. He wore a constant gaze of mistrust and reflection, even with friends and acquaintances. It looked as if the wind and sun had branded sinuous fissures on his brow at the beginning of time.

He surveyed the workers from left to right and back again . . . slowly . . . pensively. We stood precipitously on that fine line, when looking at him or not looking at him was equally dangerous. He seemed satisfied enough and brought his hand up to his mouth, coughing to clear his throat before speaking. But rather than clear a smoother passageway, his cough stimulated more coughing. Coughing moved into convulsion. It sounding like Mister Vorster was being felled by disease. You could hear him fighting with himself, the coughing was stealing this important moment; trying to dilute the power of his presence. He bent over and coiled one final squeeze of his chest. The coughing subdued, backing down and retreating like an aggressive young male lion that had been confronted by the leader of the pride. His poise returned and he spoke - loud and slow, clearly enunciating every consonant and syllable.

"He clasps the crag with cooked hands; close to the sun in lonely lands, ring'd with the azure world, he stands. The wrinkled sea beneath him crawls; he watches from his mountain walls, and like a *thunderbolt* . . . he falls."

He shouted the word thunderbolt loudly and pulled hard on Mallie and Toppie who growled wildly, straining on their leads, showing large, polished incisors; willing him to let them loose. His words echoed around the courtyard, bouncing off the wall behind me three or four times, not yet giving time to decipher his words.

'I'll be watching you,' said Mister Vorster, summarising Tennyson's poem in a simple sentence.

'Don't *pick* my grapes. Delicately caress them like a newborn child is in your hands . . . If you do this, one day you can say you were part of Glen Cleaver's legacy - a unique and majestic legacy,' he said, before passing a brown envelope to Master Boss with a veiled warning about the consequences of a failed crop.

'Award winners, Danie. Nothing less.'

26
District Six

As luck would have it, by the late morning of the tenth day of harvest, the Roggeland men cleared Cederberg in half the time expected and the bunkhouse was put on high alert for picking Drakensberg. We found ourselves sitting it out once again in the press shed; disheartened castaways recently landed on a deserted, barren island with nothing to do but lie sleepless on cold concrete and retell stories that had been heard a hundred times before.

'Mister Vorster always takes his time with Drakensberg,' proclaimed old Duke, lying on his back with his hands behind his head looking into the rafters.

Johnson was inclined to agree. 'I seen him in the last few years - among them vines every hour, pacing up and down with that leather bag over his shoulder,' he said, nodding back at Duke. Sometimes I reckoned those two loved the fact they were old timers, what with all the history and the stories they told about the place. They could have made half the stuff up and none of us would have been any the wiser.

Ringidd confirmed Duke's suspicion an hour or so later, relieving Victor and I of our boredom to fetch an urn of soup and some bread from the kitchen. We left the double doors of the press shed as Mister Vorster was walking across the courtyard. He was wearing a thin visor and metal-rimmed, sunglasses on his head, carrying a leather satchel over his shoulder - full to brimming with an assortment of mauve and white, box-like protrusions. Victor put his hand out in front of my stomach preventing my next step, cautioning me about walking directly into a firing line. We stood and waited like two little tug boats in Cape Town harbour giving way to a grand ocean liner heading out to sea. When he turned the corner, we walked on.

'What's the stuff in his bag?' I asked Victor.

'Weird scientific equipment.'

'Like what?'

'For taking samples of the earth and grapes an' stuff.'

'How do you know that?' I was always dumbfounded by Victor's knowledge. He only had a few months on me and this was also his first harvest.

'Willem told me all about it. His father's been testing him on it for years because he's going to have to do it himself one day.'

'Why's Willem gotta do it?' I asked.

'Don't know - he's just gotta do it when he's older . . . when Mister Vorster gets older.'

Mary opened the door to us at the estate kitchen. Her usually milk chocolate skin was pale-white and clammy, like a fried egg without the yolk. The friendly, affectionate women we knew had disappeared ever since the evening we saw her run out of the kitchen.

'Go fill the urn Mary and get these two a bowl of soup and bread with butter,' said Miss Johanna. 'How much grapes you picking this week then?' she asked.

'Too many,' I replied. 'They put us with the Roggeland workers, Miss Johanna. They don't trust us with the award winners,' said Victor.

'And they got Victor and me doing heavy lifting,' I interrupted. 'Baskets, crates and sacks of grapes - same size as Charlie's been lifting,' I said.

Miss Johanna opened her eyes and pursed her lips, acting like she was all impressed, but I knew she was just trying to be nice. There was not much point us two talking about hard work, when she probably had it twice as bad.

'You picked Drakensberg yet?' she asked.

'No. We find out this afternoon or tomorrow morning, Duke says,' said Victor.

'Ain't no surprises there. Drakensberg's not been picked in the first week of harvest ever since I worked here. You watch, Roggeland will finish up by Thursday and you in the bunkhouse will still be here 'til Sunday. I don't know why they don't share the load sometime.'

I got the feeling Miss Johanna had given this opinion a dozen times before. We were more interested in the butter melting into the toasted bread that Mary had placed in front of us. It had crisped up real special and I dunked it straight into my bowl, soaking up the velvet butternut squash soup like a dry sponge.

The large metal urn we carried back was heavy as hell, and damned hot on the underside. We kept changing from one side to the other for the heat - and just as well Miss Johanna gave us dishtowels to protect our hands. I had six loaves of bread in a cloth bag over my shoulder which kept swinging around my knees, forcing me to walk in tiny steps to make any forward progress. We can't have been away much longer than half-an-hour, but Mister Vorster was already stomping back down the track on the slope beside Drakensberg with the top-flap of his satchel banging uncontrollably with each step. He was carrying two small white boxes and a glass beaker in one hand. For a small second I saw the look of Willem in him, the same as when he had bounded away with his prized butterfly at the end of our afternoon at the pool. It was the first time I had seen enthusiasm in his face. Don't get me wrong, it was still accompanied by that stern, uncompromising sanctimony, but it was enthusiasm all the same.

'Let's get back before him,' urged Victor. Our arms and legs were stinging and numb by the time we reached the wide open double doors and stepped into the cooling shade of the press shed with the nourishment. Our efforts did not reap any gratitude; the bunkhouse hoarded round the soup with metal cups like impatient crowds at Tolongo's water taps . . . at least there was a semblance of order at the water taps.

'Get back to the wall,' shouted Ringidd. 'Soup's for Roggeland. Bunkhouse eating later.' He nodded over at two of the Roggeland workers in the shadows and the bunkhouse vultures receded.

Victor's assessment was correct. Mister Vorster went up to Drakensberg to take a scientific sample. He returned to the lab in the back of the estate offices and tested everything himself - acidity levels, moisture contents, temperature levels and a host of other complicated variables. It would have been easier for him to order a worker to collect the samples, or get Ringidd or Master Boss to drive the tractor up to meet him - but no, this was his job, and his alone. Drakensberg produced his best wines - award winning Chenin blancs, the source of his wife's cherished bottle of 1954.

By three o'clock in the afternoon no decision was forthcoming. At least six hard hours were needed to gather every grape from Drakensberg and it was becoming less and less likely. If we commenced in the next hour, sunset would arrive half-way through picking, resulting in a dramatic change of temperature that could split the quality and characteristics of the harvest - something Mister Vorster would avoid at all costs. Ringidd reckoned if the weather held we would be hard at it from one hour after sunrise the following morning. As soon as he had spoken, Master Boss walked through the doors and handed an envelope to Ringidd. It was good news for us, but not for Mister Vorster. Before Master Boss left he told one Roggeland foreman the reason for the delay; a change of just two degrees in temperature is enough to significantly transform the chemical structure of a grape at the point of picking. Blessed nature. Our instruction was to *stand down* for the evening.

The power of those two words slapped every man from debilitated to invigorated. Twenty minutes later, most were lying flat on their bunks while

Victor, Charlie, Franklin and I traipsed to the estate kitchen. Ringidd declined to drive us back up to the bunkhouse and we found ourselves rolling a wheelbarrow uphill, cradling two hot urns of beef and potato stew.

Those still awake watched us from their bunks with an excited astonishment at the meal about to be served. The men rarely sat as quietly and contentedly whilst eating; their heads down, focused and present with each mouthful. Lean cuts of beef, potatoes and vegetables in a sea of thick, sticky gravy - and plenty of it - was a rarity in the bunkhouse, and probably in the lives of any black folks across the Cape.

Even now it is the simple things in life that quench my spirit like nothing else. Taking a walk by a river, sitting for a wholesome meal with my family, pouring a hot cup of coffee on a cold morning - there is an endless list of gifts to appreciate that all come close to free. After every last greasy spoonful was licked, the bunkhouse heaved its lungs and let out a long, regenerating sigh as if the building had been holding its breath for the last ten days. It was four o'clock in the afternoon when we ate, and most men were sound asleep by five, a couple of hours before sunset.

When we finished rinsing the plates at the sinks, Victor volunteered to check on the overalls drying out back. It took me half-an-hour to notice that he was missing. I walked out onto the edge of the dusty turning circle. I patted away a small cloud of horse flies that seemed determined to follow me on my way to the overalls. My hand clasped the blue material on the first two hooks - dry as chalk. I couldn't think why Victor would leave them outside. The heat and the breeze in the Cape can dry clothes as fast as it cakes mud on an elephants back. But experience had taught me the evening air sucks up every ounce of moisture and spits out a dew to cover anything in its path. I gathered the overalls, carried them inside and folded them myself, placing each one neatly by its owner's bed. The other noticeable absentee was Barclay. He must have tip-toed out when I was at the back, although this was a more common occurrence and much less mysterious.

Where on earth was Victor? He wasn't in the habit of running off without me since our pact of brotherhood. I stripped to my underwear beside my bunk and lifted up the thin straw mattress. Underneath, on top of the rusted metal railings, lay an old picture book that Willem had sneaked out of the estate house. The book was called *A Tree is Nice*. I can't remember the name of the author or the artist and it was written for much younger children than me, but I didn't care. Willem read it to me for the first time, then Victor took over. Victor could read better than any twelve year-old black boy I had ever met. He told me once that he used to go to school, before he came to Glen Cleaver. He finished reading the last page of the book to me for the first time out among the karee trees early one evening and talked to me about his life before Glen Cleaver. It was the only time he ever mentioned it - before or since - like he was day-dreaming.

'I was at school for six years you know - when I lived with my uncle Fundani in District Six. Two doors down was an old women called Indah. She used to take me with her once a month to visit her daughter in the Bo-Kaap district. I was six or seven and her daughter had lots of different picture books which she used to read to me on the visits. Indah's daughter didn't have a child of her own, I think that's why she took me along. She doted on me, like I was the only child in Africa. I loved those picture books and the sound of her voice when she read to me. Every word she read was in a soft, gentle, soothing voice and she always spoke much slower than she needed to, putting on funny little accents for different characters. She would have made a great mother, sometimes I wished she had taken me for her own. Her house was on the hill, with roads all paved and climbing so steep that a car engine strained to drive up. The whole area looked like a rainbow had drained from the sky and painted the houses in different colours. No two houses were the same: pink, yellow, blue, green, red, orange, purple . . . not one colour was missing.'

'What is District Six like?' I asked him, surprised by this revelation of his past. Victor looked up at me sharply, like I just caught him doing something he shouldn't have.

'What do you mean District Six?' he snapped.

'Where you lived? . . . What you just told me.' I replied innocently. Victor paused, not knowing what to say next, looking confused and a little sad.

'I told you about that?' he asked, perplexed.

'Yeah . . . just now.'

'It's none of your business, George. Okay? Don't you ever tell anyone. You understand? You promise?'

Victor really meant it. It was like we had never signed that pact in each other's blood - like I barely knew him, or him me. I didn't know what to say. He was the one that had talked all about it a moment before. What was he to expect? Maybe he was daydreaming, but that's not something he had ever done before.

'Promise me,' said Victor again.

'Yeah . . . Okay . . . I promise, Victor.' I said. 'What does it matter if I know a couple of things about you anyway?'

'I'm not going to speak about it . . . Ever . . . Okay?'

'Okay . . . Take it easy, Victor,' I urged.

From the time Victor had read that book to me a few times I could read it myself from cover to cover - all from memory of course, I couldn't actually read the printed words. One evening Charlie, Duke, Bostock, Peter and Franklin were sat on the bunkhouse steps, all crowded close around me. I had agreed to read the book to them. None of them could read and they didn't know I was recounting everything from memory. I remember Bostock saying afterwards that I would be able to get some high-paying work when I was older because I could read. The others agreed and I felt quite special for the briefest moment until I realised the biggest hoax was on me.

I had flicked through the pages of that book over one hundred times, but I never tired of it. Willem promised to get me another one, but said I would have to wait until after harvest. I opened the first page and looked at the picture of the tree with big bushy green leaves and a dog beneath it, looking up into the foliage waiting for the hidden cat, then it dawned on me - the three chwamas!

27
Guilty

I put the picture book back under my mattress and picked up my clothes. With an hour-and-a-half before sunset and no cover of darkness, it was a dangerous time to traverse the estate grounds. Franklin was staring at me with half-open eyes, through an exhausted haze, as I passed the bottom of his bunk.

'Forgot two overalls,' I said, shaking my head at the nuisance of having to go out again while everyone else caught up on sleep. He must have believed me, because he closed his eyes and turned onto his side.

The potting shed was twenty minutes away, so I could still enjoy at least an hour with Victor and the chwamas before dark. I pulled on my overalls on the bunkhouse steps and walked into the karee trees on my incognito adventure, without Victor by my side. As a teenager, it was time I learned to do things for myself, without always needing my friend by my side for safety. I could bluff my way out of a chance encounter with Ringidd, but not Mister Vorster or Master Boss. I kept to the high ground, always in the cover of the karee trees. In the fading light, it was eerie passing Overberg and Cederberg, whose empty, deathly vines had been plundered by the Roggeland workers.

The sound of voices closed towards me and my instinct was to bound quickly, deeper into the woods. A thinning bush was the nearest cover, where I waited and watched. My mind cast back to the story of my great-grandfather, a great Bantu tribesman and famous warrior. He never fought in a losing battle against neighbouring tribes but eventually his success caught up with him and a large prize was put on his head by a rival chief, who sent a raiding party to capture or kill him.

At a river on the fringes of a large forest in the Transkei, he was in transit with five other tribesmen when the large, opposing raiding party ambushed. It would have been suicide to stand and fight. My great-grandfather moved last, running in the opposite direction from the other five, discarding his spear and his shield in the process. He ran into the deepest cover of the forest where he knew he would have higher odds of surviving than out in the open. The raiding party, containing expert trackers, closed in on him to no avail. With seconds to spare, he climbed a tall tree and lay there silent and rigid for a whole day and night, until dusk the following day. With cunning and patience he returned to his village having avoided capture and almost certain death.

In my moment of panic, I whispered to my mother's great-grandfather, asking him to watch over me and to help me to escape the danger. I lacked his guile and all I could think of to do was lie still as a fallen branch and hope nobody ventured closer. Two shadowy figures appeared and sat against a tree, not far from my position. My muscles relaxed when I heard their Xhosa dialects - a man and a woman. I wiped the sweat from my brow without Mary and Barclay realising I was hidden behind them.

I stood and dusted my overalls with the intention of walking over to say hello, just as Barclay stood and stepped back from Mary. He bent down and pulled her up hard by the arms then slapped her. She fell like a sack of maize and crumpled onto the forest floor, lying face down, wailing with her head resting on her forearm. Barclay was consumed with rage. Veins pulsed in his neck and the rest of his body clenched and tensed as if he was about to unleash an even uglier wrath on the vulnerable woman at his feet. He pulled her up by her hair and Mary raised to her knees, resisting as best she could, whilst Barclay threatened to tame her like a wild animal.

'Don't look at me, whore!' he shouted, letting go of her hair. Mary wiped and smeared tears from her eyes with the sleeve of her shirt and braced herself for worse. Barclay slapped his forehead in frustration, then pulled at his short, wiry curls of hair like he was distracting and delaying his fists from inflicting a grim reprisal.

Mary stood, breathing heavily with her white shirt covered in earth, dust and foliage. She shouted in great anger and venom, but also like she was pleading for absolution.

'He . . . raped . . . me. He raped me.' She repeated the line over and over, quieter and quieter, dropping by an inch each time until she was lying on the ground. Her hands covered her face and a dull, muffled shriek seeped through the gaps in her fingers.

Barclay took a step back then swung his foot and slammed it into the trunk of the nearest tree like a blunt axe to the fell. That is when he noticed me. I was standing so deadly still that he must have thought I was an illusion. I didn't dare move. He walked towards me and grabbed my arm, pulling me over to Mary.

'What you doing here? Why you following us?' he said.

'I wasn't following you. I promise. I'm meeting Victor. He's at the potting shed.'

'Why you up here then?' he asked, not believing my first answer because of my elongated route.

'We're not meant to be out. I was being careful not to get caught by Mister Vorster or Masta Baas. I hid when I heard voices. I didn't know who it was.'

Mary stood up and made a futile attempt to hide her distress.

'Did you hear us speaking, George? What did you hear us say? Tell me!' Mary's voice was anxious and she looked frightened. Barclay was holding my arm tightly and shook it when I didn't answer.

'Tell us, George! Tell us what you heard.' He looked as angry with me as he was with Mary's revelation. I didn't know what to say next, it just blurted out unexpectedly in that same calm, assured tone that Victor used in a crisis.

'I saw my father rape a women once. Sometimes I can't sleep at night because it is like a photograph stuck on the inside of my eyelids.'

Barclay loosened his grip of my arm, then let it drop. He sat down with his back against the tree trunk and held his head in his hands.

'I gotta get out this fok bad place. Where the fok I gonna go?'

'Take me with you! We'll go together Barclay . . . start again somewhere. Just you and me . . . like we talked about,' said Mary, knowing she was fanning a dying flame, one that had vanished down into a cold dark crevasse.

'You and me?' he snarled. 'You and me and that white man's child . . . you stupid, fok whore.' His eyes were empty as he looked up at her. Mary sucked in her lips and clenched her jaw, wrapping her arms around herself. She began shaking like she had been drenched in a thunder storm.

Mary told Barclay the truth that evening, but not the whole truth. I expect she omitted the part about visiting Danie Rousseau on consensual terms for over nine months - six months after she and Barclay had first lain naked with each other in this very forest.

Mary's instinct for survival ascended and a mask of fortitude returned to her face. I've seen that capacity in many women, and it's a quality that men don't possess in as much depth. Men fight and drink, or bury their heads in the sand and act all strong and tough, but there's some deeper reserve of survival in women, even when they have been endlessly victimised and knocked down, rolled over and kicked, bleeding half-to-death. They've got this way of carrying on when many men would rather just lie down and die. I suppose if you are strong enough to bring a child into this world, you are strong enough for just about anything.

'Get Victor from the potting shed, George. You hear me? That bastard's coming . . . he's coming to feed them little pups right soon,' said

Mary, standing then turning and running down in the direction of the estate buildings.

There was an awkward silence when Mary disappeared. Barclay stretched-out on, lying on the ground. He put his hands to his head and let out a long, forlorn sigh.

'I should go back to the bunkhouse,' I said.

'Do what you like. . .'

'What you going to do?' I asked nervously.

'Need time to think.'

'Sorry I bumped into you Barclay. I really didn't mean to.'

'At least I got a witness now.'

'What do you mean?' I said. Barclay sat up.

'I'm gonna stick a pitch-fork in that swine's skull,' he said. He stood up, energised and purposeful, his eyes piercing inevitability.

'You want that bastard to catch Victor?' he said.

'No.'

'So what you gonna do about it?' he said, before running off into the trees.

'Barclay! Wait!'

'Follow me!' he shouted.

I struggled to keep up. We bounded downhill, right through the middle of the woods and through two fruitless vineyards. Barclay leapt over tree roots, fallen branches and a row of vines that were obstructing his route. In a second copse of trees, I tripped and fell. Barclay vanished. I stood up with sore, scraped hands. Light shone like a torch with dying batteries and all I sensed was an enveloping dark wanting to imprison me.

'Barclay?' I hissed loudly. His blue overalls flickered in a small gap between the trees.

'Keep up, George,' he called. I sprinted towards him.

Barclay thumbed the iron latch and pushed open the green, potting shed door. Mary was already inside, standing next to Victor at the far end, watching him place the chwamas into their box.

'Hey, George,' whispered Victor when he saw me.

'Masta Baas coming to feed the puppies real soon, Victor' I said in concern.

'I know. We better get going,' he replied.

'Have the chwamas grown, Victor? Can I see?' I said eagerly.

'Quick then, George,' said Mary. Victor put his hands back into the empty wine case and returned with one of the pups in his hands.

'Wow, he's three times bigger,' I said.

165

'And look at his big eyes. He was the runt when we found him but he's caught up real quick. I make sure he gets his own food and milk and some extras every time I come. Look how strong he is now, George.' Victor passed over the runt. I gathered him into my chest and my face so that I could inspect his eyes.

'You're a real little chwama now,' I whispered.

'He's a naughty one, George. His brothers don't bother him anymore,' said Victor.

'How do you know they are brothers, Victor?' asked Mary.

'They are chwamas . . . tough little bushmen . . . little warriors,' he replied, evidencing nothing about the sex of the dogs.

'Put him back before Masta Baas come find us,' said Mary.

'You take your time, George. Leave Masta Baas to me. He won't give us no problems with me here,' interrupted Barclay.

Victor did not know Mary was carrying Master Boss's illegitimate child and Barclay was here for vengeance. Mary began to cry.

'Leave. Just leave,' she shouted, swiping my hand hard from her shoulder and walking forward, pushing Barclay squarely in the chest. He lost his balance and knocked into the shelves, dismantling a group of metal tools and nails that fell off and clattered on the floor.

'Wait! Mary,' said Barclay. It was no use, she was determined. We turned and watched her stride up the paved tunnel in the gap between the seeding tables, towards the door. Rays of dying light shone through and the sight of Master Boss standing there swatted her like a fly. She stood in statuesque silence waiting for her breathing to restart.

'You kaffirs . . . all wretch and no vomit,' sneered Master Boss. He held a bottle of milk under his arm and a small metal dish with mashed food for the pups in his hand.

He stepped back and closed the door behind him. The key entered the lock and turned, sending a clinking echo throughout the dimly lit shed. The nearest weapon Barclay could find was a long garden hoe. He picked it up and ran past Mary towards the door in a frenzied state. He attacked with violent gusto, spitting out all of his venom, repeatedly scraping and hitting at the heavy timber like he was buried alive. The tempo and flurry of his attack did not cease for an age, but even though he was drinking from deep reservoirs of hatred, his lungs needed oxygen more than his heart needed retribution and eventually he slumped down against the door, panting and replenishing. The door was covered in cuts and scars but remained intact, strong, healthy and immovable on its large iron hinges.

Mary sat crumpled and limp on the paved floor in the middle of the shed with Victor and I shocked into silence. We huddled together with our backs pressed hard into the chicken-wire frame. Barclay searched the shelves. He found a thin, light hammer with a bulbous head, of the sort that is used to gently tap in picture hooks or tacks. He returned to the door and inspected the handle, the latch and the plinth of wood that was protecting the lock, then swung like he was in receipt of a sledge-hammer for piling fence-stakes deep into the ground. His ambition was admirable even thought it was unlikely to yield results.

He smashed off the lock casing, but gave up on the rounded doorknob, choosing instead to use the heel of his boot and high, lunging kicks. I was unsure which would give-way first, his foot or the handle. With each failed kick he shouted louder in frustration. He needed more height and dragged a table close to the door, climbed on top and jumped up, landing with his full weight onto the handle, seemingly unconcerned about any injury he might incur. The handle dropped to the floor and smashed like an egg. He then hammered and bent the turning mechanism, trapping us inside even if the door was unlocked.

'He'll come back with the others,' said Victor.

'I want him to come back,' said Barclay, defiance in his eyes.

'It's my fault. I should never have come to see the pups. I will tell Masta Baas you came to fetch me back to the bunkhouse,' said Victor, apologetically.

'Not your fault, Victor. Masta Baas the bad devil,' replied Barclay.

A thousand things were going through my head and not one was positive. I was petrified about what was to become of us and although I felt sorry for Mary and Barclay, I couldn't understand why Barclay was so angry with her. She had been raped. What crime had she committed? I leaned over to Victor, lowered my head and whispered.

'Masta Baas raped her. She is carrying a white child in her belly.'

Victor didn't move or react, but he had not misheard. He turned slowly and narrowed his eyes, grimacing, as if to question the validity of the statement. I nodded, confirming I was telling the truth and his lungs emptied themselves of air. He looked sympathetically at Mary sitting pathetically alone in the middle of the potting shed beneath the seeding trays.

It was the first time Victor had no solution to hand. He sat with his knees raised, tucked underneath his arms, alternating his stare between Mary and Barclay, lost in thought and looking like their sadness was seeping through the pores of his own skin. I was more frightened than sad if I am to be honest. The prospect of Master Boss returning with Ringidd, or the police, filled me with dread. Glen Cleaver did not know fairness or leniency. We were all going to be lumped in together and Master Boss would tell whichever story suited him. Our trespassing and Barclay's vandalism would not help matters.

Gnawing, squealing and huffing emanated from the box behind Victor and I. The pups sounded ready to leave and explore. They were strong enough to stand and stretch on their hind legs, but not quite enough to pull themselves up and out of the box.

'They slept all the time at first, but this week they only wanted to play. They climbed all over me and almost licking my skin off before you arrived,' said Victor, glad to have found an elusive, happy thought to interrupt the grim reality of our situation.

28
Cowardice

When Barclay shook his head at Mary from across the potting shed, she stood up and spat at him. I thought she would scratch his eyes out when she pounced. He parried, soaking up every hit and scrape and slap that she could muster, all the while shouting *"whore"* at the top of his voice.

'Why do you hate me?' she screamed, furious and dumbfounded that he would not comfort her on hearing about Master Boss's act of barbarism.

Victor and I pulled her off and she slumped back down onto her backside and fell into Victor's arms sobbing. Barclay sat up straight and the first hint of sadness appeared, quivering in his lips. Mary's outburst seemed to have resolved something between them. Silence resumed.

'That thing with my father I mentioned in the forest?' I said hesitantly, looking at Barclay, then Mary. Barclay's eyes flickered slightly but Mary's head remained still and heavy on Victor's thigh while his hand stroked her hair repeatedly from the top of her head to the nub of her neck. The warmth penetrating into me from Victor's deep brown eyes was all the encouragement I needed. My words began to flow and over the next fifteen minutes Barclay, Mary and Victor heard about why I hated my father so much; about how my ugly errand in the Inner Tikki had concluded in the most sinister night of my life.

'I am sorry about what happened to you, Mary,' I said. She looked at me with weary eyes and shuffled closer, reaching to take my hand in hers, affectionately stroking it with her thumb and forefinger.

'You have nothing to be sorry about, George,' she said.

Tyres rolled off the smooth concrete in the courtyard onto the gravel track leading to the walled garden and the purr of an engine came into earshot from behind the potting shed door. The vehicle stopped ten yards short and the engine switched off. Two doors slammed and chains and bolts holding the tailgate were pulled apart before it swung open. We sat in a heightened state of tension and apprehension, waiting and listening.

Ringidd was the first to speak, right up close to the door.

'Don't do nothing stupid now. You is all cumin out now,' he said.

Barclay listened to Ringidd's ultimatum, slouched down against the inside of the door. A rusty key scraped and prodded on the fringes of the keyhole, before Ringidd's unsteady hand inserted it. He turned the key and unlocked the door, paused for a few seconds, then turned the handle tentatively. It turned well enough, but because the mechanism was smashed out, there was nothing for the latch to grab onto. After a pause, muffled voices convened outside and another person leaned into the door.

'Trespassing on private property . . . damaging private property . . . I am going to fokin' crack you kaffirs. Open . . . this . . . fokin' . . . door . . . now!' shouted Master Boss in rage, kicking hard. The leather on the toe of his boot must have suffered more than the door, which didn't budge an inch. A hint of contentment sprung across Barclay's face.

The vehicle door opened and closed, the engine sparked and it drove off back towards the courtyard, returning a few minutes later. There were no voices this time, just one large smash with a heavy sledge-hammer, which thrust a steel peg like an artillery shell from a big gun, sending large shards of wood and pieces of metal onto the back wall. Barclay was lucky to have moved to the side when he heard footsteps approach, avoiding a nasty injury.

Master Boss kicked-open the door and barged inside. He lifted his wooden cudgel and unleashed fury across the side of Barclay's arm and shoulder. By the sixth or seventh hit, Barclay had picked himself up from the floor and run outside. He froze in front of Ringidd, who was threatening a second cudgel, but it was Mallie and Toppie straining on their leashes next to Mister Vorster that halted any rebellion. Cradled underneath Mister Vorster's forearm was his favourite rifle - a Winchester Model 12. The polished, mahogany butt was on a sling at his shoulder and two barrels were pointing at the ground, scraping back and forward on the front bumper of the bakkie.

Ringidd prodded Mary, Victor and I through the doorway to be greeted by Mallie and Toppie's renewed belligerence.

'Down! Heel!' shouted Mister Vorster. He knew the biggest threat had dissipated with Barclay's compliance. The dogs obeyed instantly, relaxing their muscles and lowering their heads to his knees. Mister Vorster, perched on the bonnet, withdrew a cigar from his pocket then walked onto the gravel path.

'It's my fault, sir. I've been coming to see the pups and the others only came to fetch me back to the bunkhouse, sir,' said Victor bravely. Mister Vorster stared at him choosing not to directly respond to his confessional statement.

'Courtyard!' he said.

We followed, fifty yards behind Mister Vorster. He ambled slowly, soaking up the surroundings, casually swinging his rifle on his right shoulder and hanging the cigar loosely from his mouth while plumes of smoke bellowed from the side of his head. Mallie and Toppie strolled beside him, off their leashes. This is how I imagined he enjoyed the estate late on Sunday afternoons when his workers were in the townships. It looked like he was ambling for recreation and pleasure, ready to pick off rabbits with his shotgun; those brave or stupid enough to venture out onto the lawn or into the walled garden to plunder vegetables.

Even though Victor was in front of me, I felt increasingly frightened and alone. I remembered the day I first arrived in Master Boss's office - when I urinated in my underpants with the fear of it all. This fear was different. I was becoming numb to it. The sharp edges had been rounded and the tingling anxiety I felt during my first three months was dulled. I was learning to accept the grim inevitability of Glen Cleaver.

We lined-up in front of the double doors to the press shed. Mister Vorster stood opposite with Mallie and Toppie. He was still smoking, looking relaxed and contented, as if in this moment he would choose to be nowhere else in the world. The bakkie drove into the courtyard and parked. Master Boss brought out the box of pups from the front seat - Victor's three little bushmen. The last of the sun was dropping below the horizon but the sky still exuded an ember warmth as he set down the box in the middle of the courtyard. He walked back to our line of four and gently slapped his cudgel in his open palm. Ringidd copied.

'What you've done is filthy wrong! You fokin' kaffirs are a stink. During harvest? Just before we have to pick Drakensberg?' Master Boss spoke more loudly with each new question, freely letting his disgust be known. 'And you, little kaffir? You! A while ago I was singing your praises to Mister Vorster. And this is how you repay me? he said. 'I wash my hands of you.' He raised the cudgel, gripping it hard, then smashed it down forcefully through the air, illustrating the punishment coming Victor's way.

'Daa-niee . . . ,' said Mister Vorster, shaking his head slowly from side to side and brushing his hand backwards and forwards, usurping his manager like a fly was irritating him. He inhaled one last mouthful from his thick stick of smouldering tobacco then flicked the remainder onto the ground. He walked forward, slid the dogs' leather leashes from his wrist and passed them to Master Boss.

'Chain them to the steel ringlets on the workshop wall and bring the sack - clip them in tight mind, Danie,' he ordered.

'Yes, sir.' Master Boss walked the dogs across to the workshop buildings, tied their leashes to a drainpipe, disappeared into the darkness of the workshop and returned with two heavy chains, one of which he attached to each leash. He clipped Mallie and Toppie into two steel ringlets cemented deep into the brickwork on the outside wall.

Until this point, I had spent half of my life being reprimanded - mostly by my mother for not helping with daily chores, or because I had skipped school and church or got into scrapes with one of my sisters for no reason. Those exchanges were always like a game because I knew that no real harm would come to me. This is the way for most young kids, that in growing up it is expected you will get into trouble. But standing there with Mister Vorster's stare baring down on me through that large, flat nose, I realised that those games were lost forever. I was standing alongside Victor, in an adult world where the rules of law were constituted and administered by an uncompromising tyrant.

My mind raced and my numbing emotions thawed. Prayer is not something I was accustomed to, but I found myself inside my head asking to be in front of my mother, wishing it was her reprimanding me for arranging my bottles across the shack or smacking me for absconding from school or church. A stern, righteous scolding from Mr Mpendulo, for not remembering a passage from the bible, was more welcome than this. And . . . for a fleeting second I thought about my father; about him manipulating me for his own ends. I would have gladly accepted more of that humiliation than be here, in front of Mister Vorster.

Victor stood next to me with a grave look on his face. He lived in such a different world to me; that closed world inside his head, a place that he never let anyone else into. I felt cold and began shivering all over like I was consumed by a nasty fever. I couldn't help crying. My small gulps of breath attempted to stifle the noise and conceal my petrification. But as my gates unlocked, a deep reservoir of pity pushed hard to escape from my eyes. When the first tear slid down my cheek, the second came quicker still and the third in more rapid succession than the second. Right now, I wanted to be sucked up into the sky to be blown far over the mountains by the rage of the wind dragons. Mary was at the opposite end of the line, barely managing to stand, and soon enough my tears had companions in her eyes. She was curled up over her stomach whining a painful, fearful grief.

I thought my tears would exacerbate our misfortune, and whilst the rage of the wind dragons never appeared to save me, a different rage emerged. This rage was tempered and restrained, cold and calculating, but it was rage all the same - the very worst kind of rage in my humble experience. Mister Vorster seemed preoccupied with Barclay and Victor, staring back and forward between them, considering where to start. He lost interest in Mary and I the moment we crumpled and sunk into our pitiful sorrow.

There was clearly no challenge in confronting weakness for Mister Vorster, so he left the runts to Master Boss and Ringidd. Defiance, on the other hand? He was the strongest remedy for defiance. Master Boss and Ringidd curbed ill-discipline in the workers - a mere administrative detail as far as Mister Vorster was concerned. But defiance? Well, that seemed to get his blood bubbling with excitement, yet not so much that it showed on his face or exhumed in his words. If there is anything that I can concede to Mister Vorster, it is that his actions always spoke more loudly than his words. So when his message was dark and fearsome, most of us knew, that what followed would be worse still. Actions will always give way to the truest nature of a person, much more so than the expressions on their face or the words in their mouths.

'If you broke into my great grandmother's bedroom - the wife of Glen Cleaver's founder . . . and while she slept soundly, you held her by her throat and muffled her screams with the palm of your hand as you abused her . . . it would *not* . . . be as bad, as breaking into my potting shed to meddle with *my fokin' pops* . . .'

It is strange that a simple and kind act - in visiting to care for three small puppies - can leave a person so wildly furious and tormented. This was the first time I had seen Mister Vorster erupt. During the last six months, he had behaved in a cold, distant, detached manner, although it is fair to say that the threat of something more explosive was always coded in his eyes and sculpted between the dark, sinuous lines that ran across his forehead.

It struck me that Mister Vorster must have some disease eating away at his mind. I reckoned that whatever that disease was, it must have already devoured his heart.

'Without my dogs . . . there is no harmony with you kaffirs . . . no harmony means no grapes . . . no grapes means no wine . . . no wine means no Glen Cleaver. These pups are my heritage,' he said, pointing at Victor to confirm his verdict of blame.

'Yes, you . . . little kaffir! You have soiled my heritage.'

Victor looked at Mister Vorster with the seamless fearlessness I had come to expect of him. I don't think I've ever fully experienced fearlessness for myself, so it is hard to imagine what it is like. For Victor, I think it was his acceptance of any moment that he found himself in. It was as if he did not bother with anything outside of his control; and Mister Vorster's

173

temperament was definitely outside of his control.

My crying dried to a snivel and I stood waiting to find out what would happen next. I expected that we would be beaten and whipped, then expelled from Glen Cleaver for good - sent away unemployed and unemployable. Mister Vorster was no advocate for second chances.

To my surprise and relief, in that moment, Willem walked around the corner of the office buildings, into the courtyard. He was carrying his butterfly net and notepad underneath his arm and his glass jar was swinging loosely from a wire handle in his hand. Master Boss noticed I was distracted.

'Something catch your eye, kaffir?' he asked, angry that my attention was straying from Mister Vorster. When he turned around to see what I was looking at, the sight of Willem made him jump to attention. He paced away from us all with both his hands up in front of his chest like he was going to arrest Willem when he reached him. Willem slowed to a standstill and curiosity spread across his face as he tried to work out what was going on.

'Master Willem, you are not meant to be here. Please, return to the house and your father will join you shortly.' Willem was in the centre of the courtyard, twenty yards behind his father. When Mister Vorster heard Master Boss call his son's name, he turned around to see for himself.

'Why are you here this late in the day, Willem?' asked his father, as if the implements he was carrying were not enough to answer the question.

'I'm on my way back from scouting for butterflies, sir,' replied Willem, looking at his feet. Mister Vorster rolled his eyes before continuing the conversation.

'Now that you are here, we might as well make this a family affair. Take off that ridiculous equipment and come here. It's time you saw how things really work on the estate.'

Willem obeyed his father's order, cantering to the far wall to drop his butterfly equipment and returning a moment later to be by his side. He stood still and quiet at his father's legs and looked towards us, then at the wooden box and hessian sack on the ground at his feet. He leaned forward to glimpse inside the box and saw the three pups huddled together. When he looked back up, he stared first at Victor then at me with concerned eyes, more so when he saw that I had been crying.

'What we have here, Willem, amounts to treason,' said Mister Vorster, facing back to our line of four guilty, intolerable criminals.

'You know this kaffir, don't you Willem? The one called Victor.' Mister Vorster lifted his arm and pointed across at Victor.

'I've heard of him, Father' replied Willem.

'I think you've more than heard of him, Willem. Now I'm going to teach you about this little kaffir. He's no different to any other kaffir. A kaffir is a kaffir, as always a kaffir.'

'Come here' said Mister Vorster, raising his voice. Victor stepped from the line and walked towards Willem and his father, stopping short of the box of puppies.

'Yes, sir,' said Victor.

'You've been meddling with my pups, yes?'

'Yes, sir. I visited them to feed them and pet them, Mister Vorster, sir.'

'How often, kaffir?'

'Less times than the fingers on my hands, sir,' said Victor.

'So, more than the fingers on one hand?' enquired Mister Vorster.

'Yes, sir, Mister Vorster, sir,' confessed Victor.

Mister Vorster rubbed the balding patch on his head in frustration then looked down at his son.

'This one can't even count, Willem.'

Willem half-smiled back at his father in appeasement. He must have been torn inside, having to take his father's side in front of his best friend - his blood-brother. The three of us had spoken about difficult situations up at the pool. We had agreed that whatever we said and whatever we did, we did because we would have to in front of the adults. We understood that it had no bearing on the truth about our friendship. We played the game - to survive.

'The problem I have, kaffir - which is now your problem - is that you've tainted my dogs with your kaffir love. My dogs are not bred to love kaffirs. They are bred to hate kaffirs . . . to hate only one thing . . . the colour of kaffir black.'

Victor's back was turned to me and I could not see his face, but I imagined it was another moment for his dead-pan, unwavering reaction. Mister Vorster paused and turned to Willem again.

'Do you know why Mallie and Toppie protect us from these kaffirs so diligently, Willem? . . . Why they are so loyal and obedient to us?'

'Because you are the boss, Father?' speculated Willem, to his father's delight.

'Well, that's not the whole story. There is a reason Mallie and Toppie hate kaffirs . . . I've bred it into them since birth. You will learn to do the same. Isn't it right, Danie?'

'Absolutely, sir. Thirteen years old in a few weeks, eh? No time like the present.' Mister Vorster looked glad to have Master Boss concur and turned back to Victor, pointing his finger so that it was nearly touching between his eyes.

'You will make amends for me, little kaffir. Lift the box and walk towards Mallie and Toppie until I tell you to stop.'

Victor bent down, picked up the box and walked forward. He looked down at the chwamas who could not have known what was happening.

'Stop!' shouted Mister Vorster. 'Put the box down and come back here.' Victor placed down the box of pups about three yards from Mallie and Toppie. Both dogs knew what was inside and quickly stirred, yelping and grunting and sniffing at the air in front of them. They lunged forward testing the restraint of the thick chains fixed to the wall. Mister Vorster picked up the hessian sack and turned to Master Boss.

'Cudgel, Danie.' Master Boss passed over the short, hard baton. Mister Vorster wrapped the leather strap tight around his wrist, with the ebony nestled close to his skin, then he released the sling of his shotgun and swung it off his shoulder. It dropped and cradled underneath his opposite arm. From the pocket of his shorts he pulled two cartridge shells, breached open the weapon and inserted one cartridge into each barrel before closing it with the safety-catch unengaged.

I felt like the blood had drained, not just from my head, but from my body, to hide in a pool at my feet. Mister Vorster was going to shoot Victor stone dead - right there in the middle of the courtyard. I wanted to shout and run at him, to knock him over and trample him into the ground - like a tribal warrior that my ancestors might be proud of. Not one of my muscles dared so much as twitch. I was carved like a heavy statue, planted to the spot with deep foundations. I dared as much to turn my eyes slowly towards Barclay and Mary. They both looked deflated and defeated with eyes pointed down at their feet in that familiar obsequious obedience, despite the atrocity that was unfolding.

A mild grin curled at the edge of Ringidd's lips, relaying his sense of superiority. I don't know if it was respect, power or obedience that he hankered for, but I know that he would have loved to have been born white. Johnson even said that Ringidd talked about inventing some sort of bleaching cream to make his skin whiter.

Mister Vorster leaned forward and squatted a little so that his head was at the same height as Victor's. I couldn't hear what he whispered, but it looked like he was giving instructions. To my surprise, he passed Victor the cudgel then picked up the hessian sack and threw it at him. Victor didn't have time to catch the sack and it landed on his head, obscuring his view. He pulled it off and walked slowly towards the box of pups.

'They better be clipped in secure, Danie,' said Mister Vorster, checking again with his estate manager. Master Boss walked over to the metal ringlets and inspected them for a second time, pulling hard and fiddling.

'I don't think our tractor could pull these chains from the wall, sir.'

'Very good,' replied Mister Vorster. 'Carry on, kaffir.'

I still hadn't worked out exactly what was happening, but it transpired that Victor's punishment was a cruel device - beyond what my imagination could have cultivated. His punishment was also the three young chwama's punishment - a specific part of their development and conditioning, in breeding and engendering hatred for the black man. At eight weeks old, these little dogs were almost ready to venture away from their litter to stand on their own four paws. They had been fed and watered regularly enough, but were purposely separated from their parents with good reason - good reason as far as Mister Vorster and Master Boss were concerned. I cannot find any reason in it whatsoever.

'Let this be a lesson to you, Willem. I've said it a thousand times. Never trust a kaffir. They will lie and steal and stab you in the back if you are not careful. And they will do worse than that to their women. It's in their genes . . . Do you hear me, Willem?'

Willem hesitated and looked over at Victor with apology in his eyes. 'Yes, Father.'

'Get on with it, kaffir,' said Mister Vorster, in a low, menacing voice.

Victor had only experienced Mallie and Toppie as two sides of the same coin - in their silent dignity or whilst consumed with unbridled aggression. But now both dogs squealed and whimpered; pleading and helpless. I had never seen them like this and never imagined I would feel empathy with two beasts that would have torn my limbs from their sockets at the click of their master's finger.

In this moment I understood something that will remain with me until my final breath: Hate does not discriminate. That lack of discrimination is a laudable quality, the only laudable quality, in a trait that is the antithesis of humane. Hate does not care whether you are black or white, pink or green, dog or man, woman or child. Hate is a poison that tries hard to infect everything that surrounds it. It needs constant fuel to survive and it is the carrier of the poison who carries the biggest burden; who suffers the most virulent strain. For the lucky few who can overcome the poison of hatred, there is a journey deep into the soul; first to find it, then to ask for its absolution. Hate abounds from a crucible of fear . . . it is the preserve of broken men.

Victor picked up the first of the chwamas and before he placed it gently into the sack, he breathed deeply and looked into the eyes of Mallie and Toppie. I don't know if he was trying to reassure them that everything would be okay, or if he was trying to offer an apology by radiating reassurance and kindness from his eyes, hoping they would sense his goodness and find some capacity for forgiveness.

In the middle of the commotion, the other pups came to life and their small, soft pillows on the end of their legs clawed at the top of the box. In another two or three weeks they would probably have been strong enough to climb out, but at each attempt on this evening, they fell back in. The last pup was placed into the sack and all three must have recognised the anxious howls from their parents - a sound they had not heard since the very first moment of their births.

'Now tie it up!' said Mister Vorster.

Victor obliged and tied a loose knot at the top of the sack with a length of twine stitched into the cloth at the opening.

'What is happening, Father?' asked Willem.

'We are instilling discipline, Willem.'

'I should go to mother, Father. It's almost time for dinner,' he said, more in request than notification.

'Nonsense, boy, you wait here until this is done,' he reprimanded, pulling at Willem's shoulder, and holding him close.

Mister Vorster's attention returned to Victor holding the closed sack of pups loosely at his side. Small lumps and bumps appeared then vanished from the outside of the sack as the pups pushed and fought to find something other than the suffocating dark. High-pitched squeals and yelps echoed around the courtyard as Mallie and Toppie raced past agitated, towards panicked, straining on their leashes, confused and frightened.

'Now get on with it, kaffir. You owe me repentance,' said Mister Vorster.

When Victor put the sack on the ground in front of him, the pups stumbled to find an exit in hope of reaching their distraught parents. Mallie and Toppie's howls were a constant plea to action, urging their offspring to persist in the pursuit of safety, until the very last moment. But they had precious few seconds left when Victor lifted up the ebony baton, holding it high above the sack. His next movement would let it fall, with all his might, and give those pups a beating they would not be capable of forgetting. His task was to brand their souls with the black mark of Glen Cleaver.

'Put your back into it, kaffir. Let them see your true colours,' said Mister Vorster, taking a step back as if Victor was holding a canister of

178

gasoline about to be poured onto a fledgling bonfire. This sacred ritual, in conditioning each newborn puppy to mistrust and hate the black man, was something Mister Vorster's grandfather had initiated over half-a-century before.

Victor prepared the baton to fall and hit the sack, but something was stopping him from acting. His head turned towards me and a tear was trickling down his cheek.

'Kaffir, I'm not going to tell you again . . . do it!' Mister Vorster lifted up his shotgun and aimed the barrels directly at Victor.

Victor took in a deep breath and the cudgel fell, but only as far as the side of his thigh. His arm hung loosely, in obstinate protest.

'I would rather die than hit these pups,' said Victor as a matter of fact. He turned towards Mister Vorster and opened his arms wide, letting the cudgel swing slowly in the breeze. There were no words, but what he said was: Go on. Shoot me. Do your worst.

Mister Vorster's face instantly turned red and blotchy. The exact colour was a shade of burgundy, like some of his wines. Veins pushed out hard from his neck and he bit down on his upper lip, so hard that a smear of blood appeared from his mouth. I don't think he had ever experienced disobedience in his entire life - not even from his wife on her highest plateau of inebriation. Willem refused to look anywhere but at the ground. His eyes had welled with tears.

'This is not a game, kaffir. Do it!' shouted Mister Vorster wildly, losing control for the second time during the evening.

Mallie and Toppie were unlikely adjudicators, and sensed the stand-off, knowing that the wellbeing of their offspring hung in the balance. The volume of their howls increased further and Mallie crouched down onto her front legs with open, splayed claws, scratching incessantly at the concrete floor, as if she might dig a hole.

Mister Vorster raised his shotgun symbolically and pulled the polished mahogany butt hard into his shoulder, the last required movement before pulling the trigger. Victor saw this and threw the baton. It flew high in the air and clattered then slid across the concrete. He ran and didn't look back. The wind dragons must have come for him instead of me. He paced like a gazelle, bounding fast and high and fleet of foot towards the end of the courtyard.

The hunter took aim and the barrels of the shotgun tracked Victor's every step as he moved across the courtyard. There was plenty of time to take the shot and at such a short distance the exploding, lead ball bearings would spread out to enforce maximum and fatal damage. It was impossible

179

for Mister Vorster to miss. Victor was going to be plucked from this earth by one short crease in Mister Vorster's index finger.

He pulled the trigger - twice - but a second beforehand, lifted the barrels towards the sky and fired over the corner of the workshop roof. The lead ball bearings must have splattered like thin rain onto the karee trees in the distance.

I jumped with the piercing thud of each shot, the pulsing sound reverberating and ringing in my ears for a good while afterwards. The shock of the shots crushed Mary. She had not been able to look, covering her eyes, expecting the worst when she heard the gunfire. She assumed Victor had been killed and that his body would be seeping red wine across the courtyard floor. She slumped to the ground, wailing and screaming loudly into the concrete, still unable to remove her hands from her head.

'Oi! Kaffir! Get back here, you little fok. I'll set the dogs on you,' shouted Master Boss. Victor heard the order before he reached the corner, turned and disappeared.

I honestly thought that Mister Vorster was going to shoot him in the back. I don't know exactly why he decided not to. It might have been different had Willem not provided a major distraction and dilemma.

'I hate you. I hate you,' he shouted, darting from his father's side across the courtyard towards the estate house just as Victor ran. Willem's unexpected departure seemed to annoy Mister Vorster more than Victor's disobedience.

'Boy! Come back here! . . . Willem!' he shouted, but it was no good. Just like Victor, Willem never looked back. I felt more alone than ever. My two friends had found a temporary escape from this horror. In my heart I knew they had only delayed their suffering, most probably exacerbating it one-hundred fold. And now that they had escaped, Barclay, Mary and I were left in the eye of this monstrous hurricane.

Master Boss moved quickly to the metal ringlets on the workshop wall and grabbed Mallie and Toppie's chains to untie them. Both dogs recoiled and quietened at the sound of the shots.

'It won't take two minutes to catch that mad little kaffir, sir,' said Master Boss.

'Leave the kaffir. We'll worry about him later,' hushed Mister Vorster. 'We have a job to finish.'

Master Boss left the chains tied to the ringlet and walked back to join Ringidd. If Mister Vorster wanted the job finished, it was unlikely that he would turn to Mary. There was Barclay and there was me. For most of my life I believe I have been luckier than most. My sisters reckoned that because

I was the youngest of my siblings everything went my way - some might say I was spoiled, but that is a very relative measure for an upbringing in Tolongo.

This evening was far from one of my lucky moments. It is an evening that has haunted me until this day. I have tried to shake it. I have analysed it and reasoned with it. My mind has played a great many tricks in convincing me to accept the exceptional nature of the circumstances, but I cannot shake that feeling in my chest which comes in waves from my heart. It is not a consistent feeling. Sometimes it feels like fear, other times it is like self-loathing . . . but most of the time, it feels like shame.

Ringidd picked up the ebony baton from the far side of the courtyard.

'What do you think, Ringidd?' called Mister Vorster. As quickly as his rage had arrived, it had disappeared and the protruding veins on his neck receded. Mister Vorster's cold control returned because the job at hand seemed more important to him than the people and emotions on display during this grotesque debacle.

'That simple, little kaffir, sir. He's reliable if nothing else,' answered Ringidd, walking back towards everyone, slowing his steps melodramatically the nearer he came.

'Get rid of the other two!' said Mister Vorster to Master Boss. Master Boss looked at Ringidd, who nodded at Barclay and Mary.

'*Gedowdahere* . . . back where you meant to be . . . and count yourselves damn lucky,' he shouted. Footsteps scurried away behind me, in opposite directions.

Ringidd passed me the baton with a large smile.

'You do a good job now, George.'

'His father had no trouble with Mallie and Toppie a few years ago, sir,' said Master Boss from the sidelines.

'His father?' enquired Mister Vorster.

'Yes, sir. That kaffir, Kenneth . . . the skinny drink of water that deserted us a few months back,' replied Master Boss.

'Of course.' Mister Vorster forced out false laughter, recounting the incident. 'I could swear he enjoyed it, your father,' he said, turning to look at me as he passed on that information. History was obviously repeating itself, just like my mother warned me that it would.

'I remember the grin on his face. He enjoyed it . . . not like this pathetic coward. Now hit!' said Mister Vorster.

I can't remember much about it. I have one story in my head, but I can't recount it with the true feelings and emotions of the event. I have blocked them out. I recall taking to the task, frozen to life, like an Antarctic lake that will never melt unless it is the end of the world. The first time my wooden baton landed on the hessian bundle was a half-baked attempt.

'Within an inch of their lives; you lazy kaffir. Put your fokin' back into it!' said Master Boss.

I did not see a bundle of three adorable chwamas in front of me. I convinced myself I was hitting a sack, half-full of potatoes or maize. But potatoes and maize don't move and rebound and they are not warm and soft with shrill, innocent voices. The second time my arm came down on the pups was harder. I committed to the task with each new blow, negating the nasty repercussions from my masters. With that baton I carved a description of my character into the solid, concrete floor, all of it etched within touching distance of the assaulted pups' anxious parents.

The squeals faded with each new bludgeon and eventually fell to silent. But the crazed demented howls and blood-curling lunges from Mallie and Toppie did not abate. Mallie swung like a pendulum between extreme aggression and desperate sadness. She wanted to trade places with her young, to even the odds and make it a fairer fight. That bond between a mother and its young can engender the most selfless acts in my opinion. I have seen it with my own wife and I am sure I will see it shortly in my daughter. On this day, I denied that bond. I desecrated it. I took away any potential of its fulfillment. So the biggest word that I wrote about myself on that concrete tablet below the sack - like an ancient holy scripture - was *cowardice*. I was too frightened to be courageous, no matter how much of my soul I relinquished in the process.

After a dozen blows, sweat was dripping from my brow onto the small patches of blood that had appeared through the material at the bottom of the bag. I stood looking down at the sack. I had completed my task. In that moment of stillness and silence, as the dock of five witnesses looked upon me - three human and two canine - a tremendous clarity about the enormity of my ugliness washed over me. Warm urine trickled down my inside leg and formed in a puddle at my feet. I was panting with an open mouth and shaking from the exertion. I felt more afraid than I had before, like I had been snapped into two and would never be able to join the pieces again. I felt interminably broken.

'Now, open it!' said Mister Vorster. 'Open the sack and put each pup back into the box.'

I bent down, my hands shaking and fumbling with the string. I thought I would be sick when the knot was undone, as to look inside was the last thing on this earth that I wanted to do. Before putting my hands into the sack I looked to my side to see Toppie lying on his side, his head facing the wall as if he was going to sleep. Mallie was still facing me, aggression having left her body. She was lying wounded on her stomach, stretched out with her paws in front of her. What words can you use for an animal . . . for a dog? I don't know if they can feel things like humans. I would say she was whimpering, but the reality was that she was crying - forlorn and weeping like a mother that had just lost her child. That is how it seemed to me.

I reached into the open sack on the ground and pulled out the first little pup. 'Please forgive me little chwama. They made me do it,' I whispered under my breath.

The pup's small, soft body was still warm, but lifeless. A smear of blood trailed across the palm of my hand from his mouth when I placed him in the box. The second pup was much the same. Saliva and blood had drooled across his back and matted the fine hairs. Like his brother, his body was warm, but his eyes were closed and there was no sign of breathing.

'I'm sorry, chwama. Truly, I'm sorry,' I whispered again and passed the eight-week-old pup into the box. The small, stiffening body slumped down next to his brother and I was aware of Mister Vorster speaking to Master Boss.

'I've told you before, Danie, he's soft! I blame his fokin' mother. She's near gone and raised a kaffir-lover. He's all butterflies and botanicals . . . What am I to do?'

'Yah, but he's a good enough kid.' Master Boss daren't speak badly of his boss's son even if he was being encouraged by the man himself.

Mister Vorster lit another cigar and exhaled a large cloud of pent-up tension. He blew the smoke down towards me and the smell hung on the warm evening air.

'Looks like a trip to the river, Danie,' concluded Mister Vorster after looking into the box, confirming two dead pups. When I reached in for the last pup my eyes closed tight. I could not bear to acknowledge a third dead body - the third life I had cowardly stolen. I picked it up much like the other two and turned around, still with my eyes closed, feeling with my free hand to find the top of the box. I hunched down and placed the last broken chwama on top of his brothers. Mallie howled loudly and sprang to attention. She knew something I didn't.

'Who would have believed it? Perhaps we have a Lion-tamer after all, Danie,' said Mister Vorster.

I opened my eyes and stared into the box. At first glance, the last chwama's body was lying still like the others, but his eyes were half-open and blinking gently as if waking from a long, deep sleep. The small, fluffy chest underneath his chin rose up and down as the pup begged for breath.

I suspected his life was hanging in the balance. For all of that physical uncertainty, his memory was surely intact; forever marked by the sight and smell and touch of his young, black assailant. I could see it in his eyes, they were flickering hate, conveying a deep mistrust and loathing for the colour black.

I shouted out loud with my own eyes: *You live, hear me. Make sure you live, little chwama.*

'If this little one survives that beating, we may have a real fighter on our hands, sir' said Master Boss. Ringidd smiled and nodded enthusiastically in servile agreement.

'Perhaps . . . as long as we've erased any sign of that little kaffir's affections,' he said. 'Take the other two to the river, Danie, and put this one back into the potting shed with some milk and a blanket for the evening. The vet can check on it in the morning . . . if it's still alive.'

29
Farewell

It was a slow, shameful walk up the track towards the bunkhouse; so slow that I hoped never to arrive, so shameful that I questioned whether I deserved to be alive. My legs traipsed gradually up the familiar, shallow incline just as the moonless sky was giving birth to a dark night. Anticipating the early start for picking Drakensberg, on what everyone hoped was the last day of harvest, I convinced myself that everyone in the bunkhouse - apart from Barclay - would be sound asleep. If I crept in quietly, slid into my bunk and fell straight asleep, unless my dreams decided to trip me up, I would have eight hours in a vacuum without suffering.

It was Victor and Willem I was most worried about. How on earth could I face them again? They were going to find out what had happened soon enough, and then they would hate me forever. I imagined them draining me of the blood we had mixed together and reversing our pact of brotherhood. There was no space in my head to consider that Victor had his own grave problems still to deal with.

The sound of lone footsteps came in my direction from the path on the slope ahead. I tip-toed to the nearest tree and sat down quietly behind it, afraid of having to confront any ill-feeling, which I assumed everyone would be spraying in my direction. Ten yards from my hiding place, I heard a person stumble and trip on the root of a tree, then fall roughly onto the ground. A string of curse words in that deep, uniquely distinguishable voice of Charlie's followed as he pulled himself back onto his feet and dusted his overalls.

'Charlie?' I whispered.

'George? That you, George?' Charlie replied, unsure of where exactly the sound had come from. My silhouette appeared from behind the tree.

'I think we is heard gunshots, George, and then just now Barclay walks in all bad angry. Him not saying nothing but I can see him all bad eyes - them eyes of witch-doctor with all bad medicine. Victor with you?'

I didn't know where to start. 'They made me do it, Charlie. I didn't want to. They said my father had done it and that he enjoyed it.' My words flew out steeped in despair then I began to cry. Charlie bent down, put an

185

arm on my shoulder and brought his face to meet my own.

'Easy man, George. Tell me. Tell me all bad happened,' he said, softly with his slow, deep pulsing voice reverberating throughout my head and chest. He pulled my arm and led me a few steps off to the side and into the trees.

'Sit here, George. We don't want Ringidd come by.' He pulled my arm, urging me to sit next to him. We sat with our backs against a creaking, spindly trunk.

'Come, George. You is tell me,' he said.

'I can't tell you, Charlie. I am a coward and everyone will hate me. Victor and Willem will hate me most,' I said, overflowing with self-pity.

'You don't need to tell, if not wanting,' he said. This was just the support and acceptance I needed. I began to tell him about the pups and that Mary was carrying Master Boss's child. He listened quietly and patiently.

He must have heard plenty of similar stories, and was more interested in lancing the abscess in my heart, making sure it would have a chance to heal. Sharing my experience of these traumatic events seemed to take away some of their power.

When I had finished, Charlie's vacant expression was replaced with a pensive glare. I don't know what he was thinking, but I could tell it was nothing trivial.

'Can I ask you something, Charlie?' I interrupted.

'Of course you can ask me, George man.'

'You won't be angry?' I wanted his assurance.

'Angry? I not knowing what you asking. But I am promise not get angry, George.'

'Thanks, Charlie,' I said with relief. I had wanted to ask him the question ever since he had grabbed my arm while I trampled on his plastic sheeting on that windy night in Tolongo.

'It was not the Tokoloshe that damaged your eye and left the scars, was it, Charlie?' The question took him by surprise. I didn't think I was being too personal, but perhaps it was strange to ask something so obvious after so long in knowing someone.

'What do you know about them Tokoloshe, George?' he said, evading the question.

'My mother said the Tokoloshe are evil spirts and that the shamens put a curse on you because you are not a Christian . . . and because you were a bad Zulu.'

'You seen the bricks lifting my bunk? Protecting me from the Tokoloshe?' he said.

'I've seen them. I knew they were for the Tokoloshe,' I admitted.

Had it not been so dark, Charlie's expression might have given me earlier warning, but he decided to lead me down this dead-end lane for a while longer.

'Yes, it is true, George, man. Them Tokoloshe comes in the night. Them creeps all silent. Only them Zulu is see them . . . not them Xhosa. But Shamens say if them Xhosa become good friends with them Zulu . . . them Tokoloshe is make them also a curse.'

'You saying they could put a curse on me, Charlie? And Victor too?' This was not good news, and I now regretted raising the subject.

'We is good friends . . . no, George?'

'Yes . . . we are, Charlie. You are the only adult friend I have.' There was a mixture of fear and disbelief on my face. Charlie couldn't see much in the dark, but he sure could hear it in my voice. Then he laughed. Booming, uncontrollable laughter that he tried to curtail with his hand because of the sensitive situation we were in. At first I thought he was laughing because a curse had been put on me and that I might have to live with it for the rest of my life. What a cruel twist of fortune - to be guilty on account of a friendship.

I've never been the quickest to work out if somebody is having fun with me. 'You is telling me everybody in Tolongo think I have them one eye and them scars because of them Tokoloshe?' he asked.

'That's what they say, Charlie. My mother told me.' It didn't make me feel any less silly that others believed and peddled the same myth.

'Them is funniest I heard in all long times,' he said.

'I *knew* it wasn't the Tokoloshe, Charlie. I knew it!' I said, magnanimous.

'No man, George. Them is no Tokoloshe, man. Them is a story told to frighten little Zulu children and make them good behaving.' He paused, unsure if he should continue, so I took the first step.

'It happened here . . . didn't it Charlie?' I said tentatively.

The white of Charlie's eye disappeared and his eye-lid and mouth closed. He breathed deeply then opened his good eye and faced me once more. He didn't speak.

'You don't need to tell me if you don't want to, Charlie.' I said, copying his line, although I knew he didn't need my permission one way or the other.

'Four years ago, them dogs called Broer and Suster . . . brother and sister. Them was getting old and Mister Vorster decided better replaced by younger dogs . . . which is Mallie and Toppie see. Them is tested them on them *biggest brute* . . . is what Mister Vorster called me.'

187

'I'm sorry Charlie.' I said, shocked and saddened.

'But Charlie?' I asked.

'Yes, George.'

'Why have you got the bricks under your bed if the Tokoloshe are not real?' I asked, keen to close the book on this final mystery.

'Have you done sitting down low with them long legs?' he explained. It all made perfect sense.

'I only got one good eye, George, but I not blind like them other men.' Charlie stood up and walked back onto the path. 'You is no coward, George. You is brave . . . don't forget that you is brave. It don't not matter what nobody says. You is brave, see?' I nodded back slowly, thankful for his words, although it would take a long while for me to believe them.

'Where is Victor, George?' he asked.

'I don't know for sure . . . maybe at the oak trees above Drakensberg,' I said.

'Let's go see,' said Charlie.

Charlie and I followed the boundary above the tree-line in the dark, high on the estate, when Victor walked right up to us.

'Christ man, Victor' said Charlie, startled. Victor was just as spooked. Neither party heard the other approaching until it was too late for a diversion.

'I thought you were a baobab tree, Charlie,' said Victor.

'You is all too clever funny, Victor. Going to get you in all bad trouble someday,' said Charlie, half-serious.

'No more trouble than I'm already in,' said Victor. Then he looked at me, pausing, unsure how best to raise the topic. He decided that full frontal was the only way.

'Did Barclay do it, George?' asked Victor, referring to the beating of the pups.

I looked back at him without an answer. He saw the pain in my eyes and worked it out for himself. 'I'm sorry,' he said to me.

'You're sorry? What are you sorry for? You are not a coward like me.' I said.

'But if I had done what they wanted, they would have left you alone, George.' I didn't want the conversation to continue and he sensed it. But he did have one final, unavoidable question that he could not help to ask. 'Did they all . . .' he couldn't complete the question, but I knew what he wanted to know.

'One is alive. They put him back into the potting shed and if he's still breathing in the morning, a doctor will come to check him.'

Primitive life resurrected in Victor's eyes as he received this news, then a lustre spread across his face like a high midday sun splaying the petals of a well-watered soul.

'Strong little chwama! I knew some good would come of it if I fed and cared for them. I bet he's the runt. Did you recognise him, George?'

'No. It all happened so quickly and I could barely look at them.'

'The runt is a tribal warrior - a survivor. It'll take more than Vorster's cudgel to break him. Yeah, this is good news, George' he said, smiling. He seemed genuinely buoyed, but I also thought he was trying to make me feel better after such trauma.

I did not share Victor's enthusiasm. That single, conscious pup was at best a fortunate, unintended consolation - and most likely a very temporary consolation. I did not have the heart to mention that his dear pup would most probably be dead by morning.

'Can we go back now?' I asked. 'I could swallow an urn of soup and a loaf of bread,' I suggested, relieved that Charlie and Victor would be with me to face the bunkhouse and especially thankful that Victor did not hate me. There was no reply. Charlie looked at Victor, knowing something I didn't.

'I'm leaving, George' said Victor. Charlie remained silent, letting me absorb Victor's words.

'Leaving?' I spluttered. 'You're coming back, right?'

'I'm leaving for good, George. I've crossed a line and Mister Vorster won't let me cross back.' He sounded surprisingly relieved that the decision had been made.

'Where will you go? To District Six?' I enquired, hoping to trip up his plans.

'I don't know, George. I'm following my heart. It will guide me.'

'Your heart can't feed you and keep you warm' I replied.

'I'd rather be hungry and cold and free, than fed and warm and a slave,' he replied confidently. I should have known by now that something profound and irrefutable would come from his lips.

I looked back at him blankly, not knowing what to say. There was so much that I had to say to him; so much I still wanted to ask him. His friendship was not something I was going to give up on without a fight, not in a million years, but that was me thinking for myself again. It took thirteen years of my life to realise it was time to put myself to one side and repay Victor's trust and loyalty.

Nothing else was said as the three of us walked back towards the bunkhouse. Victor travelled as far as the edge of the tree-line, but that is where he decided to part company. Charlie was first to say goodbye. He put

189

his hand on Victor's short wiry head of hair and rubbed it hard and affectionately, then he took both his cheeks tightly into the palm of his hands.

'You go safe now, Victor man. Them is all good times waiting for you, man,' he said.

'Thanks, Charlie . . . Will you do me one favour?' he replied.

'Yes, man, Victor. Anything you want.'

'Will you look after George for me?' Victor turned to me. He had not meant his request to be patronising.

'I making sure George is all good happy times, Victor, man. Them all good happy times for George. Don't not worry 'bout nothing,' he replied.

'Thanks, Charlie,' said Victor.

'Will I ever see you again, Victor?' I didn't want to ask the question, it simply blurted out. I was dreading the answer, even though I knew it already. Victor looked at me and smiled warmly, offering his hand - the one with a small scar from a pen-knife on its palm.

'Blood-brothers forever, George. Nobody can take that away from us.' We shook hands more tightly than I thought possible and the handshake lingered for a long while as Victor stared into me and continued to smile.

'Blood-brothers forever, Victor' I replied.

I didn't want to let his hand go but I knew that I must. He turned and paced quickly into the trees and the enveloping black. It was the first time in the last few hours when I had not descended into a withering pool of tears. Charlie put his hand on my shoulder, empathising with the loss of my friend.

'Don't worry about Victor, George. He got wise Zulu ancestor spirits taking care of him. I saw them in a dream . . . sitting on him shoulders and dancing like white clouds in his eyes . . . strong, strong spirits from long ago olden times,' he said. But I was not yet ready to pass over full responsibility for Victor to his ancestral spirits. I ran forward into the dark forest.

'Victor! Wait! Victor!' The dark gave the impression he was much further ahead than the reality. He stopped and stood silently waiting for me to appear.

'There is a hill just outside Tolongo . . . on the way to the city, only twenty minutes' walk from the train station. I'll be on that hill at midday, for an hour, on the first Sunday of each month. That's where I'll be, if you ever need to find me.

'A hill?'

'Yes. I promise. That's where I'll be. I'll wait for you Victor . . . every first Sunday.'

'Maybe one day I'll see you there, George . . . I can't promise it though.'

'You don't need to promise me. It's only if you need me. Maybe one day I can help you . . . like you helped me.'

Victor held out his hand, but I ignored it and pulled him in close for a hug. He felt a little stiff at first, but quickly let his body relax. For the first time in a long while he looked a little sad, perhaps because of the kindness I had shown him. I can't tell you how glad I felt to be able to show him some kindness at last - or at least the promise of some kindness in the future.

He bounded off again, more tentatively than before, but didn't turn back to witness me standing watching him go. Soon he was among the trees, following a route towards the clearing where a path led downhill into the middle of the estate.

'On the hill beside Tolongo . . . it's the only one for miles . . . first Sunday of each month, Victor,' I shouted one last time, but he was out of earshot and my words were sucked into the dark wall of splayed branches and leaves.

'Is done, George. Let's get back before Ringidd come sniffing,' said Charlie.

I lingered for a moment longer, looking into the darkness, surrounded by the repeat of crickets and grasshoppers - the only sound among the silence. Part of me felt sad and alone, but part of me felt a little stronger for the first time in my life - like the small drops of blood Victor had exchanged in my palm were beginning to assert themselves in my veins.

30
Drakensberg

In the early hours of the next morning, the intermittent glow of a paraffin lamp shone through the creaking door of the bunkhouse as it opened.

Ringidd walked in and placed the lamp on a table then screwed up the wick, generating a high, angry flame and a tall, thin, inky plume of smoke. I slept badly, after a nightmare had awoken me in the middle of the night, and was lying there watching Ringidd while everyone else was asleep.

Ringidd waved a heavy brass bell attached to a wooden handle, up and down like a king's assistant, and poor Duke shouted out in shock and sat up rigid like he was having a heart attack. The ringing woke everyone from their sedation. I rubbed my eyes, yawned and continued to lie and drift finally towards sleep. Barclay walked over, nudged me and whispered.

'Get up, George. You'll get all the sleep you want after tonight.' He then looked up at Victor's empty, unslept bed with wide questioning eyes. I shrugged my shoulders. Charlie coughed subtly from two bunks down to get Barclay's attention. He gently shook his head from side to side, stressing Barclay should ignore his discovery for the moment. Barclay nodded, confirming he understood.

'Victor! George! Hurry up. Tea, coffee and pap. There is four loaves of bread and four pawpaw in the bag,' called Ringidd loudly. He walked into the middle of the room then sauntered half-way down the line of bunks.

'Yes, Mister Ringidd, sir,' I called out, walking to the end of my bunk so that he could see me, hoping he would not notice Victor was missing.

'Good dreams in the night, eh, George?' he said with a sarcastic smirk. 'You need to toughen up, boy,' he said. 'You should have seen him yesterday,' he continued, looking around the bunkhouse, wanting everyone's ears. 'He was *dripping* man - dripping like a teething baby.' He raised his voice making sure everyone could hear, shook his head and chuckled. Not one person acknowledged his comment, indicating where their loyalties lay. Franklin, whose bunk was nearest to Ringidd, sat up and pulled on his overalls and his shoes like there was not another person in the bunkhouse.

'All quiet and meek is it?' said Ringidd. 'Today you pick Drakensberg,' he informed us. 'Therefore, I urge you, brothers and sisters, in view of God's mercy, to offer your bodies as a living sacrifice, holy and pleasing to God - this is your true and proper worship . . . Romans twelve, verse one,' he sneered.

'Johnson?' he called, waiting for a response. Johnson looked up slowly.

'Have the men in the press shed before six o'clock,' he ordered. 'Mister Vorster wants Drakensberg cleared by lunch . . . says there is a chance of a thunderstorm later on.'

'Lunch? You crazy, Ringidd?' replied Johnson. 'Ain't half of Drakensberg going to be cleared by twelve men before lunch,' he protested, stating an obvious fact.

'That's why Mister Vorster gone arranged twenty Roggeland workers shipped over here this morning. I heard them drive in fifteen minutes ago. Miss Johanna probably already giving them breakfast in press shed.'

'Mister Vorster never trusted outside workers with Drakensberg in the past,' chipped in old Duke.

'I don't want no fuss hear, Duke,' snapped Ringidd. Duke sighed and turned his back, then Ringidd walked to the door. Before he left, he turned having forgotten something important.

'Victor?' he called out into the bunks, waiting for a reply.

'Victor! Answer me, boy!' shouted Ringidd. 'Goddamn it, boy.' He paced towards the bunks, hunched-over and ready to grab Victor for himself.

'He's gone to the pits, Mister Ringidd, sir,' I said before he had reached our bunks.

'What in hell he doing shitting out dark this time morning?'

'He's been up and down all night with a bad stomach, Mister Ringidd, sir.' I lied again.

'Goddamn it. You tell him he's sitting out Drakensberg this morning. Mister Vorster wants to see him at the estate house, eight o'clock sharp. He's to knock on the front door, not by the kitchen entrance, see? Got that, boy?' he said.

'Yes, sir. Eight o'clock. Front door to see Mister Vorster,' I repeated.

'If he not there, boy, you is cleaning out those pits for the next two weeks - clean enough to eat pap out of, hear?'

'Yes, sir Mister Ringidd, sir,' I acknowledged.

Just then, completely unexpectedly, Charlie laughed out loud, standing in the gap between the bunks two spots down. And it was not one of those nervous laughs that appears during serious or inappropriate circumstances. I don't know exactly why he started to laugh. Maybe it was the audacity of my lies, or because Ringidd had been so stupid and gullible to swallow them - I really don't know either way. What I do know is that it was the first time someone had laughed inappropriately in front of Ringidd without any fear of the consequences. And as Charlie's laughter grew, almost uncontrollably, so did its infection among the rest of us. I gulped and pressed my lips tight together trying to prevent myself from exploding, but it was no use. Barclay was next, then Bostock, Franklin and a couple of the younger guys. Half of the room was howling along with Charlie and the few that managed restraint could still not wipe the smirks from their faces.

At first, Ringidd was shocked and perplexed, but this quickly turned to anger and frustration. He took a couple of steps nearer to the edge of Charlie's bunk and looked straight at him whilst holding onto the end of the iron frame with one hand to steady himself.

'What's so damn funny, Zulu?' he asked. 'You laughing at me? Think I'm funny,' he raised his voice to be heard above the increasingly loud laughter.

'Good Goad, no Baas. Not laughing at you, Baas,' replied Charlie, wiping his one good eye and scratching the top of his head, before crouching over once more and trying to prevent the muscles in his stomach from cramping.

'Then what you laughing at, you big lump fool?' said the impotent Ringidd.

'Argh. Awe. . . .' Charlie could hardly get the words out. 'Happy Baas. All good happy.' His own reply sent him further into choking convulsions, and most of the others with him.

Ringidd stood in the middle of our ring being soaked in the spit of our humiliation. He looked around and saw that his power had disappeared. Fear and mistrust crept into his eyes.

'You is possessed by demons, Zulu. They is taking you, man,' shouted Ringidd, quickly walking backwards to the door without taking his gaze from Charlie for a second. He scrambled out, slamming the door hard-shut behind him. The laughter continued for a few minutes after he had gone. Most of us couldn't work out why we were laughing - all we knew is that it felt good. There was rare cause for feeling good at Glen Cleaver, so I for one didn't want the feeling to fade.

'Victor's a long time at the pits,' observed Johnson, pointing out he knew I had lied about his whereabouts.

'Where he gone, Charlie?' asked Franklin.

'He's not coming back is all you need know,' replied Charlie with an expression far removed from laughter.

'And it's time for more than Victor to leave,' said Barclay.

194

'What you saying, Barclay?' quizzed Johnson, suggesting it was pointless to even mention the topic.

'I'm finished with this place. You watch me. Not long now,' said Barclay.

'And what plan you got, Barclay? Gonna ask Mister Vorster for a suitcase of them new, shiny Rand notes and get him drive you back Tolongo himself?' said Johnson.

'No. I'm gonna raise his devil from hell on this place . . . then I'm leaving for good. And I know there's others want the same.' Barclay looked around the room of men. Everyone was listening earnestly, but nobody spoke up.

'At least half of you. I can see it,' Barclay said, diagnosing the look in some eyes.

'I hear this sort of talk every few years - some rebel or other with big ideas - Sammy and Ronald were the last two. Always comes to nothing,' said old Duke.

'It's not nothing this time, Duke. You watch me,' said Barclay.

'I'm watching good. I been watching for thirty-nine years,' said Duke, patronising Barclay like he had every answer.

'Yeah, I know it. And its Glen Cleaver you'll see the second before you die . . . but not me,' said Barclay.

'I don't care much what you do, Barclay,' interrupted Johnson. 'There is six hours of harvest and we get paid . . . You start your fires after Master Boss has put money in my pocket . . . understand?' he said.

Barclay stared back at him. The scorching rage in his bones would not be extinguished by a few brusque words from Johnson.

31
Loyalty

The brightness in the press shed pierced my eyes, which struggled to adjust to the severity of the low canopy of light bulbs; over one-hundred, all switched on and reflecting off the pristine, whitewashed walls. Barclay and Peter slid the doors closed behind me and every man from the bunkhouse gravitated slowly towards the Roggeland workers. They were sitting on the cold, concrete floor, quenched and fed and waiting to work. Some faces were familiar from the first ten days of harvest, but I knew none of their names.

A middle aged, short man stood up and shuffled towards Johnson. He introduced himself quietly, as Joel, then ushered Johnson sideways and whispered something into his ear. Johnson asked a few questions, some of which the man seemed unable to answer.

News travels fast in small communities, especially when it involves some sort of scandal. Johnson returned to our group a few moments later with some pieces of the jigsaw. It was Willem that gave me the full picture for me a few hours later.

By a very unfortunate coincidence, a bakkie-load of Roggeland workers had stumbled upon Victor only an hour before. They were on their way to Glen Cleaver, ten miles away, just before the Wellington Road junction. Their vehicle pulled onto a farm track, just off the main road, to pick up the last worker of the morning. The worker was in good time and quickly climbed onto the back and slammed the inside of the tailgate to signal it was safe to drive on. From the time the vehicle had pulled over until the time it moved off again can have been no more than thirty-seconds, and everybody apart from that last worker was huddled together, half-asleep. As the bakkie turned and pulled onto the main road back towards the junction, its headlamps scythed across the opposite side of the road. There was mostly nothing to see but for pale, dry grass and bush and a heavy wooden pole hammered loosely into the ground with the word *bus* scribbled onto it in faded white paint. Johnson told us it was a limited service used by the nearest farm's workers to get back to the homesteads on the outskirts of Wellington, Paarl and Worcester, each Saturday afternoon.

The driver of the bakkie did not notice anything suspicious because his seat was low to the ground. But the last worker was sitting up straight, high and uncharacteristically alert in the back. He saw what he thought was the silhouette of a body, but that's not why he slammed the side of the vehicle, wanting it to stop. Lying next to the rough black outline was a wooden box, branded with the crest of Glen Cleaver.

The bakkie stopped and the white foreman in the passenger seat rolled down his window.

'Christ man, Joel! Piss before you jump on,' he shouted to the back.

'Not needing piss, Baas. Think I seen a body and a box from Glen Cleaver up by bus stop, Baas,' replied the worker.

'You better not be feeding me kak, man! Reverse Lester!' he said to the driver, rolling up the window. The vehicle reversed twenty or thirty yards and turned so that the lights were on the wooden pole. The foreman got out and asked the driver to keep the engine running. Half the workers also jumped off - because the exhaust fumes were bellowing in their faces - rather than because of an insatiable curiosity.

'Show me, Joel, man!' ordered the foreman, waiting for the witness to lead the way.

'Just up there, 'bout twenty yards behind the pole, Baas,' said Joel.

Victor was lying sound asleep on his side, wrapped in a blanket. He was totally unaware of two men edging closer. The foreman was first to peer into the disused wine crate and saw a bruised, bloodied pup on a bed of straw, covered in a moth-eaten rag. Next to the pup was a flask and the crusts of two thick sandwiches and four oatmeal biscuits wrapped in brown paper.

'That's that kid from Glen Cleaver,' said Joel.

'What the fok happened here?' mumbled the foreman. 'I can promise you one thing, this little kaffir is not up to any good,' he said. Victor was still sound asleep, completely unaware of the vehicle's headlights beaming onto his face and the voices talking directly above him.

'Wake him up,' ordered the foreman.

'Is he alive?' asked Joel.

'Fok man! Can't you see him breathing. Get on with it man, Joel,' he said, impatiently this time. Joel hesitantly lifted his boot and placed the sole on Victor's shoulder, pushing it gently. It took a few more forceful prods to get a response. Victor's eyes must have opened to see two black shadows obscuring the blinding headlamps.

'You've got some explaining to do, kaffir. Get on the bakkie. Joel, take the box,' said the foreman.

Victor pulled the blanket from his shoulders and stood. The searing pain from the blisters on his feet was unbearable. 'What's wrong, kid?' asked Joel.

'Blisters,' replied Victor, but he was more interested in the fate of the box and its contents. 'Take care of the box,' he requested.

Joel took Victor's arm, giving him something to hold onto for support. 'I can walk by myself,' said Victor. They watched him hobble slowly in pain to the back of the van and fall over the tailgate.

There were a dozen questions from the workers in the twenty rickety minutes it took to reach the grand entrance below Glen Cleaver's drive. Victor didn't answer one of them. Joel told Johnson that he didn't say a single word for the whole bakkie ride. His expression was the same throughout, even when the vehicle drove up to Mister Vorster's front door.

The foreman picked up the wine crate and walked with Victor to the front door and rang the bell. A shrill buzz echoed inside the Vorster's hallway, then a light came on from a window on the first floor, followed a minute later by a bright outside-light, above the front door.

Neither Victor nor the foreman expected Willem to open the door, dressed in his pyjamas, dressing gown and slippers. He must have thought he was staring at a ghost or an exact painted replica of Victor, finding it hard to speak. He expected Victor would be in the centre of Cape Town by now, booked into a hostel on the docks having tucked into a hearty meal. The three-hundred Rand he stole for him from his mother's bedroom cabinet would have lasted for weeks, if he avoided thieves.

The foreman must have taken Willem's shock as lacking confidence. 'Is your father available?' he asked. There was no need for the question - Mister Vorster was half-way down the stairway with small blobs of shaving cream stuck to the lobes of his ears and the underside of his jaw. When the foreman and Victor came into Mister Vorster's view, he didn't flinch for a second.

'What *have we* here?' he said with a pleased growl.

'Many apologies, Mister Vorster, sir. My name is Jeppie Van Zyl from the Roggeland collective - my men are working for you today, and we picked this rogue up on the way. He was sleeping rough by the Wellington junction. We can't get a squeak out of him, sir . . . not a word. I thought it best to inform you.'

'Thank you Mr Van Zyl. That was the correct thing to do. Much obliged,' replied Mister Vorster, swallowing hard and draining his mouth of saliva like his favourite steak was steaming on a silver salver in front of him.

Willem moved to hide behind his father, who walked forward to see what was in the box. Victor involuntarily flinched backwards, thinking the worst.

'Calm down. I only want to look inside,' reassured Mister Vorster, peering into the box. He put in an arm and inspected the package of finished sandwiches and biscuits, then lifted up the pup and saw a thin pile of crisp Rand notes underneath.

'Is he alive?' asked Mister Vorster.

'Yes. I've helped him stay alive from the first time I saw him,' replied Victor, his first words since getting onto the Roggeland bakkie.

'A pure-breed lion tamer if ever I've seen one. Such a shame,' mumbled Mister Vorster without belittling himself by entering into conversation on the subject with the little kaffir in front of him.

'Thank you, Mr Van Zyl. You are dismissed. I will see you shortly in the press shed. We pick Drakensberg today - the most important day of the year as far as I am concerned . . . although don't tell my wife . . . she thinks it's our wedding anniversary.' The foreman chuckled nervously and Mister Vorster patted him once on the back as he stepped off.

'Thanks again, eh,' said Mister Vorster, forcing a smile.

He watched as the vehicle drove off, then turned to Victor and Willem. His rueful smile was still visible. 'It's been a memorable twenty-four hours . . . for all the wrong reasons. Am I right?' he said, expecting a reply.

'Yes, Father,' replied Willem. Victor didn't answer.

'Come inside, Victor. You, Willem and I have important matters to resolve.'

Victor thought twice about stepping off without his helpless little comrade in the box, but Mister Vorster intervened on his behalf.

'Bring the pup with you,' he said. Victor picked up the box and looked into it hoping to find some strength from his little chwama - whatever he had to offer.

'I will speak with Willem privately before we reconvene, Victor, so this is a precaution . . . your recent behaviour gives me no other option.' Mister Vorster opened a small door leading into the cupboard underneath the wide stairway and Victor walked in with the crate. The door was closed and locked behind him.

'I'll let you out when I've spoken to Willem,' said Mister Vorster from the hallway. Victor met the comment with silence.

'Why is that kaffir boy in my cupboard?' asked Gwendoline Vorster from behind the bannister on the landing above the stairway.

'Estate business . . . nothing to worry about. Go back to your bedroom,' said her husband. He put an arm around Willem and walked with him towards the kitchen.

199

'I heard that line about our wedding anniversary . . . you are full of *kak* . . . that's what I know about our last seventeen years of marriage.' Willem's mother liked to have the last word when her husband was concerned, but he was in no mood to be outdone. He faced up towards the landing, while she was strolling back to her bedroom, the place she had slept, alone, for the last thirteen years.

'I thought you would have been *too pissed* to remember anything about our marriage,' he shouted. Willem engaged a muting switch in his head which he used to filter out these sorts of conversations. He had been exposed to their constant, personal bickering since his very first memory. No wonder he spent so much time roaming the estate chasing butterflies and jumping off the high ledge into the silent depths of our secret pool.

In the kitchen, Mister Vorster flicked on the lights and dragged two chairs from the table.

'Sit!' he said, walking over to the stove and pulling a mug from the cupboard, before picking up a heavy, steel pot of coffee from the hotplate and pouring himself a cupful.

Willem sat quietly and obediently, fidgeting with his fingers, picking dirt from underneath each nail with such force that they were in danger of being ripped straight off. His father sat opposite.

'You are fidgeting, boy. Sit on your hands if you have to,' he said, before the inquisition commenced. Willem took the hint and placed his hands underneath his thighs. All the while, recurring voices in his head were telling him to lie, to stick to the story, plead innocence, deny everything - but this morning, the voices were timid and vulnerable . . . they had not been given a chance to warm up. Victor getting caught had not been part of the plan.

Mister Vorster sipped his coffee, testing the veracity of the temperature on his lips, before dumping in a full mouthful. He held the hot liquid in his mouth for a moment, looking pensive and nervous, then let it flush quickly down his throat like caustic cleaner unblocking a drain, readying him for speech.

'I am only going to ask you once, Willem . . . only once.' He made his point slowly and deliberately. Willem's lip quivered as he nodded his head in agreement.

'Before you answer, you need to know the seriousness of the ramifications if you lie to me . . . Because Willem, I can handle almost anything this world can throw at me . . . but there is one thing I cannot live with . . . a family member lying to me.'

The comment invited sadness into his eyes and Willem swore he saw them fill for a few seconds, but not enough for a tear to fall. He had seen his father angry, frustrated and irate, but never sad or vulnerable. These emotions were entirely new and much more intimidating than anything else. Father and son were meeting briefly in a space of unencumbered intimacy with no place for either of them to hide. For a small moment, the powerful, controlling man opposite Willem, was childlike.

'I only have two family members . . . and to the best of my knowledge only one possesses their rectitude . . . that person is sitting in front of me right now, Willem. Do you know what that word means?' asked his father. Willem rotated his head ever so slightly, from side to side.

'It means there is no higher virtue than righteousness. . . . Did you know that?' said Mister Vorster. Willem's head twitched in the same manner as before.

'If you take nothing else, take that with you to your grave, boy.' His father finished the lesson, sighed heavily and sipped more coffee. Willem saw his father's hand shaking slightly when he took the cup down from his lips to place it onto the table. His father leaned forward onto the edge of his seat, bringing his thick, weathered fingertips together like he was about to recite a prayer.

'Are you ready, Willem?'

'Ye-Yes, Father,' he stuttered, feeling his heart pulse in the end of his toes and his lungs retract to the size of a bottle cork.

'In truth, my question is more of an observational statement. A simple yes or no will do. And I implore you, Willem . . . do the right thing.' Willem nodded immediately back at his father, not knowing whether he had enough breath to utter a single word. He felt like he was drowning - suffocating under the weight of his father's sombre tutorial. Then his father's words appeared, exorcised like demons.

'The little kaffir, Victor, is your friend and you helped him get away from here with my pup?'

Willem was not being insolent in withholding his answer, he was completely overcome with nerves. 'Yes? . . . or no? . . .' shouted his father, making matters worse. Just as Willem had sucked in enough air for his lungs to be able to answer, his father retracted the question. Willem's hesitancy had thrown him. He could not bear for his son's answer to be the wrong one. He could not bear the possibility that he might be anything other than completely loyal to him.

'Don't answer. Before you do, I will give you some help.' Mister Vorster already knew the answer beyond any reasonable doubt. His first piece of concrete evidence was when Heert Goosen had called at his front

201

door a few months earlier to say he had been walking his dog at the reservoir and seen his son playing on the pier with two kaffir boys. Goosen thought Mister Vorster would have wanted to know and was correct in his assumption.

'The kaffir . . . he's wearing your hunting boots . . . the ones you were given last Christmas.' Mister Vorster sunk down in his chair, deflated. Willem exhaled and breathed in fully, partly in relief that the answer was already known to his father, but also because he would have fainted otherwise. He steadied himself and spoke.

'Yes, Father, he's my friend and I helped him . . . he's my best friend . . . my blood-brother.'

'Your . . . *what*?' whispered his father like he was talking to an imaginary figure.

'My blood-brother. We are blood-brothers. You know?' Willem opened the palm of his hand and pointed to the faint scar under the thumb. A single tear rolled slowly down his father's cheek. There was no anger in his eyes, only disappointment; the sort of gut wrenching disappointment a father might feel in his first seconds of looking down upon the remains of his still-born child - all hopes for a future cruelly and irreversibly snatched away by some confounding force.

Through his emerging grief, Mister Vorster stood up and wiped his eye with the back of his hand. He returned his chair to its position underneath the table then faced Willem.

'Let the kaffir . . . let Victor . . . out of the cupboard. Stay here with him until I return from my briefing in the press shed.'

32
The Lion Tamers

At exactly half-past eight o'clock, just as the second hand on the kitchen clock clicked onto the hour, Miss Johanna led Willem and Victor into the dining room. Mister Vorster was sitting at the head of the table drinking more coffee, this time from a fine, white, china cup and saucer.

'Western Province put seven tries over Free State . . . doesn't surprise me. Luc Van Heerden scored twice - his father owns Gerbervale in Stellenbosch . . . great rugby family, terrible winemakers,' mumbled Mister Vorster, continuing to scour the back pages of the Paarl Post for another headline to prick his interest.

Miss Johanna pulled out the chair one down from top of the table, for Willem to sit by his father's side. She unfolded a linen serviette and placed it on his lap then attended to Victor who was standing patiently behind the chair next to Willem. He was dressed in Willem's borrowed clothes - pressed grey slacks and a short-sleeved white shirt, both of which were the right length but hung off his skinny frame like a pillowcase on a broomstick.

The large black plimsolls on Victor's feet were a welcome change from Willem's boots which were a size too small - a guaranteed recipe for cultivating nasty blisters during a ten-mile trek of escape. Before breakfast, Mary and Willem helped pull off the boots to his considerable discomfort and plunged his feet into a bucket of warm, salty water. Half-an-hour later, the pain had eased and the risk of infection reduced.

A young, new member of the kitchen staff followed in behind Miss Johanna and addressed Mister Vorster before the boys.

'How would you like your eggs, sir'

'Scrambled. Hard scrambled. Bacon with the rind nicely crisped, just before burnt . . . Johanna knows how it's done. The boys will have the same,' said Mister Vorster.

'Ever eaten a breakfast like this before, Victor?' asked Mister Vorster.

'No, sir,' Victor replied. 'I once had tenderloin steak and mashed potatoes - when I lived with my uncle.'

'Did you? Why does that not surprise me? You have big aspirations

203

for yourself, eh?

'I don't know, sir,' he replied.

'Willem leaves for Ascension College in six weeks' time. That great institution makes boys strive for much more than they would ever imagine is possible. Do you know how much money it costs to attend Ascension for one year? . . . One thousand, six hundred rand per term. That works out as . . .'

Victor interrupted. 'Four thousand, eight-hundred rand each year.'

Mister Vorster was taken aback. 'Correct . . . and Ascension teaches much more than basic arithmetic.'

'Where is the puppy, sir?' asked Victor, completely out of sync with the conversation. Willem wished he hadn't asked that question and flicked his foot from underneath the table, hitting Victor's ankle.

'The dog is not your concern, Victor - but he is safe and you will see him later. You can't keep an animal in the kitchen when food is being prepared. Animals carry all sorts of diseases, you should know that if you have an interest in them.'

Willem heard his mother's voice behind the door to the kitchen. She was starting the day in her usual way, fussing over the details of the breakfast and quizzing her staff on the menu and about preparations for the day ahead. She walked in carrying a glass of fresh orange juice with her hair tied in a small ponytail, wearing heavy makeup, a silk, cream blouse and a tight fitting, long pale-blue pencil skirt. The outfit made her look ten years younger.

'Good morning, Mother,' said Willem.

'We have a guest?' was her reply. 'Am I not to be informed about any guests we are to have in the house?' She looked at her husband with a strained smile, clearly having no prior notice from him or the staff.

'There are some rather exceptional circumstances, Gwendoline,' said her husband.

'And what might those be?' she asked, being the only person across Glen Cleaver not to have heard of Victor's escape with the stolen pup and his subsequent capture.

'I'll tell you later . . . let's get breakfast into our stomachs first. I will be with the boys after breakfast,' he said, looking at his son. 'Then overseeing Drakensberg until every last grape is in the presses.' His wife was not in the least bit interested in his itinerary.

'I'm meeting Eleanor for coffee . . . don't know when I'll be back,' she said as if her decision had just been made that second. She stood behind her chair without unfolding her serviette or having sipped any of her orange juice.

'Good luck with your important business, Koibus,' she said, squeezing out a final portion of sarcasm before leaving - still without having looked at her son. The remaining three then heard loud, uninhibited shouting directed at Miss Johanna - all of which preceded a heavily slammed back door.

In the scheme of this morning's events, Mrs Vorster's neurotic outburst was a minor distraction. Victor had hardly noticed that she was in the room and had already gulped down a plate of eggs and bacon, three slices of heavily buttered toast with blackcurrant jam and a large glass of orange juice. Everyone sat in an awkward silence and the new member of staff stood in the background observing the scene like a cardboard cut-out. Mister Vorster nodded to her when his plate was clean, then wiped the corners of his lips with his serviette and pushed his plate forward a few inches. He stood up, stretched his arms wide open, then placed his palms squarely down onto the table.

'Time we put this nasty business to bed, don't you think?' he said.

Willem and Victor nodded in unison. Mister Vorster's balanced approach was new territory for the boys, and unable to dilute their scepticism. With each passing hour, Willem was feeling more relaxed, because his dirty secret - his friendship with Victor - was finally out in the open. It must have helped slightly, being in the familiar and comfortable surroundings of his own home. This was not the case for Victor, he was in the lion's den, waiting for something more sinister to unravel when Mister Vorster eventually discarded his conciliatory mask.

'Come through to my study,' said Mister Vorster.

They left the table and followed into the grandiose front hallway. Victor was not a guest in the true sense of the word, but he behaved like a friend of the family; one of those boys from Paarl Gimnasium that visited with his parents on Sunday afternoons for tea and scones after church. The first and last time Victor had been in the hallway was to find Willem's bedroom, to console him after the unexpected news he would be leaving for Ascension College after the summer.

Mister Vorster pulled a key from his pocket, unlocked the door and strolled into a beautifully presented room. It was usually out of bounds and locked. Willem knew little about what his father got up to in the room. His inklings suggested paperwork and personal letter-writing, sketching of new bottle labels and taking important telephone calls. Sometimes business people and local politicians visited and legalities were signed in the study in the old fashioned way, with a signature from a fountain pen next to a wax seal, de-bossed with the mark of the gold signet ring his father had inherited from his great-grandfather.

Mister Vorster referred to the study as his *'thinking window'*. The reason for the name was obvious when you sat behind the leather-topped, mahogany desk and looked out of the window, down the entire length of Glen Cleaver's driveway and across the valley below. The valley was circled by rough ground and high hills on either side, all belonging to Glen Cleaver, even though none of it was any use for planting vines.

The boys sat and sank into the low, brown, soft-leather settee and waited while Mister Vorster poked around in the drawer at his desk. Light wooden panels clad the walls of the room and especially fitted floor-to-ceiling shelves ran the length of one side, weighed down with hundreds of books, carefully organised in alphabetical order. Victor had heard about libraries on his visits with Indah to her daughter's place in the Bo-Kaap district. She had new books every week and Victor could not understand how she had enough money to afford them, until she explained they were borrowed from the local library. Ever since then, Victor had always dreamed of visiting a library, and now here he was, right in the middle of one, all because he had caused a load of trouble for himself.

'I know exactly what I'm looking for, but it may take a moment. I haven't looked at this book for years,' said Mister Vorster, kicking a set of wheeled steps to the side, then climbing up and reaching for the highest shelf.

Willem elbowed Victor and winked, his way of saying: '*I told you everything would be okay.*' Mister Vorster was balancing on the tip of his toes with an arm outstretched, blindly feeling for the prize.

'Ah-ha . . . here it is!' he said triumphantly, before climbing down and pulling a dry cloth from the desk drawer. He carefully dusted the front and back covers of the book.

'Make me a space,' he said, now in front of the boys on the settee. Willem shuffled to the side and his father landed - like a tonne bag - and wriggled to find a comfortable position in the crater he had formed. He placed the hardback book on his knees, front cover up and read out the title, strap-line and author's name.

'*The Lion Tamer - the history and breeding of the Rhodesian Ridgeback by Cornelius Van Rooyen*'

His thumb and forefinger flicked slowly through the pages from the beginning. He stopped at one page with pictures of ebony-coloured, dog-like figurines standing on their hind legs like humans, dressed in gold-leafed tunics.

'Go behind the settee, Willem,' said his father. Willem stood up and stepped behind to see the wine crate with the young pup sound asleep inside. 'Bring him over to me.'

Willem picked up the warm bundle, which barely stirred, then passed him gently with both hands to his father. It was the first time Victor looked uneasy as he sat watching Mister Vorster handle the little pup. Victor would never trust a man who had sentenced his helpless, pawing companion to such a despicable fate, only a day before. He wanted to snatch him back and run into the bush, but the time for ill-conceived heroics had long passed.

'We can trace this one back seven-thousand years . . . the earliest Egyptians domesticated the drop-eared hound, which is believed to have had a ridge.' He held the pup up to inspect it as he spoke, then handed him back to Willem and continued on flicking through the pages.

'It was three-hundred years ago that our fore-bearers came across the beasts - all thanks to the savage Hottentots - right here among our own hills,' stated Mister Vorster.

In school history classes Willem had been told about the Hottentots as one of three large tribes in southwestern Africa; nomadic black savages that had lived in the region for nearly two-thousand years. I knew them as the Khoikhoi - a tribe of animal grazers and hunters who latterly joined forces with the Xhosa people to fight against the white man when they stole the Cape as their colony, one-hundred and fifty years earlier. The Khoikhoi were master marksmen and proved to be a real thorn in the side for white armies as they set about ravaging our people and expelling them from their lands.

'We learned from those Hottentot savages that their dogs were invaluable protectors - and so began a programme of breeding. The Rhodesian Ridgeback is bred all across southern Africa and became a first-class guard dog in South Africa; on pastoral farms in Matabeleland, on boundary fences around the mines in the Krugersdorp and the Witwatersrand . . . and all the way down here to wine country,' said Mister Vorster. 'This brings me to the problem I have with the messy business of your behaviour, Victor,' he said, closing the book and placing it on the low table in front of the settee.

'The Rhodesian Ridgeback is the most faithful of all living creatures. This dog will run all day on scraps of food and a few drops of water . . . under a baking Kalahari sun or on an icy morning on the high veld . . . and he'll *never* get sick. . . . If a pride of lions or a pack of hyenas is bearing down on his master, this dog will step in to protect him. It will fight to the death - without question. And in a few cases, it will *triumph* against the mighty lion.

I've seen it with my own eyes . . . that's how the Rhodesian Ridgeback earned the title *'Lion Tamer'* . . . So as you might imagine Victor, it is no small matter that you would disrupt my breeding cycle.' Mister Vorster pushed himself up and out of the settee, standing menacingly above the boys.

'I would never have brought the pups to any harm,' said Victor.

'But you already have, boy! These are attack dogs, not cuddly toys,' he replied, pointing at the pup on Willem's lap and waiting for his composure to return.

'You can't break into private property, steal and go on the run without serious consequences . . . But I don't only blame you, Willem has played his part, of that I am sure,' he said. Protestations would have been churlish, so we sat quietly, awaiting his final verdict.

'You are lucky I am in a generous mood. The weather is perfect for the last day of harvest and I can almost taste another award winner. But a crime is a crime . . . and every person has to be called to account . . . to make amends. Are you willing to make amends, young Victor?'

'I think so,' Victor replied, without knowing what he might be agreeing to.

'Very good. After this we will wipe the slate clean, eh? Start afresh?'

'Yes, sir,' said Victor.

Willem did not know what amends *he* was going to have to make. Perhaps his truthful disclosure earlier that morning was enough; and with the grounds of Ascension College being eight-hundred miles from Glen Cleaver, Willem's father had extinguished any possibility that his friendship with Victor could continue - even if he still had a job in the bunkhouse, which looked highly unlikely.

'I've got something to show you. You can bring the pup, Willem,' said his father.

All three walked out of the main door in a line, Willem at the back with the little chwama held softly over his shoulder. Victor was hobbling behind Mister Vorster at the front. Despite wearing Willem's plimsolls, each of Victor's steps looked painful, as he forced himself through the searing hot pain of raw blisters. He crunched across the gravel, then onto hard, dry ground, struggling to keep up. By the time they had walked through the courtyard and onto higher ground, Willem was increasingly curious.

'Where are we going, Father?' he asked.

'It's a surprise. There is a wonderful spot I used to play at as a child. I haven't been up there for over thirty years.' It did not take long for Willem to work out where his father was taking them . . . his secret pool, that sacred place where he, Victor and I had formed the most cherished of friendships.

I was standing, watching, holding a pair of cutters with a sore, bent back, hidden among a busy crowd of pickers and baskets on Drakensberg, as Mister Vorster, Willem and Victor walked up the track adjacent to the vines. There was no sign of trauma in Willem's face, and with the little chwama asleep on his shoulder, a tinge of hopefulness spread throughout my body. That warm feeling appeared so rarely these days that I wanted to bottle it and drink it until I was bloated. Victor gave me much more cause for concern. It was strange to see him in Willem's clothes. Gone was his understated confidence. He looked defeated, walking with a pronounced limp, wincing each time his foot landed. He was the last person I had expected to see.

Mister Vorster led them up through the shadow of the oak trees and across dry grass, scrub and wild fynbos blanketing the hillside. To the trained eye, there was a faint path, trodden by the soles of feet, that regularly meandered towards the pool.

Mister Vorster arrived at the top of the precipice that led down into the water. He stood in silence and breathed in the view of the deep blue water below and the pale blue canvass above.

'Quite something, isn't it? No matter how dry it gets in summer, this pool is always full. It's like a secret Kalahari watering hole.'

'It's amazing, Father,' said Willem, maintaining his act of innocence.

Victor didn't speak. He knew that to share his experience of this place would have sullied Mister Vorster's fond memories forever.

'I used to dive-bomb off here with my friends every summer holidays when I was back from Ascension . . . the *Tin Openers*, we called ourselves. For the life of me, I can't even remember why we came up with that stupid name.' For a few seconds Mister Vorster looked stranded on an island of pleasant reminiscence, until the reason for our trip came gushing back, more vociferous and impatient than before.

'But we are not here for high-jinks, are we boys? We are here to complete the breeding cycle. You need to make your amends with me, little kaffir.' He pointed aggressively at Victor, rage brimming in the veins of his neck.

Willem recognised the tone in his father's voice and his false sense of security vanished, replaced by a rising fear in his chest. Victor looked at Willem, disconcerted and confused.

'There is only one way to tell if that pup is a Lion Tamer, my little kaffir. The good dogs swim, the bad ones don't. It's as simple as that,' said Mister Vorster with menace in his eyes.

209

Willem understood the insinuation. His father had brought them here to drown the little pup. Victor would have to do it; throw it from twenty-feet high, down into the cold, suffocating water. It had no chance, not even if its injuries had healed. Willem instinctively stepped back from his father. He removed the pup from his shoulder and cradled it tightly, defensively into his chest.

'Come, boy! Don't you dare fokin' disobey me!' hissed his father.

'How can you do this?' Willem pleaded initially . . . before refusing. 'I won't let you!'

'Won't let me? You won't *fokin' let me!*' A plum hue was visible under the skin on Mister Vorster's brow. 'Your disgraceful taste for mutiny will be your final flourish, boy.' He crept slowly forward towards his son. 'Without your birthright, I'd throw you in with that fokin' pup myself.'

Willem turned to run. His first step dragged on a clump of grass and he stumbled, falling softly to the ground, careful to protect the young, innocent pup in his arms. His father was on top of him instantly, forcefully grabbing and twisting his forearm.

'Arrgh . . . you're hurting me,' shouted Willem as his muscles relinquished and the pup fell free. He stayed on the ground, watching his father amble towards Victor. Victor was standing helplessly but calmly, observing Mister Vorster as much in curiosity as disdain.

'*Hardship* forms character, little kaffir . . . not *comfort.*' Mister Vorster held the pup out invitingly towards Victor, with his bare, muscular forearm. He then lifted it underneath the belly, allowing the legs to dangle freely in the air. The little chwama's eyes blinked with awareness, although his limbs bore no faculty due to the extent of his injuries. 'Throw him into the pool and make your amends. If he swims, I have a *Lion Tamer.* If he sinks . . . then all you had, was a *petting lamb.*'

Victor didn't flinch; his eyes offering little more than vague curiosity.

'Oh . . . *poor little kaffir!* Don't have the stomach for it? . . . Well, I do . . .' Mister Vorster clutched the rear of the pup's neck, turned to the pool and swung his arm backwards, like he was tossing-away one of his half-smoked cigars.

Anger and defiance exploded from Victor's eyes. This demented, tribal warrior had been waiting and preparing for this battle his whole life. He bounded forwards, solely focused on Mister Vorster's arm which would soon dispatch Victor's beloved pup into the ether. As Mister Vorster's arm accelerated, the young pup's eyes closed firmly, resigned to its fate and the impending trajectory.

Victor's attempt to save the young chwama was a noble but futile act; his goliath opponent instinctively braced himself, turned sideways and dropped his shoulder. Mister Vorster soaked-up the collision like it was a mild inconvenience. Victor shuddered into his dense, heavy body and immediately rebounded in pain.

Mister Vorster's slaughterous arm carried forward unperturbed then his grip released. The helpless, brown pup flew silently, up, out and over Victor's head. It hung in view for less than a second before gravity necessitated that its lungs become intimately acquainted with the water below.

Victor stood dazed, stumbling in front of Mister Vorster. That is when a rigid, heavy forearm slammed into the side of his head. It connected with the entire length of his jaw-line, from the tip of his chin to high above his ear.

'Fokin' vermin!' shouted Mister Vorster, perfectly timing the insult to land with the strike of his arm.

Victor's legs gave-way like a young springbok absorbing a hunter's accurately dispatched rifle-shot; his body relinquished, but his mind had not yet registered the severity of the strike. He descended headfirst towards the flat rocky ledge that he had jumped-off a hundred times before. His skull smashed onto the sharp, umber rock with a deathly effectiveness; cracking like an ostrich egg courting a sharp axe. The momentum carried Victor's body over the ledge and down into the cold blue.

A loud, cumbersome splash - of Victor's dead weight hitting the water - reverberated upwards and merged with the echo of Willem's pulverising scream. The scream soon vanished among the screeching calls of hundreds of birds rising from the undergrowth to flee the scene. Frantic black dots peppered the azure sky in all directions as Willem jumped onto the ledge and peered over. He saw Victor's body floating, face-down on the surface. Water filled his lungs and warm blood decanted from his forehead. Victor's faithful, young chwama had arrived a few seconds beforehand, plopping into the pool like a small, innocuous pebble, before spinning downwards to settle in a cold, dark, invisible resting place. Victor's body sank to join his little chwama, on the floor of the pool.

'No!' screamed Willem. He stepped out from the ledge fully clothed, sucked-in a large breath and slipped through the air with arms flailing. He landed with pointed toes and submerged. His first attempt to retrieve Victor's body was his best; he got hold of an arm and an ankle, but the soaking weight dragged him down to the bottom. He surfaced to breathe then repeated his attempt again, and again. No amount of adrenaline can grow a second set of lungs and after a handful of dives, Willem could not swim halfway towards Victor's remains resting on the bottom.

Mister Vorster had walked briskly down the steep bank of the stream below the pool to find an entrance to the stream. He walked upstream towards the pool, stepping from rock to rock, then waded into the water, splashing and swimming towards Willem who was treading water in the middle. Still fully clothed, he gulped and dived down headfirst, returning to the surface, struggling with Victor's body in his arms.

'Help me! Help me!' he shouted at Willem, gasping for air, mucus streaming from his sinuses.

With no reserves of energy, Willem offered little support. At the shallows, his father lifted Victor's body, slung it over his shoulder and carried it downstream, narrowly avoiding a fall. He retraced his steps, dragging and scraping the carcass over dust and dirt, up onto the bank. The stiffening body no longer belonged to Victor.

When Willem ran past his father, tears were streaming down his face.

'Christ, Willem! It was an accident. It was a fokin' accident, boy' said his father. Willem kept on running, never looking back. The growing, insurmountable distance between father and son could not silence Mister Vorster's protestations.

'WILLEM! WILLEM! Jesus Christ! If he'd only done what he was told, this would never have happened . . . WILLEM!' Mister Vorster continued shouting for his son, even when he was beyond the oak trees and far out of sight and sound.

'WILLEM! It was an accident . . . an accident, I tell you! I'll have to live with this you know!' he shouted, repeating the sentiment over and over. Perhaps if he repeated those words for long enough he might eventually believe them.

33
The Study

On the dusty, hillside track leading up beside Drakensberg, Mallie and Toppie lay on their sides, sheltering from the sun underneath the tractor's trailer. Master Boss was nearby, slumped in the shade of the tractors bloated rear tyre. I was picking grapes in a row of vines, directly in sight. Workers were widely dispersed; a crowd of blue collars, black heads and woollen hats, sailing across a calm sea of green foliage.

Mallie and Toppie rolled onto their forelegs with stiffened ears and moved their gaze to the oak trees above the vineyard.

'What you two sniffing at?' said Master Boss, reluctant to get up out of the shade.

The dogs walked, whimpering with concern, into the open from the rear of the trailer, arousing Master Boss's suspicions. I peered over the vines to see Willem's blonde head of hair moving fast along the top of Drakensberg, towards the path. He ran down the slope to the tractor with his arms flailing like a rag-doll's. Mallie and Toppie ran forward, jumping and bouncing back and forth unpredictably, with a mixture of excitement and concern. Willem's sole purpose was to get past and continue downhill.

'What's going on, Willem?' asked Master Boss, looking confused rather than concerned even though Willem was clearly distraught.

Willem slowed to a walk, then began running again as he reached the tractor. Master Boss did not like being ignored and ran to block his route, then grabbed the tops of Willem's arms to prevent him from going any further.

'Whoa, hold up, boy. What's going on?' he said firmly.

'Get off me,' Willem screamed, using clenched fists to hit Master Boss's arms away. His fists had no effect, but Master Boss's hands fell limp to his side voluntarily. Willem pushed him to one side and continued running and sobbing.

Whatever it was, it was bad, that much I knew. I dropped low to the ground and crawled along my row, to the far side of the vineyard, away from Master Boss. When I sat up and poked by head through the foliage, Willem was beside the estate building, not yet out of sight. Mallie and Toppie raced each other towards the forlorn, sodden, weary figure now standing

213

underneath the umbrella of the oak trees. Mister Vorster was watching the distance grow between himself and his son.

'Ringidd!' shouted Master Boss.

'Coming, Danie,' he said, scraping past a handful of perplexed Roggeland pickers.

'Get this lot into the presses,' he said, pointing to the full baskets of grapes on the trailer. 'Take Roggeland to the press shed and everyone else back to the bunkhouse. Then go tell Miss Johanna to bring everyone an early lunch. When you're done, go to the office and wait for me there. Understand?'

'Yes, Danie,' Ringidd replied, without urgency, slowly beckoning the pickers with a limp hand as Master Boss jogged to Mister Vorster underneath the trees.

Workers carried baskets of grapes, of varying weights, back to the trailer and gathered in two huddles awaiting instruction. Charlie, Johnson, Barclay and Bostock climbed onto the trailer to secure the baskets before the tractor chugged alive and Ringidd guided it down the track in neutral, feathering the brake pedal to make sure his cargo had the smoothest ride - the grapes that is, not the men. The workers following behind looked like a tribal procession, slow-marching their way to a burial site.

In the commotion, nobody but Charlie registered my disappearance. He stood up tall, subtly scanning the brown spaces between the innumerable leafy rows of vines. He didn't find me; grapes were kissing my cheeks I was pressed in so close. I ripped out some leafy stalks, splayed their branches, and held a leafy green fan in my hand, as camouflage. When I popped up, I couldn't see a soul, not on the higher ground by the oak trees, nor down on the lower ground towards the estate buildings.

I dropped my bouquet and ran to the track, with a nagging feeling that Mallie or Toppie's eerie sixth sense might catch me out. For the first time in a long while, I had forgotten myself because my thoughts were with my two friends.

I reached the back door to the kitchen and barged inside. Beyond the vestibule, the new girl dropped an urn of soup she was dragging across the tiles. Hot liquid splashed onto her shins and she shrieked, then a river of steaming yellow spread out across the floor.

'What in hell's name you doing, boy?' shouted Miss Johanna, but I was already on the other side of the room, opening the door to the corridor. I ran to the Vorster's hallway.

'Willem! Willem! It's George, Willem!' I shouted.

A key turned in the lock of the study door. It opened slowly and

Willem stood under the frame holding a golf club. His eyes were raw and bloodshot and there were cuts and bruises on his knuckles.

'He killed him, George . . .' Willem dropped the club and slumped to the floor.

The news hit me like a wrecking ball to the chest.

'Wh-what?' I stuttered, even though I heard him perfectly the first time.

Miss Johanna stood in her apron holding a white kitchen towel at the end of the corridor. She had heard every word and shuffled towards us. The sharp smell of alcohol was like a warning shot for her eyes, which would shortly witness the devastation. Willem had stolen the spare key to the study and vented blind fury. Almost every inch of the room was dismantled and unrecognisable. You could not see the floor for scattered books, torn papers, upturned furniture, and broken wine bottles. Willem had poured out the entire contents of twelve bottles of Glen Cleaver's Vintage Reserve - Mister Vorster's pride and joy. Red wine was dripping from the walls into shallow pools on the floor. The two remaining bottles of Mister Vorster's grandfather's 1897 vintage were in pieces, and their contents were slowly blending with the vintage reserve.

'You gotta go, George . . . they is coming,' whispered Miss Johanna. She saw Master Boss and Willem's father walking towards the front door of the house through the study window.

'I'm not going without you, Willem,' I said.

We ran.

34
Tractor

I didn't cry because I refused to believe it. *What would Victor do in the same circumstances*, I asked myself, running into the woods with Willem. *He would do what is right, is what he would do,* I told myself. We reached cover and a deep, dark canyon of wallowing grief beckoned. But I was not yet ready to jump in.

'We'll be safe if we can get to Charlie,' I said, knowing there was no other place to go but the bunkhouse.

'I don't care where we go,' said Willem.

'We'll have to go round the long way to avoid Ringidd.'

'I don't care a damn about Ringidd,' replied Willem, cutting the conversation dead. We walked further from the estate house, deeper into trees.

'What about your father? Will he come for us?' I asked.

'Probably.'

We zig-zagged across the eastern edge of Glen Cleaver's grounds, returning near to Drakensberg. Hidden among the trees below the plantation, Willem stopped walking.

'Shhhh. Listen,' he said.

'What?'

'Listen,' he said again. 'It's the tractor. It's coming towards us.'

We moved behind a thicket and waited. The noise got steadily louder, then the tractor came into view. It turned at the foot of the track and crunched into the lowest gear to climb up the slope. Master Boss was driving, pulling Ringidd on the trailer behind. He lay flat on his back, supporting his head on a ruffled pile of white sheeting with bent knees and his ankles tucked into his backside. The sides of the trailer were lowered, fixed to hooks on the chassis and the only other object on top of the flat wooden surface was a small green jerry-can cradled underneath Ringidd's armpit.

'Where's it going?' I asked, watching the tractor bellow thick, black smoke and slowly crawl forward, as it worked hard on the steepening gradient in the scrub beyond the track. It climbed all the way up to the oak trees and stopped. Ringidd jumped off and Master Boss reversed and turned the tractor to face back downhill. He applied the hand-brake and turned off the engine. Ringidd waited under the trees until Master Boss joined him and they walked away out of sight, across the estate boundary.

'It's safe to go, Willem,' I said.

'I want to wait here,'

'Why? We can get to Charlie - he'll help us.'

'I want to see what they're up to.'

We sat silently for another few minutes. The picture of Victor's face and the echo of his words began spinning around my head.

'Do you think the picking will start again?' I asked. Willem ignored me. I didn't push, knowing he must still be in shock. When he finally spoke he started the story from early evening the night before, less than an hour after Charlie and I had said goodbye to Victor. His monotone recount changed as he relived Victor's last few breath-filled moments at the pool. He could not contain his distress and anguish, coughing and choking on his words. I shuffled close, put my arm around his shoulder and pulled his head into my chest while he sobbed. I sat with my friend, comforting him as best as I could until he composed himself, sitting up from my side and wiping his eyes.

'I'm sorry, George.'

'You've nothing to be sorry about,' I replied.

'I wish that Victor had killed my father - not the other way around,' he said, smearing his runny nose with the back of his hand.

'You've got to run away from here, George . . . and never come back,' he said.

'I know.'

'I can help you,' he said. 'Does anyone in the bunkhouse drive?'

'I think Barclay does,' I said . . . 'And I heard Bostock used to drive a bakkie on the farm he worked on near Worcester.'

'I'll be at the bunkhouse before midnight. My parents are in bed by ten . . . so make sure you are ready. No more than five . . . and you must have a driver.'

'I know Barclay will come . . . and Charlie. I won't go without Charlie. He promised Victor he would look after me . . . he won't break a promise, not to Victor,' I said.

'You can't come back. You understand that, don't you?' he said. I nodded.

'What about you? What are you going to do?'

'I'll be at boarding school in six weeks. I never thought I would be glad about that.'

'You could come live with me and Charlie in Tolongo.'

'Thanks, George. When I'm old enough, I promise I'm leaving here. I'm going to buy a ticket for a ship to sail me away . . . America, that's where I'll go,' he said, pulling out a thin slice of biltong from the top pocket of his shirt. He ripped off half and we sat together chewing.

Willem nudged me when he saw Master Boss and Ringidd reappear from the trees. They were straining hard to carry Victor, wrapped up tightly in the white sheet, with a large red blotch that had appeared at one end. They swung the body on the count of three and threw it up onto the trailer like the rotting carcass of a young impala. Hate is a strong word, and one I have learnt to shy away from, but when I saw them bundle him up like that, I remember thinking that some people are beyond redemption. Hate is like a poison when it incubates in a person, but in this moment, as I watched Master Boss and Ringidd, all I saw was a complicit, conscious evil that was most definitely worthy of hatred; my hatred, Willem's hatred, anyone's hatred.

'He really is dead,' I said in disbelief. 'I've never seen a dead body before' I mumbled.

'I saw my grandmother after she died. She was lying in an open coffin before they buried her . . . wearing a white dress with her hair all done up and bright red lipstick that made her mouth look twice the size. She looked like a ghost. They kept her in our drawing room for a night before the funeral. My mother and father were in there by themselves first, then they called me in, then some of the staff. My father put on my grandmother's favourite record - The Duke Ellington Orchestra, that's how old Duke in the bunkhouse got his name when he arrived - and we all stood there, around her coffin listening to the music, acting like we were sad she was gone . . . All anybody ever said when she was alive was how much they hated her.' He paused for a second to let the ghoulish scene sink in. 'Let's cut across. They won't see us in the vines,' he said.

I didn't feel like moving, but Willem jogged off ahead of me, walking deep into a row of vines in the middle of Drakensberg. We sunk down together, with a view of the track at the other end of the row. When our heads crept up above the cover, Ringidd was securing Victor's body with a piece of rope fixed either side of the trailer. The tractor's engine chugged to life and slowly rolled downhill, pulling the butcher's cart behind it.

'Where are they taking him?' I asked.

'I don't know, but we should tell the police.'

'The police?'

'Victor was murdered, George,' said Willem, without a shred of

218

doubt.

'Will the police come for a kaffir?'

'Of course. For anyone,' said Willem.

'How do you know that?'

'It's the law . . . and it happens in the Hardy Boys,' he said.

'The Hardy Boys?' I looked at him like he was speaking another language.

'You know? The brothers in America. I gave Victor one of their books to read to you,' he said, looking dismayed.

'That book without pictures?' I asked.

'Yeah . . . the ones with the words . . . like it's so weird to find in a book.'

'I only liked the ones with the pictures,' I said.

'The Hardy Boys are boys like us. Their father is a police detective and they solve murders and mysteries and always report them to the police,' he explained.

'But won't the police take your father away, Willem?

'I hope so. I hope they lock him in jail forever,' he replied.

The tractor slowly meandered downhill as Master Boss searched for the least disruptive route. The noisy, rattling engine reverberated through the ground beneath us and we could smell the black exhaust fumes in the air around us. The trailer clattered, bounced and rocked from side to side so ferociously that Victor's body shuffled halfway across the back. Ringidd was sitting on the shins trying to stop it from falling. Victor's head slipped over the side and the white sheet came loose, repeatedly hiding and revealing his lifeless face as it hung, swinging and banging in time to the wheels rolling over the terrain. Blood from the large gash on the side of his forehead had congealed and a small cloud of flies were gorging on the feast.

Seeing my friend's dead remains had been so unexpected that I felt sick. I lay on the dirt, held my stomach and wretched, discharging on the earth below me. The noise was muffled by the tractor's engine. Thankfully, Willem had not seen what I had. He turned towards me as I scrunched up in pain, accepting there was nothing he could do. By the time the tractor engine was a gentle rumble in the distance I was stretched out flat on my back with my eyes closed and my hands clasped, resting on my clammy forehead. Each breath I took was deep and slow and searching for one fresh, untainted pocket of air to fill my lungs. Nothing could remove the picture of Victor's head hanging from that trailer. And although I was too far away to smell anything apart from the exhaust fumes, the picture imprinted a mark upon my nostrils. It is a smell that is hard to describe, but I imagine it is what death smells like. It was a grey, decaying smell; like life receding and recycling, like an ugly grub undergoing premature metamorphosis without the energy to complete the process.

This picture of Victor is the last one I had. I was forced to remember him that way for all too long - in my dreams, in my nightmares. There was a time when I thought that last glimpse of his face would be indelibly marked on my conscience - like a torturous, hopeless reminder of all that is wrong with this world.

I never found out whether it was the crack on his head or the water in his lungs that killed him. I tell myself that it was the head injury and that his life ended like a switch turns off a light. In that case he would not have seen his little chwama sink to that undignified end before his own.

35
Woodpile

The tractor disappeared. With no sign of life on the estate, we walked along the rear wall of the press shed and heard voices rumbling inside.

In the courtyard, five Roggeland workers were standing by the doors smoking. We ignored them and continued on to the estate offices.

'Will you come in to make the phone-call?' asked Willem.

'What phone-call?' I enquired.

'The police. There is a phone in the office.'

'What if Mallie and Toppie are inside?'

'They're in the kennels if my father or Danie are not around,' reassured Willem. Everything was as he said; one phone on the table and no dogs.

Willem sat behind the desk and picked up the phone as I snooped around.

'What's the number for the police?' asked Willem.

'How would I know?'

Willem grimaced and slapped his forehead.

'There must be a directory,' he muttered, standing to check the shelves behind him.

'Here is it.'

He held up a small, stapled booklet, no more than twenty pages deep. He found two numbers on the first page, below *Community Contacts*.

'Commissioner Du Toit or the police house?'

'I don't know.'

'I'm going straight to the top,' he said. His index finger rotated the circular dial as he put the handset to his ear, waiting for it to connect. I had never used a phone and could hardly believe that Willem could speak to someone that was not here in the room. Nobody answered.

'Maybe he's at the police house.' He dialled the next number.

'Sergeant Steyn,' said a man, answering abruptly and catching Willem by surprise. From the tone of the sergeant's voice, the call was an unwelcome interruption.

'I am phoning to report a murder,' said Willem.

'Who is this?' replied the sergeant, recognising the caller was a boy.

'There has been a murder on the Glen Cleaver estate. You have to come quickly,' said Willem without giving his name.

'*Who is this?* If it's a prank, you are in trouble, boy,' said Sergeant Steyn.

'Did you not hear me? *I said . . . there has been a murder. Glen Cleaver*. Come and do your damn job.' Willem slammed down the receiver leaving the police officer hanging on the end of the line.

'Domkopf!' said Willem.

'Do you think they will come?'

'He'd be pretty stupid not to,' said Willem.

'Can we get out of here now?' I said, popping my head around the door to check the walkway was clear.

'Midnight at the bunkhouse . . . okay, George?' said Willem.

'I'll be ready, Willem. I promise.'

Willem held out his right hand for me to shake. I reciprocated, but Willem laughed and pulled my hand towards him and bear-hugged me.

'Blood-brothers, George . . . forever,' he said.

'Blood-brothers,' I replied. Willem walked away, striding like a different person to the one I knew. His usual, directionless, purposeless meander was replaced with a purposeful march, like a straight-backed soldier ready for a fearless confrontation with his enemy - his father, I imagine.

'Be careful, Willem,' I called after him. He didn't look back, simply raised his arm with his index finger pointed assuredly to the sky and continued bounding forward.

As I entered the track to the bunkhouse under the cover of the karee trees, I heard cars driving quickly up the towards the estate house. I am sure the first was Mrs Vorster, followed in close succession by the police.

Just past Ringidd's place, I heard the tractor again. It was driving down a rough, overgrown track from a clearing up in the trees. I ducked down and watched Master Boss flicker between gaps in the trees. The tractor was pulling an empty trailer and I was instantly confused as to why Ringidd and Victor's body were not with it. When the rumble of the engine and the clinking of the trailer faded, I retraced its tracks. My feet crunched on a dry, bouncy carpet of dead leaves and twigs that snapped underneath me. There was still little sign of life, as if the insects and birds had migrated. The picture of Victor's severed forehead came into my mind once again and that smell reappeared at my nostrils. I clasped my stomach and steadied myself, feeling that I could be sick again.

In a clearing, Ringidd was standing next to a rotting woodpile in the middle. Willem said that every few years the local community used the clearing to light a bonfire during Halloween. Everyone paid money to attend and kids got dressed up as witches or ghouls with painted faces. The event was meant for the children, but the adults used it as an excuse to drink beer and wine while their kids spooked each other and gorged themselves on sweets and toffee-coated apples. The evening ended with everyone gathered in the middle with their heads turned up towards the night sky to watch a firework display, ignited from the hillside above the woods.

Considering Ringidd's feeble and decrepit physique, he had miraculously heaved Victor's limp body onto the woodpile. He twisted the sheeting tightly at either end like the wrapper of a caramel and tied it with twine. The pile was not level and Victor's legs slipped and lay precariously, like they would pull his torso over. Ringidd stepped onto the logs and fumbled around with the body, pushing it up and wedging the legs into place with a strenuous effort.

He gathered the jerry-can, unscrewed the lid and freely, generously splashed gasoline over the wood. Diesel fumes slapped my nostrils as he took the packet of matches from his pocket. He struck one match, then a second. Only the third ignited. He flung it onto the pile, triggering a violent explosion. Flames jumped out in all directions then just as quickly shrunk as a small, black mushroom-cloud formed above.

The first thing to burn with any enthusiasm was the white sheet and Victor's overalls. They must have soaked up the diesel, quickly turning ashen and falling away to reveal Victor's naked body. His two legs slipped again; black and pink in equal measure. Why did they kill my friend? Why were they burning his body? I turned and ran and did not stop until I reached the bunkhouse, bouncing up the steps and barging the door open. The whole room was scattered with men; at their beds, standing, sitting drinking coffee. Startled faces and silence rippled through the room.

'Mister Vorster killed Victor. He killed him! They are burning his body in the forest,' I shouted through a mist of tears.

Charlie stood up and ran towards me. He shook me steady. 'Show me, George. Show me.'

He turned and looked at the others. 'Come if you want.'

I didn't need to show where, because he could see and smell the line of smoke rising high from the clearing in the trees. He ran, quickly followed by Barclay, then Bostock and finally, by Franklin. The only person I felt safe to be with was Charlie, so I ran after him, at half the pace.

When I reached the clearing, the woodpile was roaring strong and high. It had taken only a few short minutes for Victor's charred body to become indistinguishable from the blackened, flaming logs surrounding him.

It was Ringidd's misfortune not to have left the clearing after the fire was lit. He must have tried to run when he saw Charlie and Barclay bound into the clearing, but a lame old baboon is no match for two wild, hungry lions. Charlie pinned him against a tree trunk, lifting him two feet off the ground. His free hand was wrapped around his neck, suffocating him. He relaxed his grip just as Ringidd was about to lose consciousness and he fell to the ground, breathing in air like a newborn child taking its first breaths.

'Don't ever come back, Ringidd. Hear?' said Charlie.

Ringidd was in no state to speak, but nodded frantically.

'You come back here . . . near the bunkhouse . . . or near Glen Cleaver . . . and I will kill you with them bare hands.' He splayed the palms of his hands out in front of Ringidd's face to reinforce the point.

Ringidd would have been pleased if there had been a mirror in the clearing because he looked whiter and paler than I thought possible for a black man.

'Go. Go find a hole to hide in,' said Charlie. When Ringidd didn't move, he kicked him, hard. 'Go, I'm said.'

Ringidd scratched at the earth below him, trying to find some purchase with his fingers to pull himself up. He didn't have the strength, so crawled and kept crawling towards the beginning of the overgrown path.

Barclay, Bostock and Franklin stood around Charlie. In his anger, Charlie's bad eye - normally hidden and closed over with skin - was now wide open revealing his white, blind eyeball. His muscles had enlarged as fury pumped adrenalin around his body, excavating large pulsing veins in his forearms below the cuffs of his blue overalls, rolled to the elbow.

He walked slowly across the clearing and the others followed. I watched from the far side then joined them. Charlie walked right up to the fire, so close that he put his arms up in front of his face to protect himself from the heat. I thought he was going to try and climb up there and drag Victor off, but it was too ferocious for that. He turned to see me standing a few yards behind, then walked over and took my arm, pulling me gently forward, close to the fire, to stand beside him. My big, loyal giant of a friend slumped down onto his knees on the grass in front of the woodpile and whispered something to himself. We stood silently, hypnotised by the flames, the crackling and the sparks. My mind was blank, relieved of all past memories and future worries. In those few seconds I had my first real taste of life, the truest taste of it.

'We come back after dark . . . send Victor to his ancestors. They will gather for him. Everyone comes for the bravest warriors,' said Charlie.

'Willem said he will help five of us to leave tonight, before midnight,' I said on our way back to the bunkhouse.

'How he going to do that, George' asked Bostock.

'You drive, don't you? And Barclay?' I asked.

'I don't drive so good. What about you, Barclay?' said Bostock.

'I drive, man. But I ain't not driving out from here until we got payback for Victor and Mary,' said Barclay.

'What payback man, Barclay?' asked Charlie in his usual slow, deep and now sceptical voice.

'We can fight them if we get all the men. We can break into the workshop and the potting shed and get tools, then smash up the estate, empty the wine tanks and lynch them,' he raved.

'I say we take the Vorsters, Masta Boss and Ringidd, strip them naked, tie them and drag them all the way up to the clearing and hang 'em,' said Franklin.

'Or burn them on the same pile as Victor,' interrupted Bostock.

'All you gonna do get shot by one Mister Vorster's guns, Franklin. He be sleeping with it every night now,' said Charlie. 'I bet he got Mallie and Toppie at them end his bed too,' he warned.

Franklin looked disappointed and a little foolish to have been put in his place so succinctly, he was never the type to go on a rampage of this sort. Barclay on the other hand, well I wouldn't have put that past him, even if it resulted in his death. If you had told me he was capable of such a thing a week ago I would have said it was impossible - but sometimes the measure of a man changes with the severity of his circumstances.

'If there only space for five, who goes?' asked Bostock.

'Me, George, Barclay, Franklin and you . . . that's it . . . don't none mention it to the others hear?' threatened Charlie. We all nodded in agreement.

36
From the Fringe of the Fire

'After food, I want you to go down with Barclay and collect herbs from the garden,' said Charlie, looking at me and Barclay.

'The walled garden?' I asked.

'Yes.' he said, lifting the metal bucket to rinse it at the sink.

'What herbs, Charlie?' I asked, confused about the request rather than worried about the dangers.

'Thems that smells strong. I don't know no names,' he said.

Food was served from the remaining stew and pap in the large urn, with two loaves of bread from the wicker baskets that had been delivered from the kitchen after lunch. The stew was a notch warmer than cold, but undeniably more nutritious and flavoursome than the meals we cooked for ourselves. I had no appetite. For the last six hours I had been walking around in a perpetual state of queasiness.

'Eat up, George,' said Charlie. He walked over to the table, having seen that I was shuffling food around my plate as my mind wandered to an imaginary cave in the clouds. He bent down and put his inflatable lips to my ear.

'Time for to be strong, George. We is leaving tonight . . . you not getting far on them cup water,' he whispered. I forced a mouthful down my throat and the sludge hit my stomach making me feel worse than before. I pushed the plate away in protest then walked outside for some fresh air, summoning all my concentration to stop me from throwing up.

The first thin arc of a new moon and a handful of the brightest stars came in and out of view as a few large, well-defined clouds were blown gently across the night sky. I sat there mesmerised by the enormity of it all and for a second I saw the clouds and the shadows converge to paint a picture of Victor's face. He was smiling, subtly reprimanding me for looking so sad. 'Cheer up, George . . . it ain't so bad.' I heard him say.

Even in death Victor knew the right thing to say. He had been robbed of his life, and here I was embroiled again in an impenetrable bubble of self-pity.

'Maybe I'm just not as strong as you, Victor, I thought to myself. Our imaginary conversation continued.

226

'But that's it, George . . . don't you see?'

'See what?'

'You know it, George. You already know it.'

'Know what Victor? . . . Know what? . . . Stop talking in riddles.'

'You don't have to be anything more, or anything less, than you already are George . . . that is the secret . . . remember it.'

I stared out onto the turning circle, trying to absorb and decipher the advice. When my gaze returned to the night sky, the clouds had parted.

I slumped down onto the steps and cried, allowing myself to finally grieve, seven hours after hearing the tragic news of his death. I missed my friend so much.

'I lost my brother. He was nine and I was eleven,' said Franklin, standing at my side smoking a cigarette. In my consumed state I hadn't heard him open or close the door, nor smelt the ammonia trail of his cigarette. Franklin was not a person of many words, but it was all I needed to hear. I found some comfort that I was not alone in the burden of such painful emotions.

Charlie stomped around the bunkhouse swinging his metal bucket by his side, stopping at the end of each bunk then repeatedly hitting the bucket with a metal spoon to get each person's attention. He wanted donations of umqombothi. I say donations, but there was nothing voluntary about it. His low, deep voice issued one repeated command . . . *'Umqombothi! - All that you have.'*

Charlie was angry at the indifference most men had shown about Victor's *accident* and was looking for the slightest excuse to start swinging his oversized fists at anyone that stepped an inch out of line. Nobody wanted to part with their dwindled stash after so many hard days at work, but it didn't make the slightest whit of difference to Charlie on this particular evening.

'Charlie will say goodbye to Victor proper, George,' said Franklin, walking back inside. When the door closed behind him I sat up straight and stuttered air into my lungs, the way it happens after a long cry. I felt better for the release, if a little drained. Before I stood up to get Barclay to chaperone me to the herb garden, I had unfinished business to conclude with my friend.

'I'm not going to let you down, Victor,' I murmured under my breath. 'No more feeling sorry for myself, I promise.' I stood there letting the words sink in and wiped my eyes. Inside, Charlie stood at the table with his bucket half-full. Eugene, Peter and Duke were the last three in line, each holding old, recycled bottles of umqombothi that had miraculously appeared at the point Charlie was going to upturn their bunks.

227

Barclay and I returned from the walled garden less than an hour later and reported that two bakkie loads of Roggeland workers had just left the estate. Mister Vorster must have used them to clear the last grapes from Drakensberg, and to avoid spreading any more news of Victor's murder. Most of the men lay exhausted on their bunks, falling asleep. Bostock and Franklin were fully dressed, having discarded their blue overalls for ragged grey slacks and crumpled old collared shirts. They were sitting at the table with Charlie who had also discarded his overalls for the first time since I had known him. He was wearing baggy, worn denim jeans and a tight black, v-neck sweater with holes in each elbow and nothing beneath. I placed two large bunches of the herbs onto the table in front of him.

'Them very good, George,' he said, lips curling at their ends hinting that he was pleased rather than angry and cantankerous for the first time today.

He took a large bread knife, bunched up the herbs and diced them into a pile then placed them into a wooden bowl next to his bucket of umqombothi. He brought it to his face and inhaled like he was trying to suck the vegetation through his nostrils.

'Smell it, smell it,' he urged. 'Them very good, George. Very good.'

Each one of us inhaled as Charlie held out the bowl and passed it around our faces. The large green clumps omitted a strange but not unpleasant smell. I didn't have a clue which herbs I had put down on the table, but they must have been a wild concoction of lavender, dill, mint, rosemary, basil, sage . . . pretty much everything that Miss Johanna was asked to grow by Mrs Vorster.

'Go get them lamps, George,' said Charlie, pointing to the two brass paraffin lamps hanging by their wire handles on nails near the bunkhouse door.

Charlie took them from me, unhooked the wire handle and lifted out the glass casings. He withdrew the sodden wicks, put them in his pocket and poured all the remaining paraffin into the bowl of herbs. The small green mountain of cuttings disappeared and was replaced immediately by a rippled, green lake. Charlie picked up his metal spoon then stirred and prodded the mixture as we looked on with curiosity.

When he finished stirring, he stood up, grabbed a rag cloth from the back of a chair and walked with the bowl to the sink. He laid the cloth in the sink and poured the contents onto it. The mixture of paraffin and herbs fell and splashed, leaving slushy green remains. Charlie picked up the cloth containing the soaked herbs and twisted it into an increasingly small ball. Paraffin dripped through the material into the sink and the smell overcame the bunkhouse. After twisting and squeezing, he returned to the table, opened the cloth and shook a damp grassy paste back into the bowl.

'Time to go,' Charlie said, passing Bostock the bowl. 'I'll take them umqombothi.'

We followed Charlie, swinging his bucket of umqombothi, down the track in the dark without paraffin lamps to guide us. A hundred yards past Ringidd's two-roomed hut, we turned onto the rough overgrown track that led to the clearing. Ringidd must have heeded Charlie's earlier warning, because there were no lights shining and the regular crackling from his radio was absent.

The flames at the woodpile had long died down, but a bright red glow from the larger logs in the middle of the ashes guided us like a beacon, across the clearing. Charlie found a large stick and prodded the middle of the fire setting off an avalanche of ash to expose a hot furnace underneath. He shielded his face from the heat and I took a few steps back to make sure my skin would not blister.

'Poke them logs into the middle,' said Charlie, pointing and passing the stick to Barclay. We spread out around the fire and those brave enough picked up the fresh ends of logs and chucked them into the middle. I sat on the ground and kicked in one or two with the ends of the oversized boots Charlie had told me to wear. The smoke followed me around, stinging my eyes and I sat there coughing and blinking, searching for a pocket of air.

New flames soon rose from the fresh logs in the middle of the furnace and Charlie placed his metal bucket of umqombothi nearby. It quickly stained black, torched by the hot flames and smoke. The sour, maize beer nearest the metal of the bucket bubbled energetically - like the blackberries and sugar I saw Miss Johanna's women boil up in a pot for jam in the estate kitchen. Charlie reached in with a stick, hooked the bucket's handle, then dragged it carefully and safely from the flames.

Barclay, Bostock, Franklin and I looked on patiently and silently as Charlie made his preparations. He picked up the bowl of green sludge and scraped up hot ashes from the fringe of the fire, took a metal spoon from his pocket and mixed the ashes and the sludge of herbs and paraffin. The smell of his magical potion introduced itself. Charlie pulled a stick from the fire, now burning with a flame a foot high, and put the bowl onto the ground, bringing the flaming stick down on top of it. The paraffin ignited with a large flash and burnt off in a few seconds. When the flames died, the contents gently glowed and the unforgettable, powerful, viscous trail of burial incense spread among us. Charlie took off the black woollen cap from his head, crouched down on his ankles above the bowl and fanned it backwards and forwards. The embers glowed more brightly, and big clouds of the incense drifted upwards.

'They are ready for us,' he said.

'Who are ready, Charlie?' asked Bostock.

'Victor's ancestors . . . they are *all* here . . . *thousands of them.* They are rustling in the leaves on every tree around this clearing. Listen,' he said, circling for a complete view of our audience in the trees.

The leaves on the karee trees swayed and fluttered and their branches gently creaked. I cannot confirm the presence of Victor's ancestors with the same steadfast belief of Charlie, but it was comforting to think that he was being greeted by a procession of guardians to help him on the next leg of his journey.

'Tonight, Victor home. He finished visiting this world,' said Charlie. 'Tribal elders not sending a person to their ancestors in smoke . . . but is too late for Victor to be sealed in the ground of his homeland . . . the white man's took his homeland. Victor's ancestors is Khoikhoi, Xhosa and Zulu all mixed together. In township thems called mongrel, but Victor them purest breed. Him ancestors knows it . . . and thems all here tonight,' said Charlie.

He untied a small length of twine holding a metal cup from the top of his trousers, then filled it from the warm bucket of umqombothi. In one breath with his eyes shut, he mindfully drank from the cup of warm beer.

'Welcomes home . . . my little friend, Victor,' said Charlie, lifting his empty cup towards the sky. He filled it again and passed it to Barclay. Every man drank before me, but none felt it necessary to add any extra words. I did not expect Charlie to fill the cup for me, but he held it out and invited me forward. I stepped out of the shadow, into the light of the fire, received the cup and drank. The last time I had tasted alcohol was at the annual braai, with Victor.

I swallowed two whole mouthfuls. 'Some for me and some for Victor,' I said, throwing the remaining liquid onto the fire, sparking a small burst of flames and smoke. The beer sizzled and evaporated.

'I won't let you down, Victor. That is one promise I know I will definitely keep,' I whispered so that nobody else could hear, then stepped back from the fire.

'I heard my father talking to Danie.' The quiet voice came from behind us. Our heads turned and there was Willem, standing about ten yards behind our backs, watching the fire. 'He didn't say where the fire was, but I followed the smell from the track,' he explained to the five black faces standing in the flickering, orange smoke in front of him.

Nobody spoke. Charlie took the cup from me and dunked it into the umqombothi for one last time, then invited Willem forward. He stood next to me and drank, struggling to accept the bitter, fermented maize.

Willem raised the empty cup into the air with his arm.

'To my best friend . . . my butterfly in a glass jar, who finally floated free . . . I'm so sorry, my friend.'

We all stood and looked into the fire for what felt like an age. I didn't want to leave; the fire was warm and comforting . . . it was also transforming my friend, Victor. I was so glad that Willem had shared this moment.

'I have keys for the workshop, the garage and my father's car. Meet me behind the workshop in an hour. You will have to take Mary as well,' said Willem.

'How big the car?' asked Barclay.

'Comfortable for five . . . six at a squeeze,' replied Willem.

'You can put me in the trunk for all I care,' said Bostock.

Nobody seemed against the idea, not even Barclay. It was the least we could do after all that Mary had endured.

'Can I borrow your bowl please, Charlie?' I asked.

'What for?'

'Just something I want to do,' I said, for the first time with enough confidence that I didn't have to explain myself. Charlie turned it upside down and the burnt ash and herb cake fell out onto the floor like dried elephant dung. He passed it to me.

'One hour . . . behind the workshop! Don't be late,' Charlie said to everyone before we dispersed. I sat at the fire until everyone had walked out of view at the track then filled the bowl with ashes and walked briskly toward our pool beyond the high boundary of oak trees.

37
Daimler

I was the last to arrive. Charlie, Bostock, Barclay and Franklin were sitting on the ground with their backs against the red brick wall at the rear of the workshop.

'Where you been, George?' said Bostock.

'At the pool where Victor died. I scattered his dust on the ground beside it. At least part of him has left Glen Cleaver. Mr Mpendulo in Tolongo says every person returns to the earth when they die. I know that's the place that Victor would have chosen. We used to play there in secret . . . Willem, Victor and me.'

'When was you playing up there?' asked Franklin.

'On weekends when you were back in the township . . . sometimes after work,' I said.

'Them some things 'bout Victor and George nobody knows,' said Charlie.

'Victor and Willem taught me to swim up there,' I said, proudly.

'You can swim?' said Bostock in astonishment.

'Yeah. One afternoon I jumped off the high pier at the dam and swam in ice cold water.' The looks on their faces said they didn't believe me.

'I never swam once,' said Bostock, looking at me like he was in the presence of a spirited adventurer that had conquered virgin lands.

Footsteps padded lightly and quickly, approaching from the track around the nearest corner. Charlie and Barclay stood up tense and aggressive. They relaxed when Mary and Willem appeared at the corner. Mary sucked her lips into her mouth and pouted vulnerability with a dropped, demure head. She was wearing denim trousers and a plain orange t-shirt. Her hair was hanging, straggled below her shoulders and her face was dirty and smeared. Like this, she belonged to the Inner Tikki rather than the grand kitchen in Glen Cleaver's estate house.

I nodded my head and smiled at Mary and she expanded her lips wide in acknowledgement. The others were more concerned with our imminent escape and did not react. Willem got straight to the point.

'This is for the workshop,' he said, passing a key to Charlie. He delved back into the leather satchel hanging from his shoulder and pulled

232

out another two. 'For the garage doors and the car,' he said, holding the keys up for us to see. 'There is a connecting door to the garage from inside the workshop. The garage doors are chained and padlocked . . . I can't find the key for the padlock . . . sorry,' he said.

'No matter,' said Barclay. 'I can use a sledgehammer.'

'The noise of smashing might wake up Danie or my father - so do it last of all, then drive out fast. Don't look back. Head towards Paarl then turn onto the old road for Cape Town, just after the Wellington Junction. If you can get that far you can make it all the way to Tolongo.'

'Why you doing this for some *lowly kaffirs*?' said Barclay in an ungracious, cynical tone, sounding like he had Willem in the same category as every other piece of rotten white flesh he had ever met. Willem paused and reflected for a few seconds.

'I'm not doing anything for you . . . I'm doing it for Victor and George,' he said. Barclay huffed in response, as if Willem still somehow represented the enemy, even when that blatantly contravened the facts.

'You gonna be in all bad trouble, Master Willem,' said Charlie.

'Not if you do what I say,' replied Willem. Gone was his floaty, carefree attitude. This mission had been planned down to every detail.

'Unlock the doors then give me back the keys. Stay hidden in the garage for twenty minutes. I'll put the keys back and get into bed. After twenty minutes is up, smash the locks. Make it look like you broke in. Mallie and Toppie might start barking, but it's a chance worth taking,' he said.

'How we going to check twenty minutes is up? Only clock is in the bunkhouse,' said Franklin. Willem undid the brown leather strap of his watch, slid it from his wrist and passed it to me.

'It's for you, George . . . something to remember me by,' said Willem.

Even though it was made of metal or gold, the watch was slim and delicate. I put it around my wrist and Willem helped me to fix the small, fiddly buckle on the strap.

'I'll tell you when the time starts - only after I get the keys back,' said Willem.

Willem explained that when the large hand reached the top of the circle, twenty minutes would be up. I had never owned a watch. I had never owned anything come to think of it, apart from those discarded, coloured bottles that I collected in Tolongo.

'What about the police?' I asked, spitting the words out like a gatling gun, conscious that I was taking up precious minutes. 'Are they going to take your father and Masta Baas away?' In all of the anticipation and heightened emotion of the evening, I had nearly forgotten about the phone-call he had made, and the two cars I saw racing up the driveway.

'You mad man, George?' said Charlie, surprised that I could have dreamed up such a notion. I was instantly defensive.

'Willem called the police himself, Charlie. I was with him,' I replied. Willem had still not answered.

'The police are here to protect them white men from us, not them other way around,' scolded Charlie.

'Willem?' I looked at him for some support and verification that justice was going to be served.

'Yeah, the police came quick - Commissioner Du Toit himself, following my mother - just after I left you. I hid in my mother's bedroom . . . I hadn't seen father since the pool. I thought he was going to go mad and beat me half to death or something. But he didn't. Mother sent me down to him after fixing him a cup of tea. Father was standing with him at the front door waiting for me. He didn't look at me once when I walked down the stairs, not until he was sitting in front in the drawing room with Commissioner Du Toit.'

'The Commissioner's the police boss.' I said, clarifying for everyone's benefit.

'It was different to what I thought, George. He said that if Victor was alive he would have been prosecuted for theft, vandalism of private property, disobedience, insolence and another twenty things I hardly knew the meaning of. He said that the whole thing was an accident brought about by Victor . . . *a kaffir's curse* he called it'

'What he mean by that? That Victor's death was coming to him anyway?' said Franklin.

'Something like that,' said Willem.

'But you told him the truth, Willem. Didn't you?' I pleaded.

'There was no point, George. He wasn't there to listen. Him and my father sat right in front of me telling me how lucky I was not to be prosecuted myself. And Du Toit was licking up every drop of kak oozing from my father's mouth like it was the gospel. I never saw two people suck up to each other like those two bloated limpets.'

'So they ain't gonna arrest nobody for killing Victor?' asked Franklin.

'They're calling it an accident, but as far as they're concerned it was like Victor was never here. There are no records of him being alive - no passbook, no family relatives, no address in the townships. They said he was an orphan from a closed-down charity project in Cape Town.'

'An orphan?' I muttered. 'But Victor told me about his uncle in District Six.'

'They never mentioned anything about District Six - all they said was he never had a mother or a father, that was why he was so unstable and unpredictable.

'I don't believe them. None of it matters anyway - what matters is that he was killed when all he did was stick up for anything good,' I said.

'You don't have to tell me, George . . . but it's no use. It'll never be any use . . . Du Toit was putting the frighteners on me - kept saying about how he was turning a blind eye because he is such good friends with my father. If I promised not to mention Victor again and work hard at Ascension College then he said he would drop the charges against me - reckoned Ascension would help me grow up and see the error of my ways . . . but he doesn't know who he's dealing with . . . sitting there sipping his fruit juice thinking he was the king of the world,' said Willem, his face turning red in anger.

We had all been hanging on his every word. None of us knew what it was like to be Willem; putting up with all those different people's expectations, half of them strangers that only rubbed shoulders because they lived in the valley. Willem's always been told he's gotta be this and he's gotta be that; talk this way, walk that way, dress like a figurine toy, comb your hair, shake hands with a strong grip, respect your elders - even when those folks would never put him before their own interests. I truly don't know which life I would rather live; Willem's in Glen Cleaver, or mine in Tolongo. Both seem sort of miserable in their own way. I would probably take Tolongo if push came to shove . . . at least there's a sort of an honesty about that miserable existence; it's much harder to pretend you are something you're not in Tolongo . . . even though my Aunt Nobule always tried her damnedest.

The highest expectations most people have in Tolongo, is for regular food and a dry, safe, private place to sleep each night . . . but it is fair to say that for most, that simple dream is unobtainable. People can't afford to think forward in Tolongo - not like Willem who has his whole life mapped out for him by his mother and his father. In Tolongo, those sorts of dreams are a fruitless torment. My mother saw those dreams in my father at the very beginning; the colours in his head started out bright and vivid, like a rainbow, but each year they faded and faded, until all he could see was black and grey. Those dark shades quickly turned to a total blindness for life; an inevitable consequence of his growing self-loathing and immersion in self-medication.

'You haven't heard the worst,' said Willem. 'Just before Du Toit was leaving the house, he turned to me and my father at the front doors and said that in a few years - when I was all grown up - we would probably share a beer at a braai and have a good laugh about the whole thing.'

'What did you say to that?' I exclaimed in further disbelief and growing anger.

'Nothing. I just stared back at the piece of kak,' said Willem.

'George? Willem? We gotta go!' said Charlie, interrupting the suspense and bringing us back to the pressing moment.

We walked quietly and nervously into the courtyard following Charlie and Willem. Charlie unlocked the workshop door and Barclay pushed past him, going straight to the sledgehammer hanging on the wall behind.

'You all go and wait for me in the garage.' he said.

'No, Barclay man, come wait here with us. Don't go do nothing stupid now,' insisted Charlie.

'I not doing nothing stupid, Charlie, man. Back in a few minutes.' Barclay was not intimidated and there was no way of stopping him. He walked across the courtyard towards the press sheds and in one fell swoop, smashed the padlock. It rattled across the concrete floor. Barclay opened the doors just enough to slip inside then shut them again behind him and turned on one section of lights.

Willem showed us the connecting doorway to the garage, entered with us and turned on the light. The large berth was sparse with only a few stacked wine crates on one wall and the highly polished, burgundy automobile lying asleep under a blanket in the middle.

'Don't worry, you can't see the light from outside with the doors shut,' Willem reassured.

'This what Ringidd driving you all to church?' asked Charlie, pointing to the car.

'Yeah,' whispered Willem becoming overly cautious. 'It's a Daimler. My father only uses it for family occasions.' Bostock walked alongside, stroking his hand across the roof as Willem unlocked the driver's door and reached inside to flick the lock in the back seat.

'Do you hear that?' said Franklin from the back of the room, next to Mary.

'What?' said Charlie. We stood like statues and pricked up our ears. There was a sound of muffled banging coming from the press sheds. Barclay was hard at work.

'You won't hear that from the house,' said Willem, quashing our concern.

'What about the car key, Master Willem?' asked Bostock.

'What do you mean?' he said.

'You can't take it back with you. We need it for the engine,' he explained.

Willem's face fell. He closed his eyes and sighed.

'Are you being serious?' he said, opening his eyes again. It was now obvious that Willem had never driven a car and despite his best intentions, getting us into the car was not the same as getting us to drive away with it.

'Can you not start the engine then give me the key back?' he asked, clutching at the invisible.

'It don't work that way, Master Willem,' said Bostock. 'We gotta have the key in the ignition for it to drive.'

'Say I took it, Master Willem,' said the female voice in the background. It was the first time Mary had spoken since she and Willem had joined us. Willem turned around to look at her. 'I know where the keys are kept. On the hooks underneath the stair,' she said to Willem smiling and letting him know that the claim would be credible. Relief spread across Willem's face. Mary's admission had brushed away any trace of his involvement.

'I better get back,' said Willem.

Franklin was the first to say goodbye. He took Willem's hand and shook it vigorously with both of his. Bostock did the same, then Charlie.

'You is a brave warrior, Master Willem. Like them powerful Zulu warrior. My ancestors is find you and thank you in the next life . . . I'm sorry we no better thanking you in this life,' said Charlie.

'You don't need to thank me, Charlie. Just look after George, will you?' asked Willem.

'I don't know why you and Victor think I need looking after so bad? I can look after myself you know,' I said.

'I know you can,' said Willem, responding with a high voice a little too quickly. 'But it's good to have someone looking out for you,' he persuaded.

'Who's going to look out for you?' I asked.

'You and Victor would look out for me if you could. That's enough for me . . . it's more than most others have,' he said.

'I'll walk you to the courtyard,' I said. Willem nodded in agreement. He reached the connecting door to the workshop and stopped, turning to the three men and the lady who had already climbed into the car and were shuffling on the tanned, leather upholstery making themselves comfortable.

'Good luck,' he said.

We walked past workbenches, pots of whitewash next to buckets of brushes soaking in methylated spirit and open bags of caustic lime-powder piled up underneath the benches. There was an assortment of welded metal piping, technical equipment and high stacks of sawn wood to navigate around to get outside. Willem opened the door and walked into the courtyard first.

'You don't need to worry about me, you know,' said Willem.

'I know.' I replied. 'I will probably read in the newspaper about a famous butterfly expert in twenty years' time. Victor always said you would to do something great in your life.'

'You'll have to learn to read first then?' joked Willem.

'You're right' I chuckled. 'Maybe that's what I'll do.'

'Take care of yourself, George . . . blood-brother's forever, right?' he said, lifting his palm.

'Forever.'

Our hands met and squeezed warmly. The thought of my blood entwined with his and Victor's felt special to me. But it is ironic that the bond that Victor, Willem and I had built up over those ten months was not because of our entwined blood, but in spite of it. I feel proud that Victor, Willem and I chose our bond of friendship . . . our love for each other . . . by our own free will. When we did, we released an eternal magic into the air; and that magic is flying around us now with such a powerful fragrance that it can never die out. I believe I inhale a small fragment of it each time I breathe.

'I have something for you,' I said to Willem pulling a gift from the pocket of my scuffed, stained trousers. My creative genius is so elusive that Willem didn't recognise what I had made, even when I held it out clearly in front of him.

'It's meant to be a butterfly. I know it's not very good. I grabbed together a few stalks of fynbos and some flowers near the pool and tied them together,' I explained.

'I like it . . . it's like the Green-Veined Emperor . . . thanks, George.' I didn't need him to be so polite, although I do think he was touched by the gesture, even if my sculpting prowess left much to be desired. He put my rogue butterfly into his brown satchel and buckled the flap.

'Make sure they don't leave before twenty minutes - just to be safe. Okay?'

'Okay,' I said, looking at the new watch on my wrist. 'Not until the big hand reaches the top,' I promised. I don't think either of us knew what to say next. We had endured too many gut-wrenching goodbyes in the last two days.

'Everything's going to be okay you know, George. When things are tough, just think of Victor and me. We'll be with you, even if you can't see us.'

'And you think of me too, Willem. 'Cos I'll be with you, even if you can't see me.'

'You'll see me again sometime, George,' he said, with an out-of-place look of confidence.

'You really think so?' I asked.

'I *know* it.' He turned and bounded on sprung heels to the corner of the courtyard and turned onto the path to the estate house.

Fifteen minutes later, Barclay stepped into the garage with the sledgehammer still dripping at his side. He was panting through a wide, white smile with eyes as wide as the headlamps on the Daimler. He stood there seeming eager for one of us to ask him what he had been up to, but nobody was forthcoming. Charlie got out of the passenger side and walked around to the front of the car where he inspected the seam between the two garage doors.

'You start them engine, Barclay, and I go round front smash them chains and open door. Soon as I back in car, we getting out of here like kudu chased by lions - hear?'

Barclay ambled over to Charlie and stood in front of him with us all looking on through the windscreen - everyone apart from Bostock that is - he was squeezed in so tight to the dark trunk he was practically licking the fabric of the lining.

'What's going on?' said the muffled voice from behind our seats. I gave him a running commentary as best I could, but the rumbling engine put an end to it.

'You hit that chain good and proper now, Charlie . . . just like I did on those tank valves inside the press shed. Every last one is gushing out like a fire-hose right now . . . no Drakensberg award winners this year . . . not unless you suck it out the drains or lick it off the concrete,' said Barclay.

His revenge did not match the suffering he or Mary had endured at Glen Cleaver, but it was still the sweetest trick any of us had tasted for a very long time. Wide grins spread across Barclay and Charlie's face. I successfully recounted the news to Bostock in the trunk and in his rapture he whooped and banged hard on the back of our seats. Mary was the only one continuing to sit in apprehensive and bemusement as she questioned what was so funny.

'I wish I saw the look on Vorster's face when he opens them doors in morning,' said Franklin - loud enough that Bostock and the two out front could hear.

'If you see that, means we not made it out of here. Laugh all you want in Tolongo,' snapped Mary. She was right. We were still not free and the most dangerous step had still to be taken. The laughter sobered and a recognition returned - that our biggest vengeance had not yet been realised; a daring escape in Mister Vorster's precious, stolen automobile.

Charlie grabbed the handle of the sledgehammer and walked back out to the courtyard, closing the connecting door from the workshop to the garage behind him. We cannot have been waiting for much more than a minute, but it felt like a lifetime. Barclay turned the ignition and the engine purred. He flicked a switch on the dashboard and the headlamps came to life. The engine had only turned over for a few seconds when he began hitting the steering wheel hard with his palms.

'Hurry up, Charlie, man,' he said, raising his voice.

'What if somebody sees him out there? Or if Master Willem's been caught at the estate house or something?' said Franklin.

'Shut up, Franklin,' shouted Barclay. 'No good creating a panic.' Franklin didn't respond and a wave of tension broke throughout the car. Just as I was thinking one of us should check on Charlie, the heavy head of the sledgehammer tore the padlock and chain from its bolted latch on the garage doors. Both doors swung open forcefully and Charlie appeared in the middle of the doorway, lit up by the headlamps like an abnormally large witch-doctor ready to dance in orange flames on hot coals for his ancestors. He nodded determination then ran to the passenger door, jumped inside and slammed it shut.

'Go. Go, Barclay, man,' shouted Charlie.

Barclay didn't need any encouragement. He was already in first gear and revving the engine past screeching. The car shot forward like a toy leaving a coiled spring, but we could not avoid the garage door which rebounded part of the way in on itself following Charlie's powerful opening. There was a loud crash as we smashed the door sideways, ripping it from one of its hinges. My head banged hard off the inside roof of the car as we bounced, then I turned and looked out the back window to see the door half-collapsed over the entrance-way. We were in one piece, but the collision smashed the passenger headlamp to pieces. We now had forty miles to drive on dark, barren roads with a single torch to guide us. This was a minor inconvenience, although it did occur to me that you don't see fancy cars driving around with broken lights in the middle of the night. The broken light was a calling card that would grab the attention of any other drivers out on the road at such a late hour.

We skidded and scraped down the track, first past Master Boss's house then past the front of the estate house. Barclay had not driven for a few years, I could tell. He was twisting, turning, braking and accelerating leaving a wake of dust clouds on the track behind us. Behind the dust I could see the flicker of growing flames from the courtyard.

'Did you set fire to the press shed, Barclay?'

He turned around for the briefest second with raised eyebrows. Not that I should have been surprise. It wasn't only fine wine that Mister Vorster was going to have lost come morning.

There was no sign of life at Master Boss's place, but his house was mostly hidden in the trees, so there was no real way of knowing. We skidded too fast and too loud onto the gravel turning circle in front of the estate house and the car spun half-way round on itself, nearly facing back up to where we had come from. The spinning wheels shoveled two deep tracks in the gravel as the car skidded and came to a complete standstill. Franklin, myself and Mary were pushed so hard up against each other as it happened that I felt like a piece of meat between two slices of bread being pushed hard between someone's hands. Mary was much softer eating than Franklin, that's for sure. She put her arm around me and held me tight, even after our involuntary squeezing had stopped.

There was a bad smell of burning rubber and Barclay was beginning to panic and curse. We can have been no more than twenty yards from the front door of the estate house.

'Something's fok'd here, man, Charlie.' Barclay was shouting and making excuses for the fact we had come to a standstill right in the firing line.

'Come on, Barclay, man,' shouted Charlie. 'Get going man!' he shouted again. The rest of us were sitting in the back, gagged by our hearts choking us in our throats. All I could hear from Bostock was loud banging from the inside of trunk and muffled shouts that we could not decipher.

A light was switched on in the upstairs hallway of the house. Mary saw it first and it sent her into a panic.

'Vorster's coming! He sees us,' she shouted. Barclay was still revving the engine hard, trying to get into gear, but Mary wanted to run.

'I'm getting out,' she shouted. 'It's gone to hell.' She reached across for the handle of the door. Charlie's arm lunged into the back and grabbed her.

'You stay here now!' he shouted, pulling her back towards me in the middle seat. 'Hold onto her, George, don't let go.'

Just at that moment, the source of all our problems branded Barclay like a molten cattle-prodder. 'Fok!' he screamed, reaching down to release the lever of the handbrake. It had been engaged since the start and the car was not steering or gliding properly because of it. The smell of burning suggested there was not much brake left. Barclay got the car into gear and for a second time we catapulted forward - this time less like a frantic mountain dassie evading the talons of a fish-eagle with hungry chicks, and more like an ocean liner leaving the calm waters of harbour.

Our audience of one was not waving fond goodbyes from the harbour wall. Mister Vorster stood in the doorway to the estate house in his dressing gown with his shotgun at his side. We were at too great a distance for any damage to be done, but he tried nonetheless; shotgun pellets spattered onto the roof of the car like light hail-stones. Halfway down the driveway, with a score of oak salutes on either side of us, the house disappeared from view. I was still holding on tightly to Mary who was now sobbing. I think the thought of having to remain in that place had been too much for her to bear.

We rolled quietly through the high, white stone pillars marking Glen Cleaver's entrance and Barclay turned right, onto a freshly tarred road. The noise of the engine purred quietly and we sailed peacefully on the flat, windless sea in collective silence towards the old road for Cape Town. The faint smell of relief during our hour-long, circumnavigated journey was hardly noticeable and it was only after we had abandoned the car and found safety and anonymity in Tolongo's Inner Tikki - the place I now call my home - that my first full breath evaporated slowly and gratefully, and forever memorably past my lips.

38
Fynbos

30 January 2016

I awaken early, before first light, and drive into the centre of Cape Town, then park in a quiet, residential street in the Malay district. It is a short walk downhill to the bus stop near Long Street. The bus takes me inland from Cape Town on the N1, a modern two and three-lane highway, towards the distant silhouette of the Du Toitskloof mountain-pass. Long stretches of the central reservation are laden with colourful flowers in full bloom that warm my soul; scything through the monotony of dusty, fallow fields, baked grassland and swathes of corn, like a rainbow does a brooding sky.

Sunken in the nest of the Hottentots Mountains, Franschhoek feels like the well-hidden egg of an orange-breasted sunbird. On stepping from the bus, the smell of pine needles and oak immediately flares my nostrils, baked grass tickles my calves on the verge, bright wild flowers on the mountainsides soothe my eyes and the lullaby of birdsong feathers my ears. A field of mature vines ripples over the valley floor, resplendent with plump, silken grapes hanging from heavy bunches. Even the rich, fertile soil has a smell; it is leathery and luxurious, like the hand-crafted hide-interior of an expensive automobile. I feel far removed from the life I lived here fifty-five years ago. Sometimes I question if I didn't live it all in a dream.

The main street is smattered with elderly ladies, the wives of retired farmers or landowners; all clad in expensive, formal dresses or blouses and skirts, leisurely browsing at shop windows on their way to the first social gatherings of the morning, in one of five or six coffee houses. The ladies pass in a plague of perfume, polluting the air. They are as indifferent to me as they are to the tourists venturing out after breakfast in baggy shorts and flip-flops, coloured T-shirts and baseball caps. Some of them have fancy cameras on wide, branded straps hanging around their necks, others carry cell-phones for the same purpose.

The weak currency has given rise to burgeoning international tourism and demand for new shops, restaurants and hotels. Two black men own and manage an award-winning chocolatier business; people as far as America and Europe know about it. I also read in the Cape Argus that a

243

restaurant in the town, owned and managed by an interracial couple, was voted among the top fifty in the world by a reputable, international magazine. If you had foretold these things, even two decades ago, I would not have believed a word.

Many houses, offset from the road, are in the Dutch colonial style; whitewashed and clothed in prominent arches with balustrades that rise from their roofs like a cardinal's ceremonial headdress. Parked cars have been imported from all corners of the globe, and the signs pinned above the shop entrances are bright, shiny and plastic. But somehow this place has managed to resist the culture of change and development that subsumes other towns. Time has paused in Franschhoek and I have always thought it belongs to the beginning of the twentieth century.

A local Afrikaner, probably a farm or vineyard owner, is walking towards me. He bulges proudly around his midriff but is otherwise strong and lithe from a life of regular, hard work. His collared, white cotton shirt is stretched-tight by his stomach and his khaki shorts are held up with a heavy, brown, leather belt, pulled tight below the belly that hangs over it. His sandals may have been sewn together with leather wire cut from the same material as the belt. He is the silverback. This man is the one above all others that doesn't like change. Nobody likes change for change's sake, but this man doesn't like change in any circumstances. He is in the mould of Mister Vorster; a relic that has not yet died out. There are fewer of them to be found now, because Franschhoek has attracted an international community and the silverback has found it hard to keep up. He is suspicious of incomers; like the English physician who lives in town but travels to London for two week's work each month, returning to consult with his patients over the internet. That is the sort of lifestyle that wealth and technology and the jet engine can afford a person. It is not a life I would choose, but I am not that man and certainly do not have his capabilities. Perhaps if I had, I might think differently on the matter, but my preference, more than ever, is for a simple life.

It takes an hour to walk up the dusty, unobtrusive path that ascends from the reservoir and meanders next to the stream, towards the pool. In my ripe, old-age, the walk gets longer and steeper with each new year. God only knows how I've lasted so long. My sisters departed this earth within a year of each other, before I reached middle-age; my mother, twenty years before that. There is nothing especially tragic or unfortunate about their deaths, I assure you. These are the lengths for an average life in our parts, for our people. I am the anomaly, the lucky one, the one with a library of memories.

Beside the pool, my floral epitaph is more glorious and expansive than I could have imagined, shining proudly against the green and brown pastel mountains. It carpets an area as big as a tennis court. The sight amazes me; the natural world truly is a wonder. The colourful invaders look like they belong, having reclaimed their rightful place among the inhospitable, indigenous vegetation - seducing it slowly and surely with an unequalled vibrancy. The reason I chose fynbos is because it is a stubborn little warrior. It has small leaves that are hard wearing - like the spines of an acacia bush - and it can endure almost anything that is thrown at it, including wildfire. Even the most insurmountable confrontation can strengthen its grip - its determination to succeed. I love to grow things; plants, flowers, fruits, vegetables . . . anything really . . . but flowers especially. It was the fragrance from a white rose that charmed my nostrils for the first time, inside Glen Cleaver's walled garden. I was hypnotised by the experience and all of my adult life has been spent in horticulture, chasing that same elixir. I have been lucky enough to make a reasonable living from such a glorious pursuit. In rare moments of dissension, Thembi tells me I love flowers more than I love her . . . but she always apologises, knowing well that it is a wildly inaccurate and unfair reflection.

Growing flowers is not unlike growing grapes. It's partly science, but mostly art and must be underpinned by love or passion. Without that foundation of love, you cannot survive the uncertainty, the lack of control, the need to defer to some higher game of cause and effect. A successful harvest - of flowers, and more so of grapes - hinges upon a great many variables, most of which lie well without the control of a person. That is the thing with nature you see, it gives the appearance of unfolding by some meticulous design, but it is never that contrived. Mankind may meddle to the best of his ability, but the final determination belongs to nature. Nature will decide whether the vintage is withered, or strong, or sweet, or thin, or bitter or acrid and undrinkable.

So why does mankind fall short? Why can it not accept itself; relinquish to the inevitable cycle . . . of life, then death. We are clingers; constantly grasping at a life and constantly fearful of a death . . . constantly needing to matter. In the higher forms of nature, of life - the flowers, the grapes, the trees - there is not the burden of choice. Their nature is unencumbered by the illusion of a better life. My plants put down roots into the earth, drink when it rains, smile in the sunshine and wither and die in the frost. This is nature's strength; in accepting its journey, living as it was created - nothing more and nothing less.

Mankind has conceived itself to be like the oak tree or the mountain top. What room is there for the sapling, or the blade of grass, or the termite that gets stamped upon by the foot of a springbok? If we are all oak trees or the mountain, we may be strong enough to weather the storm, to shield against frost, to survive in thin air or to soak up greater energy from the sun . . . but the oak trees and the mountains did not arrive with those things in mind. Why then, does mankind not accept its vulnerability; revel in the beauty of the frail and the mundane? Why do we not look upon the blade of grass as we look upon the fragrant, colourful, outstretched petals of a rose? Why do we only look down at the grass when the cherry blossom has fallen and scattered? But nature does not see with the eyes of mankind. Nature unfolds as nature unfolds. And yet this mankind is part of the same nature. We are not born into the earth, we are born out of the earth . . . like the flowers and the grapes and the trees. That is what puzzles me most.

* * * * *

I scrape a shallow hole in the dry ground and secure the roots of one final, new plant, take off my shoes and socks then step into the cool stream above the ledge to fill my flask. The water is not yet for my drinking. I return to my plant and give it a sip. The next hour is spent doing the same for the others; gingerly stepping across the slope, sprinkling cool water from left to right.

The plants are not getting their thirst quenched, but it is enough for them to taste; enough to sustain their hope through the hottest months. Perhaps it is these sprinklings that give them an advantage over the other vegetation. It is the least I can do. My fynbos is unrelenting. It has decided to spread its wings, like a young cape sugarbird that has flown the nest and ventured further afield, unafraid to cross new boundaries and put down new roots. It is spreading so fast and so thickly that it must be in the prime of its life. And just like a parent, as I have taken great pleasure and satisfaction in seeing my daughter grow into a confident, happy and resilient young woman, so I am happy and satisfied that these flowers are also flourishing; sustaining themselves under the weight of their own purpose.

When the nourishing is complete, I sit, dangling my feet over the high ledge above the pool, next to a trickle of water that is falling over the lip. The sun is now unyieldingly hot and I undo a couple of buttons on my shirt; a hopeless attempt to trap some of the obscure, lethargic breeze. I drink from my flask and devour my favourite chicken and mayonnaise salad sandwich, which Thembi kindly prepared.

What a view, and I am the only one to see it. Mountains face me from across the valley and the stream looks like a long, thin, black thread attached to a large ball of wool at the bottom, rudely discarded onto the floor by nature's seamstress. The fish-eagle I saw perched on a tree beyond the dam is now circling in the thermals high above, surveying the landscape for a meal. The eagle is the only bird I can see but I can hear many other species of the Hottentots, gently chirping from the undergrowth as if they are all perched comfortably upon my shoulders. I am fully at peace.

It is time to leave, so I stand and amble towards Glen Cleaver's oak boundary as if I have all the time in the world. I don't know why I feel so nervous about seeing Willem. Come to think of it, he's my oldest living friend, but I am worried he will not recognise me after so long. I reach the trees and walk underneath the canopy of leafy branches into the shade. I approach a small ebony plaque that has been nailed onto one of the trunks. It is engraved with the names and dates of the births and deaths of Koibus and Gwendoline Vorster and has been inscribed:

"Earth hath no sorrow that heaven cannot heal."

I am reminded of the letter Willem read out on the night of the Truth and Reconciliation Commission hearing – the one from his father. Themula dug up the transcript, by permission of the Commission, and I have kept it ever since:

"Dear Willem,

I write you because I am dying. I don't know if I'm lucky to know it in advance, but I feel it coming quicker now; tomorrow I may not have a chance. Wine-grower's lung the doctors call it. The fungus on grapes, a curse of my vocation in life!

It has been seventeen years since I last saw you (and I'm not counting your mother's funeral). I don't know where you are, but I expect the lawyers will get this into your hands somehow, along with my betrothal, after I pass. I hope you can stomach to receive it. You can start afresh with Glen Cleaver; be a different custodian to the one I am. These times are changing, and I am too old and frail to stand in the way.

Although you returned home from Ascension at the end of each term, you really left me after that fateful day. Since then, you looked at me with vacant eyes and only spoke in one or two syllables at a time . . . But that day was not lost on me either. Every time I cough, I hear the splashes of that boy's body falling into the pool - like he is trying to force his way up

247

from my lungs and choke me to death. I am tired of the coughing and the memory of it all.

His name was Lungelo Shasisi - a young boy pushed onto Danie Rousseau by an old orphanage caretaker who moved up from Cape Town to Paarl with five other kids and wanted rid. I don't know much apart from his parents died before he could crawl. I would ask the caretaker, but I expect he is resting high above, all dressed in white . . . and I am about to pass through the smouldering gates below.

This boy, Victor - Lungelo, I know he wasn't only an orphan. I know he was your friend. As God is my witness, I am sorry . . . one day I hope you can forgive me.

Your father,
Koibus Vorster"

* * * * *

Beyond the trees, I step out onto Mister Vorster's cherished Drakensberg plantation. Green velvet is painted in narrow lines across the steep-sided hill, bathed in the descending sun. I follow the track downhill and part of me expects Mallie and Toppie to come running towards their intruder, or to have Ringidd or Master Boss shout orders from across the vines. Peace and silence endures.

An old vineyard to my right-hand side - Cathkin if my memory serves me correctly - has been replaced with a plantation of olive trees. To its side, a dozen poly-tunnels appear to be hovering, near the track. At the end of the potting shed, the woodland has been felled and cleared, and the ground reconfigured and beautifully landscaped. A children's adventure playground has been installed with tree-houses, rope swings, ladders and one of those long, wire slides that scares people half-to-death for their peculiar idea for fun and amusement. Dozens of families are scattered on picnic tables or blankets, enjoying food and wine whilst attempting to control their vibrant children, without success. The only faces I can see are happy ones.

I join the road to the main house and want to pinch myself to check that I have not travelled back in time. Two workers dressed in pristine blue overalls are walking towards me. They have crisp, denture-white t-shirts underneath their overalls and bright yellow gumboots on their feet. Each overall has Glen Cleaver's beautifully embroidered crest on the chest pocket and a larger motif on the back. The men smile and say *good afternoon* as they walk past.

The estate house is without a trace of age or ill-repair. I take three steps up onto the side of the terrace and walk along towards the front door, passing the window into Mister Vorster's old study - his *thinking window.* I stop and look inside. The room has been converted into a children's playroom. There is a rocking-horse in the middle and plastic vehicles and toys on the floor and stacked in wicker baskets beside shelves of children's books. The sky-blue walls are decorated randomly with multi-coloured stickers; alphabet letters, numbers and hot-air balloons. The playroom door is wide open and in the hallway, two young children with clean, blonde hair are skirting around after each other on tricycles, shouting and yelping like young pups on the loose.

A small, framed cabinet is fixed on the far wall. At first glance, the object behind the glass looks like it belongs to a school nature project, but when I inspect it more closely, pinned against the white back-drop is the fynbos butterfly I made for Willem, fifty-five years ago. I can just make-out the words *Green-Veined Emperor,* engraved on the brass plaque below.

The sight of my crude gift, in such a prominent place after all this time, makes my heart sing - loudly, from the lowest to the highest notes, touching each one in between. I stand mesmerised, although it looks even less like a butterfly after all this time. I don't register the child rolling into the middle of the room on her tricycle, nor climbing up onto the rocking-horse. She looks straight at me in a pretty white frock with a flushed red face and hair stuck to the sides of her cheeks. I smile and she smiles back, then carries on rocking, as if I am imagined.

At the front door, I breathe deeply and my finger rises to meet the white enameled buzzer. I tell myself to press it, but something is holding me back. My finger is less than an inch away. All I need to do is let it fall forward a fraction. How hard can it be? Willem will open the door and greet me with a warm smile and a hearty embrace. I have come to the edge, but there is nobody here to push me. Victor would have pressed that buzzer by now. He would be sitting in there on the comfiest seats, drinking wine or coffee and munching on thick-crust sandwiches, stirring up his next adventure with his friend. But I am not Victor. I am Lifa.

My hand falls and I find myself walking away, down Glen Cleaver's dusty driveway, in the shade of the oak trees that now feel more like welcoming friends than guardians of this place. I feel grateful and contented and cannot help thinking about the newborn baby that will soon spring into my life. Thembi and I are travelling to be near Themula and our son-in-law in Port Elizabeth for the birth. We are very excited. Themula wants a boy and has already been referring to the bump in her stomach as *him*. I don't care whether it is a boy or a girl and neither will she when she finally hears those newborn cries of helplessness and the feeling of her child's warm, delicate skin muzzle in her chest. I haven't told her that though, she has plenty of time to learn these things for herself. When I am lucky enough to meet Themula's little miracle for the first time, I vow to cradle that child in my arms and smile and whisper repeatedly: *I love you.*

Before the estate house is entirely out of sight, I turn for one final glance. A large silhouette of a man stands behind the thinking window. I refocus, there is only one person that silhouette can belong to. Willem lifts his hand and waves at me in a wide, slow arc. My calf-muscles tense, I rise up onto my toes and stretch my arm as high as it will go. I punch the air with a clenched fist and a strong, rigid arm. On my wrist is the watch he gave me, fifty-five years earlier. It has a different strap, but the mechanism could not be more true and faithful.

We stand in union for a few, still seconds until my arm drops. I hope Willem is smiling as widely as me. I am so glad to see my friend after all this time, and to know that he has seen me, if only for the briefest moment.

As I turn to continue down the last stretch of driveway, I notice the sound of leaves rustling in the trees and wonder if Victor and his ancestors are watching . . . humming their approval . . . echoing eternity.

THE END

Printed in Great Britain
by Amazon

16745869R00144